KIDNAPPED

W9-CBD-321

Robert Louis Stevenson

Kidnapped

or the Lad with the Silver Button

Introduction by Margot Livesey

*Edited, with a Preface and Notes, by
Barry Menikoff*

THE MODERN LIBRARY

NEW YORK

2001 Modern Library Paperback Edition

Copyright © 1999 by Barry Menikoff
Introduction copyright © 2001 by Margot Livesey
Biographical Note copyright © 2001 by Random House, Inc.

All rights reserved under International and Pan-American Copyright
Conventions. Published in the United States by Random House, Inc.,
New York, and simultaneously in Canada by Random House of Canada
Limited, Toronto.

Modern Library and colophon are registered trademarks of Random
House, Inc.

This work was originally published in hardcover in 1999 as *Robert Louis
Stevenson's Kidnapped: or the Lad with the Silver Button* by Huntington Library,
San Marino, California. This paperback edition is published by
arrangement with Barry Menikoff.

Grateful acknowledgment is made to the following for permission to
reprint previously published material:

FRONTISPIECE: Original etching of Robert Louis Stevenson by William
Henry Warren Bicknell. Used by permission of the Houghton Library,
Harvard University.

PAGE LXXXV: Detail from map reproduced in first English edition of
Kidnapped. Used by permission of the Huntington Library.

Library of Congress Cataloging-in-Publication Data
Stevenson, Robert Louis, 1850–1894.
   [Kidnapped]
   Kidnapped, or, The lad with the silver button / Robert Louis
Stevenson.— 2001 Modern Library pbk. ed. / introduction by Margot
Livesey; edited, with a preface and notes, by Barry Menikoff.
      p. cm. — (Modern Library classics)
   ISBN 0-375-75725-2
   1. Scotland—History—18th century—Fiction.
2. Teenage boys—Fiction. 3. Kidnapping—Fiction. I. Title: Kidnapped.
II. Title: Lad with the silver button. III. Menikoff, Barry. IV. Title. V.
Series.

PR5484 .K5 2001
823'.8—dc21

Modern Library website address: www.modernlibrary.com

Printed in the United States of America

98765432

ROBERT LOUIS STEVENSON

Robert Louis Stevenson, a versatile and prolific writer best remembered for his novels of romantic adventure, was born in Edinburgh on 13 November 1850. The son of a prosperous civil engineer who specialized in the construction of lighthouses, he was expected to follow the family profession but ended up studying law at Edinburgh University. Still, when he was a young man his agnosticism and bohemian existence led to painful clashes with his strict Calvinist parents. Stevenson spent much of his life battling a severe lung disease (probably tuberculosis) and traveled constantly in search of a climate that would prove congenial to his health. His first full-length book, *An Inland Voyage* (1878), grew out of a canoe trip he took through Belgium and northern France; a later tour through the wilds of southern France produced *Travels with a Donkey in the Cévennes* (1879). Stevenson journeyed to San Francisco in 1879 to marry Fanny Osbourne, an American divorcée ten years his senior. *The Silverado Squatters* (1883) recalls the couple's eccentric honeymoon at an abandoned silver mine on Mount Saint Helena. After returning to Europe in 1880 the Stevensons moved about, living in Switzerland, France, and England.

"Fiction is to grown men what play is to the child," Stevenson once said. He launched his career as a storyteller with "A Lodging for the Night" (1877), a short story set in fifteenth-century Paris that recounts an episode in the life of French poet François Villon. He went on to write ghost stories, medieval romances, moral allegories, tales of psychological horror, and fables drawn from Scottish folklore. In 1882 he brought out *New Arabian Nights,* an extravagant series of adventures that pays tribute to one of the favorite books of his childhood. G. K. Chesterton remarked, "I will not say that the *New Arabian Nights* is the greatest of Stevenson's works; though a considerable case might be made for the challenge. But I will say that it is probably the most unique; there was nothing like it before, and, I think, nothing equal to it since." Stevenson's other compilations of short fiction include *More New Arabian Nights: The Dynamiter* (1885) and *The Merry Men and Other Tales and Fables* (1887). "[Stevenson's] short stories are certain to retain their position in English literature," judged Arthur Conan Doyle. "His serious rivals are few indeed. Poe, Nathaniel Hawthorne, Stevenson; those are the three . . . who are the greatest exponents of the short story in our language."

The publication of *Treasure Island* in 1883 brought Stevenson enormous acclaim. Written as an entertainment for his twelve-year-old stepson, the rousing tale of pirates and buried treasure proved universally popular. "Over *Treasure Island* I let my fire die in winter without knowing that I was freezing," recalled J. M. Barrie, and Henry James predicted, "*Treasure Island* will surely become—it must already have become and will remain—in its way a classic." "[Stevenson is] a master of narrative," observed V. S. Pritchett. "He places his scenes at a fitting distance from each other, with an unflurried order and particularity, so that we do not blunder into them but are quietly brought to the point where the view is best. . . . He is a writer of brilliant beginnings. He catches the sensation of being athletically alive, which is especially the gift of youth. In *Treasure Island* this sense of physical action is wonderful and youth's dominant preoccupation with its own fear and courage plays naturally upon it. The timidity, the pride, the caution, the heady excitement of youth, its day dreams and admirations, are wonderfully rendered." Novelist William Golding agreed: "When one turns to *Treasure Island*, one sees immediately that Stevenson was the professional knowing precisely what effects he wanted and how he was going to get them. Every chapter is shaped and fitted into the general structure like the timbers of a ship."

Stevenson soon enhanced his reputation with *The Strange Case of Dr. Jekyll and Mr. Hyde* (1886), a psychological thriller that sprang from the deepest recesses of his own subconscious. A brilliantly original study of the dual aspects of human nature, it endures today as the quintessential Victorian parable of good and evil. "Robert Louis Stevenson has become immortalized by way of his private fantasy—which came to him, by his own testimony, unbidden, in a dream," observed Joyce Carol Oates. "The visionary starkness of *The Strange Case of Dr. Jekyll and Mr. Hyde* anticipates that of Freud: there is a split in man's psyche between ego and instinct, between civilization and 'nature,' and the split can never be healed." Vladimir Nabokov considered it "his most wonderful book," comparing Stevenson's "shilling shocker" to *Madame Bovary* and *Dead Souls* as "a fable that lies nearer to poetry than to ordinary prose fiction."

A few months later, in another burst of creative energy, Stevenson completed *Kidnapped* (1886). Set in the Scottish

Highlands during the aftermath of the Jacobite rebellion of 1745, this classic of high adventure interweaves the drama of Scottish history with the psychological moral growth of its adolescent hero, David Balfour. J. M. Barrie rated *Kidnapped* "the outstanding boy's book of its generation," and Mark Twain wrote to Stevenson, "My wife keeps re-reading *Kidnapped* and neglecting my works. And I have not blamed her; I do it myself." V. S. Pritchett reflected that "*Kidnapped* is far more than a boy's book. . . . [It] contains a universal statement about the loyalties and uncertainties of youth." And Stevenson biographer Ian Bell noted, "*Kidnapped* says as much about Stevenson as any autobiography. In David Balfour and Alan Breck he gave substance to two sides of his own character, adventurer and rationalist, man of duty and man of passion." Stevenson subsequently turned out three more tales embedded in the fierce loyalties and violent enmities of Scottish history: *The Master of Ballantrae* (1889), *Catriona* (1893), and the unfinished *Weir of Hermiston* (1896).

Though perhaps best known for his fiction, Stevenson was also a celebrated essayist as well as a popular poet. In collections such as *Virginibus Puerisque and Other Papers* (1881), *Familiar Studies of Men and Books* (1882), and *Memories and Portraits* (1887) he offered idiosyncratic views on everything from dreams, umbrellas, political activism, and jingoistic Victorian mores to the art and craft of fiction. "[Stevenson's] essays are tremendously bold in their biographical and interpretive outlines," said *The Times Literary Supplement*. "[They attest to his] human curiosity, his intimate, affectionate embroilment with behavior and character, his wonderful phrase-making and inventiveness of language." As a poet Stevenson enjoyed his greatest success with *A Child's Garden of Verses* (1885), an extraordinarily evocative picture of the joys and heartaches of childhood that appealed to both imaginative children and nostalgic adults. His other volumes of poetry include *Underwoods* (1887), *Ballads* (1890), and *Songs of Travel* (1896).

In 1888 Stevenson set sail from San Francisco for the South Pacific, where he spent the last six years of his life. *In the South Seas* (1896), a posthumously issued travelogue, vividly recounts his journey there. During this period he collaborated with his stepson, Lloyd Osbourne, on *The Wrong Box* (1889), a black comedy involving a mismanaged trust fund and a recalcitrant corpse; *The Wrecker* (1892), a story of modern crime and adventure on the Pacific; and *The Ebb-Tide* (1894), a dark tale probing the nature of evil that anticipates the fiction of Joseph Conrad. In addition he published *Island Nights' Entertainments* (1893), a collection of short stories that included "The Bottle Imp" (1891) and "The Isle of Voices" (1893), two tales based on Polynesian superstitions, along with "The Beach of Falesá" (1892), a masterful meditation on the growing gulf between native Polynesians and the white imperialists who had invaded their world. He also completed two works of nonfiction: *Father Damien* (1890), a famous defense of the Belgian priest who devoted his life to the care of lepers, and *A Footnote to History* (1892), a piercing examination of political turmoil in Samoa. Robert Louis Stevenson died of a cerebral hemorrhage at his estate in Vailima, Samoa, on 3 December 1894. The next day Samoan chieftains honored Stevenson, whom they hailed as *Tusitala,* or "Teller of Tales," with burial in a tomb atop Mount

Vaea. *The Letters of Robert Louis Stevenson,* an eight-volume compilation of his correspondence, was issued in 1994 to mark the centenary of his death.

"Stevenson can claim to have mastered the whole gamut of fiction," judged Arthur Conan Doyle. "No man has a more marked individuality, and yet no man effaces himself more completely when he sets himself to tell a tale." And John Galsworthy stated, "As a teller of a tale Stevenson is the equal of Dumas and Dickens. . . . He had but one main theme, that essential theme of romance, the struggle between the good and the bad, of hero against villain. . . . Stevenson was so vivid and attractive as a person, so picturesque in his travels and his ways of life, so copious and entrancing in his essays and his letters, and so pleasing as a poet, that his general self overshadows him as a novelist. But compare with his novels all the romantic novels written since . . . and you will see how high he stands. Next to Dumas, he is the best of all the romantic novelists [and] of British nineteenth century writers, he will live longer than any except Dickens." His biographer David Daiches concluded that "Stevenson produced some of the most memorable fiction in our language. . . . He transformed the Victorian boys' adventure into a classic of its kind."

CONTENTS

INTRODUCTION

Margot Livesey

I

When I was growing up in Scotland, Robert Louis Stevenson was the first author whom I knew by name, and he remains the only one whom I can truthfully claim to have been reading all my life. From an early age, my parents read to me from *A Child's Garden of Verses*, and I soon learned some of the poems by heart.

> I have a little shadow
> that goes in and out with me,
> And what can be the use of him
> is more than I can see.

Perhaps I recognized, even then, Stevenson's unique gift for keeping a foot in two camps. While the poems vividly captured my childish concerns, somewhere in the margins shimmered the mystery of adult life. A few years later *Kidnapped* was the first chapter book I read, and I can still picture the maroon binding and the black-and-white drawings that illustrated David Balfour's adventures. At the age of seven, a book without pictures would have been out of the question, but, in fact, they turned out to be superfluous. I could imagine everything that happened just from the words on the page, although I must admit to the small advantage that the view from my bedroom window—bare hills, rocks, heather—was very much like the landscape of *Kidnapped*.

At first glance such early acquaintance might seem like a good omen for an author's reputation. In actuality, that Stevenson is so widely read by children has tended to make him seem like an author from whom, as adults, we have little to learn. It is worth noting that his contemporaries would not have shared this prejudice. Nineteenth-century readers did not regard children's books as a separate species. Stevenson's own father often reread *The Parent's Assistant*, a volume of children's stories, and Leslie Stephen, Virginia Woolf's father, writes of staying up late to finish *Treasure Island*.

Like the shadow of his poem, Stevenson's reputation has waxed and waned at an alarming rate. He died in a blaze of hagiography, which perhaps in part explains the fury of later critics. F. R. Leavis in *The Great Tradition* dismisses Stevenson (in a footnote, no less) as a romantic writer, guilty of fine writing, and in general Stevenson has not fared as well as his friend Henry James. People comment with amazement that Borges and Nabokov praised his novels. Still, his best work has remained in print for over a hundred years, and he is among that small group of authors to have given a phrase to the language: Jekyll and Hyde.

Besides our perception of Stevenson as a children's author, two other factors may have contributed to his ambiguous reputation. Although his list of publications is much longer than most people realize—he wrote journalism and travel pieces for money—he failed to produce a recognizable oeuvre, a group of works that stand together, each resonating with the others. In addition, the pendulum of literary taste has swung in a direction that Stevenson disliked and was determined to avoid: namely, pessimism. After reading *The Portrait of a Lady* he wrote to James begging him to write no more such books, and while he admired the early work of Thomas Hardy, he hated the darker *Tess of the d'Urbervilles*. The English writer John Galsworthy commented memorably on this aspect of Stevenson when he said that the superiority of Stevenson over Hardy was that Stevenson was all life, while Hardy was all death.

II

Robert Louis Stevenson was born on 13 November 1850 in Edinburgh. His father, Thomas, was a lighthouse engineer who was responsible for the deep-sea light at Skerryvore, a place commemorated in *Kidnapped;* Stevenson later gave the name to his house in Bournemouth. His mother, Meg, was the youngest of the thirteen children of the Reverend Dr. Lewis Balfour. From *A Child's Garden of Verses* we know of Stevenson's early illnesses (although nowhere else in his work would we suspect how much of his life was spent in bed). His attendance at school was erratic, and his largely solitary childhood was filled with make-believe games.

He began writing at an early age, dictating "A History of Moses" to his mother at the age of six. A year later, on the title page of his second major work, "The Book of Joseph," he described himself as the author of "A History of Moses." His parents were proud of his precocious literary endeavors, but it never occurred to them that their son would be a writer; Louis was destined to follow in his father's footsteps as a lighthouse engineer. To this end, he studied science at Edinburgh University, very lackadaisically by all accounts, and accompanied his father to various lighthouses. Much of his fiction draws on the wild landscapes he saw on these journeys.

As a student still living at home, Louis had a complicated relationship with his parents. His parents were both deeply religious (Thomas believed that dogs had souls), and in our more secular age we can only imagine their dismay when they discovered that their son was a founding member of a student society that preached atheism. Under questioning, Louis admitted he had indeed lost his faith; terrible scenes ensued. Happily, his visits to prostitutes did not also come to light.

The result of these quarrels was a physical collapse on Louis's part, which led to his being sent to recuperate in the south of France. There he described himself as imitating Hazlitt, Lamb, Wordsworth, Thomas Browne, Defoe, Hawthorne, and Baudelaire, among others, in a determined effort to improve his writing. He also recorded his study of Thoreau and Whitman; the latter he regarded as crucial to developing a morality independent of the church.

Over the next couple of years Stevenson wrote several essays, including a controversial one on Robert Burns and another on Victor Hugo's romances. With his parents' permission, he gave up science in favor of law and in 1875 was admitted to the Scottish Bar. A brass plaque appeared outside the family home, but Stevenson made almost no effort to practice. The financial support of his parents was both necessary and forthcoming for most of his life. At the age of thirty-five he wrote, "I fall always on my feet, but I am constrained to add that the best part of my legs seems to be my father."

In 1876 Louis returned to France with a view to making the journey that would form the basis of his first published book, *An Inland Voyage*. With his friend Simpson, he set out to explore by canoe the canals and rivers of northwest France. Besides abysmal weather, little of note occurred as they passed from one river to the next, but Louis did indeed transform his journals (and those of Simpson) into a book. And at the end of the journey he met the woman who was arguably to change his life.

Fanny Osbourne was an American, ten years his senior, married, and with two children. She was staying in Grez, a town noted for its Anglo-American artistic community, when Louis arrived to visit his cousin. Fanny, who was already estranged from her husband, later claimed that Stevenson fell in love with her at first sight, but this seems to be pure fabrication. She was initially more attracted to his cousin, and on his side Louis appears to have been just as interested in her seventeen-year-old daughter as in Fanny herself.

That autumn, however, he visited Fanny in Paris. She gives an odd picture of her mercurial suitor: "I do wish," she wrote, "Louis wouldn't burst into tears in such an unexpected way." Stevenson also suffered from cataracts of laughter, for which, he said, the only cure was to have someone bend his fingers backward. Although many of the couple's letters have been lost, the two almost certainly became lovers at this time.

In 1878 Fanny returned to America and Stevenson to Scotland. Later that year he was back in France, purchasing a donkey. He named her Modestine, and together they made a twelve-day journey through the Cévennes. Several reviewers remarked on the pervasive sexuality of *Travels with a Donkey*, and

Stevenson himself said that "lots of it is mere protestations to Fanny."

We do not know on what terms the two parted, but in August 1879 Fanny sent a telegram, and in the most romantic gesture of his life, Stevenson embarked secretly for America. The long voyage followed by the train journey across the country dealt a serious blow to his health; by the time he reached Fanny in Monterey, he needed a nurse more than a wife. He described their marriage the following year as "a sort of marriage in extremis."

Fanny has been a major battleground for Stevenson biographers: did she help or hinder his genius? Whatever came later, it seems clear that this was a love match. Before meeting her, Stevenson had published only a few travel pieces and essays; he had no real source of income other than his parents and was never far from being an invalid. As for Fanny, she was for Stevenson the apogee of several significant relationships with older women. He lived in her company for fourteen years and wrote the works by which we know him.

Throughout their married life the Stevensons moved frequently, driven by Louis's love of Scotland, his need for a healthy climate, his desire for stimulating company. Winter in his homeland was out of the question, and several attempts proved that summer was too. The dreadful weather in *Kidnapped*—the novel is set in summer, but cold rain falls frequently—is perhaps partly revenge. In 1894, after four years of moving between Scotland and Europe, the Stevensons settled in the English seaside town of Bournemouth. There Louis spent much of the next three years in bed, often frighteningly ill; he later described himself as living like a weevil in a biscuit. But in spite of poor health he was wonderfully productive. In rapid succession he published *A Child's Garden of Verses, Dr. Jekyll and Mr. Hyde,* and *Kidnapped.* By the time he left Britain in 1887 he was a well-known writer.

Thomas Stevenson died in May of that year, and with his death, Louis at last felt free to leave Britain. In August he and Fanny sailed to America. Judging by the note he scribbled, thanking James for his farewell gift of a case of champagne, the voyage began in high spirits: "It is a fine James, and a very fine Henry James, and a remarkably fine wine; and as for the boat it is a damn bad boat." The Stevensons spent the winter in the Adirondacks and eventually, by a zigzag route, made their way to the South Seas and Samoa, where in 1889 Stevenson bought the Vailima estate and built a house. For the reading public the myth had come true: the author of *Treasure Island* was now living on his own island.

A famous photograph taken in 1892 shows the household on the porch of Vailima. No one is smiling. Stevenson is thoughtful, his mother prim; Fanny and her daughter, Belle, stare gloomily toward the camera. Her son, Lloyd, stands with arms folded and eyes narrowed, behind Stevenson. The Samoans, wearing lavalavas and garlands, are similarly somber. The camera has captured not the idyllic aspects of life at Vailima but the domestic strains, of which we get distressing glimpses in Louis's correspondence.

During these years Fanny became increasingly prey to nervous illnesses. Stevenson wrote that she made every talk an argument and then a quarrel. Meanwhile, Belle was driven by her husband's philandering to seek divorce. And although earning more than ever before, Stevenson was worried about money. These difficulties go some way toward explaining why, in spite of better health, so little of his memorable work comes from this period.

On 3 December 1894, Stevenson worked on his novel *Weir of Hermiston* in the morning, wrote letters in the afternoon, and died in the evening. He was helping Fanny make mayonnaise, adding the oil drop by drop, when he collapsed. By dawn the following day the Samoans were at work with knives and axes, cutting a road up the slopes of Mount Vaea. His coffin was carried in relays to the summit that afternoon.

III

Like many great writers, Stevenson had only a few subjects, which he was slow to discover: "I . . . sit for a long while silent on my eggs. Unconscious thought, there is the only method." He was thirty-one when he began what would be his first success, *Treasure Island*. The genesis of the novel is revealing. The family was staying in the small Scottish town of Braemar, and one rainy afternoon Stevenson drew a map of an island and began to make up a story to entertain his stepson, Lloyd. Thomas Stevenson, who was visiting, enthusiastically contributed details. Early chapters were read aloud to the appreciative family. The novel went on to be serialized in a boys' magazine and in 1883 was published as a book to surprising success.

It is surely no accident that Stevenson found narrative luck on the first occasion of which we have any record of his father's approval. The quarrel with Thomas, a quarrel that Louis's ill health repeatedly forced both parties to abandon, was one of the great driving forces and barriers in his work. Only after Thomas's death was he able to keep a father alive in his fiction. Meanwhile, in *Treasure Island* (as in *Kidnapped*) he solved the dilemma by killing off the hero's father as soon as possible. Then, in the presence of his real father, Louis made rapid progress, successfully synthesizing the romantic heritage of Sir Walter Scott and Alexandre Dumas, the spiritual heritage of John Knox, and his own sense of how much might be gained and lost by a desperate voyage.

One of the most significant accomplishments of *Treasure Island* is Stevenson's refusal to emulate his Victorian predecessors and preach a narrowly moral tale, a refusal that he continued in *Kidnapped*. I must confess I returned to the novel with some trepidation, half-expecting to take my seven-year-old self to task. But from the beautiful, stately opening pages wherein David Balfour leaves his home for the last time, I was captivated. I appreciated, as I had not previously, the complexities of Highland history and the fine characterization of David and his friend Alan Breck.

The novel is set in 1751, soon after Bonnie Prince Charlie's doomed attempt to win back the Scottish crown from England. (The two countries had been united under King James in 1603.) The rebellion not only sent Prince Charlie and the clan chiefs who followed him into hiding but led to severely repressive measures being visited upon those parts of Scotland that supported him. Both the uprising and the outcome served to further divide the country into the Lowlands—loyal to the English King George—and the Highlands—loyal to the Stewarts.

As a child, I was oblivious to all this. I read first and foremost for the story, and the story remains gripping. A boy of sixteen, newly orphaned but not cast down, sets out to find his one remaining relative. Instead of being made welcome by his uncle Ebenezer, David finds himself taken captive aboard a ship bound for America. He is destined to be sold into slavery. But in the fog the *Covenant* runs down a small boat; a single man is saved who turns out to be a Jacobite, a staunch supporter of the exiled prince. When David hears the seamen plotting to steal Alan Breck's money belt, he impulsively allies himself with the newcomer. "I have no credit by it; it was by no choice of mine, but as if by compulsion, that I walked right up to the table and put my hand on his shoulder."

The two survive the battle of the roundhouse only to be separated by shipwreck. After a miserable period during which David is stranded on the small, uninhabited island of Earraid (Stevenson spent time there while his father was building a lighthouse), he is reunited with Alan at the very moment when the Red Fox, King George's cruel factor in the region of Appin, is murdered. Together the two draw the pursuers away from the assassin and take flight across the heather. With many ups and downs in their fortunes, and their friendship, they escape the English soldiers and make their way to safety.

But the story is not simply a historical adventure story. Stevenson's lustrous prose, his realism, and his psychological acuity elevate the novel to literature. In his essay on Stevenson, published in 1887, Henry James finds two weak spots in *Kidnapped*—the opening chapters with Uncle Ebenezer, he claims, are hackneyed, and the book stops without ending—but he goes on to argue that "the remaining five sixths deserve to stand by *Henry Esmond,* as a fictive autobiography in archaic form. . . . There could be no better instance of the author's talent for seeing the actual in the marvellous, and reducing the ex-travagant to plausible detail."

This combination of the actual and the marvelous is in-deed one of the great pleasures of *Kidnapped:* the characters sup cold porridge, forget their water bottles, and worry about their clothes even as they flee for their lives. As in all great quest nov-els, the outer journey serves to reveal the inner; for the most part the narrative takes violence seriously. The death of the poor cabin boy, Ransome, at the hands of the drunken first mate is handled with considerable subtlety, and David is a clumsy fighter, aghast to find himself hurting people.

Shortly before his death Stevenson wrote:

> I cannot get used to this world, to procreation, to heredity, to sight, to hearing; the commonest things are a burthen. The prim obliterated polite face of life, and the broad, bawdy, and orgiastic—or maenadic—foundations, form a spectacle to which no habit reconciles me.

As any visitor to Edinburgh will have observed, the city itself embodies this conflict: on one side of Princes Street Gardens lies the respectable, orderly New Town, where Stevenson grew up with his parents; on the other, the dark, warrenlike streets and closes of the Old Town, where he drank with his friends, visited prostitutes, and attended classes at the university. Aware-ness of this discrepancy between the polite face of society (his father) and the turmoil beneath (himself) haunted Stevenson throughout his life and is manifest in much of his work, most notably, of course, *Dr. Jekyll and Mr. Hyde.* How amused he would have been to find himself posthumously achieving the pinnacle of respectable fame: the Royal Bank of Scotland used his portrait on the one-pound note. (Sir Walter Scott, I regret to say, got the five-pounder.)

Kidnapped itself is full of references to this doubleness. Captain Hoseason, for example, is described as being two men, and he "left the better one behind, as soon as he set foot on board his vessel." And almost all the major characters have this kind of split in their natures. Alan Breck is a fearless fighter but afraid of the stormy sea. Mr. Riach, one of the two mates on the *Covenant,* is gentle and lively when drunk, cruel and dour when sober. Duality not only is crucial to the characters but also governs, under many guises, the world they inhabit.

At the microlevel we have the conflict between English and Scots as a literary language. Stevenson was an ardent proponent of the latter while at the same time very aware that this could make his work inaccessible. At the macrolevel, much of the plot of *Kidnapped* revolves around the enmity between the cold, proper Lowland Scots, sensibly resigned to English rule (David Balfour), and the fiery Highlanders, clinging to the dream of a Stewart king (Alan Breck). The friendship between the two repeatedly comes back to their many differences and how these differences both divide and unite them.

Of course, these aspects of the novel were invisible to my younger self. So too were other virtues. Rereading, I was struck by the use of what I want to call narrative space; many writers have a fine sense of place and atmosphere, but Stevenson seems to me to have something beyond those gifts. It is no accident that *Treasure Island* began with the drawing of a map and that *Kidnapped,* while impeccable in its geography, is set before the great Scottish mapmakers had tamed the landscape, thus allowing Stevenson a free hand to display his remarkable talent for making the terrain through which his characters pass both shape and reveal their actions. And all of this is conveyed not in labored paragraphs of description but in small, perfectly placed details.

Which brings me to my next point: Stevenson's glorious prose. His style, praised and envied by his contemporaries, is unobtrusive, flexible, and brilliant. One of his most deeply held beliefs was that the success of the novel rested not on any attempt to imitate the dazzle and confusion of life but on "its immeasurable difference from life. . . . A novel stands or falls by its significant simplicity." This significant simplicity is, I think, a major part of what allows *Kidnapped* to be read so successfully by both adults and children. The novel unfolds in a crystalline prose that allows us to witness the events as if we were watching them acted out on a stage.

One other effect of Stevenson's lucid style, whether intentional or not, is to make us overlook the basic fact that *Kidnapped* is a historical novel; the equivalent subject now would be the Civil War. This oversight is due, I think, not merely to our obtuseness but to Stevenson's genius. He presents the characters and their adventures in a manner that is lively and unstrained by nostalgia. The central event of the novel—the notorious Appin murder, which occurred a century before Stevenson's birth—is shown to us through the innocent eyes of David Balfour as if it had happened yesterday.

Like *Treasure Island, Kidnapped* was first serialized in a boys' magazine. It was published in 1886 to enthusiastic reviews and has remained popular ever since. Stevenson went on to write several stories, travel pieces, a history of Samoa, and two novels, *The Master of Ballantrae* and *Catriona* (published in the United States as *David Balfour*) as well as his unfinished masterpiece, *Weir of Hermiston*. The canon has taught us to value the body of work over the single volume, but looking at our brimming bookshops and libraries, surely we can afford to esteem quality, even if it comes without quantity. As we love Mary Shelley for *Frankenstein*, di Lampedusa for *The Leopard*, Fournier for *The Lost Domain*, so we can love Stevenson for his few bright books. And how happy the author haunted by dualism would be to discover that his work belongs properly to both young and old, for Stevenson is full of something we can't get enough of at any age: life.

Binding for the first American edition (New York, 1886).

EDITOR'S PREFACE

I

Why *Kidnapped*? At the start of the twenty-first century, when the displacement of Gutenberg's culture by that of the flashing pixel seems assured, why produce a new edition of one of the most familiar novels in English? The simple answer is that a book remains our most compact cultural artifact, portable like a cellular phone, and (in the form of a master novel) reflective of a period's social and intellectual history. *Kidnapped* is a ready transport to a distant past, joining the reader with a sixteen-year-old "boy" who, in the aftermath of a small war, finds himself wandering the remote islands and highlands of Scotland with a renegade soldier. This may sound like the stuff of romance, but in truth it has the potency of myth. There is no other explanation for the lasting appeal of a book that has been translated into a host of world languages. Like its author, who continues to fascinate biographers, *Kidnapped* quickens the imagination of contemporary readers: they are none of them bored, and many read the book with avidity. It may be simple enough to say this, but the point should not be underestimated. Virtually every college reader in this age of the speeding image needs to be coaxed, at times even coerced, into paying attention to static images. That a late-nineteenth-century text, of a story set almost 150 years earlier, could entice a reader raised on television and film is no small achievement. Although Stevenson obviously could not foresee his late-twentieth-century readers, his imagination was modern enough to accommodate them. The economy and rapidity of his action, the vividness and limpidity of expression, and the entire story sustained by suspense—all these qualities are precisely suited to a contemporary reader's visual experience. This is not to say that Stevenson was a screenwriter ahead of his time (although the cinematic qualities of his fiction have always been exploited) but that he intuitively understood what readers required—he once remarked that an author must be willing to spend five hours to save a reader five minutes—and what, a century after his death, they came to demand. For if sober critics droned on about the complexity and density and greatness of the Victorian triple-decker, Stevenson instinctively knew that fundamentally those tomes were beyond reason: "To be clear and to be expressive and always to be brief—those were his primary aims."[1]

If Stevenson was writing at the dawn of the new style, of the break with Victorian decoration and ornament, he was himself the originator of that style. It was a style that modeled itself on the best of English prose, past and present, from the well known ("Shakespeare and Thomas Browne, and Jeremy Taylor and Dryden's prose, and Samuel Johnson") to the esoteric ("it is very well worth while to read Napier. His 'History of the Peninsular War' seems to me a fine solid piece of work"), and it

1. New York *Daily Tribune,* 10 December 1894, p. 16.

was itself the model for the new style in English prose.[2] Stevenson's writing was everywhere admired and often adulated. From George Meredith to Viola Paget to Henry James, from Andrew Lang to Marcel Schwob to Natsume Sōseki ("Among the writings of the West, I like Stevenson's style the best. It has strength and conciseness, and it is never tedious or effeminate"),[3] from autograph hunters to book collectors, writers and readers all saw Stevenson as someone who was leading English prose, and basically English fiction, into new territory. Kipling learned to write short stories from him. Jack London thought he and Kipling were the dominant models in English for fiction. As late as the mid-1930s Malcolm Cowley, looking back over his early years in Pittsburgh, listed Stevenson and Kipling as the first two writers that his "lost" generation read on their own.

But if these writers are themselves now old, it is instructive to identify their positions in literary and cultural studies. With the legitimation of popular culture, Kipling and London, who immediately followed Stevenson, have suddenly become more attractive and serious. And the modern novel, which for the majority of the twentieth century was defined as the novel of James and Conrad and Joyce, of Woolf and Faulkner and Lawrence, has now been redefined, or at least expanded, to include a tributary that runs from Stevenson to Kipling to London to Hemingway and on through Graham Greene. This parallel tradition contains the elements that contemporary readers find most compelling: stories that engage their attention

2. "Mr. R. L. Stevenson on the Cultivation of Style," *Publishers' Circular,* 17 June 1893, p. 668.

3. *Chūō Kōron,* January 1906. I am indebted to my colleague Nobuko Ochner for the reference and the translation.

because they take place in the real world, are narrated fluently, and hold a great capacity for visualization as they are read. These are the stories that become the films, and indeed are themselves the films within the stories. *Kidnapped* is a prototype of this form.

On 29 May 1886, *Young Folks Paper,* the weekly that was serializing *Kidnapped; or the Lad with the Silver Button,* published a letter from a reader named Edwin Hope: "I have never read anything of Mr. Stevenson's before, and his intensely powerful style strikes me with the added force of novelty. There is a vivid *directness* and simplicity in the style, with the true quaint flavour of the period in it, which seems to me the perfection of storytelling. It is the same merit which is so strong in the ever-fresh 'Robinson Crusoe' and 'Gulliver's Travels' " (vol. 28, no. 809). The novel, which had been running since the start of the month, had "already won very high encomiums from a number of readers" (according to the editor in this same issue), but Edwin Hope has the distinction of offering the first printed commentary on the text. Both by the substance and tone of his letter, the writer is considerably more mature than the title of the weekly publication would lead one to expect. Indeed, judging solely by the letters and the editorial commentary in "Our Letter-Box," the readership of James Henderson's magazine was older than its name implied. At one point the editor addressed this issue directly: "The title of *Young Folks* cannot certainly be limited to children. The title was selected because it embraced a much wider circle. 'Young folks' can be applied with as much propriety to young men and young women as to children. . . . Our readers [include] all classes, ages, sizes, and sects. We have no specially privileged class" (3 July 1886, vol. 29, no. 814). Twenty years later the Manchester literary club published an appraisal of the journal that James Henderson had founded after he moved from Manchester to London: " 'Young Folks' Paper' was . . . a high-class weekly journal for family reading, and in its day it stood without rival. A very considerable portion of its space was devoted to poetry and to essays dealing with literary subjects."[4]

The conviction that *Kidnapped* is a children's book derives from two major sources: its initial publication in *Young Folks* and Stevenson's own dedication-preface to the first edition, identifying the purpose of the novel: "to steal some young gentleman's attention from his Ovid, carry him awhile into the Highlands and the last century, and pack him to bed with some engaging images to mingle with his dreams." Apart from the obvious pose of the declaration, a manner that has a long tradition behind it in the field of the "romance," any reader may wonder at the choice of Ovid as the classical author whom the young gentleman was being seduced away from. After all, Ovid presents a relatively simple Latin for reading purposes, but more importantly he represents a racy and even titillating writing, one that the young gentleman might be reading under the covers, and the thought of drawing the boy's attention away from libidinous delights and directing it toward a realistic exploration of Scottish history can hardly be viewed as a treat, and certainly not as a favor. In brief, Stevenson is doing precisely the opposite of what he claims: rather than turning his reader away from study and enticing him into the world of pleasure, he is closing the classical pages of pleasure and opening a book with a potentially powerful instructional value.

4. Tinsley Pratt, "A Chapter in the Life of R. L. Stevenson," *Manchester Quarterly* 25 (1906), pp. 502–03.

There is no question that Stevenson's Dedication, together with the publication of *Treasure Island* and *A Child's Garden of Verses,* and the periodic references in his letters to the composition of a "boys' book," have been the principal reasons for the classification of *Kidnapped* as a children's book, and this despite the fact that from the time of its publication and throughout Stevenson's life the novel was consistently treated as an adult text. The New York *Tribune* addressed this issue directly in its review: "While avowedly intended for boys, [it] is as certain as any of Mr. Stevenson's previous books to find the majority of its readers among grown-up people" (18 July 1886, p. 6). The New York *Times* was a bit more oblique: " 'Kidnapped' may have a little touch of 'Treasure Island' in it, but for a man to have written 'Treasure Island' and to have then produced as dramatic a story as 'Kidnapped' is to have done a good deal" (1 August 1886, p. 9). Henry James jotted elliptically on a back page of the copy inscribed to him a note on the "coquetry of his pretending he writes 'for boys' " (see illustration, page lxii). In his published essay on Stevenson, James dropped both the informality and the implication that the novelist might be dissembling: "the execution is so serious that the idea (the idea of a boy's romantic adventures) becomes a matter of universal relations."[5]

Yet for more than a century *Kidnapped* has been marketed and cataloged as a children's classic, a notable example being the Scribner's edition illustrated by N. C. Wyeth, regularly displayed in bookstores at Christmas when parents are eagerly in search of anything that will raise the cultural level of their chil-

5. *The Century Magazine,* vol. 35, no. 6 (April 1888), p. 871.

dren. With the book institutionalized as a children's classic, it is virtually impossible to alter, let alone eradicate, that perception. In other words, *Kidnapped* becomes the book that it has been received as, and for a substantial portion of the population, including the public that has never read it, the book is what its cultural reception reads it as. Yet there is an adult audience that occupies another space and reads the text with a more open attitude, one that displaces or discounts the years of received or ossified criticism. Perhaps Stevenson's own readers were closer to the book's impulses than later generations; perhaps it is important to return to that earlier period, not to recover their experience, which would be futile, but to comprehend their wonder before a wholly original form of writing.

For some the story of David Balfour is so well known that its very familiarity works against it. For those reading it for the first time it may have the excitement attendant upon the new, but at the end one must wonder at the distance between the suspense here and that manifested in a thriller by Alfred Hitchcock or Michael Powell, not to mention someone like Brian De Palma. Perhaps it is unfair to contrast a book with a film, but we read every text in the context of our whole experience, and Stevenson's book must surely seem tame by comparison. Indeed, it would be strange if an innocent reader were not querulous about the fuss over *Kidnapped* when the title-word has such frightening meanings for a contemporary audience. But if the gap between the late-Victorian reader's expectations of dramatized terror and our own seems unbridgeable, we should remember that there are still significant differences even between what Stevenson was doing and what his audience expected. For one thing, the kind of terror that Stevenson provided in *Dr.*

Jekyll and Mr. Hyde, his greatest commercial success, was viscerally distinct from that in *Kidnapped.* There Stevenson was working in a genre—almost a subgenre—that focused on horror, whether we call it "Gothic" or the "shilling shocker," an early version of the "nightmare" films of today, or the horror films of Hollywood in the 1930s. Certainly Stevenson was more artistic, and certainly *Dr. Jekyll and Mr. Hyde* is more than Hollywood kitsch, but the continuous remakes of the story suggest that the essential nature of the market was never revised or questioned: it was a film sold as a product to frighten if not terrorize its audience, whatever the intentions of the filmmakers with respect to the moral or allegorical implications of the story. That Stevenson was capable of writing stories that elicited such responses is hardly surprising, given his nurturance on tales of witchcraft and possession that his nurse, Alison Cunningham (whose name is appropriated in *Kidnapped*), read and told him as a child. And stories of possession and the supernatural like "Thrawn Janet" and the "Tale of Tod Lapraik" are enough to remind us that he was quite willing to play with the reader's emotions in a way that was not far removed from the practice of Poe, whose shadow hovered over many of his early stories.

But the method in *Kidnapped* was different. Without question Stevenson was determined to create a *realistic* experience of fear and terror—not sensational, not melodramatic, but a meticulous melding of the exact detail with a measured tone in order to effect the proper sensation: the bolt of lightning that saves David from a near-fatal fall at the top of the stairs in the House of Shaws; the rats "scurrying" over his face after he is shanghaied and thrown in the putrid bowels of the ship; the "raw, red wound" on Ransome's leg, the stigma of Shuan's physical abuse but a badge of courage for the orphan whose mind was more profoundly damaged; or the "rope's end" that Ransome himself carried to "wollop" the boys even smaller than him, thus repeating an unending cycle of abuse. The seamless integration of these details within the narrative constitutes a pattern of Stevenson's style, a lean and poetic realism that is both plain and movingly affective at the same time, a style that despite the time of the story (1751) and the moment of composition (1886) most closely resembles the modernist experimental fiction of Ernest Hemingway.

When David comes to his lawyer at the end of his adventure, he is questioned sharply about his experience: " 'You say you were shipwrecked,' said Rankeillor: 'where was that?' 'Off the south end of the isle of Mull,' said I. 'The name of the isle on which I was cast up is the Island Earraid.' 'Ah!' says he smiling, 'you are deeper than me in the geography' " (p. 250). David's answer was clearly more than Rankeillor bargained for. In a way, the lawyer offers a grudging if oblique compliment to his young client, telling him in effect that the details of these small and obscure western islands are of no importance to the main issue under contention: who *is* this person in his office, and is he the rightful heir to the estate of Shaws? But that was Stevenson's characteristically oblique way of noting one of the major motifs of his text—not only a book whose characters traverse a broad swath of Scottish land but one where the place-names of everything from a clachan to a town, from a loch to an isle, from a battlefield to a gallows site are identified with a fidelity to their location and their history that can be appreciated only by reference to a historical gazetteer.

David Daiches was succinct when he called *Kidnapped* "a

topographical novel about Scotland in 1751."[6] Stevenson was insistent that his book be accompanied by a map, and publication was held up until a map could be produced that would effectively trace David Balfour's "wanderings," much like the wanderings of epic heroes in the past. Any number of radio broadcasts of the adventures of David Balfour have followed his route through the western isles and across the Highlands, a route that has also become a tourist attraction. Not only have writers followed in the footsteps of Stevenson but people have signed up to follow in the footsteps of his pen-and-ink creations. On a banal level this is a testament to how well travel agents have been able to commodify a novel into a viable marketing tool. But on a more profound level it reflects how deeply Stevenson embedded his country's physical history—for topography to him *was* history—into the consciousness of his people. Mull and Morven, Earraid, Queensferry, Balquhidder—these all exist in the national cultural life of Scotland, separate from their real life, by dint of their imaginative reconstruction in a fictional text.

II

Stevenson has always been noted for his descriptive power. It cannot be repeated too often that he was a major force in the reconstitution of travel writing, and that description was one of the elements that gave his writing such appeal. Edinburgh on foot, Belgium balanced in a canoe, the Cévennes on a donkey's back—all these places were captured by someone with a painter's eye and a poet's pen. That this talent—Stevenson

---

6. *Literary Landscapes of the British Isles: A Narrative Atlas* (London: Bell & Hyman, 1979), p. 205.

would have insisted it was a skill he taught himself, although it can be seen in his earliest correspondence—would be transferred from his letters to his travels to his fiction is hardly surprising. "The Pavilion on the Links," with its empty spaces and shifting sands, and *The Merry Men*, whose powerful riptides constitute a sonata to the sea, are two of his earliest and most brilliant ventures in the field of Scottish descriptive writing. In time, Stevenson became a model for all the manuals on writing fiction, and if the formal analysis of place or setting had not disappeared, or gone into desuetude, we might still see examples from his work. But who today wants to read long passages of description? Indeed, one of the nineteenth-century novel's most cherished techniques is not just dated, a bit antique, but completely irrelevant: what does one need with prose description when we have photography and cinema? In effect, the writers who held the highest position in Victorian fiction were among those whose fall has been the hardest. Scott and Dickens and Eliot were too long by far, and it was the descriptive passages that were the easiest to get rid of because they were the most incidental to the narrative.

What made Stevenson such an exception to this process? If indeed he was the model for the how-to books, why did his descriptive prose survive the excision of the readers? Put another way, why was he quoted so regularly in the early twentieth century for a technique that was already being viewed as something of a relic? For one thing, Stevenson himself saw description as an anomaly in late-nineteenth-century fiction. He knew that the pen could not compete with the eye. He had no intentions of making his prose serve the purpose of a camera, a device he was much taken with and used extensively to record his private life. Instead, description was made to serve atmosphere and emotion beyond all else; it was never designed to pictorially reproduce a natural scene. In a long note inscribed on the flyleaf of his autographed copy of *Kidnapped,* Will Low recalled telling Stevenson (when the novelist visited him in Paris shortly after the book's publication) how vivid a "picture" had been formed in his mind of Alan and David's flight through the heather. Stevenson then challenged his friend:

> "Well," he exclaimed "now turn to the book and tell me if you can find a half page of description." This we did together and I found that a word here and there, and *the sensations felt* by the pursued, were all that had given me this strong sense of the character of the country. R.L.S. was much pleased for at the time his motto was "Death to the optic nerve"; and he had cunningly replaced any form of definite description of the scenes in which his characters moved, by the portrayal of their emotions roused by these external conditions.[7]

Since David Balfour covers a broad swath of Scotland on foot, it is inevitable that the landscape figures centrally in both his eyes and his thoughts. He is repeatedly struck by the *desolation* of the territory, first when he is cast ashore on Earraid ("I thought in my heart I had never seen a place so desert and desolate" (p. 115) and later as he flees with Alan "over the most dismal deserts in Scotland" (p. 212). Not only is the country "broken" and "uneven" but it is dominated by "wild rivers"

---

7. February 1912. Silverado Museum, Saint Helena, California.

and "eerie mountains" that are even more forbidding. David's perception of this land "as waste as the sea" (p. 193) is remarkably consistent throughout the narrative.

> It was near noon before we set out: a dark day, with clouds and the sun shining upon little patches. The sea was here very deep and still, and had scarce a wave upon it; so that I must put the water to my lips, before I could believe it to be truly salt. The mountains on either side were high, rough and barren, very black and gloomy in the shadow of the clouds, but all silver-laced with little water-courses where the sun shone upon them. It seemed a hard country, this of Appin, for people to care as much about as Alan did. (p. 145)

Each of the first three sentences of this brief paragraph begins with an unremarkable observation ("It was near noon," "The sea was . . . deep and still," "The mountains . . . were high"), while the fourth and final sentence offers a summary judgment on all that went before. David has just entered the country of Appin, where the murder of Colin Campbell is about to occur. The time, so carefully indicated, is a detail that Stevenson drops into nearly every chapter, a means of enforcing the psychological realism and maintaining a tight rein on the structure. And the images, while foreshadowing the "death of the Red Fox," are equally representative of the natural elements that recur throughout the text. The bright sun shining, the sea so still that it might pass for fresh water, the black mountains—the scene is more suggestive than descriptive; it is not a picture that Stevenson captures but a mood, and it is characteristic that both the attractive and the ominous elements coexist, or are conjoined in the scene itself. So the dark mountains are laced with rivulets that, under the reflection of the sun, are silver to the eye, thus encasing in prose Stevenson's deep conviction that in nature, as in human experience, duality is all. But no scene, however suggestive-descriptive, is complete without commentary or interpretation: "It seemed a hard country, this of Appin, for people to care as much about as Alan did." For David, a young man desperately in search of his origins, and almost preternaturally sensitive to scenes of intimacy ("a scroll of smoke . . . meant a fire, and warmth, and cookery, and some living inhabitant that must have lit it; and this comforted my heart wonderfully" [p. 21]), the vastness and emptiness of the spaces only heightened his feelings of coldness and loneliness. What he does not yet understand, as Stevenson does, is that people's attachment to their country often has little to do with the ease of the land: that *place* may have a more profound meaning for their lives than can be found in any calculus, and that despite the charms (and protection) of the country across the water, as Alan grudgingly admits, Scotland has a deeper hold on one's affections: " 'France is a braw place, nae doubt; but I weary for the heather and the deer' " (p. 102).

Stevenson's gift for evocation, achieved by the combination of prose rhythm and poetic image, is so subtle and compelling that a reader might easily overlook its role in developing and furthering the narrative. Nothing in a Stevenson text is merely technical, nothing is without meaning, and that is especially the case in a novel as densely compacted of ideas as *Kidnapped*, one that joins historical incident with psychological truth. The novel is based upon a famous political trial in Inveraray in 1752,[8] and focuses on the period immediately following the defeat of the Jacobites in 1746 after their final failed effort to retrieve the crown of England for the house of Stewart. It would be fruitful to examine the narrative in this context. In our own time we have forgotten how deeply historical Stevenson was, how familiar he was with all aspects of Scottish life and culture, and how determined he was to represent it in his fiction. Indeed, the choice of subject of *Kidnapped* is nothing less than a testament to his own country's history, ensuring that its transmission be shaped by a Scottish as opposed to an English reading. Stevenson provides that reading, and for all those devoted to the eighteenth century, and the unending studies of the last Jacobite rebellion, and the clan system, and the divergences between the Highlands and the Lowlands, and the clash between two cultures, and between three countries, *Kidnapped* is a model text.

Yet it is also a text that lives outside its own history, and independently of our knowledge of the real Colin Campbell's murder, or Robin Oig's hanging, or Alan Breck's exile, even though those hard facts are not just integral but essential to the narrative. The novel has clearly flourished in an array of national cultures where the barest outlines of the historical events are Greek to the audience. Even North American readers can hardly be expected to know the incidents that the story purports to narrate. What, then, enables it to move readers in spite of (or apart from) its historical vestments? Perhaps it is the unobtrusive way in which fundamental realities about the conditions of the world are introduced into the narrative. For issues

---

8. See the first entry in the Notes, "the Appin murder . . . printed trial."

that Stevenson uncovers under the guise of adventure, indeed in the form of adventure, such as innocence terrorized, or cruel and capricious violence, to name just one constellation, are profoundly affecting as experiences and timeless when considered as philosophical reflections. This is a story that begins with the offstage presence of death and the palpable feeling of abandonment: David Balfour has just become an orphan. The question of how he will manage makes for interest, as Henry James might say, but in the world according to Stevenson, nothing comes without pain and certainly not without grief. For the conditions of life are hard—Stevenson called it a "battlefield" in *The Suicide Club*—and victory, which at best is nothing more than survival, is not for the faint of heart.

One of the most striking characteristics of *Kidnapped* is the starkness of its realism, a feature recognized immediately upon its publication: "Perhaps the greatest compliment that can be paid Mr. Stevenson is to say that he has the true Defoe manner, for there are all those little side issues, trifles, as it were, which he often introduces, which makes the whole thing, though you know it to be fiction, to read as if it were fact."[9] Although the realism touches all aspects of the narrative, from historical events to portraiture,[10] it can be seen in some of the smallest details as well. There is Cluny Macpherson, rebel, imprisoned in his own "Cage," half noble, half pathetic, offering David a meal of collops with a squeeze of lemon juice ("cookery was one of his chief fancies" [p. 204]), a small luxury he could not afford a few years earlier when Prince Charles visited him on the run from

9. New York *Times*, 1 August 1886, p. 9.
10. Henry James, marking the famous quarrel chapter between David and Alan, noted on his page, "do psychological truth of this."

the English (" 'for at that time we were glad to get the meat and never fashed for kitchen' " [p. 205]). Or David alone on the isle Earraid, cold, weary, and wet, who "knew indeed that shellfish were counted good to eat" (Stevenson had read that in Edmund Burt)[11] and who then winds up nearly "retching" to death. So much for the truth of books. Unlike in fanciful fiction, David never knows what to expect from his diet of raw fish; "sometimes all was well and sometimes I was thrown into a miserable sickness; nor could I ever distinguish what particular fish it was that hurt me" (p. 119). This might be read as emblematic of one of the book's central principles: David Balfour lives with the same kind of uncertainty as do people in life. Stevenson places us in David's position so that we are roughly in the same state of confusion and ignorance as he is when confronted by his uncle, or Captain Hoseason, on Earraid or in the Highlands. The purpose of the narrative is to make us first experience the action, then only gradually come to understand its meaning, so that the lesson of life is that we engage first, and only later do we understand. In effect, Stevenson illustrates a general principle of life, that our knowledge cannot come before our experience; or put another way, existence precedes understanding.

We must be careful how far we take this argument, or at least not rigidify it. For Stevenson was a deep believer in the embodiment of intelligence in books. We cannot say that he argues for experience at the expense of knowledge. When David finally

---

11. In "the little Fishing Towns ... such numbers of half-naked Children, but fresh coloured, strong and healthy, I think are not to be met with in the In-land Towns. Some will have their Numbers and Strength to be the Effects of Shell-fish"; [Edmund Burt], *Letters from a Gentleman in the North of Scotland*, 2 vols. (London: S. Birt, 1754), 1:33–34.

gets off Earraid, he says that had he been sea bred he would not have spent a day on the isle, but if he had only "sat down to think" he "must have soon guessed the secret and got free" (p. 125). For boys of the sea it is a matter of knowledge that comes by way of experience; for David, lacking the experience, it is a problem to be deduced through the use of intelligence, a process that is about the best one can hope for in an imperfect world, or in a world where the experiences of life come quicker than the occasions for reflection. If anything is true about *Kidnapped,* it is that the narrative and dramatic movements are virtually in tandem, and continue almost nonstop until the final three chapters. One of the reasons the novel has been so long-lived is precisely because of this movement, because the action appears continuous from the time David sets off on his journey until the moment he crosses the Forth. Within the chapters are any number of incidents that are each one a micronarrative within the larger story. And the effect of all these microstories that crowd and populate the text? Are they just ploys to keep the reader turning the page? To some degree that is true. But it is only a half-truth. For Stevenson never uses a detail for its own sake. Virtually every incident in *Kidnapped* is designed to either reveal personality or express an idea or illustrate a point about history, literature, law, manners, religion, or folklore. Like Henry James, Stevenson was committed in his fiction to the aesthetic principle of formal congruence.

One of the most striking illustrations of Stevenson's realism is the portrait of the *Covenant*'s cabin boy. David meets him first when he brings a message to Shaws and then talks with him on the road to Queensferry.

He said his name was Ransome, and that he had followed the sea since he was nine, but could not say how old he was, as he had lost his reckoning. He showed me tattoo marks, baring his breast in the teeth of the wind and in spite of my remonstrances, for I thought it was enough to kill him; he swore horribly whenever he remembered, but more like a silly schoolboy than a man; and boasted of many wild and bad things that he had done, stealthy thefts, false accusations, ay, and even murder; but all with such a dearth of likelihood in the details, and such a weak and crazy swagger in the delivery, as disposed me rather to pity than to believe him. (p. 46)

The picture of this boy is not only graphic but heartbreaking. Yet even here the role he enacts is a function of Stevenson's larger design, to expose the tyrannical authority of the ship's officers and their complete abandonment of any responsibility for their actions. *Kidnapped* treats of law and lawlessness. The *Covenant,* by trading in human cargo, is operating way beyond the bounds of the law. By lighting on the cabin boy Stevenson sears into David's mind ("the poor child still comes about me in my dreams" [p. 64]) the cruelty and terror visited upon the weak and helpless by those in power and control. Ransome's experience can be read plausibly as emblematic of the terror exhibited by James Stewart and his wife, the terror of the Highlanders defeated and disarmed before the English mace and crown, a government prepared to dispatch them arbitrarily to trial, and, if need be, to the gallows.

David's initial encounter with Ransome does not give him any clear idea as to why he seems unlike any boy he has ever

KIDNAPPED:

BEING

MEMOIRS OF THE ADVENTURES OF DAVID BALFOUR

IN THE YEAR 1751.

BY ROBERT LOUIS STEVENSON,

Author of "Treasure Island," "Prince Otto," "The Strange Case of Dr. Jekyll," &c.

PUBLISHED FOR THE AUTHOR

BY

JAMES HENDERSON, RED LION HOUSE, RED LION COURT, FLEET STREET,
LONDON, E.C.

*Title page from the edition published by James Henderson solely for the purpose of copyright.
The text included the first ten chapters of the novel.*

met. The style and manner of speech, the physical characteristics and behavior, even the nature of the conversation all strike a plain-speaking and clear-thinking lad like David as utterly bizarre. Ransome's reason has been short-circuited, his mind unbalanced; David refers to his "crazy" walk, his "crackbrain humour." Ransome's condition, as David and we discover, was the result of such relentless physical abuse that the loss of reason was the only way he stayed alive: by forgetting or disremembering the beatings given him by Shuan he was able to continue doing his job, which was essentially that of a galley slave. David would on occasion insist on making Ransome recognize what was happening, and then the boy would cry out in rage, and rush to do something—what could he do, really?—but immediately he would forget again, and revert to a kind of helpless passivity. One of Stevenson's deftest touches is the capture of Ransome's disordered mind—the jumble of vague memories of home (his father a clockmaker, a starling whistling an old ballad) joined to the lowest, most brutal fragments of sailors' talk, so exaggerated as to sound absurd, yet all with more than we would wish of truth.

III

Since *Kidnapped* is marked with incidents of violence as well as danger, it is no surprise that fear and courage are among the most powerful recurrent emotions. Although the successive dangers contribute to the perception that the story is directed to boys, in reality those selfsame incidents highlight the central issue of manhood, which is what David must achieve. Early on he is exposed to his uncle Ebenezer, who responds viscerally to the bolt of lightning that saves David's life: "Now whether my uncle thought the crash to be the sound of my fall, or whether he heard in it God's voice denouncing murder . . . he was seized on by a kind of panic fear, and . . . ran into the house and left the door open behind him" (p. 39). As soon as he discovers that David is still alive, "there came into his eyes a terror that was not of this world" (p. 40). Although Ebenezer Balfour is often dismissed as an overdone villain, the staple of popular fiction, Stevenson etches him with an exactitude that belies that casual view. His miserliness is detailed with an engraver's accuracy— measuring out the beer, husbanding the candles—while his negativity is enforced by his insistent repetition of *no:* "Na, na; na, na" (p. 32). What is more extraordinary is how the man has changed over his life, for the idea that he was once young, and in love with David's mother, and courted her only to lose out to his brother and get Shaws instead, is a lesson that David has to absorb by the end of the novel, when he learns the full story of his family history from Rankeillor. But in the meantime, or in the novel's real time, which is that of the sequence of actions as they were experienced, albeit narrated retrospectively, David is watching a man in the grip of an emotion that was well described by Seneca in Epistle XIII: "No fear is so ruinous and so uncontrollable as panic fear. For other fears are groundless, but this fear is witless."[12] The door left open behind him, the look in his eyes that was not of this world—these reveal a man incapable of confronting any kind of opposition without resort to "panic fear." Ebenezer's way of dealing with the world is with slyness and deceit, a type of negative behavior that conforms to the portrait Stevenson sketches of his house in near ruins, and

12. "On Groundless Fears," *Seneca and Lucilium Epistulae Morales,* trans. Richard M. Gummere (London: William Heinemann, 1925), vol. 1, p. 79.

is confirmed by his betrayal of David to Captain Hoseason. Although Stevenson never uses the word *coward* to describe Ebenezer, the idea is implicit in the action.

David is beached on Earraid just past midnight. "To walk by the sea at that hour of the morning, and in a place so desert-like and lonesome, struck me with a kind of fear." The dread of the night and the solitariness fill him with emotion: "I was afraid to think what had befallen my shipmates, and afraid to look longer at so empty a scene" (pp. 116–17). The desolation of the place, joined to the terror of the unknown, possibly more frightening than any real danger, forces David to think about what he should do to hold himself together. He instinctively realizes that the best thing he can do is avoid thinking about the things he fears: the death of his shipmates and the unforeseen dangers of the island. Why he should be afraid to think of the crew's death might seem strange, since they had "stolen" him from his country, were complicit in the murder of Ransome, and twice attempted to kill him and Alan in the roundhouse. Yet David had learned while on the *Covenant* that "rough" though they were, sailors were not all that different from other men ("No class of man is altogether bad") and had their own small virtues, "kind when it occurred to them, simple . . . [with] some glimmerings of honesty" (p. 62). Thus he feels bonded with them in shipwreck—he still thinks of them as ship*mates*— despite their battles in the roundhouse. David does not want to think of their fate because then he would have to reflect on his own. The fear of death is profound, and Stevenson presents it with a quiet yet emphatic simplicity: " 'He was a fine man too . . . but he's dead' " (p. 47); "He gave the captain a glance that meant the boy was dead, as plain as speaking" (p. 68).

Death is a leveler, and no man, however bad, deserves anything but pity at the final accounting. We know this to be one of Stevenson's most profound convictions, one that runs through his fiction from "The Pavilion on the Links" (1878) to "The Beach of Falesá" (1892).

For David to become a man he must first recognize fear, which could be overpowering in its physicality ("If I did not cry out, it was because fear had me by the throat" [p. 38]), and then strive to conquer it. When one of the sailors drops through the skylight during the battle in the roundhouse, David puts a pistol to his back: "only at the touch of him (and him alive) my whole flesh mis-gave me, and I could no more pull the trigger than I could have flown" (p. 87). The prospect of killing an actual man paralyzes David. But the sailor has no such qualms, and he roars out an oath: "and at that either my courage came again, or I grew so much afraid as came to the same thing; for I gave a shriek and shot him in the midst of the body." It is nothing less than proverbial to say that courage is triggered by fear, and here Stevenson dramatizes that commonplace. This scene is a major one in David's development, caught as he is between a boy's and a man's world. So when he reflects on the men he has killed it seems a "nightmare," and he feels in effect the fear that follows upon crime and is its own punishment: "I began to sob and cry like any child" (p. 92).

David is put in a crucible of dangers, and in order to survive he must learn not just to defend himself but to live with the actions of his defense. One of his great natural talents is his intelligence, and he is always trying to understand and adapt his behavior to his experiences. One discovery he makes is that men are afraid of different things. As the *Covenant* is in the midst of dangerous reefs, he comes to see that the captain and the ship's officer, neither of whom had shown well in battle, were nonetheless "brave in their own trade," whereas Alan, out of his element, was white with fright (p. 111). Stevenson here exhibits his habit of isolating the various abilities of a person and appraising them for their merits. Captain Hoseason, his portrait drawn in steel point, is far from attractive. Yet as the novelist reminds us repeatedly, the worst man may have not only a kindlier side but a useful or worthy talent. In Hoseason's case it is seamanship, and his fearlessness on deck in the face of dangerous rocks reveals a bravery that David sees as genuinely admirable, impressive in its own way as Alan's martial skill.

What is courage? David repeatedly learns that whatever it is he must either acquire it or find it within himself. At one point, when Alan is giving him lessons in swordplay, and berating him all the while for his clumsiness, David thinks to himself: "I was often tempted to turn tail, but held my ground for all that, and got some profit of my lessons; if it was but to stand on guard with an assured countenance, which is often all that is required" (p. 183). David naturally enjoys a bit of amusement at this unintended lesson: that self-confidence, perhaps even bluff, goes a long way in this world, and the presence of courage may be nothing more than its absence, albeit with a good face. But true courage cannot be left to pose alone, which is tantamount to leaving it to chance. It is only in the face of mortal danger that one discovers the resources within. Stevenson dramatizes this most brilliantly in the scene in "The Rocks," when David and Alan are forced to leap from one rock to another across a roaring river. "When I saw where I was, there came on me a deadly sickness of fear, and I put my hand over my eyes"

(p. 172). Alan forces brandy on David to calm his fear, but finally there is nothing for him to do but face the jump. "I was now alone upon the rock . . . if I did not leap at once, I should never leap at all. I bent low on my knees and flung myself forth, with that kind of anger of despair that has sometimes stood me in stead of courage" (p. 173). Unlike Indiana Jones, David does not leap with insouciance or sangfroid, but out of compulsion; he is impelled forward by the brandy, by the example of Alan before him, and by the realization that if he does not jump now, he will never jump at all. Is this courage? Can courage be defined by a behavior not altogether freely chosen? The answer is yes, and Stevenson has Alan provide a classic formulation: "To be feared of a thing and yet to do it, is what makes the prettiest kind of a man" (p. 174). To face down danger and not be paralyzed by fear—that is the test of manhood. It is a test that modern writers following Stevenson have explored in their own terms, not the least being Hemingway's extensive study of bullfighters in *Death in the Afternoon*. David is not a sailor, nor a warrior, nor a runner, nor a jumper, but he is called upon to act as if he had all their technical and athletic skills. Consider all the times he faces death: from his first encounter with his uncle Ebenezer to his clubbing and sickness on board the *Covenant*, the battle in the roundhouse, shipwreck, facing down a Highlander with a dirk, the blind catechist who is ready to shoot him, the redcoats who pursue him through the heather, his leap over the roaring water, and a final illness in Cluny's "Cage." Truly a cat's nine lives. It is not surprising that he sometimes breaks down, that he gets petulant and quarrelsome with Alan, or that the unrelenting stitch in his side, joined with the incessant rain, makes him want to give up the whole flight entirely.

Rather what is unusual is that he keeps on going. He does not stop running, he does not abandon Alan, and he never succumbs to the "weariness" that dogs him all along the way. For courage is not just facing down danger but the capacity to endure pain and suffering and not be defeated. For Stevenson, as later for Hemingway and Camus, this is nothing more than a modern version of stoicism.

IV

Stevenson had a wonderful sense of humor, as all who knew him attested. He was a marvelous raconteur, could be outrageously playful (as shown by the elaborate pranks carried out in his young Edinburgh days with his cousin Bob), and had a tongue that alternated between jest and bite. The range of his comedy and satire can be found in all the volumes of his *Letters* and in the mordancy of *New Arabian Nights* and the farce of *The Wrong Box*. If these last two texts are well known, there are others that are barely so, like *St. Ives*, with its extravagant parody of popular romances. The simple truth is that traces of humor can be found in most of Stevenson's writing, and *Kidnapped* is no exception. In this case it is so pervasive, however sparcly remarked, as to warrant discussion in its own right.[13]

One of the most quotable lines from *Kidnapped* appears just after Colin Campbell has been shot, and David discovers Alan at the scene. Having satisfied himself that his friend did not pull the trigger, he then asks him if he can "swear" that he does

13. The first printed letter to *Young Folks* called attention to the "fine leaven of *humour*" running all through the story-in-progress: "It is Scotch humour, keen flavoured, gripping the palate" (May 29, 1886). Christopher Morley, in an introduction to *Kidnapped* for the Limited Editions Club, wrote that Stevenson was never given "due acclaim" for his humor, although Morley found it limited in the novel to chapters 25 and 26 (New York, 1938, p. ix).

not know the man who was seen fleeing: " 'No yet . . . but I've a grand memory for forgetting, David' " (p. 155). Of course the humor here is fairly obvious. In the immediate aftermath of a terrible scene, a murder "in cold blood" (to use David's phrase), Alan provides a momentary relief from the tragedy. He has already been sparring with David by his denial of any complicity in the murder: " 'I swear upon the Holy Iron I had neither art nor part, act nor thought in it' " (p. 155). The sword is of course exactly what Alan would swear upon, since it is what defines him, in one sense, and what he may well hold most sacred. The fact that he throws in a Scots legal phrase, "art nor part," which means he was not an accomplice in the act, and hence is not culpable, is a nice touch that Stevenson provides for the benefit of historical accuracy. But the "grand memory for forgetting" is strictly Alan, his way of saying "I am as great at the forgetting as I am at the fighting," and it is amusing not just as an oxymoron but because it reveals a bit of Alan's character, the way he juxtaposes and tries to reconcile opposites, a habit that David sees as the contradiction between courage and vanity, as in Alan's hiding his hat under his greatcoat lest it be destroyed by water, or in his calling Mr. Riach a "small" man: "It was droll how Alan dwelt on Mr Riach's stature, for to say the truth, the one was no smaller than the other" (p. 161).

Stevenson takes a single word like *grand* and invests it with the speaker's irony. So when David has failed at his task of watching for the redcoats Alan says to him: "man! but ye're a grand hand at the sleeping!" (p. 176). By this time the word assumes a mocking note (it was used first by Ebenezer Balfour in describing the stairs—"They're grand"—and then by David after his near fall—"This was the grand stair!" (p. 38), just as Hemingway uses the word *fine* in "Hills Like White Elephants" to imply ironic meanings. Still it is not just irony that Alan's talk carries but good humor, even a kind of self-mockery—"I've a grand memory for forgetting"—as if the word itself is a sign of the speaker's awareness of his own boastfulness. David of course does not know whether to laugh or get angry at Alan, a condition he finds himself in repeatedly. During the quarrel chapter Alan cannot accept the fact that David is nearly a foot taller than he: " 'Ye're no such a thing! . . . There may be a trifling maitter of an inch or two; I'm no saying I'm just exactly what ye would call a tall man, whatever" (p. 223). The amusingly tentative way Alan goes about denying the obvious, as if to dismiss all argument, helps to defuse the tension and begin the work of repairing their relationship. So when Alan finally admits the difference in height, lest a new quarrel ensue, David says, "I could have laughed, had not my stitch caught me so hard; but if I had laughed, I think I must have wept too" (p. 223). As elsewhere, the space between tragedy and comedy is very close, and it is not always clear whether one is enjoying the fun of a ridiculous incident or sorrowing at the near escape of a painful one.

Stevenson's humor covers a range of ironic tones, from genial comedy to sarcasm to dry wit, with even a touch of the gallows. In each case the humor is calibrated to the context. David and Alan are trying to get help from a Highlander during their flight. The convoluted process of communicating by means of physical signs demonstrates Alan's inventive survival skills and gives them both an opportunity for resting and "drolling" a while: " 'it would certainly be much simpler for me to write to him, but it would be a sore job for John Breck to read it. He would have to go to the school for two-three years; and it's possible we might be wearied waiting on him' " (pp. 185–86). Later, by contrast, the two are almost at sword's point, each gibing the other, until Alan throws out his now-famous tag, " 'I am a Stewart . . .' " Unable to bear it any longer, David cuts him off with a marvelous insult: " 'I ken ye bear a King's name. But . . . I have seen a good many of those that bear it; and the best I can say of them is this, that they would be none the worse of washing' " (p. 220). And an example from the islet chapter, where David is so disheartened by his miserable situation that when he sees a proud and powerful stag looking for all the world like a lord astride his demesne, all he can do is admit the animal's superior ability to adapt to the conditions of life: "I saw a red deer . . . standing in the rain on the top of the island; . . . I suppose he must have swum the straits; though what should bring any creature to Earraid, was more than I could fancy" (p. 121). This is not just the mark of a shrewd lad, which we know David to be, but of a young man with a gift for language and a desire to exploit that gift. Thus the biting insult and the mock wonder are equally illustrative of David's fluency in expressing the complexities of his emotions. He expends his wit even at moments of great danger: "Alan's society was not only a peril to my life, but a burthen on my purse" (p. 190). This is drier than the gallows humor of James Stewart (" 'It would be a painful thing for our friends if I was to hang' " [p. 166]), as David seems unable to decide which is worse, Alan as a danger to his life or a drain on his purse. The line recalls a familiar if not proverbial phrase—"your money or your life"—which was used subsequently in one of the signature routines of a great modern comedian.

David and Alan at last cross the Highland line, with just a body of water left between them and safety. As David looks across to the other shore, with its prospect of freedom and wealth, he muses on his present homeless state, a beggar in rags, and an outlaw as well. The chapter "We Pass the Forth" serves as a pause in the plot, providing a respite for the fugitives from the fatigue of the flight, and a bridge to the final cluster of chapters, in which David recounts his adventures and recovers his estate. It is also a smart and entertaining comic interlude. The male bonding that has dominated the narrative to this point is here broken, or at least interrupted, by an attractive and resourceful woman who proves instrumental in transporting David and Alan across the Forth. If Stevenson had in mind the bravery of Flora Macdonald, and the compassion of Cummy, then he could do no better than his creation of Alison of Limekilns. And in the process he slips in a bit of banter that teasingly touches on issues of sexuality.

The comedy begins with Alan and David's repartee on the logic of traversing a body of water (" 'If it's hard to pass a river, it stands to reason it must be worse to pass a sea' " [p. 236]) and broadens to the good-natured epithets that Alan hurls at David in exasperation at his young friend's ignorance of female psychology (" 'ye have a fine, hang-dog, rag-and-tatter, clapper-maclaw kind of a look to ye, as if ye had stolen the coat from a potato-bogle' " [p. 238]). It reaches a high point in Alan's covert wooing of the innkeeper's daughter, whom he is determined to use to secure a boat and carry them across the Forth. To do that he assumes her natural sympathy for a poor, woe-begone lad like David (whose condition he theatrically exaggerates) and, working on her good looks, as well as David's ungainliness, he entices both her curiosity and her pity. If Alan's "play-acting" (as he calls it) is deceptive, and offensive to his young companion's sense of honesty, he reminds David of the alternative: " 'if ye have any affection for my neck (to say nothing of your own) ye will perhaps be kind enough to take this matter gravely' " (p. 239). The wry remark is a way of lancing the reality of death. Stevenson's comedy, as we have seen, is never far from its near cousin, and the wit and raillery often serve to make the prospect of tragedy bearable. But his art conceals this complexity. Just as the simplicity of the style masks the studied diction and the rhythmic syntax, so too does the subtle blending of comedy and tragedy deflect from the clearness of understanding that is at the heart of each of the modes. Of course, to separate the humor from the pathos would wrench the meaning from the text, for in the end comedy is the balm for sadness, just as tragedy is a beacon in the midst of laughter.

But Stevenson was not beyond the display of comic effect for its own sake, as Alan here pleads with the young woman for help.

If we lack that boat, we have but three shillings left in this wide world; and where to go, and how to do, and what other place there is for us except the chains of a gibbet—I give you my naked word, I kenna! Shall we go wanting, lassie? Are ye to lie in your warm bed and think upon us, when the wind gowls in the chimney and the rain tirls on the roof? Are ye to eat your meat by the cheeks of a red fire, and think upon this poor sick lad of mine, biting his finger ends on a blae muir for cauld and hunger? Sick or sound, he must aye be moving; with the death grapple at his throat he must aye be trailing in the rain on the lang roads; and when he gants his last on a rickle of cauld stanes, there will be nae friends near him but only me and God. (p. 243)

Alan is making this most extraordinary appeal to an innocent lass whose heart (he presumes) she puts before her head. The passage is a parody of sentimental fiction, or more precisely of the techniques and attitudes that sentimental writing indulges in: the adjective that pretends to make the noun larger but is merely a conventional epithet ("this *wide* world"); the rhetorical repetition ("and where to go, and how to do, and what other place") that tugs at the listener's heart; the picture of the victim, cold, suffering, and in want, contrasted with the warmth and comfort of the auditor, who ought to feel guilty at the inequity of their positions; and the final indignity of death on the gibbet, with the body left to hang in chains. Who could be dry-eyed at this projection of a young man's fate? And if Alan is "play-acting" here, well aware that he is conning the trusting lass, there is Stevenson behind his puppet, with a full consciousness of how much this writing is bred in the bone of popular romance. Ever the magus, however, the novelist gives his own twist to this self-reflexive exercise. For by the use of a vigorous Scots vocabulary—one that leads the *Scottish National Dictionary* to quote the same sentence twice in order to cite both "gowls" and "tirls"—he turns a sentimental parody into a miniature prose performance, one where the subject becomes the transformation of a tired literary form into a living art.

Henry James
from his friend
Robert Louis Stevenson

Skerryvore
July 21st 1886.
and I wish I had a better
work to give as good a man

KIDNAPPED

BEING

MEMOIRS OF THE ADVENTURES OF DAVID BALFOUR
IN THE YEAR 1751.

Half-title page from Henry James's inscribed copy of the first English edition.

V

From the beginning Stevenson was a favorite of sophisticated readers, and these included that vast Grub Street fraternity who reviewed books and were instrumental in creating reputations in the local and periodical press. This was also true in the United States, where virtually every new Stevenson book was reviewed in the New York *Times* and the New York *Tribune*. Stevenson's "popularity" is an extremely complicated question, and the casual notion that he was a writer who appealed to a very broad reading public is at best a problematic truth.[14] If he was not caviar, like Henry James, or ortolans, like Meredith, he was nonetheless a dry white wine that demanded a delicate and knowledgeable palate. If *Kidnapped* is commonly promoted in our time as a thrilling story in order to generate interest among the young, Stevenson's adult readers had a far easier time balancing their judgments: "The world of men and boys has appraised him long ago—the boys for the sake of the story, the men for the sake of the myrrh and aloes of the style."[15] If the note of that praise sounds a bit sweet to a contemporary ear, nevertheless it reflects a hard truth acknowledged by all serious readers at the end of the nineteenth century, including Oscar Wilde: Stevenson's prose was virtually unmatched by any living

14. *Publishers' Circular* reviewed an American magazine's list of the 150 most popular novels in America and commented on the absence from the list of *Kidnapped, Prince Otto, The Master of Ballantrae,* and *The Wrecker:* "This is likely to astonish Mr. Stevenson's admirers in Great Britain" (30 December 1893, p. 749). Just over a year later, the New York *Times* quoted figures from the *Westminster Gazette* on the sale of Stevenson's books in their English editions. Setting aside *Dr. Jekyll and Mr. Hyde,* a relatively "cheap book" that easily topped the list at 80,000 copies, *Treasure Island* was next at 52,000, with *Kidnapped* a distant third at 39,000. *New Arabian Nights,* published in 1882, was only at 12,000. Now compare *King Solomon's Mines,* published in the same year and at the same price as *Treasure Island,* then at 94,000 (5 January 1895).

15. George Stronach, newspaper clipping pasted in rear of *The Merry Men,* n.d. [December 1894], Huntington Library.

writer in English. Of course there were Meredith and James and Hardy. But the first two were truly stylists for the elite, and Hardy in his own way possessed an idiosyncratic manner. Stevenson alone wrote an English that was at one and the same time lyrical and limpid. In fact, one of the commonest words in *Kidnapped* is *plain,* a term that dignifies the garb of a good minister ("dressed decently and plainly in something of a clerical style" [p. 139]), highlights sound thinking (" 'the plain common sense is to set the blame where it belongs' " [p. 168]), and is itself a plea for clear expression (" 'Tell me your tale plainly out' " [p. 106]).

Stevenson's contemporaries, living before the First World War and that generation's antipathy to the real or illusory icons of the nineteenth century, and long before our own generation's visceral reaction to aesthetics as a standard for judgment, were acutely conscious of his facility and even a bit awed by it. " 'Kidnapped' remains his masterpiece. There his genius is to be seen at its best . . . in its most perfect and flawless expression."[16] Or this from an editorial in the Glasgow *Herald:* "The mastery of words . . . is not surpassed in distinction and music by that of any English story-teller, and it is hard to imagine a better equipment for a great novelist" (18 December 1894). But we do not have to look to the obituaries to find a consciousness among his contemporaries of his linguistic originality. Shortly after the publication of *Travels with a Donkey* Stevenson received a letter from his good friend and traveling companion for *An Inland Voyage,* Walter Grindlay Simpson: "As for your language it is perfect. Critics say it is pedantic. Away with them. You

16. New York *Daily Tribune,* 30 December 1894, p. 16.

merely use dictionary words when they are necessary and what the critics resent is that your vocabulary is larger than that of a ploughman or a merchant."[17]

If Stevenson prided himself on anything it was his precision as a writer, chastising Edmund Gosse for using the wrong word ("never again write 'noticeable'; I have but to remind you that 'notable' is the word")[18] and complaining about the nineteenth century's "slovenly" literary habits. "I have only one feather in my cap, and that is I am not a sloven." He credited that to his study of the classics:

> Although I am in the position of Shakespeare—I have little Latin and less Greek—yet the benefit which I owe to my little Latin is inconceivable. It not only helps one to arrive at the value of words, but you must remember that we are only the decayed fragments of the Roman Empire from which we have all that we value ourselves upon, and I always believe we can never be so well employed as in endeavouring to understand as well as we can the original meaning of that system of things in whose ruins we live.[19]

Stevenson begins with Shakespeare and Jonson and ends with a presentiment of T. S. Eliot. Since he was living under the falling shadow of the *fin de siècle* he felt nothing more pressing than the need for exactitude in language. These remarks were made to

---

17. 10 June 1879. Beinecke Library, Yale University (B5501).

18. Stevenson, *The Letters of Robert Louis Stevenson,* ed. Bradford A. Booth and Ernest Mehew, 8 vols. (New Haven: Yale University Press, 1994–1995), 4:200.

19. "Mr. R. L. Stevenson on the Cultivation of Style," *Publishers' Circular,* 17 June 1893, p. 668.

a journalist in New Zealand just eighteen months before his death in Samoa. He had begun to see his work outside the frame of his century's experience and within the larger context of Western history. He highlighted the linguistic nature of his writing as a wedge into its deeper structure, for meaning and intention were embedded in history, and history was nothing if not constituted of words. Thus to know the origins of our language was to know something of ourselves.

On 14 February 1886, Stevenson wrote to Charles Baxter about his new book:

> What's mair, Sir, it's Scōtch: no strong, for the sake o' they pock-puddens, but jist a kitchen o't, to leeven the wersh, sapless, fushionless, stotty, stytering South-Scotch they think sae muckle o'. Its name is Kidnaaapped; or Memoyers of the Adventyers of Darvid Balfour in the year seventeen hunner and fifty wan. There's nae sculduddery aboot that, as ye can see for yoursel. And if you hae no objection, I would like very much to put your name to it.[20]

From the beginning Stevenson took pains to ensure that each book of his had a dedication, and in the early years he even tried to fit the text to the person. *New Arabian Nights* was for his cousin Bob, in memory of their salad days, while *Treasure Island* went to his enthusiastic and energetic stepson, Lloyd Osbourne. No one could have been a better match for *Kidnapped* than Charles Baxter. Their friendship dated from their college

---

20. *Letters*, 5:206.

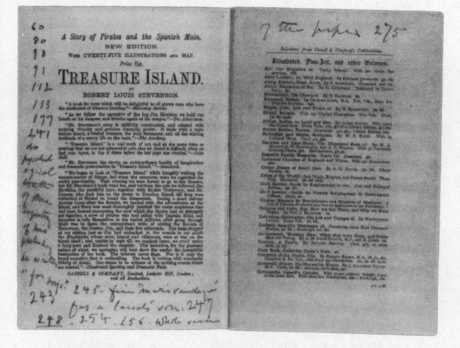

Henry James's markings on the advertising pages of his copy of Kidnapped. *These notes were used for the essay on Stevenson that James first published in the* Century Magazine *in April 1888.*

days and was maintained without interruption through their adult years. If Baxter became in the end Stevenson's most trusted financial adviser and business agent, it was not that role that made the dedication so just: the two men were deeply nationalistic about Scotland (Baxter lived his entire life in Edinburgh) and they enjoyed nothing more than sporting with each other in their native tongue. Stevenson's letters were often a rollicking tumble of Scots words and phrases, and were implicated with a shared set of nationalistic attitudes. If Stevenson recalls for Baxter (in the dedication) the old clubs of their youth, or the intellectual giants whose legacy they cherished and whose achievements they were just beginning to emulate, he also reminds him (and himself) of his own distance from "those places that have now become . . . a part of the scenery of dreams."

But the dedication was a broad public statement, written at Bournemouth, in another land and largely for another people, and with all the constraints of a public discourse. In the confines of a private letter, on the other hand, Stevenson could leave England and reenter the land of his birth. And he could freely express himself. Of course, he had been doing that all through the composition of *Kidnapped*, painstakingly legitimating the Scots language, but in his letter the point is made with crystal clarity. After assuring Baxter that he does not have to worry about any damage to his professional reputation because the text is neither "indecent" nor "irreligious," Stevenson then identifies the salient feature of a book dedicated to a habitué of the Parliament close—"it's Scotch." What follows is a brilliant minidiatribe against the English. Stevenson employs a succession of words that go far to characterize his prospective audience's ability to understand or even tolerate the "strong"

Scots that he and Baxter are comfortable with. The fault, of course, lies with the "pock-puddens," a contemptuous term for the English that is often defined as a jocular expression but in Stevenson's use conveys all the contempt and none of the jocularity.[21]

So (he implicitly argues) he has used just enough "Scotch" to "kitchen" or spice—and now follows a string of adjectives that intensify the derision in *pock-puddens*—the dull, tasteless, insipid, uninspired, stammering, and halting kind of Scots they think so much of. "South-Scotch" is Stevenson's term for "English-Scotch," some hybrid creation of English speakers who want to ornament the language, which the great Cockburn protested against in 1844: "Railways and steamers, carrying the southern [i.e., English] into every recess, will leave no asylum for our native classical tongue" (*SND*). *Southern* was a term almost as contemptuous as *pock-puddens*, and was used thus by Sir Walter Scott: "A sturdy Scotsman, with all sort of prejudices against the southern, and the spawn of the southern" (1818; *OED*). Stevenson is protesting with all the force of his native tongue what passes for the English understanding of "Scotch" in literature. He is in fact railing against the taming of the Scottish language for the sake of a tepid English taste for local color. If anyone wonders where Stevenson gathered the rhetoric years later to denounce the Reverend Dr. Hyde in his famous defense of Father Damien, one need look no further than this wonderful sentence (which is quoted on three separate occasions in the

---

21. All the examples in the *Scottish National Dictionary* (*SND*) support Stevenson. Edmund Burt says that all over Scotland his countrymen are "dignified with the title" which "signifies a glutton" (ca. 1730). Scott uses it pejoratively ("The Englishers . . . the pock-puddings ken nae better") and Stevenson himself is cited, having compacted all his countrymen's animosity for the English into the expression.

SND). The power and vigor of the expression, the intensity of feeling, are directed not simply against the false "South-Scotch" that Stevenson decries but against the attitudes and conditions that compel an artist to acquiesce in that kind of writing: it can even be seen as the visceral reaction of a "colonized" subject to a form of "imperial" oppression.

Stevenson chafed all his life at the array of social, sexual, and political mentalities that controlled and censored literature, yet there is no question but that he conformed to them. This does not mean that he did not at times break out in anger, although the outbursts were confined almost exclusively to the privacy of his correspondence. The irony, and truly the brilliance of his achievement in *Kidnapped*, is that he was able to accomplish his genuine objectives in spite of these enormous obstacles. Far from being softened, the language of the novel is bold and hardy throughout. Finally, as the writer mock-jests with Baxter, his book has no "sculduddery"; it is not, in other words, obscene or smutty. By deliberately using such a coarse word (which also means *fornication*) Stevenson affirms his right to speak openly and freely in his own language. And yet even here the long process of planing the edges of this deeply recalcitrant writer never ceases. In DeLancey Ferguson and Marshall Waingrow's 1956 edition of the letters to Baxter they gloss "sculduddery" as "bawdy," while Ernest Mehew, in the latest edition, avoids any definition altogether.

From early on Stevenson proclaimed the virtue of Scots as a literary language, using it sparingly in "The Pavilion on the Links," extensively in *The Merry Men*, and exclusively in "Thrawn Janet." He submitted the last story to Leslie Stephen at the *Cornhill*, "but as it is all in Scotch he cannot take it, I know. It was *so good,* I could not help sending it."[22] Of course the story was accepted, but Stevenson's remark reflects his awareness of the difficulty the language presented to a foreign (i.e., English) reader, and so he would occasionally insert a definition within the sentence: "I found a den, *or small hollow,* where there was a spring of pure water" ("Pavilion"; italics added). Or from *Kidnapped:* "we spent a great part of our days at the waterside, stripped to the waist and groping or (as they say) *guddling* for these fish" (p. 183; italics added). But this kind of internal glossing, while artistic at best, was simply unworkable when the vocabulary and idiom and syntax were predominantly Scots. As proud as Stevenson was of working in his native tongue— " 'Tod Lapraik' is a piece of living Scots; if I had never writ anything but that and 'Thrawn Janet', still I'd have been a writer"[23]—it was plain that it could not be read, let alone understood, without a Scots dictionary, or at least a glossary. Stevenson was conscious of this, as he was of the grumbling on the part of English readers about a language they had little knowledge of and less interest in. When Marcel Schwob wrote to him asking if he could translate any of his books, Stevenson suggested *Kidnapped* or *The Master of Ballantrae,* but then warned him: "In both these works you should be prepared for Scotticisms used deliberately."[24]

But the matter of language goes beyond mere usage, beyond the fact that Scots *pyat* is used in place of *magpie* (p. 147) or that *clachan* substitutes for "what is called a hamlet in the English" (p. 184). For Stevenson language is the texture and structure of

22. *Letters,* 3:188.
23. *Letters,* 8:38.
24. *Letters,* 7:70.

thought, and the words we use and the way we use them, their rhythm and inflection, are as important as what they mean. They tell us who we are. In an inspired touch Stevenson shows us what we lose when our voice is stilled. He places David Balfour in the same position to the exotic Highlanders as the English reader is to the text. David is helpless before all these people whose Gaelic "might have been Greek and Hebrew for me" (p. 124), just as the reader is baffled by a plethora of alien words. A telling example is the scene where the fishermen are laughing at David, who is panic-stricken on the islet. The Scot feels their behavior as deliberate cruelty; the Gaels think the lad with the waving arms a figure of great fun. Neither comprehends the other, and a simple experience is thus apprehended in diametrical terms. For without a common tongue we are all living in a Tower of Babel, confused by others and caught in the web of our own words. David's frustration, and his sense of isolation, is heightened as he travels through an uncharted territory where everyone speaks a "strange" language and where his own speech is equally "strange" to everyone else. He has a brief respite from these feelings when he meets Mr. Henderland, only because the Lowland minister "spoke with the broad south-country tongue, which I was beginning to weary for the sound of" (p. 140).

It was while hiding on a naked rock in the heat of the day, when the redcoats were jabbing their bayonets in the surrounding heather, that David faced another linguistic experience.

It was in this way that I first heard the right English speech. . . .

'I tell you, it's 'ot!' . . . and I was amazed at the clipping tones and the odd sing-song in which he spoke, and no less at that strange trick of dropping out the letter h. To be sure, I had heard Ransome, but he had taken his ways from all sorts of people, and spoke so imperfectly at the best, that I set down the most of it to childishness. My surprise was all the greater to hear that manner of speaking in the mouth of a grown man; and indeed I have never grown used with it; nor yet altogether with the English grammar, as perhaps a very critical eye might here and there spy out even in these memoirs. (pp. 177–78)

This passage appears two-thirds of the way into the narrative, and is the first time that "English" is formally cited as a language. In other words, for the first two-thirds of the novel David Balfour, along with everyone else, is implicated in the two languages of his own country, Scotland, and only now, when he is nearly cheek by jowl with a live English soldier, does he realize that the language of *that* country, of the supporters of King George, of whom he counts himself an adherent, is quite simply different from his own. It comes as a genuine shock to him. And his assumption that it is the "*right* English speech" only further confounds him; for if the English spoken by the soldier is proper English, why then does it sound so "odd" both in its inflection as well as in its pronunciation? (David, of course, was not equipped to identify the class of the speaker, but Stevenson cleverly maintains his character's integrity while offering the reader an early Shavian observation.)

Stevenson has suddenly brought the two cultures of Scotland, of the Highlands and the Lowlands, into contact with the third culture of England, thus bringing into the foreground the reality of not two countries but three. Of course David and Alan, along with everybody else through the first nineteen chapters, are speaking English, but it is from David's point of view an improper or imperfect sort of English, as David periodically translates for his reader the occasional Scots word, just as Stevenson provides the occasional gloss. In reality this passage makes explicit issues about language that are played out in the novel, not the least of which is the sense of inferiority that the narrator has with respect to his command of English, an inferiority he attributes to his weakness in grammar but which in reality Stevenson subverts for the reader. When David says he has never grown "used with it" in reference to the inflection and pronunciation of the soldier, the reader might pause and think, "used *to* it," but the phrase is actually good Scots, meaning "to make familiar with, to accustom to," and is cited in the *SND* and *EDD* as dialectal, with Stevenson quoted from *Underwoods* in the *SND*. What the author is doing is clear and opaque at the same time: he is asserting the legitimacy of his own language, its forms and expressions, its rhythms and inflections, while giving apparent credence to an unsuspecting reader that David does not have a solid command of English grammar. It is a tactic that only the most deliberate and self-reflexive of writers would undertake, and few could manage as artfully. It is a small irony that a number of Stevenson's forms of speech that may be considered Scots or idiosyncratic or both were altered by editors and compositors in the setting of the novel, since it hardly needs saying that it was an English publishing apparatus that put the book in print. But through it all there is more than mere gamesmanship on the writer's part, for Stevenson addresses the central questions of how we use our language and what it means to us. David was quick enough to guess that Ransome's speech was a bastardization that derived from a variety of social experiences, and he was not prepared to accept it as definitive. If this passage means anything, it is a sly shedding of the sense of inferiority that the Scots speaker has to the English.

Kidnapped is a text constitutive of and informed by three major languages—Scots, English, and Gaelic—with a fourth, Latin, thrown in for good measure. Obviously not all are given equal status; Stevenson was unfamiliar with Gaelic, and the proverbial Latin phrases were designed more for gentle satire than to make a case for another language's place in the province of the book. Yet even here Stevenson was insinuating an important point: for as he said repeatedly, we are but the ruins of an ancient culture, and those familiar tags from Virgil and Horace and Martial, tossed off so casually by Rankeillor, remind us of who we are and where we come from. They remind us, too, of an older book and another wandering, timeless hero: David's odyssey, after all, has a long and glorious history behind it.

Autograph title page.

A NOTE ON THE TEXT

Stevenson was a writer whose precise attention to minute detail was recognized long before he became an international star. Yet despite the prodigious Stevenson archives in the United States and Scotland, there is surprisingly little hard evidence on how his manuscripts became printed books. We know from anecdotal remarks that he was intensely conscious of the process and extremely vigilant in demanding that the compositors and proofreaders follow his copy. A candid obituary in the Aberdeen *Journal* provides a telling example of his attitude:

> Stevenson's handwriting was a horror to typewriters and compositors, yet he was a most particular man about his proofs, and grew very irate and sarcastic on the subject of typographical errors. His readers must have noticed that he was most accurate and systematic in his punctuation. In spite of the fact that it was often impossible for the unhappy compositor to distinguish between a comma and a period, a capital and a small letter, on the MS., nothing annoyed the author so much as a mistake of the kind. (18 December 1894)

That so pointed an observation could be made in a remote Scottish newspaper strongly suggests that the complexities of working with Stevenson's autographs were common knowledge to the wider Grub Street world, as indeed they were to his closer connections. E. L. Burlingame, Stevenson's longstanding editor at Scribner's, illustrated the writer's combativeness during the composing process: "I have tried in vain to find a corrected proof-sheet, for these were very characteristic. Occasionally he would put sportive addresses on the side to the proof-reader, now and then extremely caustic ones—one especially that I think the reader cut off and kept to nurse animosity upon, for I have never seen it since" (untitled address, November 13, 1900; Anson Burlingame Papers, Library of Congress).

This edition of *Kidnapped; or the Lad with the Silver Button* is based on the autograph manuscript in the Huntington Library (HM 2410). It reproduces for the first time Stevenson's text as he wrote it. The extant holograph, constituting chapters 1 through 27, is in places heavily revised, in others clear and fluent. Given the heavy use of the holograph during the production of the book—editorial queries in the margins that sent the pages back to Stevenson for response—the document itself is in relatively good condition. Not the pristine condition of his later holographs, to be sure, but then *Kidnapped* was written before every scrap from Stevenson's hand was saved as if it were holy writ or precious metal. For me, working with the manuscript was a privilege as much as a labor. Stevenson's handwriting, cramped and tiny though it is, has a kind of elegance to it, and in time the eye accommodates the quirks of his hand, and the ear becomes familiar with the voice that moves the script. No one can come away from studying the manuscript without deep admiration for Stevenson's intensity of concentration and the shading and polish he exerted on even the smallest vision or revision. In following the autograph this edition acknowledges the broadest range of Stevenson's artistic intentions.

Punctuation and capitalization. Stevenson wrote for the ear, he punctuated by ear, and he often capitalized by ear. His system of punctuation, while initially odd-looking, sounds quite natural when "read" audibly. At times individual compositors for the periodical *Young Folks* and the first English edition punctiliously followed Stevenson's text; but in the main they altered and regularized the punctuation. For this edition only minor emendations to the original punctuation were necessary: missing periods and quotation marks were added, and apostrophes were introduced or emended. Capitalization was a more complicated matter. As the Aberdeen newspaper noted, Stevenson's capitals were often indistinguishable from his small letters. But his use of them was deliberate and purposeful. *King*, for example, is declaimed by Alan Breck with a kind of a swagger, as he repeatedly reminds David that he "bears a *King's* name," with a capital *K.* On the other hand, *whig* is rarely uttered without a sneer, or written with anything but a small letter. This edition restores Stevenson's capitals and small letters to their original form.

Spelling and compounds. Stevenson read capaciously in older books, and his spelling was a by-product of that reading. It might reflect the period of the novel (*burthen* in place of *burden*); it was occasionally archaic (*Glascow*) and frequently Scots (*muir*

From "I Run a Great Danger in the House of Shaws," Kidnapped.
Holograph, p. 22.

rather than *moor*). I have retained all the forms that have linguistic authority, while clear spelling errors have been corrected (*murmured, but* for *butt, dizy*). One spelling matter needs separate comment: Stevenson was unvarying in writing *nieghbour, niether, siezed,* and *Lieth*. Although this habit drove Sidney Colvin to carp constantly about his friend's weakness in orthography, it is plausible that for Stevenson there was an aural basis for the spelling. But these words are so rife that I have emended them in order to avoid obtruding their (mis)spelling on the reader. In the matter of compound words and hyphenation, Stevenson's practice was more modern than the compositors'. He used fewer hyphens, preferring either to compound or to write two words rather than one. Here, too, we can see him "speaking" the word in his mind and compounding or not depending upon the breath or pause between the two words. Occasionally he inserted a hyphen after the prefixes *mis* (*mis-chief*) and *dis* (*dis-appointment*), another sign that he used accidental marks to serve an oral and dramatic style. Of course, in a handwritten novel of nearly one hundred thousand words he was not always consistent (*redcoats, red coats, red-coats*), and I have not attempted to impose consistency on him.

Language. The subject of *Kidnapped,* to borrow a smart conceit from Vladimir Nabokov, is Stevenson's love affair with the Scots and English languages. There is not room enough here to analyze the linguistic differences between Stevenson's manuscript and the serial and first book editions, but they are substantial and significant. Words on the holograph were deleted or altered, and others not there were added. From simple misreadings to deliberate revisions, from small changes in vocabulary to the elimination or recasting of sentences, the printed editions represent major departures from Stevenson's handwritten text. The changes bore particularly on his deliberate and pervasive use of Scots. The dialectal syntax was modified to make it more correct ("a bit fun" or "a bit pressure" was changed to "a bit *of* fun"), or a Scots diminutive was read as an authorial error (*awhilie* to *awhile*), or small Scots words were turned into English ones (*weel* to *well*, *twa* to *two*). In two cases important words were dropped altogether, because they were either too hard to decipher or incomprehensible or both (*allenarly, notour*). But it would be a mistake to think that it was simply the unfamiliar or even more uncomfortable Scots that was the source of the problem. For Stevenson's English was corrected as well. Whether it was squeamishness ("*nurse* the bairn" became *keep*) or delicacy ("traded upon her *innocence*" became *ignorance*), whether it was insensitivity to poetic shading ("a few lights *showed*" was changed to *shone*) or just a dull and common ear (*sparking* to *sparkling*), the revisions plane the contours and coarsen the surfaces of Stevenson's style. These changes—and some few may well have been Stevenson's own revisions between the serial and book publications—were not the result of arrogant or supercilious compositors (although the editor of *Young Folks* might fall into that category) so much as the consequence of a production practice that authorized the makers of books to aid and improve the writers. But Stevenson was one of those rare authors who needed little if any assistance, and never was an apprentice to anyone but himself.

This edition restores all the language of the holograph. Stevenson's hand makes it a judgment call to distinguish *further* from *farther*. And two words were problematic. "I looked, too, at

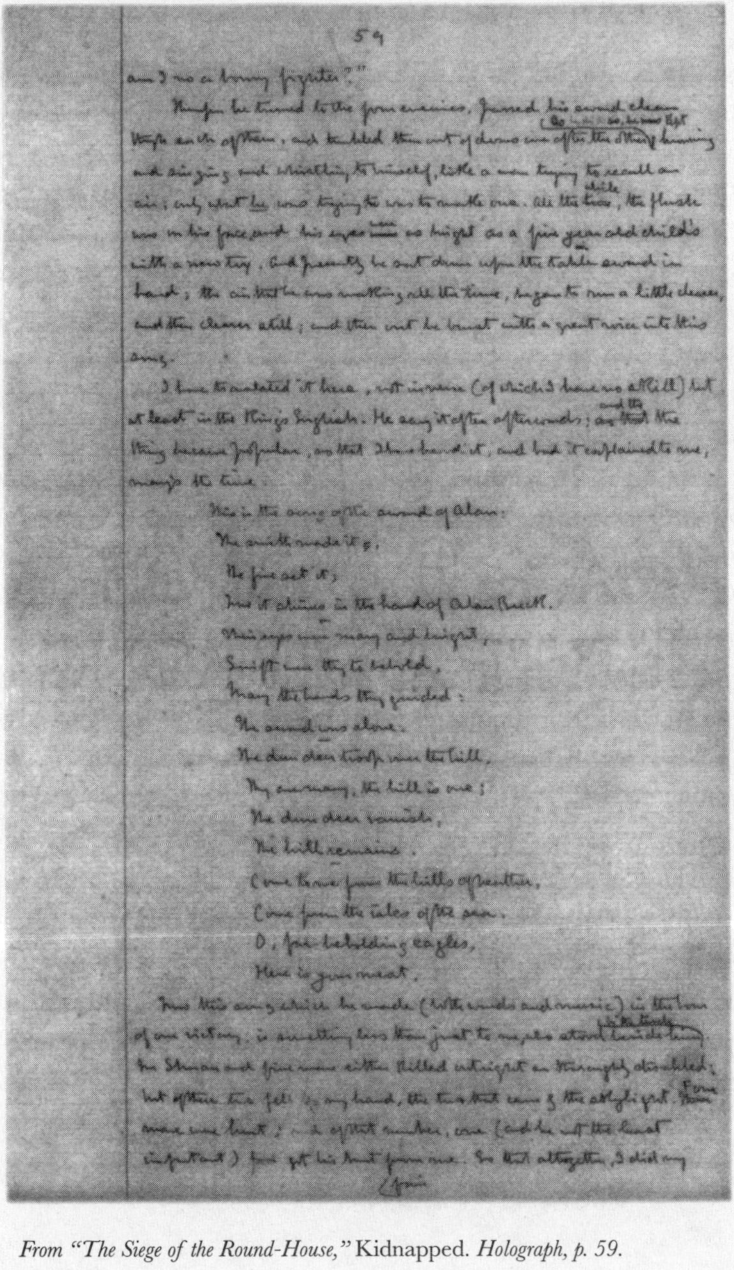

From "The Siege of the Round-House," Kidnapped. *Holograph, p. 59.*

the seamen with the skiff; big, [   ] fellows" (p. 51). *Young Folks* and Cassell both print *brown*, but the word could plausibly be read as *braw*. I have, however, followed the printed texts. The other word proved indecipherable. The sentence reads: "Presently, he [   ] towards me sideways, but keeping his eyes away" (p. 37). Both serial and book print: "Presently, he *looked* towards me sideways," and then delete the remainder of the sentence. I have printed the word as *walked*.

Since the Huntington Library holograph is incomplete, ending with chapter 27, I have based the last three chapters of this edition on the *Young Folks Paper* serial. Minor emendations have been made to that copytext, in accordance with Stevenson's practice in the autograph: periods were dropped after the courtesy title ("Mr"), hyphens removed in seven words, and one spelling change made (*blythe* for *blithe*).

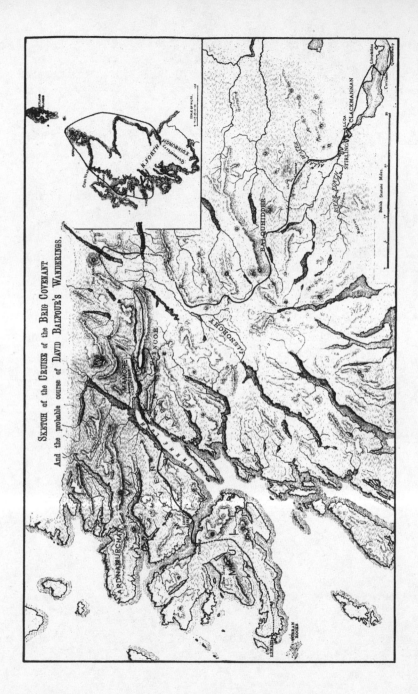

SKETCH of the CRUISE of the BRIG COVENANT
And the probable course of DAVID BALFOUR'S WANDERINGS.

KIDNAPPED

KIDNAPPED

BEING

Memoirs of the Adventures of David Balfour

IN THE YEAR 1751:

How he was Kidnapped and Cast away; his Sufferings in a Desert Isle;
his Journey in the Wild Highlands; his Acquaintance with ALAN BRECK
STEWART and other notorious Highland Jacobites; with all that he
Suffered at the hands of his Uncle, EBENEZER BALFOUR OF SHAWS,
falsely so-called: Written by Himself, and now set forth

BY

ROBERT LOUIS STEVENSON.

CASSELL & COMPANY, LIMITED:
MDCCCLXXXVI.

[All Rights Reserved.]

KIDNAPPED

Being memoirs of the adventures of David Balfour in the year 1751: How he was Kidnapped and Cast away; his Sufferings in a Desert Isle; his Journey in the Wild Highlands; his Acquaintance with Alan Breck Stewart and other notorious Highland Jacobites; with all that he Suffered at the hands of his Uncle, Ebenezer Balfour of Shaws, falsely so-called: Written by Himself, and now set forth

by **ROBERT LOUIS STEVENSON**

FRONTISPIECE: *Title page from the first English edition.*

Dedication

My dear Charles Baxter,

If you ever read this tale, you will likely ask yourself more questions than I should care to answer: as for instance how the Appin murder has come to fall in the year 1751, how the Torran rocks have crept so near to Earraid, or why the printed trial is silent as to all that touches David Balfour. These are nuts beyond my ability to crack. But if you tried me on the point of Alan's guilt or innocence, I think I could defend the reading of the text. To this day you will find the tradition of Appin clear in Alan's favour. If you inquire, you may even hear that the descendants of "the other man" who fired the shot are in the country to this day. But that other man's name, inquire as you please, you shall not hear; for the Highlander values a secret for itself and for the congenial exercise of keeping it. I might go on for long to justify one point and own another indefensible; it is more honest to confess at once how little I am touched by the desire of accuracy. This is no furniture for the scholar's library, but a book for the winter evening schoolroom when the tasks are over and the hour for bed draws near; and honest Alan, who was a grim old fire-eater in his day, has in this new avatar no more desperate purpose than to steal some young gentleman's attention from his

Ovid, carry him awhile into the Highlands and the last century, and pack him to bed with some engaging images to mingle with his dreams.

As for you, my dear Charles, I do not even ask you to like the tale. But perhaps when he is older, your son will; he may then be pleased to find his father's name on the fly leaf; and in the meanwhile it pleases me to set it there, in memory of many days that were happy and some (now perhaps as pleasant to remember) that were sad. If it is strange for me to look back from a distance both in time and space on these bygone adventures of our youth, it must be stranger for you who tread the same streets—who may tomorrow open the door of the old Speculative, where we begin to rank with Scott and Robert Emmet and the beloved and inglorious Macbean—or may pass the corner of the close where that great society, the L.J.R., held its meetings and drank its beer, sitting in the seats of Burns and his companions. I think I see you, moving there by plain daylight, beholding with your natural eyes those places that have now become for your companion a part of the scenery of dreams. How, in the intervals of present business, the past must echo in your memory! Let it not echo often without some kind thoughts of your friend.

R.L.S.
Skerryvore,
Bournemouth.

Contents

1

I Set Off upon My Journey
to the House of Shaws

I will begin the story of my adventures with a certain morning in the month of June, the year of grace 1751, when I took the key for the last time out of the door of my father's house. The sun began to shine upon the summit of the hills as I went down the road; and by the time I had come as far as the manse, the black-birds were whistling in the garden lilacs, and the mist that hung around the valley in the time of the dawn was beginning to arise and die away.

Mr Campbell, the minister of Essendean, was waiting for me by the garden gate, good man! He asked me if I had breakfasted; and hearing that I lacked for nothing, he took my hand in both of his and clapped it kindly under his arm. "Well, Davie lad," said he, "I will go with you as far as the ford, to set you on the way." And we began to walk forward in silence. "Are ye sorry to leave Essendean?" said he, after awhile.

"Why, sir," said I, "if I knew where I was going or what was likely to become of me, I would tell you candidly. Essendean is a good place indeed; and I have been very happy there; but then I have never been anywhere else. My father and mother, since they are both dead, I shall be no nearer to in Essendean than in the Kingdom of Hungary; and to speak truth, if I thought I had a chance to better myself where I was going, I would go with a good will."

"Ay?" said Mr Campbell. "Very well, Davie. Then it behoves me to tell your fortune; or so far as I may. When your mother was gone, and your father (the worthy, Christian man) began to sicken for his end, he gave me in charge a certain letter, which he said was your inheritance. 'So soon,' says he, 'as I am gone, and the house is redd up and the gear disposed of,' (all which, Davie, hath been done) 'give my boy this letter into his hand and start him off to the house of Shaws not far from Cramond. That is the place I came from,' he said, 'and it's where it befits allenarly that my boy should return. He is a steady lad,' your father said, 'and a canny goer; and I doubt not he will come safe and be well liked where he goes.' "

"The house of Shaws?" I cried. "What had my poor father to do with the house of Shaws?"

"Nay," said Mr Campbell, "who can tell that for a surety? But the name of that family, Davie boy, is the name you bear; Balfours of Shaws: an ancient, honest, reputable house, peradventure in these latter days decayed. Your father, too, was a man of learning as befitted his position; no man more plausibly conducted school; nor had he the manner or the speech of a common dominie, but (as ye will yourself remember) I took aye a pleasure to have him to the manse to meet the gentry; and those of my own house, Campbell of Kilrennet, Campbell of Dunswire, Campbell of Minch and others, all well-kenned gentlemen, had pleasure in his society. Lastly, to put all the elements of this affair before you, here is this testamentary letter itself, superscrived by the own hand of our departed brother."

He gave me the letter which was addressed in these words: "To the hands of Ebenezer Balfour Esquire of Shaws, in his house of Shaws, these will be delivered by my son David Balfour." My heart was beating hard at this great prospect, now suddenly opening before a lad of sixteen years of age; the son of a poor country Dominie in the Forest of Ettrick.

"Mr Campbell," I stammered, "and if you were in my shoes, would you go?"

"Of a surety," said the Minister, "that would I, and without pause. A pretty lad like you should get to Cramond (which is near in by Edinburgh) in two days of walk. If the worst came to the worst, and your high relations (as I cannot but suppose them to be somewhat of your blood) should put you to the door, ye can but walk the two days back again and risp at the manse door. But I would rather hope that ye shall be well received, as your poor father forecast for you; and for anything that I ken, come to be a great man in time. And here Davie laddie," he resumed, "it lies near upon my conscience to improve this parting, and set you on the right guard against the dangers of the world."

Here he cast about for a comfortable seat, lighted on a big boulder under a birch by the trackside; sate down upon it, with a very long, serious upper lip; and, the sun now shining in upon us between two peaks, put his pocket handkerchief over his cocked hat, to shelter him. There, then, with uplifted forefinger, he first put me on my guard against a considerable number of heresies, to which I had no temptation, and urged upon me to be instant in my prayers and reading of the bible. That done, he drew a picture of the great house that I was bound to, and how I should conduct myself with its inhabitants.

"Be soople, Davie, in things immaterial," said he. "Bear ye this in mind, that, though gentle born, ye have had a country rearing. Dinnae shame us, Davie,—dinnae shame us! In yon great, muckle house, with all these domestics upper and under, show yourself as nice, as circumspect, as quick at the conception and as slow of speech, as any. As for the laird—remember he's the laird; I say no more: honour to whom honour. It's a pleasure to obey a laird; or should be, to the young."

"Well, sir," said I, "it may be; and I promise you, I'll try to make it so."

"Why, very well said," replied Mr Campbell, heartily. "And now, to come to the material or (to make a quibble) to the immaterial. I have here a little packet which contains four things," he tugged it, as he spoke and with some difficulty, from the skirt pocket of his coat. "Of these four things, the first is your legal due: the little pickle money for your father's books and plenishing, which I have bought (as I have explained from the first) in the design of re-selling at a profit to the incoming dominie. The other three are gifties that Mrs Campbell and myself would be blythe of your acceptance. The first, which is round, will likely please ye best at the first off-go; but O Davie laddie, it's but a drop of water in the sea; it'll help you but a step and vanish like the dew. The second which is flat and square, and written upon, will stand by you all through life, like a good staff for the road, and a good pillow to your head in sickness. And as for the last, which is cubical, that'll see you, it's my prayerful wish, into a better land."

With that he got upon his feet, took off his hat and prayed a little while aloud and in affecting terms for a young man setting out into the world; then suddenly took me in his arms and embraced me very hard; then held me at arm's length, looking at me with his face all working with sorrow; and then whipped about and, crying good-bye to me, set off backward by the way that we had come at a sort of jogging run. It might have been laughable to another; but I was in no mind to laugh. I watched him as long as he was in sight; and he never stopped hurrying nor once looked back. Then it came in upon my mind that this was all his sorrow at my departure; and my conscience smote me hard and fast, because I (for my part) was overjoyed to get away out of that quiet countryside, and go to a great, busy house, among rich and respected gentlefolk of my own name and blood.

"Davie, Davie," I thought, "was ever seen such black ingratitude? Can you forget old favours and old friends at the mere whistle of a name? Fy, fy; think shame!"

And I sat down on the boulder the good man had just left, and opened the parcel to see the nature of my gifts. That which he had called cubical, I had never had much doubt of; sure enough it was a little bible, to carry in a plaid-neuk. That which he had called round, I found to be a shilling piece; and the third which was to help me so wonderfully both in health and sickness all the days of my life, was a little piece of coarse yellow paper, written upon thus in red ink:

"To Make Lilly of the Valley Water.

Take the flowers of lilly of the valley and distil them in sack, and drink a spooneful or two, as there is occasion. It restores speach to those that have the dumb palsey: It is good against the Gout; it comforts the heart and strengthens the memory; and the flowers put into a Glasse close stopt, and set into ane hill of ants for a month, then take it out and you will find a liquor which comes from the flowers, which keep in a vial; it is good, ill or well, and whether man or woman."

And then in the Minister's own hand was added: "Likewise for sprains, rub it in; and for the cholic, a great spooneful in the hour."

To be sure I laughed over this; but it was rather tremulous laughter; and I was glad to get my bundle on my staff's end, and set out over the ford and up the hill upon the farther side; till, just as I came on the green drove-road, running wide through the heather, I took my last look of Kirk Essendean, the trees about the manse, and the big rowans in the kirkyard where my father and my mother lay.

I Come to My Journey's End

O n the forenoon of the second day, coming to the top of a hill, I saw all the country fall away before me down to the sea; and in the midst of this descent, on a long ridge, the city of Edinburgh smoking like a kiln. There was a flag upon the castle, and ships moving or lying anchored in the firth; both of which, for as far away as they were, I could distinguish clearly, and both brought my country heart into my mouth.

Presently after, I came by a house where a shepherd lived, and got a rough direction for the neighbourhood of Cramond; and so, from one to another, worked my way to the westward of the capital by Colinton, till I came out upon the Glasgow road. And there, to my great pleasure and wonder, I beheld a regiment marching to the fifes, every foot in time; an old, red-faced general on a gray horse at the one end; and at the other the company of Grenadiers with their Pope's-hats. The pride of life seemed to mount into my brain at the sight of the red coats and the hearing of that merry music.

A little farther on, and I was told I was in Cramond parish and began to substitute in my inquiries the name of the house of Shaws. It was a word that seemed to surprise those of whom I sought my way. At first I thought the plainness of my appear-

ance, in my country habit and that all dusty from the road, con-
sorted ill with the greatness of the place to which I was bound.
But after two or maybe three had given me the same look and the
same answer, I began to take it in my head there was something
strange about the Shaws itself.

The better to set this fear at rest, I changed the form of my
inquiries; and spying an honest fellow coming along a lane on
the shafts of his cart, I asked him if he had ever heard tell of a
house they called the house of Shaws?

He stopped his cart and looked at me, like all the others. "Ay,"
said he: "What for?"

"It's a great house?" I asked.

"Doubtless," says he; "the house is a big, muckle house."

"Ay," said I; "but the folk that are in it?"

"Folk?" cried he. "Are ye daft? There's nae folk there—to
call folk!"

"What?" says I. "Not Mr Ebenezer?"

"Ou, ay," says the man, "there's the laird, to be sure, if it's him
you're wanting. What'll like be your business, mannie?"

"I was led to think that I would get a situation," I said, looking
as modest as I could.

"What?" cries the carter, on so sharp a note that his very horse
started; and then, "Well, mannie," he added, "it's nane of my
affairs; but ye seem a decent-spoken lad; and if ye'll take a word
from me, ye'll keep clear of the Shaws."

The next person I came across was a dapper little man in a
beautiful white wig, whom I saw to be a barber on his rounds;
and knowing well that barbers were great gossips, I asked him
plainly what sort of a man was Mr Balfour of the Shaws?

"Hoot, hoot, hoot," said the Barber; "nae kind of a man, nae kind of a man at all:" and began to ask me very shrewdly what my business was; but I was more than a match for him at that, and he went on to his next customer no wiser than he came.

I cannot well describe the blow this dealt to my illusions. The more indistinct the accusations were, the less I liked them; for they left the wider field to fancy. What kind of a great house was this, that all the parish should start and stare to be asked the way to it? or what sort of a gentleman, that his ill-fame should be thus current on the wayside? If an hour's walking would have brought me back to Essendean, I had left my adventure then and there, and returned to Mr Campbell's. But when I had come so far a way already, mere shame would not suffer me to desist till I had put the matter to the touch of proof; I was bound, out of mere self respect, to carry it through; and little as I liked the sound of what I heard, and slow as I began to travel, I still kept asking my way and still kept advancing.

It was drawing on to sundown, when I met a stout, dark, sour looking woman coming trudging down a hill; and she, when I had put my usual question, turned sharp about, accompanied me back to the summit she had just left and, in the bottom of the next valley, pointed to a great hulk of building standing very bare upon a green. The country was pleasant round about, running in low hills, pleasantly watered and wooded, and the crops, to my eyes, wonderfully good; but the house itself appeared to be a kind of ruin; no road led up to it; no smoke arose from any of the chimneys; nor was there any semblance of a garden. My heart sank. "That!" I cried.

The woman's face lit up with a malignant anger. "That is the house of Shaws!" she cried. "Blood built it; blood stopped the building of it; blood shall bring it down. See here!" she cried

" 'That is the house of Shaws!' she cried."

Young Folks Paper, May 1, 1886.

again, "I spit upon the ground, and crack my thumb at it! Black be its fall! If ye see the laird, tell him what ye hear; tell him this makes the twelve hunner and nineteen time that Jennet Clouston has called down the curse on him and his—house, byre and stable, man, guest and master, wife, miss or bairn—black, black be their fall!"

And the woman whose voice had risen to a kind of eldritch sing-song, turned with a skip, and was gone. I stood where she left me, with my hair on end. In these days, folk still believed in witches and trembled at a curse; and this one, falling so pat, like a wayside omen, to arrest me ere I carried out my purpose, took the pith out of my legs.

I sat me down and stared at the house of Shaws. The more I

looked, the pleasanter that countryside appeared; being all set with hawthorn bushes full of flowers; the fields dotted with sheep; a fine flight of rooks in the sky; and every sign of a kind soil and climate. And yet the barrack in the midst of it went sore against my fancy.

Country folk went by from the fields as I sat there on the side of the ditch, but I lacked the spirit to give them a good-e'en. At last the sun went down, and then, right up against the yellow sky, I saw a scroll of smoke go mounting; not much thicker, as it seemed to me, than the smoke of a candle; but still there it was, and meant a fire, and warmth, and cookery, and some living inhabitant that must have lit it; and this comforted my heart wonderfully, more, I feel sure, than a whole flask of the lily of the valley water, that Mrs Campbell set so great a store by.

So I set forward by a little, faint track in the grass that led in my direction. It was very faint indeed to be the only way to a place of habitation; yet I saw no other. Presently it brought me to stone uprights, with an unroofed lodge beside them, and coats of arms upon the top. A brave entrance, it was plainly meant to be; but never finished; instead of gates of wrought iron, a pair of hurdles were tied across with a straw rope; and as there were no park walls, nor any sign of avenue, the track that I was following passed on the right hand of the pillars and went wandering on toward the house.

The nearer I got to that, the drearier it appeared. It seemed like the one wing of a house that had never been finished; what should have been the inner end stood open on the upper floors, and showed against the sky with steps and stairs of uncompleted masonry; and many of the windows were unglazed, and bats flew in and out like doves out of a dovecote.

The night had begun to fall, as I got close; and in three of the lower windows, which were very high up, and narrow, and well barred, the changing light of a little fire began to glimmer.

Was this the palace I had been coming to? was it within these walls that I was to seek new friends and begin great fortunes? Why, in my father's house on Essen-waterside, the fire and the bright lights would show a mile away; and the door open to a beggar's knock.

I came forward cautiously, and giving ear as I came, heard some one rattling with dishes; and a little, dry, eager cough, that came in fits; but there was no sound of speech, and not a dog barked.

The door, as well as I could see it in the dim light, was a great piece of wood all studded with nails; and I lifted my hand, with a faint heart under my jacket, and knocked once. Then I stood and waited. The house had fallen into a dead silence; a whole minute passed away, and nothing stirred but the bats overhead. I knocked again; and hearkened again. By this time my ears were grown so accustomed to the quiet, that I could hear the ticking of the clock inside, as it slowly counted out the seconds; but whoever was in that house, kept deadly still and must have held his breath.

I was in two minds whether to run away; but anger got the upper hand; and I began instead to rain kicks and buffets on the door, and to shout out aloud for Mr Balfour. I was in full carreer, when I heard the cough right overhead, and, jumping back and looking up, beheld a man's head in a tall night-cap and the bell mouth of a blunderbuss at one of the first story windows.

"It's loaded," said a voice.

"I have come here with a letter," I said, "to Mr Ebenezer Balfour of the Shaws. Is he here?"

"From whom is it?" asked the man with the blunderbuss.

"That is neither here nor there," said I, for I was growing very wroth.

"Well," was the reply, "ye can put it down upon the doorstep and be off with you."

"I will do no such thing," I cried. "I will deliver it into Mr Balfour's hands, as it was meant I should. It is a letter of introduction."

"A what?" cried the voice sharply.

I repeated what I had said.

"Who are ye, yourself?" was the next question, after a considerable pause.

"I am not ashamed of my name," said I. "They call me David Balfour."

At that, I made sure the man started, for I heard the blunderbuss rattle on the windowsill; and it was after quite a long pause, and with a curious change of voice, that the next question followed:

"Is your father dead?"

I was so much surprised at this, that I could find no voice to answer, but stood staring.

"Ay," the man resumed, "he'll be dead, no doubt; and that'll be what brings ye chapping to my door." Another pause; and then, defiantly, "Well, man," he said, "I'll let you in!" and he disappeared from the window.

❦ 3

I Make Acquaintance of My Uncle

Presently there came a great rattling of chains and bolts, and the door was cautiously opened and shut to again behind me as soon as I had passed.

"Go into kitchen, and touch naething," said the voice; and while the person of the house set himself to replacing the defences of the door, I groped my way forward and entered the kitchen.

The fire had burned up fairly bright, and showed me the barest room I think I ever put my eyes on. Half a dozen dishes stood upon the brick; the table was laid for supper with a bowl of porridge, a horn spoon and a cup of small beer. Besides what I have named, there was not another thing in that great, stone-vaulted, empty chamber, but lockfast chests arranged along the wall and a corner cupboard with a padlock.

As soon as the last chain was up, the man rejoined me. He was a mean, stooping, narrow-shouldered, clay-faced creature; and his age might have been anything between fifty or seventy. His night-cap was of flannel, and so was the night gown that he wore, instead of coat and waistcoat, over his ragged shirt. He was long unshaved; but what most distressed and even daunted me, he would neither take his eyes away from me nor look me fairly in the face. What he was, whether by trade or birth, was more than I could fathom: but he seemed most like an old, unprofitable serving man, who should have been left in charge of that big house upon board wages.

"Are ye sharp-set?" he asked, glancing at about the level of my knee. "Ye can eat that drop parritch."

I said I feared it was his own supper.

"O," said he, "I can do fine wanting it. I'll take the beer though, for it slockens my cough." He drank the cup about half out, still keeping an eye upon me as he drank; and then suddenly held out his hand. "Let's see the letter," said he.

I told him the letter was for Mr Balfour; not for him.

"And who do ye think I am?" says he. "Give me Alexander's letter!"

"You know my father's name?" I cried.

"It would be strange if I didnae," he returned, "for he was my born brother; and little as ye seem to like either me, or my house, or my good parritch, I'm your born uncle, Davie my man, and you my born nephew. So give us the letter, and sit down and fill your kite."

If I had been some years younger, what with shame, weariness and disappointment, I believe I had burst into tears. As it was, I could find no words, neither black nor white; but handed him the letter and sat down to the porridge with as little appetite for meat as ever a young man had.

Meanwhile my uncle, stooping over the fire, turned the letter over and over in his hands. "Do ye ken what's in it?" he asked, suddenly.

"You see for yourself, sir," said I, "that the seal has not been broken."

"Ay," said he, "but what brought you here?"

"To give the letter," said I.

"No," says he, cunningly, "but ye'll have had some hopes, nae doubt?"

"I confess, sir," said I, "when I was told that I had kinsfolk well-to-do, I did indeed indulge the hope that they might help me in my life. But I am no beggar; I look for no favours at your hand, and I want none that are not freely given; for as poor as I appear, I have friends of my own that will be blythe to help me."

"Hoot-toot," said uncle Ebenezer, "dinnae fly up in the snuff at me. We'll agree fine yet. And, Davie my man, if you're done with that bit parritch, I would just take a sup of it myself. Ay," he continued, as soon as he had ousted me from the stool and spoon, "they're fine, halesome food, they're grand food, parritch." He murmured a little grace to himself and fell to. "Your father was very fond of his meat, I mind; he was a hearty if not a great eater; but as for me I would never do mair than pyke at food." He took a pull at the small beer, which probably reminded him of hospitable duties; for his next speech ran thus: "If ye're dry, ye'll find water behind the door."

To this I returned no answer, standing stiffly on my two feet and looking down upon my uncle with a mighty angry heart. He, on his part, continued to eat like a man under some pressure of time, and to throw out little darting glances now at my shoes and now at my home-spun stockings. Once only when he had ventured to look a little higher, our eyes met; and no thief taken with a hand in a man's pocket could have shown more lively signals of distress. This set me in a curious muse, whether his timidity arose from too long a disuse of any human company; and whether perhaps, upon a little trial, it might pass off, and my uncle change into an altogether different man. From this I was awakened by his sharp voice.

"Your father's been long dead?" he asked.

"Three weeks, sir," said I.

"He was a secret man, Alexander; a secret, silent man," he continued. "He never said muckle when he was young. He'll never have spoken muckle of me?"

"I never knew, sir, till you told it me yourself, that he had any brother."

"Dear me, dear me," said Ebenezer. "Nor yet of Shaws, I daresay?"

"Not so much as the name, sir," said I.

"To think o' that!" said he. "A strange nature of a man!" But for all that, he seemed singularly satisfied, but whether with himself, or me, or with this conduct of my father's, was more than I could read. Certainly, however, he seemed to be outgrowing that distaste, or ill-will, that he had conceived at first against my person; for presently he jumped up, came across the room behind me, and hit me a smack upon the shoulder. "We'll agree fine yet!" he cried. "I'm just as glad I let you in. And now come awa' to your bed."

To my surprise, he lit no lamp or candle, but set forth into the dark passage, groped his way, breathing deeply, up a flight of steps, and paused before a door which he unlocked. I was close upon his heels, having stumbled after him as best I might; and he bade me go in for that was my chamber. I did as he bid, but paused after a few steps, and begged a light to go to bed with.

"Hoot-toot," said uncle Ebenezer, "there's a fine moon."

"Neither moon nor star, sir, and pit-mirk," said I. "I cannae see the bed."

"Hoot-toot, hoot-toot," said he. "Lights in a house is a thing I dinnae agree with. I'm unco feared of fires. Good night to you, Davie my man." And before I had time to add a further protest, he pulled the door to, and I heard him lock me in from the outside.

I did not know whether to laugh or cry. This room was as cold as a well; and the bed, when I had found my way to it, as damp as a peat-hag; but by good fortune I had caught up my bundle and my plaid, and rolling myself in the latter, I lay down upon the floor under lee of the big bedstead and fell speedily asleep.

With the first peep of day, I opened my eyes to find myself in a great chamber, hung with stamped leather, furnished with fine embroidered furniture and lit by three fair windows. Ten years ago, or perhaps twenty, it must have been as pleasant a room to lie down or to awake in, as a man could wish; but damp, dirt, disuse and the mice and spiders had done their worst since then. Many of the window panes, besides, were broken; and indeed this was so common a feature in that house, that I believe my uncle must at some time have stood a siege therein from his indignant neighbours, perhaps with Jennet Clouston at their head.

Meanwhile the sun was shining outside; and being very cold in that miserable room, I knocked and shouted till my jailer came and let me out. He carried me to the back of the house where was a draw well, and told me to "wash my face there, if I wanted;" and when that was done, I made the best of my own way back to the kitchen, where he had lit the fire (for he kindled it afresh for every meal, to save a penny's worth of fuel in a month) and was now making the porridge. The table was laid with two bowls and two horn spoons, but the same single measure of small beer. Perhaps my eye rested on this particular with some surprise, and perhaps my uncle observed it; for he spoke up as if in answer to my thought, asking me if I would like to drink ale—for so he called it.

I told him such was my habit, but not to put himself about.

"Na, na," said he, "I'll deny you nothing in reason." He fetched another cup from the brick; and then to my great surprise, instead of drawing more beer, he poured an accurate half from one cup to the other. There was a kind of nobleness in this that took my breath away; if my uncle was certainly a miser, he was one of that thorough breed that make the vice respectable.

When we had made an end of our meal, my uncle Ebenezer unlocked a drawer and drew out of it a clay pipe and a lump of tobacco, from which he cut one fill before he locked it up again, and then sat down in the sun at one of the windows and silently smoked. From time to time, his eyes came coasting round to me and he shot out one of his questions. Once it was, "And your mother?" And when I had told him that she too was dead, "Ay she was a bonny lassie!" Then, after another long pause, "Whae were these friends o' yours?"

I told him they were different gentlemen of the name of Campbell; though indeed there was only one, and that the minister, that had ever taken the least note of me; but I began to think my uncle made too light of my position; and finding myself all alone with him, I did not wish him to suppose me helpless.

He seemed to turn this over in his mind; and then "Davie my man," said he, "ye've come to the right bit when ye come to your uncle Ebenezer. I've a great notion of the family, and I mean to do the right by you; but while I'm taking a bit think to mysel' of what's the best thing to put you to—whether the law, or the meenistry, or maybe the army, whilk is what boys are fondest of—I wouldnae like the Balfours to be humbled before a wheen Hieland Campbells, and I'll ask you to keep your tongue between your teeth. Nae letters; nae messages; no kind of word to onybody; or else—there's my door."

"Uncle Ebenezer," said I, "I've no manner of reason to suppose you mean anything but well by me. For all that, I would have you to know that I have a pride of my own. It was by no will of mine that I came seeking you; and if you show me your door again, I'll take you at the word."

He seemed grievously put about. "Hoots-toots," said he, "ca' cannie, man—ca' cannie! Bide a day or two; I'm nae warlock to find a fortune for you in the bottom of a parritch bowl; but just you give me a day or twa, and say naething to naebody, and as sure as sure, I'll do the right by you."

"Very well," said I. "Enough said. If you want to help me, there's no doubt but I'll be glad of it, and none but I'll be grateful."

It seemed to me, too soon I daresay, that I was getting the upper hand of my uncle; and I began next to say that I must have the bed and bed clothes aired and put to sun-dry; for nothing would make me sleep in such a pickle.

"Is this my house or yours?" said he, in his keen voice; and then all of a sudden broke off. "Na, na," said he. "I didnae mean that. What's mine is yours, Davie my man, and what's yours is mine. Blood's thicker than water; and there's naebody but you and me that ought the name." And then on he rambled about the family, and its ancient greatness, and his father that began to build the house, and himself that stopped the building as a sinful waste; and this put it in my head to give him Jennet Clouston's message.

"The limmer!" he cried. "Twelve hunner and fifteen—that's every day since I had the limmer rowpit! Dod, David, I'll have her roasted on red peats before I'm by with it! A witch—a notour, proclaimed witch! I'll aff and see the session clerk." And with that he opened a chest, and got out a very old and well preserved blue coat and waistcoat, and a good enough beaver hat; both without lace; these he threw on anyway; and taking a cane from the cupboard, locked all up again, and was for setting out, when a thought arrested him. "I cannae leave you by yoursel in the house," said he. "I'll have to lock you out."

The blood came up into my face. "If you lock me out," I said, "it'll be the last you see of me in friendship."

He turned very pale and sucked his mouth in. "This is no the way," he said, looking wickedly at a corner of the floor, "this is no the way to win my favour, David."

"Sir," says I, "with a proper reverence for your age and our common blood, I do not value your favour at a boddle's purchase. I was brought up to have a good conceit of myself; and if you were all the uncle, and all the family, I had in the world ten times over, I wouldn't buy your liking at such prices."

Uncle Ebenezer went and looked out of the window for a while; I could see him all trembling and twitching like a man with palsy.

When he turned round, he had a smile upon his face. "Well, well," said he, "we must bear and forbear. I'll no go; that's all that's to be said of it."

"Uncle Ebenezer," I said, "I can make nothing out of this. You use me like a thief; you hate to have me in this house; you let me see it, every word and every minute; it's not possible that you can like me; and as for me, I've spoken to you as I never thought to speak to any man. Why do you seek to keep me, then? Let me gang back—let me gang back, to the friends I have and that like me!"

"Na, na; na, na," he said, very earnestly. "I like you fine; we'll agree fine yet; and for the honour of the house I couldnae let you leave the way ye came. Bide here quiet: there's a good lad; just you bide here quiet a bittie; and ye'll find that we agree."

"Well, sir," said I, after I had thought the matter out in silence, "I'll stay a while. It's more just I should be helped by my own blood than strangers; and if we don't agree, I'll do my best it shall be through no fault of mine."

❧ 4

I Run a Great Danger

in the House of Shaws

For a day that was begun so ill, the day passed fairly well. We had the porridge cold again at noon, and hot porridge at night: porridge and small beer was my uncle's diet. He spoke but little; and that in the same way as before, shooting a question at me after a long silence; and when I sought to lead him in talk about my future, slipped out of it again. In a room next door to the kitchen, where he suffered me to go, I found a great number of books, both latin and English, in which I took a great pleasure all the afternoon. Indeed the time passed so lightly in this good company, that I began to be almost reconciled to my residence at Shaws; and nothing but the sight of my uncle, and his eyes playing hide and seek with mine, revived the force of my distrust.

One thing I discovered, which put me in some doubt. This was an entry on the fly leaf of a chapbook, one of Patrick Walker's, plainly written by my father's hand, and thus conceived: "To my brother Ebenezer on his fifth birthday." Now, what puzzled me was this: that as my father was of course the younger brother, he must either have made some strange error, or he must have written, before he was yet five, an excellent, clear, manly hand of writing.

I tried to get this out of my head; but though I took down many interesting authors, old and new, both history, poetry and story book, this notion of my father's hand of writing stuck to me; and when at length I went back into the kitchen, and sat down once more to porridge and small beer, the first thing I said to uncle Ebenezer, was to ask him if my father had not been very quick at his book.

"Alexander? No him!" was the reply. "I was far quicker mysel; I was a clever chappie when I was young. Why I could read as soon as he could."

This puzzled me yet more; and a thought coming into my head, I asked if he and my father had been twins.

He jumped upon his stool, and the horn spoon fell out of his hand upon the floor. "What gars ye ask that?" he said, and caught me by the breast of the jacket and looked this time straight into my eyes: his own, which were little and light, and bright like a bird's, blinking and winking strangely.

"What do you mean?" I asked very calmly, for I was far stronger than he and not easily frightened. "Take your hand from my jacket. This is no way to behave."

My uncle seemed to make a great effort upon himself. "Dod, man David," he said, "ye shouldnae speak to me about your father. That's whaur the mistake is." He sat awhile and shook, blinking in his plate; "He was all the brother that ever I had," he added, but with no heart in his voice; and then he caught up his spoon, and fell to supper again, but still shaking.

Now this last passage, this laying of hands upon my person and sudden profession of love for my dead father, went so clean beyond my comprehension that it put me into both fear and hope. On the one hand, I began to think my uncle was perhaps insane and might be dangerous; on the other, there came up into my mind (quite unbidden by me, and even discouraged) a story like some ballad I had heard folk singing, of a poor lad that was a rightful heir and a wicked kinsman that tried to keep him from his own. For why should my uncle play a part with a relative that came, almost a beggar, to his door, unless in his heart he had some cause to fear him?

With this notion, all unacknowledged, but nevertheless getting firmly settled in my head, I now began to imitate his covert looks; so that we sat at table like a cat and a mouse, each stealthily observing the other. Not another word had he to say to me, black or white, but was busy turning something secretly over in his mind; and the longer we sat and the more I looked at him, the more certain I became that the something was unfriendly to myself.

When he had cleaned the platter, he got out a single pipeful of tobacco, just as in the morning, turned round a stool into the chimney corner and sat awhile smoking with his back to me.

"Davie," he said, at length, "I've been thinking." Then he paused, and said it again. "There's a wee bit siller that I half promised ye before ye were born," he continued; "promised it to your father; O, naething legal, ye understand; just gentlemen daffing at their wine. Well, I keepit that bit money separate (it was a great expense, but a promise is a promise), and it has grown by now to be a maitter of just precisely—just exactly—" (And here he paused and stumbled)—"of just exactly forty pounds." This last he rapped out with a sidelong glance over his shoulder; and the next moment, added almost with a scream: "Scots!"

The pound Scots being the same thing as an English shilling, the difference made by this second thought was considerable; I could see, besides, that the whole story was a lie, invented with some end which it puzzled me to guess; and I made no attempt to conceal the tone of railery in which I answered: "O, think again, sir! Pounds sterling, I believe."

"That's what I said," returned my uncle: "pounds sterling! And if you'll step out by to the door a minute, just to see what kind of a night it is, I'll get it out to ye and call ye in again."

I did his will, smiling to myself in my contempt that he should think I was so easily to be deceived. It was a dark night, with a few stars low down; and as I stood just outside the door, I heard a hollow moaning of wind far off among the hills. I said to myself there was something thundery and changeful in the weather, and little knew of what a vast importance that should prove to me before the evening passed.

When I was called in again, my uncle counted out into my hand seven and thirty golden guinea pieces; the last pound was in his hand in small gold and silver, but his heart failed him there, and he crammed the change into his pocket. "There," said he, "that'll show you! I'm a queer man, and strange wi' strangers; but my word is my bond, and there's the proof of it."

Now, my uncle seemed so miserly that I was struck dumb by this sudden generosity and could find no words in which to thank him.

"No a word!" said he; "nae thanks; I want nae thanks. I do my duty; I'm no saying that everybody would have done it; but for my part (though I'm a careful body, too) it's a pleasure to me to do the right by my brother's son; and it's a pleasure to me to think that now we'll can agree as such near friends should."

I spoke to him in return as handsomely as I was able; but all the while I was wondering what would come next, and why he had parted with his precious guineas; for as to the reason he had given, a baby would have refused it.

Presently, he walked towards me sideways, but keeping his eyes away; "And see here," says he. "Tit for tat."

I told him I was ready to prove my gratitude in any reasonable degree, and then waited, looking for some monstrous demand. And yet when at last he plucked up courage to speak, it was only to tell me (very properly, as I thought) that he was growing old and a little broken, and that he would expect me to help him with the house and the bit garden. Yet he never looked at me, not even when I answered and expressed my readiness to serve.

"Well," he said, "let's begin." He pulled out of his pocket a rusty key. "There," says he, "there's the key of the stair tower at the far end of the house; ye can only win into it from the outside, for that part of the house is no finished. Gang ye in there, and up the stairs, and bring me down the chest that's at the top. There's papers in't," he added.

"Can I have a light, sir?" said I.

"Na," said he, very cunningly. "Nae lights in my house."

"Very well, sir," said I. "Are the stairs good?"

"They're grand," said he; and then as I was going, "Keep to the wall," he added, "there's nae bannisters. But the stairs are grand underfoot."

Out I went into the night. The wind was still moaning in the distance, though never a breath of it came near the house of Shaws. It had fallen blacker than ever; and I was glad to feel along the wall, till I came the length of the stair-tower door at the far end of the unfinished wing. I had got the key into the keyhole and had just turned it; when all upon a sudden, without sound of wind or thunder, the whole sky lighted up with wild fire and went black again. I had to put my hand over my eyes to get back to the colour of the darkness; and indeed I was already half blinded, when I stepped into the tower.

It was so dark inside, it seemed a body could scarce breathe; but I pushed out with foot and hand, and presently struck the wall with the one and the lowermost round of the stair with the other. The wall, by the touch, was of fine hewn stone; the steps too, though somewhat steep and narrow, were of polished masonwork, and regular and solid underfoot. Minding my uncle's word about the bannisters, I kept close to the towerside, and felt my way up in the pitch darkness with a beating heart.

The house of Shaws stood some five full storeys high, not counting lofts. Well, as I advanced, it seemed to me the stair grew airier and a thought more lightsome; and I was wondering what might be the cause of this change, when a second blink of the summer lightning came and went. If I did not cry out, it was because fear had me by the throat; and if I did not fall, it was more by heaven's mercy than my own strength. It was not only that the flash shone in on every side through breaches in the wall, so that I seemed to be clambering aloft upon an open scaffold; but the same passing brightness showed me the steps were of unequal length, and that one of my feet rested that moment within two inches of the well.

This was the grand stair! I thought; and with the thought a gust of a kind of angry courage came into my heart. My uncle had sent me here, certainly to run great risks, perhaps to die. I swore I would settle that "perhaps," if I should break my neck for it; got me down upon my hands and knees; and as slowly as a snail, feeling before me every inch and testing the solidity of every stone, I continued to ascend the stair. The darkness, by contrast with the flash, appeared to have redoubled; nor was that all; for my ears were now troubled and my mind confounded by a great stir of bats in the top part of the tower; and the foul beasts, flying downward, sometimes beat about my face and body.

The tower, I should have said, was square; and in every corner, the step was made of a great stone of a different shape to join the flights. Well, I had come close to one of these turns, when feeling forward as usual, my hand slipped upon an edge and found nothing but emptiness beyond it. The stair had been carried no higher: to set a stranger mounting it in the dark was to send him straight to his death; and (although, thanks to the lightning and my own precautions, I was safe enough) the mere thought of the peril in which I might have stood and the dreadful height I might have fallen from, brought out the sweat upon my body and relaxed my joints.

But I knew what I wanted now, and turned and groped my way down again, with a wonderful anger in my heart. About half way down, the wind sprang up in a clap and shook the tower and died again; the rain followed; and before I had reached the ground level, it fell in buckets. I put out my head into the storm and looked along towards the kitchen. The door, which I had shut behind me when I left, now stood open and shed a little glimmer of light; and I thought I could see a figure standing in the rain, quite still, like a man hearkening. And then there came a blinding flash, which showed me my uncle plainly, just where I had fancied him to stand; and hard upon the heels of it, a great tow-row of thunder.

Now whether my uncle thought the crash to be the sound of my fall, or whether he heard in it God's voice denouncing murder, I will leave you to guess, as I have often tried to do, for yourselves. Certain it is, at least, that he was seized on by a kind of panic fear, and that he ran into the house and left the door open behind him. I followed as softly as I could, and coming unheard into the kitchen, stood and watched him.

He had found time to open the corner cupboard, and bring

out a great case bottle of Aqua Vitae; and now sat with his back towards me at the table. Ever and again he would be seized with a fit of deadly shuddering, and groan aloud, and carrying the bottle to his lips, drink down the raw spirits by the mouthful.

I stepped forward, came close behind him where he sat, and suddenly clapping my two hands down upon his shoulders— "Ah!" cried I.

My uncle gave a kind of broken cry like a sheep's bleat, flung up his arms, and tumbled to the floor like a dead man. I was somewhat shocked at this; but I had myself to look to first of all, and did not hesitate to let him lie as he had fallen. The keys were hanging in the cupboard; and it was my design to furnish myself with arms before my uncle (or rather, what I now saw him to be, my enemy) should come again to his senses and the power of devising evil. In the cupboard were a few bottles, some apparently of medicine; a great many bills and other papers, which I should willingly enough have rummaged, had I had the time; and a few necessaries, that were nothing to my purpose. Thence I turned to the chests. The first was full of meal; the second of moneybags and papers tied into sheaves; in the third, with many other things (and these for the most part clothes) I found a rusty, ugly-looking Highland dirk without the scabbard. This I concealed inside my waistcoat, and turned to my uncle.

He lay as he had fallen, all huddled, with one knee up and one arm sprawling abroad; his face had a strange colour of blue and he seemed to have ceased breathing. Fear came on me that he was dead; then I got water and dashed it in his face; and with that he seemed to come a little to himself, working his mouth and fluttering his eyelids. At last he looked up, and saw me, and there came into his eyes a terror that was not of this world.

"Come, come," said I; "sit up!"

"Are ye alive?" he sobbed, "O, man, are ye alive?"

"That am I," said I. "Small thanks to you!"

He had begun to seek for his breath with deep sighs. "The blue vial," said he—"in the aumry—the blue vial;" his breath came slower still.

I ran to the cupboard and (sure enough) found there a blue phial of medicine, with the dose written on it on a paper; and this I administered to him with what speed I might. "It's the trouble," said he, reviving a little. "I have a trouble, Davie. It's the heart."

I set him on a chair, and looked at him; it is true I felt some pity for a man that looked so sick, but I was besides of righteous anger; and I numbered over before him the points on which I wanted explanation: why he lied to me at every word; why he feared that I should leave him; why he disliked it to be hinted that he and my father were twins ("Is that because it is true?" I asked); why he had given me money to which I was convinced I had no claim; and last of all, why he had tried to kill me. He heard me all through in silence; then he sought to speak; and then in a broken voice, he begged me to let him go to bed. "I'll tell ye the morn," he said, "as sure as death, I will." And so weak was he that I could do nothing but consent; I locked him into his room, however, and pocketed the key; and then returning to the kitchen, made up such a blaze as had not shone there for many a long year, and wrapping myself in my plaid, lay down upon the chests and fell asleep.

ᕈ5

I Go to the Queen's Ferry

Much rain fell in the night; and the next morning there blew a bitter, wintry wind out of the northwest, driving scattered clouds. For all that, and before the sun began to peep or the last of the stars was vanished, I made my way to the side of the burn and had a plunge in a deep, whirling pool. All aglow from my bath, I sat down once more beside the fire, which I replenished, and began gravely to consider my position.

There was now no doubt about my uncle's enmity; there was no doubt I carried my life in my hand, and he would leave no stone unturned that he might compass my destruction. But I was young and spirited, and like most lads that have been country-bred, I had a great opinion of my shrewdness. I had come to his door no better than a beggar and little more than a child; he had met me with treachery and violence; it would be a fine consummation to take the upper hand and drive him like a herd of sheep.

I sat there, nursing my knee and smiling at the fire; and I saw myself in fancy smell out his secrets one after another, and grow to be that man's king and ruler. The warlock of Essendean, they say, had made a mirror in which men could read the future; it must have been of other stuff than burning coal; for in all the shapes and pictures that I sat and gazed at, there was never a ship, never a seaman with a hairy cap, never a big bludgeon for my silly head, or the least sign of all those tribulations that were ripe to fall on me.

Presently, all swollen with conceit, I went upstairs and gave my prisoner his liberty. He gave me good morning civilly; and I gave the same to him, smiling down upon him from the heights of my sufficiency. Soon we were set to breakfast as it might have been the day before.

"Well, sir," said I, with a jeering tone, "have you nothing more to say to me?" And then as he made no articulate reply, "It will be time I think to understand each other," I continued. "You took me for a country Johnnie-Raw, with no more mother-wit or courage than a porridge stick. I took you for a good man, or no worse than others at the least. It seems we were both wrong. What cause you have to fear me, to cheat me, and to attempt my life——"

He murmured something about a jest, and that he liked a bit fun; and then, seeing me smile, changed his tone and assured me he would make all clear as soon as we had breakfasted. We sat sometime facing each other; I saw by his face that he had no lie ready for me, though he was hard at work preparing one; and I think I was about to tell him so, when we were interrupted by a knocking at the door.

Bidding my uncle sit where he was, I went to open it, and found on the doorstep a half-grown boy in sea-clothes. He had no sooner seen me than he began to dance some steps of the sea-hornpipe (which I had never before heard of, far less seen) snapping his fingers in the air and footing it right cleverly. For all that, he was blue with the cold; and there was something in his face, a look between tears and laughter, that was highly pathetic and consisted ill with this gaiety of manner.

"What cheer, mate?" says he, with a cracked voice.

I asked him soberly to name his pleasure.

"O, pleasure!" says he; and then began to sing:

> "For it's my delight, of a shiny night
> In the season of the year."

"Well," said I, "if you have no business at all, I will even be so unmannerly as shut you out."

"Stay, brother!" he cried. "Have you no fun about you? or do you want to get me thrashed? I've brought a letter from old Heasy-oasy to Mr Belflower." He showed me a letter as he spoke; "And I say, mate," he added, "I'm mortal hungry."

"Well," said I, "come into the house and you shall have a bite if I go empty for it."

With that I brought him in and set him down to my own place, where he fell to greedily on the remains of breakfast, winking to me between whiles, and making many faces; which, I think, the poor soul considered manly. Meanwhile my uncle had read the letter and sat thinking; then suddenly, he got to his feet with a great air of liveliness, and pulled me apart into the farthest corner of the room.

"Read that," said he, and put the letter in my hand.

Here it is, lying before me as I write:

> "The Hawes Inn at the Queen's Ferry.
> "Sir, I lie here with my hawser up and down, and send my cabin boy to informe. If you have any fur-

ther commands for over-seas, today will be the last
occasion, as the wind will serve us weel out of the
firth. I will not seek to deny that I have had crosses
with your doer, Mr Rankeillor; of which, if not speedily redd up, you may looke to see some losses follow.
I have drawn a bill upon you as per margin, and am,
Sir, your most obed⁺, humble servant—Elias Hoseason."

"Ye see, Davie," resumed my uncle, as soon as he saw that I
had done, "I have a venture with this man Hoseason, the captain
of a trading brig, the *Covenant* of Dysart. Now, if you and me was
to walk over with yon lad, I could see the captain at the Hawes,
or maybe on board the *Covenant*, if there was papers to be signed;
and so far from a loss of time, we can jog on to the lawyer, Mr
Rankeillor's. After a' that's come and gone, ye would be swier to
believe me upon my naked word; but ye'll can believe Rankeillor. He's factor to half the gentry in these pairts; an auld man,
forby: highly respeckit;—and kenned your father."

I stood awhile and thought. I was going to some place of ship-
ping, which was doubtless populous and where my uncle durst
attempt no violence, and indeed even the society of the cabin
boy so far protected me; once there, I believed I could force on
the visit to the lawyer, even if my uncle were now insincere in
proposing it; and perhaps in the bottom of my heart I wished a
nearer view of the sea and ships. You are to remember I had lived
all my life in the inland hills, and just two days before, had my
first sight of the firth, lying like a blue floor, and the sailed ships
moving on the face of it, no bigger than toys. One thing with
another, I made up my mind.

"Very well," says I, "Let us go to the Ferry."

My uncle got into his hat and coat and buckled an old rusty cutlass on; and then we trod the fire out, locked the door and set forth upon our walk.

The wind, being in that cold quarter, the north west, blew nearly in our faces as we went. It was the month of June; the grass was all white with daisies and the trees with blossom; but to judge by our blue nails and aching wrists, the time might have been winter and the whiteness a December frost.

Uncle Ebenezer trudged in the ditch, jogging from side to side like an old ploughman coming home from work. He never said a word the whole way; and I was thrown back for talk on the cabin boy. He said his name was Ransome, and that he had followed the sea since he was nine, but could not say how old he was, as he had lost his reckoning. He showed me tattoo marks, baring his breast in the teeth of the wind and in spite of my remonstrances, for I thought it was enough to kill him; he swore horribly whenever he remembered, but more like a silly schoolboy than a man; and boasted of many wild and bad things that he had done, stealthy thefts, false accusations, ay, and even murder; but all with such a dearth of likelihood in the details, and such a weak and crazy swagger in the delivery, as disposed me rather to pity than to believe him.

I asked him of the brig (which he declared was the finest ship that sailed) and of Captain Hoseason, in whose praise he was equally loud. Heasy-oasey (for so he still named the skipper) was a man, by his account, that minded for nothing either in heaven or earth; one that as people said would "crack on all sail into the day of judgement;" rough, fierce, unscrupulous and brutal; and all this, my poor cabin boy had taught himself to admire as something seamanlike and manly. He would only admit one flaw in his idol. "He aint no seaman," he admitted; "that's Mr Shuan that navigates the brig; he's the finest seaman in the trade, only for drink; and I tell you I believe it! Why, look 'ere;" and turning down his stocking, he showed me a great, raw, red wound that made my blood run cold. "He done that—Mr Shuan done it," he said, with an air of pride.

"What!" I cried, "do you take such savage usage at his hands? Why, you are no slave to be so handled!"

"No," said the poor moon-calf, changing his tone at once, "and so he'll find! See 'ere!" And he showed me a great case knife, which he told me was stolen. "O," says he, "let me see him try; I dare him to; I'll do for him! O, he aint the first!" And he confirmed it with a poor, silly, ugly oath.

I have never felt such pity for anyone in this wide world, as I felt for that half-witted creature; and it began to come over me that the brig *Covenant* (for all her pious name) was little better than a hell upon the seas. "Have you no friends?" said I.

He said he had a father in some English seaport, I forget which. "He was a fine man too," he said; "but he's dead."

"In heaven's name," cried I, "can you find no reputable life on shore?"

"O no!" says he, winking and looking very sly, "they would put me to a trade. I know a trick worth two of that, I do!"

I asked him what trade could be so dreadful as the one he followed, where he ran the continual peril of his life, not alone from wind and sea, but by the horrid cruelty of those who were his masters. He said it was very true; and then began to praise the life, and tell what a pleasure it was to get on shore with money in his pocket, and spend it like a man, and buy apples, and swagger, and surprise what he called stick-in-the-mud boys. "And then it's not all as bad as that," says he; "there's worse off than me: there's the twenty-pounders. O, laws! you should see them taking on. Why, I've seen a man as old as you, I dessay" (to him, I seemed old)—"ah, and he had a beard too—well and as soon as we cleared out of the river, and he had the drug out of his head— my! how he cried and carried on! I made a fine fool of him, I tell you! And then there's little uns, too: O! little by me! I tell you, I keep them in order; when we carry little uns, I have a rope's end of my own to wollop 'em." And so he ran on, until it came in on me that what he meant by twenty-pounders were those unhappy criminals who were sent over-seas to slavery in North America, or the still more unhappy innocent who were kidnapped or tre-panned (as the word went) for private interest or vengeance.

Just then, we came to the top of the hill, and looked down on the Ferry and the Hope. The Firth of Forth (as is very well known) narrows at this point to the width of a good sized river, which makes a convenient passage going north, and turns the upper reach into a land-locked haven for all manner of ships. Right in the midst of the narrows, lies an islet with some ruins; on the south shore, they have built a pier for the service of the ferry; and at the end of the pier, on the other side of the road and backed against a pretty garden of holly-trees and hawthorns, I could see the building which they call the Hawes Inn.

The town of Queensferry lies farther west; and the neighbour-hood of the inn looked pretty lonely at that time of day, for the boat had just gone north with passengers. A skiff, however, lay beside the pier, with some seaman sleeping on the thwarts; this, as Ransome told me, was the brig's boat waiting for the captain; and about half a mile off and all alone in the anchorage, he showed me the *Covenant* herself.

There was a sea-going bustle on board; yards were swinging into place; and as the wind blew from that quarter, I could hear the song of the sailors as they pulled upon the ropes. After all I had listened to upon the way, I looked at that ship with an extreme abhorrence; and from the bottom of my heart, I pitied all poor souls that were condemned to sail in her.

We had all three pulled up on the brow of the hill; and now I marched across the road and addressed my uncle. "I think it right to tell you, sir," says I, "there's nothing that will bring me on board that *Covenant*."

He seemed to waken from a dream. "Eh?" he said. "What's that."

I told him over again.

"Well, well," said he, "we'll have to please ye, I suppose. But what are we standing here for? It's perishing cold; and if I'm no mistaken, they're busking the *Covenant* for sea."

~6

What Befell at the Queen's Ferry

As soon as we came to the inn, Ransome led us up the stair to a small room, with a bed in it, and heated like an oven by a great fire of coal. At a table hard by the chimney, a tall, dark, sober looking man sat writing. In spite of the heat of the room, he wore a thick sea-jacket buttoned to the neck and a tall hairy cap drawn down over his ears; yet I never saw any man, not even a judge upon the bench, look cooler or more studious and self possessed than this ship captain.

He got to his feet at once, and coming forward, offered his large hand to Ebenezer. "I am proud to see you, Mr Balfour," said he, in a fine, deep voice, "and glad that ye are here in time. The wind's fair and the tide upon the turn: we'll see the old coal bucket burning on the Isle of May before tonight."

"Captain Hoseason," returned my uncle, "you keep your room unco hot."

"It's a habit I have, Mr Balfour," said the skipper. "I'm a cold-rife man by my nature; I have a cold blood, sir; there's neither fur, nor flannel, no, sir, nor hot rum, will warm up what they call the temperature. Sir, it's the same with most men that have been carbonadoed (as they call it) in the tropic seas."

"Well, well, Captain," replied my uncle, "we must all be the way we're made."

But it chanced that this fancy of the Captain's had a great share in my misfortunes; for though I had promised myself not to let my kinsman out of sight, I was both so impatient for a nearer look of the sea, and so sickened by the closeness of the room, that when he told me to "run downstairs and play myself awhilie," I was full enough to take him at his word.

Away I went therefore, leaving the two men sitting down to a bottle and a great mass of papers; and crossing the road in front of the inn, walked down upon the beach. With the wind in that quarter, only little wavelets, not much bigger than I had seen upon a lake, beat upon the shore. But the weeds were new to me, some green, some brown and long, and some with little bladders that crackled between my fingers. Even so far up the firth, the smell of the sea water was exceeding salt and stirring; the *Covenant*, besides, was beginning to shake out her sails, which hung upon the yards in clusters; and the spirit of all that I beheld put me in thoughts of far voyages and foreign places.

I looked, too, at the seamen with the skiff; big, brown fellows, some in shirts, some with jackets, some with coloured handkerchiefs about their throats, one with a brace of pistols stuck into his pockets, two or three with knotty bludgeons, and all with their case knives. I passed the time of day with one that looked less desperate than his fellows, and asked him of the sailing of the brig. He said they would get under way as soon as the ebb set, and expressed his gladness to be out of a port where there were no taverns and fiddlers; but all with such horrifying oaths that I made haste to get away from him.

This threw me back on Ransome, who seemed the least wicked of that gang, and who soon came out of the inn and ran to me crying for a bowl of punch. I told him I would give him no such thing, for neither he nor I were of an age for such indulgences. "But a glass of ale you may have, and welcome," said I. He mopped and mowed at me, and called me names; but he was glad to get the ale, for all that; and presently we were set down at a table in the front room of the inn and both eating and drinking with a good appetite.

Here it occurred to me that, as the landlord was a man of that country, I might do well to make a friend of him. I offered him a share, as was much the custom in these days; but he was far too great a man to sit with such poor customers as Ransome and myself; and he was leaving the room, when I called him back to ask if he knew Mr Rankeillor.

"Hoot, ay!" says he, "and a very honest man. And O, by the by," says he "was it you that came in with Ebenezer?" And when I had told him yes, "Ye'll be no friend of his?" he asked, meaning, in the Scotch way, that I would be no relative.

I told him no, none.

"I thought not," said he; "and yet ye have a kind of gliff of Mr Alexander."

I said it seemed that Ebenezer was ill-seen in the country.

"Nae doubt," said the landlord. "He's a wicked auld man and there's many would like to see him girning in a tow: Jennet Clouston and mony mair that he has herried out of house and hame. And yet he was once a fine young fellow, too. But that was before the sough gaed abroad about Mr Alexander; that was like the death of him."

"And what was it?" I asked.

"Ou, just that he had killed him," said the landlord. "Did ye never hear that?"

"And what would he kill him for?" said I.

"And what for, but just to get the place?" said he.

"The place?" said I. "The Shaws?"

"Nae other place that I ken," said he.

"Ay, man?" said I. "Is that so? was my—was Alexander the oldest son?"

" 'Deed was he," said the landlord. "What else would he have killed him for?" And with that he went away, as he had been impatient to do from the beginning.

Of course, I had guessed it a long while ago; but it is one thing to guess, another to know; and I sat stunned with my good fortune, and could scarce grow to believe that the same poor lad, who had trudged in the dust from Ettrick forest not two days ago, was now one of the rich of the earth, and had a house and broad lands, and if he but knew how to ride, might mount his horse tomorrow. All these pleasant things, and a thousand others, crowded into my mind, as I sat staring before me out of the inn-window and paying no heed to what I saw; only I remember that my eye lighted on Captain Hoseason down on the pier among his seamen and speaking with some authority. And presently, he came marching back towards the house, with no mark of a sailor's clumsiness, but carrying his fine, tall figure with a manly bearing, and still with the same sober, grave expression on his face. I wondered if it was possible that Ransome's stories could be true, and half disbelieved them; they fitted so ill with the man's looks. But indeed he was neither so good as I supposed him, nor quite so bad as Ransome did; for in fact, he was two men, and left the better one behind, as soon as he set foot on board his vessel.

The next thing, I heard my uncle calling me, and found the pair in the road together. It was the Captain who addressed me that with an air (very flattering to a young lad) of grave equality.

"Sir," said he, "Mr Balfour tells me great things of you; and for my own part, I like your looks. I wish I was for longer here that we might make the better friends; but we'll make the most of what we have: ye shall come on board my brig for half an hour, till the ebb sets, and drink a bowl with me."

Now I longed to see the inside of a ship more than words can tell; but I was not going to put myself in jeopardy; and I told him my uncle and I had an appointment with a lawyer.

"Ay, ay," said he, "he passed me word of that. But ye see the boat'll set ye ashore at the town pier, and that's but a penny stone cast from Rankeillor's house." And here he suddenly leaned down and whispered in my ear: "Take care of the old tod: he means mis-chief. Come aboard till I can get a word with ye." And then, passing his arm through mine, he continued aloud, as he set off towards his boat: "But come, what can I bring ye from the Carolinas? Any friend of Mr Balfour's can command. A roll of tobacco? Indian featherwork? a skin of a wild beast? a stone pipe? The mocking bird that mews for all the world like a cat? the cardinal bird that is as red as blood?—take your pick and say your pleasure."

By this time, we were at the boatside and he was handing me in. I did not dream of hanging back; I thought (the poor fool!) that I had found a good friend and helper; and I was rejoiced to see the ship. As soon as we were all set in our places, the boat was thrust off from the pier and began to move over the waters; and what with my pleasure in this new movement and my surprise at our low position, and the appearance of the shores, and the

"Sure enough, there was the boat pulling for the town,
with my uncle sitting in the stern."

Young Folks Paper, May 8, 1886.

growing bigness of the brig as we drew near to it, I could hardly understand what the captain said and must have answered him at random. I remember he was mighty pleasant, and when I disclaimed the notion of troubling him, told me I should be rich enough to pay him, if that was what I wished.

As soon as we were alongside, where I sat fairly gaping at the ship's height, the strong humming of the tide against its sides and the pleasant cries of the seamen at their work, Hoseason, declaring that he and I must be the first aboard, ordered a tackle to be sent down from the main yard. In this I was whipped into the air and set down again on the deck, where the Captain stood ready waiting for me and instantly slipped back his arm under mine. There I stood some while, a little dizzy with the unsteadiness of all around me, perhaps a little afraid, and yet vastly pleased with these strange sights: the Captain meanwhile pointing out the strangest and telling me their names and uses.

"But where is my uncle?" said I, suddenly.

"Ay," said Hoseason, with a sudden grimness, "that's the point."

I felt I was lost. With all my strength, I plucked myself clear of him, and ran to the bulwarks. Sure enough, there was the boat pulling for the town, with my uncle sitting in the stern. I gave a piercing cry—"Help, help—murder!"—so that both sides of the anchorage rang with it, and my uncle turned round where he was sitting and showed me a face full of cruelty and terror.

It was the last I saw. Already strong hands had been plucking me back from the ship's side; and now a thunderbolt seemed to strike me, I saw a great flash of fire, and fell senseless.

7

I Go to Sea in the Brig
Covenant of **D**ysart

I came to myself in darkness, in great pain, bound hand and foot and deafened by many unfamiliar noises. There sounded in my ears a roaring of water as of a huge mill dam; stunning concussions, the thrashing of heavy sprays, the thundering of the sails, and the shrill cries of seamen. The whole world now heaved giddily up, and now rushed giddily downward; and so sick and hurt was I in body, that I could scarce tell if these wild and staggering movements were merely fanciful or no.

My mind was so much confounded, that it took me a long while, chasing my thoughts up and down, and ever stunned again by a fresh stab of pain, to realise that I must be lying somewhere bound in the belly of that unlucky ship, and that the wind must have strengthened to a gale. With the clear perception of my plight, there fell upon me a blackness of despair, a horror of remorse at my own folly, and a passion of anger at my uncle, that once more bereft me of my senses.

When I returned again to life, the same uproar of the elements, the same confused and violent movements, shook and deafened me; and presently to my other pains and distresses, there was added the prostration of an unused landsman on the sea. In that time of my adventurous youth, I suffered many hardships; but none that was so crushing to my mind and body, or lit by so few hopes, as these first hours on board the brig.

I heard a gun fire, and supposed the storm had proved too strong for us, and we were firing signals of distress. The thought of deliverance, even by death in the deep sea, was welcome to me. Yet it was no such matter, but (as I was afterwards told) a common habit of the Captain's, which I here set down to show that even the worst man may have his kindlier sides. We were then passing, it appeared, within some miles of Dysart, where the brig was built and where old Mrs Hoseason, the Captain's mother, had come some years before to live; and whether outward or inward bound, the *Covenant* was never suffered to go by that place by day, without a gun fired and the colours shown.

I had no measure of time; day and night were alike in that ill-smelling cavern of the ship's bowels where I lay; and the acuteness of my sufferings drew out the hours to double. How long, therefore, I lay waiting to hear the ship split upon some rock, or to feel her reel head foremost into the depths of the sea, I have not the means of computation. But sleep at length stole from me the consciousness of sorrow.

I was wakened by the light of a hand-lantern shining in my face. A small man of about thirty, with green eyes and a tangle of fair hair, stood looking down at me.

"Well," said he, "how goes it?"

I answered by a sob; and my visitor then felt my pulse and temples, and set himself to wash and dress the wound upon my scalp.

"Ay," said he: "a sore dunt. What, man? Cheer up! The world's no done; you've made a bad start of it, but you'll make a better. Have you had any meat?"

I said I could not look at it; and thereupon he gave me some brandy and water in a tin pannikin, and left me once more to myself.

The next time he came to see me, I was lying betwixt sleep and waking, my eyes wide open on the darkness, the sickness quite departed, but succeeded by a horrid giddiness and swimming that was almost worse to bear. I ached besides in every limb, and the cords that bound me seemed to be of fire. The smell of the hole in which I lay seemed to have become a part of me; and during the long interval since his last visit, I had suffered tortures of fear, now from the scurrying of the ship's rats that sometimes pattered on my very face, and now from the dismal imaginings that haunt the pillow of fever.

The glimmer of the lantern, as a trap opened, shone in like the heaven's sunlight; and though it only showed me the strong dark beams of the ship that was my prison, I could have cried aloud for gladness. The man with the green eyes was the first to descend the ladder, and I noticed that he came somewhat unsteadily. He was followed by the Captain. Neither said a word; but the first set to and examined me, and dressed my wound as before, while Hoseason looked me in my face with an odd, black look.

"Now, sir, you see for yourself," said the first: "a high fever, no appetite, no light, no meat: you see for yourself what that means."

"I am no conjurer, Mr Riach," said the Captain.

"Give me leave, sir," said Riach; "you've a good head upon your shoulders and a good Scotch tongue to ask with; but I will leave you no manner of excuse: I want that boy taken out of this hole and put in the forecastle."

"What ye may want, sir, is a matter of concern to nobody but yourself," returned the captain; "but I can tell ye that which is to be. Here he is, here he shall bide."

"Admitting that you have been paid in a proportion," said the other, "I will crave leave humbly to say that I have not. Paid I am, and none too much, to be the second officer of this old tub; and you ken very well if I do my best to earn it. But I was paid for nothing more."

"If ye could hold back your hand from the tin-pan, Mr Riach, I would have no complaint to make of ye," returned the skipper; "and instead of asking riddles, I make bold to say that ye would keep your breath to cool your porridge. We'll be required on deck," he added on a sharper note, and set one foot upon the ladder.

But Mr Riach caught him by the sleeve. "Admitting that you have been paid to do a murder . . . ," he began.

Hoseason turned upon him with a flash. "What's that?" he cried. "What kind of talk is that for any decent man?"

"It seems it is the talk that you can understand," said Mr Riach, looking him steadily in the face.

"Mr Riach, I have sailed with ye three cruises," replied the captain. "In all that time, sir, ye should have learned to know me: I'm a stiff man, and a dour man, but for what ye say the now—fy, fy—it comes from a bad heart and a black conscience. If ye say the lad will die——"

"Ay, will he!" said Mr Riach.

"Well, sir, and is that not enough?" said Hoseason. "Flit him where ye please!"

Thereupon the captain ascended the ladder; and I, who had lain silent throughout this strange conversation, beheld Mr Riach turn after him and bow as low as to his knees in what was plainly a spirit of derision. Even in my then state of sickness, I perceived two things: that the mate was touched with liquor, as the captain hinted, and that (drunk or sober) he was like to prove a valuable friend.

Five minutes afterwards, my bonds were cut, I was hoisted on a man's back, carried up to the forecastle, and laid in a bunk on some sea-blankets; where the first thing that I did was to lose my senses.

It was a blessed thing indeed, to open my eyes again upon the daylight and to find myself in the society of men. The forecastle was a roomy place enough, set all about with berths, in which the men of the watch below were seated smoking or lying down asleep. The day being calm and the wind fair, the scuttle was open, and not only the good daylight but from time to time (as the ship rolled) a dusty beam of sunlight shone in, and dazzled and delighted me. I had no sooner moved, moreover, than one of the men brought me a drink of something healing which Mr Riach had prepared, and bade me lie still and I should soon be well again. There were no bones broken, he explained: "a clour on the head was naething. Man," said he, "it was me that gave it ye!"

Here I lay for the space of many days, a close prisoner, and not only got my health again, but came to know my companions. They were a rough lot indeed, as sailors mostly are; being men rooted out of all the kindly parts of life, and condemned to toss together on the rough seas, with masters no less cruel. There were some among them that had sailed with the pirates and seen things it would be a shame even to speak of; some were men that had run from the King's ships, and went with a halter round their necks, of which they made no secret; and all, as the saying goes, were "at a word and a blow" with their best friends. Yet I had not been many days shut up with them before I began to be ashamed of my first judgement, when I had drawn away from them at the Ferry pier, as though they had been unclean beasts. No class of man is altogether bad; but each has its own faults and virtues; and these shipmates of mine were no exception to the rule. Rough they were, sure enough; and bad, I suppose; but they had many virtues, they were kind when it occurred to them, simple even beyond the simplicity of a country lad like me, and had some glimmerings of honesty.

There was one man of maybe forty, that would sit on my berthside for hours, and tell me of his wife and child. He was a fisher that had lost his boat, and thus been driven to the deep-sea voyaging. Well, it is years ago now; but I have never forgotten him. His wife (who was "young by him," as he often told me) waited in vain to see her man return; he would never again make the fire for her in the morning, nor yet nurse the bairn when she was sick. Indeed many of these poor fellows (as the event proved) were upon their last cruise; the deep seas and cannibal fish received them; and it is a thankless business to speak ill of the dead.

Among other good deeds that they did, they returned my money which had been shared among them; and though it was about a third short, I was very glad to get it and hoped great good from it in the land I was going to. The ship was bound for the Carolinas; and you must not suppose that I was going to that place merely as an exile. The trade was even then much depressed; since that, and with the rebellion of the colonies and the formation of the United States, it has of course come to an end; but in these days of my youth, white men were still sold into slavery on the plantations, and that was the destiny to which my wicked uncle had condemned me.

The cabin boy Ransome (from whom I had first heard of these atrocities) came in at times from the round-house, where he berthed and served, now nursing a bruised limb in silent agony, now raving against the cruelty of Mr Shuan. It made my heart bleed; but the men had a great respect for the chief mate, who was, as they said, "the only seaman of the whole jing-bang, and none such a bad man when he was sober." Indeed I found there was a strange peculiarity about our two mates: that Mr Riach was sullen, unkind and harsh when he was sober, and Mr Shuan would not hurt a fly except when he was drinking. I asked about the captain; but I was told drink made no difference upon that man of iron.

I did my best in the small time allowed me to make something like a man, or rather I should say something like a boy, of the poor creature, Ransome. But his mind was scarce truly human. He could remember nothing of the time before he came to sea; only that his father had made clocks, and had a starling in the parlour which could whistle "The north countrie": all else had been blotted out in these years of hardship and cruelties. He had a strange notion of the dry land, picked up from sailors' stories: that it was a place where lads were put to some kind of slavery called a trade, and where apprentices were continually lashed and clapped into foul prisons. In a town, he thought every second person a decoy, and every third house a place in which seamen would be drugged and murdered. To be sure I could tell him how kindly I had myself been used upon that dry land he was so much afraid of, and how well fed and carefully taught both by my friends and my parents; and if he had been recently hurt, he would weep bitterly and swear to run away; but if he was in his usual, crackbrain humour or (still more) if he had had a glass of spirits in the round-house, he would deride the notion.

It was Mr Riach (heaven forgive him!) who gave the boy drink; and it was doubtless kindly meant; but besides that it was ruin to his health, it was the pitifullest thing in life to see this unhappy, unfriended creature staggering and dancing and talking he knew not what. Some of the men laughed, but not all; others would grow as black as thunder (thinking perhaps of their own childhood or their own children) and bid him stop that nonsense, and think what he was doing. As for me, I felt ashamed to look at him, and the poor child still comes about me in my dreams.

All this time, you should know, the *Covenant* was meeting continual head winds and tumbling up and down against head seas, so that the scuttle was almost constantly shut, and the forecastle lighted only by a swinging lantern on a beam. There was constant labour for all hands; the sails had to be made and shortened every hour; the strain told on the men's temper; there was a growl of quarrelling all day long from berth to berth; and as I was never allowed to set my foot on deck, you can picture to yourselves how weary of my life I grew to be, and how impatient for a change.

And a change I was to get, as you shall hear; but I must first tell of a conversation I had with Mr Riach, which put a little heart in me to bear my troubles. Getting him in a favourable stage of drink (for indeed he never looked near me when he was sober) I pledged him to secrecy and told him my whole story.

He declared it was like a ballad; that he would do his best to help me; that I should have paper, pen and ink, and write one line to Mr Campbell and another to Mr Rankeillor; and that if I had told the truth, ten to one, he would be able (with their help) to pull me through and set me in my rights.

"And in the meantime," says he, "keep your heart up. You're not the only one, I'll tell you that. There's many a man hoeing tobacco overseas, that should be mounting his horse at his own door at home; many and many! And life is all a variorum, at the best. Look at me: I'm a laird's son and more than half a doctor, too; and here I am, man-Jack to Hoseason!"

I thought it would be civil to ask him for his story.

He whistled loud. "Never had one," said he. "I liked fun, that's all." And he skipped out of the forecastle.

8

The Round-House

One night, about twelve o'clock, a man of Mr Riach's watch (which was on deck) came down for his jacket; and instantly there began to go a whisper about the forecastle that "Shuan had done for him at last." There was no need of a name; we all knew who was meant; but we had scarce time to get the idea rightly in our heads, far less to speak of it, when the scuttle was again flung open and Captain Hoseason came down the ladder. He looked sharply round the bunks in the tossing light of the lantern; and then, walking straight up to me, he addressed me, to my great surprise, in tones of kindness.

"My man," said he, "we want ye to serve in the round-house. You and Ransome are to change berths. Run away aft with ye."

Even as he spoke, two seamen appeared in the scuttle carrying Ransome in their arms; and the ship at that moment giving a great sheer into the sea, and the lantern swinging, the light fell direct on the boy's face. It was as white as wax, and had a look upon it like a dreadful smile. The blood in me ran cold, and I drew in my breath as if I had been struck.

"Run away aft, run away aft with ye!" cried Hoseason.

And at that I brushed by the sailors and the boy (who neither spoke nor moved) and ran up the ladder on deck.

The brig was sheering swiftly and giddily through a long, cresting swell. She was on the starboard tack; and on the left hand under the arched foot of the foresail, I could see the sunset still quite bright. This, at such an hour of the night, surprised me greatly; but I was too ignorant to draw the true conclusion, that we were going north-about round Scotland, and were now on the high sea between the Orkney and the Shetland Islands, having avoided the dangerous currents of the Pentland Firth. For my part, who had been so long shut in the dark and knew nothing of head-winds, I thought we might be half way or more across the Atlantic. And indeed, beyond that I wondered a little at the lateness of the sunset light, I gave no heed to it, and pushed on across the decks, running between the seas, catching at ropes and only saved from going overboard by one of the hands on deck, who had been always kind to me.

The round-house, for which I was bound, and where I was now to sleep and serve, stood some six feet above the decks, and considering the size of the brig, was of good dimensions. Inside, were a fixed table and bench, and two berths, one for the captain and the other for the two mates, turn and turn about. It was all fitted with lockers from top to bottom, so as to stow the officers' belongings and a part of the ship's stores; there was a second store-room underneath, which you entered by a hatchway in the middle of the deck; indeed, all the best of the meat and drink, and the whole of the powder were collected in this place; and all the firearms, except the two pieces of brass ordnance, were set in a rack on the aftermost wall of the round-house. The most of the cutlasses were in another place.

A small window with a shutter on each side, and a skylight in the roof, gave it light by day; and after dark, there was a lamp always burning. It was burning when I entered, not brightly, but enough to show me Mr Shuan, sitting at the table with the brandy bottle and a tin pannikin in front of him. He was a tall man, strongly made and very black; and he stared before him on the table like one stupid.

He took no notice of my coming in; nor did he move, when the captain followed and leant on the berth beside me, looking darkly at the mate. I stood in great fear of Hoseason, and had my reasons for it; but something told me I need not be afraid of him just then; and I whispered in his ear: "How is he?" He shook his head like one that does not know and does not wish to think; and his face was very stern.

Presently Mr Riach came in. He gave the captain a glance that meant the boy was dead, as plain as speaking, and took his place like the rest of us; so that we all three stood without a word, staring down at Mr Shuan, and Mr Shuan (on his side) sat without a word looking hard upon the table.

All of a sudden he put out his hand to take the bottle; and at that Mr Riach started forward and caught it away from him, rather by surprise than violence, crying out with an oath that there had been too much of this work altogether, and that a judgement would fall upon the ship. And as he spoke (the weather sliding-doors standing open) he tossed the bottle into the sea.

Mr Shuan was on his feet in a trice; he still looked dazed, but he meant murder, ay, and would have done it, for the second time that night, had not the captain stepped in between him and his victim.

"Sit down," roars the captain. "Ye sot and swine, do ye know what ye've done? Ye've murdered the boy."

Mr Shuan seemed to understand; for he sat down again and put up his hand to his brow. "Well," he said, "he brought me a dirty pannikin."

At that word, the captain and I and Mr Riach all looked at each other for a second with a kind of frightened look; and then Hoseason walked up to his chief officer, took him by the shoulder, led him across to his bunk, and bade him lie down and go to sleep, as you might speak to a bad child. The murderer cried a little, but he took off his sea-boots and obeyed.

"Ah!" cried Mr Riach, with a dreadful voice, "ye should have interfered long syne—it's too late now."

"Mr Riach," said the captain, "this night's work must never be kennt in Dysart. The boy went overboard, sir; that's what the story is; and I would give five pounds out of my pocket, it was true!" He turned to the table. "What made ye throw the good bottle away?" he added. "There was nae sense in that, sir. Here, David—draw me another; they're in the bottom locker;" and he tossed me a key. "Ye'll need a glass yourself, sir," he added, to Riach. "Yon was an ugly thing to see."

So the pair sat down and hob-a-nobbed; and while they did so, the murderer who had been lying and whimpering in his berth, raised himself upon his elbow, and looked at them and at me.

That was the first night of my new duties; and in the course of the next day, I had got well into the run of them. I had to serve at the meals, which the captain took at regular hours, sitting down with the officer who was off duty; all the day through, I would be running with a dram to one or other of my three masters; and at night I slept on a blanket, thrown on the deck boards at the aftermost end of the round-house and right in the draught of the two doors. It was a hard and a cold bed; nor was I suffered to sleep without interruption; for some one would be always coming in from deck to get a dram, and when a fresh watch was to be set, two and sometimes all three would sit down and brew a bowl together. How they kept their health, I know not; any more than how I kept my own.

And yet in other ways, it was an easy service. There was no cloth to lay; the meals were either of oatmeal porridge or salt junk, except twice a week when there was duff; and though I was clumsy enough and (not being firm on my sea-legs) sometimes fell with what I was bringing them, both Mr Riach and the captain were singularly patient. I could not but fancy they were making up lee-way with their consciences; and that they would scarce have been so good with me, if they had not been worse with Ransome.

As for Mr Shuan, the drink, or his crime, or the two together, had certainly troubled his wits. I cannot say I ever saw him in his proper mind. He never grew used to my being there, stared at me continually (sometimes, I would have thought, with terror) and more than once drew back from my hand when I was serving him. I was pretty sure, from the first, that he had no clear mind of what he had done; and on my second day in the round-house, I had the proof of it. We were alone, and he had been staring at me a long time, when all at once, up he got, as pale as death, and came close up to me—to my great terror. But I had no cause to be afraid of him.

"You were not here before?" he asked.

"No, sir," said I.

"There was another boy?" he asked again; and when I had answered him, "Ah!" says he, "I thought that," and went and sat down, without another word except to call for brandy.

You may think it strange, but for all the horror I had, I was still sorry for him. He was a married man, with a wife in Leith; but whether or no he had a family, I have now forgotten; I hope not.

Altogether it was no very hard life for the time it lasted which (as you are to hear) was not long. I was as well fed as the best of them; even their pickles, which were the great dainty, I was allowed my share of; and had I liked, I might have been drunk from morning to night, like Mr Shuan. I had company, too, and good company of its sort. Mr Riach, who had been to the college, spoke to me like a friend when he was not sulking, and told me many curious things, and some that were improving; and even the captain, though he kept me at the stick's end the most part of the time, would sometimes unbuckle a bit, and tell me of the fine countries he had visited.

The shadow of poor Ransome, to be sure, lay on all four of us, and on me and Mr Shuan, in particular, most heavily. And then I had another trouble of my own. Here I was, doing dirty work for three men that I looked down upon, and one of whom, at least, should have hung upon a gallows; that was for the present; and as for the future, I could only see myself slaving alongside of negros in the tobacco fields. Mr Riach, perhaps from caution, would never suffer me to say another word about my story; the captain, whom I tried to approach, rebuffed me like a dog, and would not hear a word; and as the days came and went, my heart sank lower and lower, till I was even glad of the work which kept me from thinking.

9

The Man with the Belt of Gold

More than a week went by, in which the ill luck that had hitherto pursued the *Covenant* upon this voyage grew yet more strongly marked. Some days she made a little way; others, she was driven actually back. We were driven so far south that we tossed and beat to and fro the whole of the ninth day, within sight of Cape Wrath and the wild, rocky coast on either hand of it; there followed on that a council of the officers, and some decision which I did not rightly understand and only saw the result: that we had made a fair wind of a foul one and were running south.

The tenth afternoon, there was a falling swell and a thick, wet, white fog that hid one end of the brig from the other. All afternoon, when I went on deck, I saw men and officers listening hard over the bulwarks—"for breakers," they said; and though I did not so much as understand the word, I felt danger in the air and was excited.

Maybe about ten at night, I was serving Mr Riach and the Captain at their supper, when the ship struck something with a great sound, and we heard voices singing out. My two masters leaped to their feet.

"She's struck," said Mr Riach.

"No, sir," said the captain, "we've only run a boat down."

And they hurried out.

The captain was in the right of it. We had run down a boat in the fog, and she had parted in the midst and gone down with all her crew, but one. This man (as I heard afterwards) had been sitting in the stern as a passenger, while the rest were on the benches rowing. At the moment of the blow, the stern had been thrown into the air, and the man (having his hands free, and for all he was encumbered with a frieze overcoat that came below his knees) had leaped up and caught hold of the brig's bowsprit. It showed he had luck and much agility and unusual strength, that he should have thus saved himself from such a pass. And yet when the captain brought him into the round-house, and I set eyes on him for the first time, he looked as cool as I did.

He was smallish in stature, but well set and as nimble as a goat; his face was of a good open expression, but sunburnt very dark, heavily freckled, and pitted with the small-pox; his eyes were unusually light and had a kind of dancing madness in them, that was both engaging and alarming; and when he took off his greatcoat, he laid a pair of fine, silver-mounted pistols on the able, and I saw that he was belted with a great sword. His manners, besides, were elegant, and he pledged the captain handsomely. Altogether I thought of him, at the first sight, that here was a man I would rather call my friend than my enemy.

The captain, too, was taking his observations, but rather of the man's clothes than his person. And to be sure, as soon as he had taken off the greatcoat, he showed forth mighty fine for the round-house of a merchant brig: having a hat with feathers, a red waistcoat, breeches of black plush and a blue coat with silver buttons and handsome silver lace: costly clothes, though somewhat spoiled with the fog and being slept in.

"I'm vexed, sir, about the boat," says the captain.

"There are some pretty men gone to the bottom," said the stranger, "that I would rather see on the dry land again, than half a score of boats."

"Friends of yours?" said Hoseason.

"You have none such friends in your country," was the reply. "They would have died for me like dogs."

"Well, sir," said the captain, still watching him, "there are more men in the world, than boats to put them in."

"And that's true too," cried the other; "and you seem to be a gentleman of great penetration."

"I have been in France, sir," says the captain, so that it was plain he meant more by the words than showed upon the face of them.

"Well, sir," says the other; "and so has many a pretty man, for the matter of that."

"No doubt, sir," says the captain; "and fine coats."

"Oho," says the stranger, "is that how the wind sets?" And he laid his hand quickly on his pistols.

"Don't be hasty," said the captain. "Don't do a mis-chief, before ye see the need for it. Ye've a French soldier's coat upon your back and a Scotch tongue in your head, to be sure; but so has many an honest fellow in these days, and I daresay none the worse of it."

"So?" said the gentleman in the fine coat, "are ye of the honest party?" (meaning, was he a Jacobite? for each side, in these sort of civil broils, takes the name of honesty for its own).

"Why, sir," replied the captain, "I am a true-blue protestant, and I thank God for it." (It was the first word of any religion I had ever heard from him, but I learnt afterwards he was a great church-goer while on shore.) "But for all that," says he, "I can be sorry to see another man with his back to the wall."

"Can ye so, indeed?" asks the Jacobite. "Well, sir, to be quite plain with ye, I am one of those honest gentlemen that were in trouble about the years forty five and six; and (to be still quite plain with ye) if I get into the hands of any of the red-coated gentry, it's like it would go hard with me. Now, sir, I was for France, and there was a French ship cruising here to pick me up; but she gave us the go-by in the fog—as I wish from the heart, that ye had done yoursel'! And the best that I can say is this: if ye can set me ashore where I was going, I have that upon me will reward you highly for your trouble."

"In France?" says the captain. "No, sir; that I cannot do. But where ye come from—we might talk of that."

And then unhappily he observed me standing in my corner, and packed me off to the galley to get supper for the gentleman. I lost no time, I promise you; and when I came back into the round-house, I found the gentleman had taken a money belt from about his waist, and poured out a guinea or two upon the table. The captain was looking at the guineas, and at the belt, and then at the gentleman's face, and I thought he seemed excited.

"Half of it," he cried, "and I'm your man!"

The other swept back the guineas into the belt, and put it on again under his waistcoat. "I have told ye, sir," said he, "that not one doit of it belongs to me. It belongs to my chieftain" (and here he touched his hat) "and while I would be but a silly messenger,

"The captain was looking at the guineas, and at the belt, and then at the gentleman's face, and I thought he seemed excited."

Young Folks Paper, May 16, 1886.

to grudge some of it that the rest might come safe, I should show myself a hound indeed, if I bought my own carcase any too dear. Thirty guineas on the sea side, or sixty if ye set me on the Linnhe Loch. Take it, if ye will; if not, why, ye can do your worst."

"Ay," said Hoseason. "And if I give ye over to the soldiers?"

"You would make a fool's bargain," said the other. "My chief, let me tell you, sir, is forfeited, like every honest man in Scotland. His estate is in the hands of the man they call King George; and it's his officers that collect the rents, or try to collect them. But for the honour of Scotland, the poor tenant bodies take a thought upon their chief lying in exile; and this money is a part of that very rent for which King George is looking. Now, sir, ye seem to me to be a man that understands things: bring this money within the reach of government, and how much of it'll come to you?"

"Little enough, to be sure," said Hoseason; and then, "If they knew," he added, drily. "But I think, if I was to try that I could hold my tongue about it."

"Ah, but I'll begowk ye there!" cried the gentleman. "Play me false, and I'll play you cunning. If a hand's laid upon me, they shall ken what money it is."

"Well," returned the captain, "what must be must. Sixty guineas, and done. Here's my hand upon it."

"And here's mine," said the other.

And thereupon the captain went out (rather hurriedly, I thought) and left me alone in the round-house with the stranger.

At that period (so soon after the forty-five) there were many exiled gentlemen coming back at the peril of their lives, either to see their friends or to collect a little money; and as for the Highland chiefs that had been forfeited, it was a common matter of talk how their tenants would stint themselves to send them money, and their clansmen outface the soldiery to get it in, and run the gauntlet of our great navy to carry it across. All this I had, of course, heard tell of; and now I had a man under my eyes, whose life was forfeit on all these counts and upon one more; for he was not only a rebel and a smuggler of rents, but had taken service with King Lewis of France. And as if all this were not enough, he had a beltful of golden guineas round his loins. Whatever my opinions, I could not look on such a man without a lively interest.

"And so you're a Jacobite?" said I, as I set meat before him.

"Ay," said he, beginning to eat. "And you, by your long face, should be a whig?"

"Betwixt and Between," said I; not to annoy him, for indeed I was as good a whig as Mr Campbell could make me.

"And that's nothing," said he. "But I'm saying, Mr Betwixt-and-Between," he added, "this bottle of yours is dry; and it's hard if I'm to pay sixty guineas and be grudged a dram upon the back of it."

"I'll go and ask for the key," said I, and stepped on deck.

The fog was as close as ever, but the swell almost down. They had laid the brig to, not knowing precisely where they were, and the wind (what little there was of it) not serving well for their true course. Some of the hands were still hearkening for breakers; but the captain and the two officers were in the waist with their heads together. It struck me, I don't know why, that they were after no good; and the first word I heard, as I drew softly near, more than confirmed me.

It was Mr Riach, crying out, as if upon a sudden thought: "Couldn't we wile him out of the round-house?"

"He's better where he is," returned Hoseason; "he hasn't room to use his sword."

"Well, that's true," said Riach; "but he's hard to come at."

"Hut!" said Hoseason. "We can get the man in talk, one upon each side, and pin him by the two arms; or if that'll not hold, sir, we can make a run by both the doors and get him underhand before he has the time to draw."

At this hearing, I was seized with both fear and anger at these treacherous, greedy, bloody men that I sailed with. My first mind was to run away; my second was bolder.

"Captain," said I, "the gentleman is seeking a dram, and the bottle's out. Will you give me the key?"

They all started and turned about.

"Why, here's our chance to get the fire-arms!" Riach cried; and then to me: "Hark ye, David," he said, "do ye ken where the pistols are?"

"Ay, ay," put in Hoseason. "David kens, David's a good lad. Ye see, David my man, yon wild Hielandman is a danger to the ship, besides being a rank foe to King George, God bless him!"

I had never been so be-davided since I came on board; but I said yes, as if all I heard were quite natural.

"The trouble is," resumed the captain, "that all our fire-locks, great and little, are in the round-house under this man's nose; likewise the powder. Now if me, or one of the officers, was to go in and take them, he would fall to thinking. But a lad like you, David, might snap up a horn and a pistol or two without remark. And if ye can do it cleverly, I'll bear it in mind, when it'll be good for you to have friends; and that's when we come to Carolina."

Here Mr Riach whispered him a little.

"Very right, sir," said the captain; and then to myself: "And see here, David, yon man has a beltful of gold, and I give you my word that you shall have your fingers in it."

I told him I would do as he wished, though indeed I had scarce breath to speak with; and upon that he gave me the key of the spirit locker, and I began to go slowly back to the round-house. What was I to do? They were dogs and thieves; they had stolen me from my own country; they had killed poor Ransome; and was I to hold the candle to another murder? But then upon the other hand there was the fear of death very plain before me; for what could a boy and a man, if they were as brave as lions, against a whole ship's company?

I was still arguing it back and forth, and getting no great clearness, when I came into the round-house and saw the Jacobite eating his supper under the lamp; and at that, my mind was made up all in a moment. I have no credit by it; it was by no choice of mine, but as if by compulsion, that I walked right up to the table and put my hand on his shoulder.

"Do ye want to be killed?" said I.

He sprang to his feet, and looked a question at me as clear as if he had spoken.

"O!" cried I, "they're all murderers here. It's a ship full of them! They've murdered a boy already. Now, it's you."

"Ay, ay," said he, "but they haven't got me yet." And then looking at me curiously, "Will ye stand with me?" he asked.

"That will I!" said I. "I am no thief, nor yet murderer. I'll stand by you."

"Why, then," said he, "what's your name?"

"David Balfour," said I, and then thinking that a man with so fine a coat must like fine people, I added for the first time, "of Shaws."

It never occurred to him to doubt me, for a highlander is used to see great gentlefolk in great poverty; but as he had no estate of his own, my words nettled a very childish vanity he had.

"My name is Stewart," he said, drawing himself up. "Alan Breck, they call me. A King's name is good enough for me, though I bear it plain and have the name of no farm-midden to clap to the hind-end of it."

And having administered this rebuke, as though it were something of a chief importance, he turned to examine our defences.

The round-house was built very strong to support the breaching of the seas. Of its five apertures, only the skylight and the two doors were large enough for the passage of a man. The doors, besides, could be drawn close; they were of stout oak, and ran in grooves, and were fitted with hooks to keep them either shut or open, as the need arose. The one that was already shut, I secured in this fashion; but when I was proceeding to slide to the other, Alan stopped me.

"David," said he, "—for I cannot bring to mind the name of your landed estate, and so will make so bold as call you David— that door, being open, is the best part of my defences."

"It would be yet better shut," says I.

"Not so, David," says he. "Ye see, I have but one face; but so long as that door is open and my face to it, the best part of my enemies will be in front of me, where I would aye wish to find them."

Then he gave me from the rack a cutlass (of which there were a few besides the firearms) choosing it with great care, shaking his head and saying he had never in all his life seen poorer weapons; and next he set me down to the table with a powder horn, a bag of bullets and all the pistols, which he bade me charge.

"And that will be better work, let me tell you," said he, "for a gentleman of decent birth, than scraping plates and raxing drams to a wheen tarry sailors."

Thereupon he stood up in the midst with his face to the door, and drawing his great sword, made trial of the room he had to wield it in.

"I must stick to the point," he said, shaking his head; "and that's a pity too. It doesn't set my genius, which is all the upper guard. And now," said he, "do you keep on charging the pistols, and give heed to me."

I told him I would listen closely. My chest was tight, my mouth dry, the light dark to my eyes; the thought of the numbers that were soon to leap in upon us kept my heart in a flutter; and the sea, which I heard washing round the brig, and where I thought my dead body would be cast ere morning, ran in my mind strangely.

"First of all," said he, "how many are against us?"

I reckoned them up; and such was the hurry of my mind, I had to cast the numbers twice. "Fifteen," said I.

Alan whistled. "Well," said he, "that can't be cured. And now follow me. It is my part to keep this door, where I look for the main battle. In that, ye have no hand. And mind and dinnae fire to this side unless they get me down; for I would rather have ten foes in front of me, than one friend like you cracking pistols at my back."

I told him, indeed I was no great shot.

"And that's very bravely said," he cried, in a great admiration of my candour. "There's many a pretty gentleman that wouldn't dare to say it."

"But then sir," said I, "there is the door behind you, which they may perhaps break in."

"Ay," said he, "and that is a part of your work. No sooner your pistols charged, than ye must climb up into yon bed where you're handy at the window; and if they lift hand against the door, you're to shoot. But that's not all. Let's make a bit of a soldier of ye, David. What else have ye to guard?"

"There's the skylight," said I. "But indeed, Mr Stewart, I would need to have eyes upon both sides to keep the two of them; for when my face is at the one, my back is to the other."

"And that's very true," said Alan. "But have ye no ears to your head?"

"To be sure!" cried I. "I must hear the bursting of the glass!"

"Ye have some rudiments of sense," said Alan grimly.

10

The Siege of the Round-House

But now our time of truce was come to an end. Those on deck had waited for my coming till they grew impatient; and scarce had Alan spoken, when the captain showed face in the open door.

"Stand!" cried Alan, and pointed his sword at him.

The captain stood indeed, but he neither winced nor drew back a foot. "A naked sword?" says he. "This is a strange return for hospitality."

"Do ye see me?" said Alan. "I am come of Kings. My badge is the oak. Do ye see my sword? It has slashed the heads off mair whigamores than you have toes upon your feet. Call up your vermin to your back, sir, and fall on! The sooner the clash begins, the sooner ye'll taste this steel throughout your vitals."

The captain said nothing to Alan, but he looked over at me with an ugly look. "David," said he, "I'll mind this." And the sound of his voice went through me with a jar.

Next moment he was gone.

"And now," said Alan, "let your hand keep your head, for the grip is coming."

Alan drew a dirk which he held in his left hand, in case they should run in under his sword. I, on my part, clambered up into the berth, with an armful of pistols and something of a heavy heart, and set open the window where I was to watch. It was a small part of the deck that I could see, but enough for our purpose. The sea had gone down, and the wind was steady and kept the sails quiet; so that there was a great stillness on the ship, in which I made sure I heard the sound of muttering voices. A little after, and there came a clash of steel upon the deck, by which I knew they were doling out the cutlasses, and one had been let fall. And after that, silence again.

I do not know if I was what you call afraid; but my heart beat like a bird's, both quick and little; and there was a dimness came before my eyes, which I continually rubbed away and which continually returned. As for hope, I had none; but only a darkness of despair, and a sort of anger against all the world that made me long to sell my life as dear as I was able. I tried to pray, I remember, but that same hurry of my mind, like a man running, would not suffer me to think upon the words; and my chief wish was to have the thing begin and be done with it.

It came all of a sudden when it did, with a rush of feet and a roar, and then a shout from Alan, and a sound of blows and some one crying out as if hurt. I looked back over my shoulder, and saw Mr Shuan in the doorway, crossing blades with Alan.

"That's him that killed the boy!" I cried.

"Look to your window!" said Alan, and as I turned back to my place, I saw him pass his sword through the mate's body.

It was none too soon for me to look to my own part; for my head was scarce back at the window, before five men, carrying a spare yard for a battering ram, ran past me and took post to drive the door in. I had never fired with a pistol in my life, and not often with a gun; far less against a fellow creature. But it was now or never; and just as they swung the yard, I cried out "Take that!" and shot into their midst.

I must have hit one of them, for he sang out and gave back a step, and the rest stopped as if a little disconcerted. Before they had time to recover, I sent another ball over their heads; and at my third shot (which went as wide as the second) the whole party threw down the yard and ran for it.

Then I looked round again into the deck house. The whole place was full of the smoke of my own firing, just as my ears seemed to be burst with the noise of the shots. But there was Alan, standing as before; only now his sword was running blood to the hilt, and himself so swelled with triumph and fallen into so fine an attitude, that he looked to be invincible. Right before him on the floor was Mr Shuan on his hands and knees; the blood was pouring from his mouth, and he was sinking slowly lower, with a terrible, white face; and just as I looked, some of those from behind caught hold of him by the heels and dragged him bodily out of the round-house. I believe he died as they were doing so.

"There's one of your whigs for ye!" cried Alan; and then turning to me, he asked if I had done much execution.

I told him I had winged one, and thought it was the captain.

"And I've settled two," says he. "No, there's not enough blood let; they'll be back again. To your watch, David. This was but a dram before meat."

I settled back to my place, re-charging the three pistols I had fired, and keeping watch with both eye and ear.

Our enemies were disputing not far off upon the deck, and that so loudly that I could hear a word or two above the washing of the seas.

"It was Shuan bauchled it," I heard one say.

And another answered him with a "Wheesht, man! He's paid the piper."

After that the voices fell again into the same muttering as before. Only now, one person spoke most of the time, as though laying down a plan, and first one and then another answered him briefly, like men taking orders. By this, I made sure they were coming on again, and told Alan.

"It's what we have to pray for," said he. "Unless we can give them a good distaste of us, and done with it, there'll be nae sleep for either you or me. But this time, mind, they'll be in earnest."

By this, my pistols were ready, and there was nothing to do but listen and wait. While the brush lasted, I had not the time to think if I was frighted; but now when all was still again, my mind ran upon nothing else. The thought of the sharp swords and the cold steel was strong in me; and presently when I began to hear stealthy steps and a brushing of men's clothes against the round-house wall, and knew they were taking their places in the dark, I could have found it in my mind to cry out aloud.

All this was upon Alan's side; and I had begun to think my share of fight was at an end, when I heard some one drop softly on the roof above me.

Then there came a single call on the sea-pipe, and that was the signal. A knot of them made one rush of it, cutlass in hand, against the door; and at the same moment, the glass of the skylight was dashed in a thousand pieces and a man leaped through and landed on the floor. Before he got his feet I had clapped a pistol to his back, and might have shot him, too; only at the touch of him (and him alive) my whole flesh mis-gave me, and I could no more pull the trigger than I could have flown.

He had dropped his cutlass as he jumped; and when he felt the pistol, whipped straight round and laid hold of me, roaring out an oath; and at that either my courage came again, or I grew so much afraid as came to the same thing; for I gave a shriek and shot him in the midst of the body. He gave the most horrible, ugly groan and fell to the floor. The foot of a second fellow, whose legs were dangling through the skylight, struck me at the same time upon the head; and at that I snatched another pistol and shot this one through the thigh, so that he slipped through and tumbled in a lump on his companion's body. There was no talk of missing, any more than there was time to aim; I clapped the muzzle to the very place and fired.

I might have stood and stared at them for long, but I heard Alan shout as if for help, and that brought me to my senses.

He had kept the door so long; but one of the seamen, while he was engaged with others, had run in under his guard and caught him about the body. Alan was dirking him with his left hand, but the fellow clung like a leech. Another had broken in and had his cutlass raised. The door was thronged with their faces. I thought we were lost, and catching up my cutlass, fell on them in flank.

But I had not time to be of help. The wrestler dropped at last; and Alan, leaping back to get his distance, ran upon the others like a bull, roaring as he went. They broke before him like water, turning, and running, and falling one against another in their haste. The sword in his hands flashed like quicksilver into the huddle of our fleeing enemies; and at every flash, there came the scream of a man hurt. I was still thinking we were lost, when lo! they were all gone, and Alan was driving them along the deck as a sheepdog chases sheep.

Yet he was no sooner out than he was back again, being as

"They broke before him like water, turning, and running, and falling
one against another in their haste."

Young Folks Paper, May 22, 1886.

cautious as he was brave; and meanwhile the seamen continued running and crying out as if he was still behind them, and we heard them tumble one upon another into the forecastle, and clap to the hutch upon the top.

The round-house was like a shambles; three were dead inside, another lay in his death agony across the threshold; and there were Alan and I victorious and unhurt.

He came up to me with open arms. "Come to my arms!" he cried, and embraced and kissed me hard upon both cheeks. "David," said he, "I love you like a brother. And O, man," he cried in a kind of ecstasy, "am I no a bonny fighter?"

Thereupon he turned to the four enemies, passed his sword clean through each of them, and tumbled them out of doors one after the other. As he did so, he kept humming and singing and whistling to himself, like a man trying to recall an air; only what *he* was trying was to make one. All the while, the flush was on his face, and his eyes were as bright as a five year old child's with a new toy. And presently he sat down upon the table sword in hand; the air that he was making all the time, began to run a little clearer, and then clearer still; and then out he burst with a great voice into this song.

I have translated it here, not in verse (of which I have no skill) but at least in the King's English. He sang it often afterwards; and the thing became popular, so that I have heard it, and had it explained to me, many's the time.

> This is the song of the sword of Alan:
> The smith made it,
> The fire set it;
> Now it shines in the hand of Alan Breck.

Their eyes were many and bright,
Swift were they to behold,
Many the hands they guided:
The sword was alone.

The dun deer troop over the hill,
They are many, the hill is one;
The dun deer vanish,
The hill remains.

Come to me from the hills of heather,
Come from the isles of the sea.
O, far-beholding eagles,
Here is your meat.

Now this song which he made (both words and music) in the hour of our victory, is something less than just to me, who stood beside him in the tussle. Mr Shuan and five more either killed outright or thoroughly disabled; but of these two fell by my hand, the two that came by the skylight. Four more were hurt; and of that number, one (and he not the least important) got his hurt from me. So that altogether, I did my fair share both of the killing and the wounding; and might have claimed a place in Alan's verses. But poets (as a very wise man once told me) have to think upon their rhymes; and in good prose talk, Alan always did me more than justice.

In the meanwhile, I was innocent of any wrong being done me. For not only I knew no word of the Gaelic; but what with the long suspense of the waiting, and the scurry and strain of our two spirts of fighting—and more than all, the horror I had of some of my own share in it—the thing was no sooner over than I was glad to stagger to a seat. There was that tightness on my chest that I could hardly breathe; the thought of the two men I had shot sat upon me like a nightmare; and all upon a sudden, and before I had a guess of what was coming, I began to sob and cry like any child.

Alan clapped my shoulder, and said I was a brave lad and wanted nothing but a sleep.

"I'll take the first watch," said he. "Ye've done well by me, David, first and last; and I wouldn't lose you for all Appin—no, nor for Breadalbane."

So he made up my bed on the floor, and took the first spell, pistol in hand and sword on knee; three hours by the captain's watch upon the wall. Then he roused me up, and I took my turn of three hours; before the end of which it was broad day, and a very quiet morning, with a smooth rolling sea that tossed the ship and made the blood run to and fro on the round-house floor, and a heavy rain that drummed upon the roof. All my watch there was nothing stirring; and by the banging of the tiller, I knew they had even no one at the helm. Indeed (as I learned afterwards) they were so many of them hurt or dead, and the rest in so ill a temper, that Mr Riach and the captain had to take turn and turn (like Alan and me) or the brig might have gone ashore and nobody the wiser. It was a mercy the night had fallen so still, for the wind had gone down as soon as the rain began. Even as it was, I judged by the wailing of a great number of gulls that went crying and fishing round the ship, that she must have drifted pretty near the coast or one of the islands of the Hebrides; and as soon as the gray came, looking out of the door of the round-house, I saw the great stone hills of Skye on the right hand.

11

The Captain Knuckles Under

Alan and I sat down to breakfast about six of the clock. The floor was covered with broken glass and in a horrid mess of blood, which took away my hunger. In all other ways, we were in a situation not only agreeable but merry; having ousted the officers from their own cabin, and having at command all the drink in the ship, both wine and spirits, and all the dainty part of what was eatable, such as the pickles and the fine sort of biscuit. This, of itself, was enough to set us in good humour; but the richest part of it was this, that the two thirstiest men that ever came out of Scotland (Mr Shuan being dead) were now shut in the fore part of the ship and condemned to what they hated most—cold water.

"And depend upon it," Alan said, "we shall hear more of them erelong. Ye may keep a man from the fighting but never from his bottle."

We made good company for each other. Alan, indeed, expressed himself most lovingly; and taking a knife from the table, cut me off one of the silver buttons from his coat.

"I had them," says he, "from my father, Duncan Stewart; and now give ye one of them to be a keepsake for last night's work.

And wherever ye go and show that button, the friends of Alan Breck will come around you."

He said this as if he had been Charlemagne and commanded armies; and indeed, much as I admired his courage, I was always in danger of smiling at his vanity: in danger, I say, for had I not kept my countenance, I would be afraid to think what a quarrel might have followed.

As soon as we were through with our meal, he rummaged in the captain's locker till he found a clothes-brush; and then taking off his coat, began to visit his suit and take off the stains, with such care and labour as I supposed to have been only usual with women. To be sure, he had no other; and besides (as he said) it belonged to a King and so behoved to be royally looked after.

For all that, when I saw what care he took to pluck out the threads where the button had been cut away, I put a higher value on his gift.

He was still so engaged, when we were hailed by Mr Riach from the deck, asking for a parley; and I climbing through the skylight and sitting on the edge of it, pistol in hand and with a bold front, though inwardly in fear of broken glass, hailed him back again and bade him speak out. He came to the edge of the round-house, and stood on a coil of rope, so that his chin was on a level with the roof; and we looked at each other awhile in silence. Mr Riach, as I do not think he had been very forward in the battle, so he had got off with nothing worse than a blow upon the cheek; but he looked out of heart and very weary, having been all night afoot, either standing watch or doctoring the wounded.

"This is a bad job," said he at last, shaking his head.

"It was none of our choosing," said I.

"The captain," says he, "would like to speak with your friend. They might speak at the window."

"And how do we know what treachery he means?" cried I.

"He means none, David," returned Mr Riach; "and if he did, I'll tell ye the honest truth, we couldnae get the men to follow."

"Is that so?" said I.

"I'll tell ye more than that," said he. "It's not only the men; it's me. I'm frich'ened, Davie." And he smiled across at me. "No," he continued, "what we want is to be shut of him."

Thereupon, I consulted with Alan, and the parley was agreed to and parole given upon either side; but this was not the whole of Mr Riach's business, and he now begged me for a dram, with such instancy and such reminders of his former kindness, that at last I handed him a pannikin with about a gill of brandy. He drank a part, and then carried the rest down upon deck, to share it (I suppose) with his superior.

A little after, the captain came (as was agreed) to one of the windows, and stood there in the rain, with his arm in a sling, and looking stern and pale, and so old that my heart smote me for having fired upon him.

Alan at once held a pistol in his face.

"Put that thing up!" said the captain. "Have I not passed my word, sir? or do ye seek to affront me?"

"Captain," says Alan, "I doubt your word is a breakable. Last night, ye haggled and argle-bargled like an apple-wife; and then passed me your word, and gave me your hand to back it; and ye ken very well what was the upshot.—Be damned to your word!" says he.

"Well, well, sir," said the captain, "ye'll get little good by swearing." (And truly that was a fault of which the captain was quite free.) "But we have other things to speak," he continued bitterly. "Ye've made a sore hash of my brig; I haven't hands enough left to work her; and my first officer (whom I could ill spare) has got your sword throughout his vitals, and passed without speech. There is nothing left me, sir, but to put back into the port of Glasgow after hands; and there (by your leave) ye will find them that are better able to talk to you."

"Ay?" said Alan; "and, faith, I'll have a talk with them mysel'. Unless there's naebody speaks English in that town, I have a bonny tale for them. Fifteen tarry sailors upon the one side, and a man and a halfling boy upon the other?—O, man, it's peetiful!"

Hoseason flushed red.

"No," continued Alan, "that'll no do. Ye'll just have to set me ashore as we agreed."

"Ay," said Hoseason, "but my first officer is dead, ye can ken best how. There's none of the rest of us acquaint with this coast, sir; and it's one very dangerous to ships."

"I give ye your choice," says Alan. "Set me on dry ground in Appin or Lismore or Ardgour, or in Morven or Arisaig or Morar; or in brief where ye please within thirty miles of my own country; except in a country of the Campbells'. That's a broad target. If ye miss that, ye must be as feckless at the sailoring as I have found ye at the fighting. Why, my poor country people in their bit cobles pass from island to island in all weathers, ay, and by night too, for the matter of that."

"A coble's not a ship, sir," said the captain. "It has nae draught of water."

"Well, then, to Glasgow if ye list!" says Alan. "We'll have the laugh of ye at the least."

"My mind runs little upon laughing," said the captain. "But all this will cost money, sir."

"Well, sir," says Alan, "I am nae weathercock. Thirty guineas, if ye land me on the sea-side; and sixty, if ye put me in the Linnhe loch."

"But see, sir, where we lie, we are but a few hours' sail from Ardnamurchan," said Hoseason. "Give me sixty, and I'll set ye there."

"And I'm to wear my brogues and run jeopardy of the red coats, to pleasure you?" cries Alan. "No, sir, if ye want sixty guineas, earn them, and set me in my own country."

"It's to risk the brig, sir," said the Captain; "and your own lives along with her."

"Take it or want it," says Alan.

"Could ye pilot us at all?" asked the captain, who was frowning to himself.

"Well, it's doubtful," said Alan. "I'm more of a fighting-man (as ye have seen for yoursel') than a sailorman. But I have been often enough picked up and set down upon this coast, and should ken something of the lie of it."

The captain shook his head, still frowning.

"If I had lost less money on this unchancy cruise," says he, "I would see you in a rope's-end before I risked my brig, sir. But be it as ye will. As soon as I get a slant of wind (and there's some coming, or I'm the more mistaken), I'll put it in hand. But there's one thing more. We may meet in with a King's ship and she may lay us aboard, sir, with no blame of mine: they keep the cruisers thick upon this coast, ye ken who for. Now, sir, if that was to befall, ye might leave the money."

"Captain," says Alan, "if ye see a pennant, it shall be your part to run away. And now as I hear you're a little short of brandy in the fore part, I'll offer ye a change: a bottle of brandy against two buckets of water."

That was the last clause of the treaty, and was duly executed on both sides; so that Alan and I could at last wash out the round-house and be quit of the memorials of those whom we had slain; and the captain and Mr Riach could be happy again in their own way, the name of which was drink.

❧ 12

I Hear of the Red Fox

Before we had done cleaning out the round-house, a breeze sprang up from a little to the east of north. This blew off the rain and brought out the sun.

And here I must explain; and the reader would do well to look at a map. On the day when the fog fell and we ran down Alan's boat, we had been running through the Little Minch. At dawn after the battle, we lay becalmed to the east of the isle of Canna or between that and Isle Eriska in the chain of the Long Island. Now to get from there to the Linnhe Loch, the straight course was through the narrows of the Sound of Mull. But the captain had no chart; he was afraid to trust his brig so deep among the islands; and the wind serving well, he preferred to go by-west of Tiree, and come up under the southern coast of the great isle of Mull.

All day the breeze held in the same point, and rather freshened than died down; and towards afternoon, a swell began to set in from round the Outer Hebrides. Our course, to go round about the inner isles, was to the west of south, so that at first we had this swell upon our beam and were much rolled about. But after nightfall, when we had turned the end of Tiree and began to head more to the east, the sea came right astern.

Meanwhile, the early part of the day before the swell came up, was very pleasant, sailing, as we were, in a bright sunshine and with many mountainous islands upon different sides. Alan and I sat in the round-house with the doors open on each side (the wind being straight astern) and smoked a pipe or two of the captain's fine tobacco. It was at this time we heard each other's stories, which was the more important to me, as I gained some knowledge of that wild, Highland country, on which I was so soon to land. In those days, so close on the back of the great rebellion, it was needful a man should know what he was doing, when he went upon the heather.

It was I that showed the example, telling him all my misfortune; which he heard with great good nature. Only, when I came to mention that good friend of mine, Mr Campbell the minister, Alan fired up and cried out that he hated all that were of that name.

"Why," said I, "he is a man you should be proud to give your hand to."

"I know nothing I would help a Campbell to," says he, "unless it was a leaden bullet. I would hunt all of that name like blackcocks. If I lay dying, I would crawl upon my knees to my chamber window for a shot at one."

"Why, Alan," I cried, "what ails ye at the Campbells?"

"Well," says he, "ye ken very well that I am an Appin Stewart, and the Campbells have long harried and wasted those of my name; ay, and got lands of us by treachery—but never with the sword," he cried loudly, and with the word, brought down his fist upon the table. But I paid the less attention to this, for I knew it was usually said by those who have underhand. "There's more than that," he continued, "and all in the same story: lying words, lying papers, tricks fit for a peddler, and the show of what's legal over-all, to make a man the more angry."

"You that are so wasteful of your buttons," said I, "I can hardly think you would be a good judge of business."

"Ah!" says he, falling again to smiling, "I got my wastefulness from the same man I got the buttons from; and that was my poor father, Duncan Stewart, grace be to him! He was the prettiest man of his kindred; and the best swordsman in the Hielands, David, and that is the same as to say, in all the world. I should ken, for it was him that taught me. He was in the Black Watch, when first it was mustered; and like other gentleman privates, had a gillie at his back, to carry his firelock for him on the march. Well, the King, it appears, was wishful to see Hieland swordsmanship; and my father and three more were chosen out and sent to London town, to let him see it at the best. So they were had into the palace and showed the whole art of the sword for two hours at a stretch, before King George and Queen Carline, and the Butcher Cumberland, and many more of whom I havenae mind. And when they were through, the King (for all he was a rank usurper) spoke them fair and gave each man three guineas in his hand. Now, as they were going out of the palace, they had a porter's lodge to go by; and it came in on my father, as he was perhaps the first private Hieland gentleman that had ever gone by that door, it was right he should give the poor porter a proper notion of their quality. So he gives the King's three guineas into the man's hand, as if it was his common custom; the three others that came behind him did the same; and then they were on the street, never a penny the better for their pains. Some say it was one, that was the first to fee the King's porter; and some say it was another; but the truth of it is that it was Duncan Stewart, as I am willing to prove with either sword or pistol. And that was the father that I had, God rest him!"

"I think he was not the man to leave you rich," said I.

"And that's true," said Alan. "He left me my breeks to cover me, and little besides. And that was how I came to inlist, which was a black spot upon my character at the best of times, and would still be a sore job for me if I fell among the redcoats."

"What?" cried I, "were you in the English army?"

"That I was," said Alan. "But I deserted to the right side at Preston Pans—and that's some comfort."

I could scarcely share this view: holding desertion under arms for an unpardonable fault in honour. But for all I was so young, I was wiser than say my thought. "Dear, dear," says I, "the punishment is death."

"Ay," said he, "if they got hands on me, it would be a short shrift and a lang tow for Alan! But I have the King of France's commission in my pocket; which would aye be some protection."

"I mis-doubt it much," said I.

"I have doubts mysel'," said Alan, drily.

"And, good heaven, man," cried I, "you that are a condemned rebel, and a deserter, and a man of the French King's—what tempts ye back into this country? It's a braving of providence."

"Tit," says Alan, "I have been back every year since forty-six!"

"And what brings ye, man?" cried I.

"Well, ye see, I weary for my friends and country," said he. "France is a braw place, nae doubt; but I weary for the heather and the deer. And then I have bit things that I attend to. Whiles, I pick up a few lads to serve the King of France: recruits, ye see; and that's aye a little money. But the heart of the matter is the business of my chief, Ardshiel."

"I thought they called your chief Appin," said I.

"Ay, but Ardshiel is the Captain of the Clan," said he, which scarcely cleared my mind. "Ye see, David, he that was all his life so great a man, and come of the blood and bearing the name of Kings, is now brought home to live in a French town like a poor and private person. He that had four hundred swords at his whistle, I have seen, with these eyes of mine, buying butter in the marketplace, and taking it home in a kale leaf. This is not only a pain but a disgrace to us of his family and clan. There are the bairns forby, the children and the hope of Appin, that must be learned their letters and how to hold a sword, in that far country. Now the tenants of Appin have to pay a rent to King George; but their hearts are staunch; they are true to their chief; and what with love, and a bit pressure, and maybe a threat or two, the poor folk scrape up a second rent for Ardshiel. Well, David, I'm the hand that carries it." And he struck the belt about his body, so that the guineas rang.

"Do they pay both?" cried I.

"Ay, David, both," says he.

"What? two rents?" I repeated.

"Ay, David," said he. "I told a different tale to yon captain man; but this is the truth of it. And it's wonderful to me how little pressure is needed. But that's the handiwork of my good kinsman and my father's friend, James of the Glens: James Stewart, that is, Ardshiel's half brother. He it is that gets the money in, and does the management."

This was the first time I heard the name of that James Stewart, who was afterwards so famous at the time of his hanging. But I took little heed at the moment, for all my mind was occupied with the generosity of these poor Highlanders.

"I call it noble," I cried. "I'm a whig, or little better; but I call it noble."

"Ay," said he, "ye're a whig, but ye're a gentleman; and that's what does it. Now, if ye were one of the cursed race of Campbell, ye would gnash your teeth to hear tell of it. If ye were the Red Fox" . . . And at that name, his teeth shut together and he ceased speaking. I have seen many a grim face, but never a grimmer than Alan's when he had named the Red Fox.

"And who is the Red Fox?" I asked, daunted but still curious.

"Who is he?" cried Alan. "Well, and I'll tell you that. When the men of the clans were broken at Culloden, and the good cause went down, and the horses rode over the fetlocks in the best blood of the north, Ardshiel had to flee like a poor deer upon the mountains—he and his lady and his bairns. A sore job we had of it before we got him shipped; and while he still lay in the heather, the English rogues, that couldnae come at his life, were striking at his rights. They stripped him of his powers; they stripped him of his lands; they plucked the weapons from the hands of his clansmen that had borne arms for thirty centuries; ay, and the very clothes off their back—so that it's now a sin to wear a tartan plaid, and a man may be cast into a jail, if he has but a kilt about his legs. One thing they couldnae kill. That was the love the clansmen bore their chief. These guineas are the proof of it. And now, in there steps a man, a Campbell, red-headed Colin of Glenure——"

"Is that him you call the Red Fox?" said I.

"Will ye bring me his brush?" cries Alan, fiercely. "Ay, that's the man. In he steps, and gets papers from King George, to be so-called King's factor on the lands of Appin. And at first he sings small, and is hail-fellow-well-met with Sheamus—that's James of the Glens, my chieftain's agent. But by and by, that came to his ears that I have just told you: how the poor commons of Appin, the farmers and the crofters and the boumen, were wringing their very plaids to get a second rent and send it overseas for Ardshiel and his poor bairns. What was it ye called it, when I told ye?"

"I called it noble, Alan," said I.

"And you little better than a common whig!" cries Alan. "But when it came to Colin Roy, the black Campbell blood in him ran wild. He sat gnashing his teeth at the wine table. What! should a Stewart get a bite of bread, and him not be able to prevent it? Ah! Red Fox, if ever I hold you at a gun's end, the Lord have pity upon ye!" (Alan stopped to swallow down his anger.) "Well, David, what does he do? He declares all the farms to let. And thinks he, in his black heart, 'I'll soon get other tenants that'll overbid these Stewarts and MacColls and McRobs'—(For those are all names in my clan, David)—'And then,' thinks he, 'Ardshiel will have to hold his bonnet on a French roadside.'"

"Well," said I, "what followed?"

Alan laid down his pipe, which he had long since suffered to go out, and set his two hands upon his knees.

"Ay," said he, "ye'll never guess that! For these same Stewarts and MacColls and McRobs (that had two rents to pay, one to King George by stark force, and one to Ardshiel by natural kindness) offered him a better price than any Campbell in all broad Scotland; and far he sent seeking them—as far as to the sides of Clyde and the cross of Edinburgh—seeking and fleeching and begging them to come, where there was a Stewart to be starved and a red-headed hound of a Campbell to be pleasured!"

"Well, Alan," said I, "that is a strange story, and a fine one too. And whig as I may be, I am glad the man was beaten."

"Him beaten?" echoed Alan. "It's little ye ken of Campbells

and less of the Red Fox. Him beaten? No: nor will be till his blood's on the hillside! But if the day comes, David man, that I can find time and leisure for a bit of hunting, there grows not enough heather in all Scotland to hide him from my vengeance!"

"Man Alan," said I, "ye are neither very wise nor very christian to blow off so many words of anger. They will do the man ye call the Fox no harm, and yourself no good. Tell me your tale plainly out. What did he next?"

"And that's a good observe, David," said Alan. "Troth and indeed, they will do him no harm; the more's the pity! And barring that about Christianity (of which my opinion is quite otherwise, or I would be nae Christian) I am much of your mind."

"Opinion here or opinion there," said I, "it's a kent thing that Christianity forbids revenge."

"Ay," said he, "it's well seen it was a Campbell taught ye! It would be a convenient world for them and their sort, if there was no such thing as a lad and a gun behind a heather bush! But that's nothing to the point. This is what he did."

"Ay," said I, "come to that."

"Well, David," said he, "since he couldnae be rid of the loyal commons by fair means, he swore he would be rid of them by foul. Ardshiel was to starve: that was the thing he aimed at. And since them that fed him in his exile wouldnae be bought out— right or wrong, he would drive them out. Therefore, he sent for lawyers and papers and redcoats to stand at his back. And the kindly folk of that country must all pack and tramp, every father's son out of his father's house, and out of the place where he was bred and fed, and played when he was a callant. And who are to succeed them? Bare-leggit beggars! King George is to whistle for his rents; he maun dow with less; he can spread his butter thinner:—what cares Red Colin? If he can hurt Ardshiel, he has his wish; if he can pluck the meat from my chieftain's table, and the bit toys out of his children's hands, he will gang home singing to Glenure!"

"Let me have a word," said I. "Be sure, if they take less rents, be sure government has a finger in the pie. It's not this Campbell's fault, man—it's his orders. And if ye killed this Colin tomorrow, what better would ye be? There would be another factor in his shoes, as fast as spur can drive."

"Ye're a good lad in a fight," said Alan; "but man! ye have whig blood in ye!"

He spoke kindly enough, but there was so much anger under his contempt that I thought it wise to change the conversation. I expressed my wonder how, with the highlands covered with troops and guarded like a city in a siege, a man in his situation could come and go without arrest.

"It's easier than ye would think," said Alan. "A bare hillside (ye see) is like all one road; if there's a sentry at one place, ye just go by another. And then heather's a great help. And everywhere there are friends' houses and friends' byres and haystacks. And besides, when folk talk of a country covered with troops, it's but a kind of a byword at the best. A soldier covers nae mair of it than his boot soles. I have fished a water with a sentry on the other side of the brae, and killed a fine trout; and I have sat in a heather bush within six feet of another, and learned a real bonny tune from his whistling. This was it," said he, and whistled me the air.

"And then besides," he continued, "it's not so bad now as it was in forty six. The Hielands are what they call pacified. Small wonder, with never a gun or a sword left from Cantyre to Cape Wrath, but what tenty folk have hidden in their thatch! But what I would like to ken, David, is just how long? Not long, ye would think, with men like Ardshiel in exile and men like the Red Fox sitting birling the wine and oppressing the poor at home. But it's a kittle thing to decide what folk'll bear, and what they will not. Or why would Red Colin be riding his horse all over my poor country of Appin, and never a pretty lad to put a bullet in him?"

And with this, Alan fell into a muse, and for a long time sate very sad and silent.

I will add the rest of what I have to say about my friend: that he was skilled in all kinds of music, but principally pipe music; was a well-considered poet in his own tongue; had read several books both in French and English; was a dead shot, a good angler, and an excellent fencer with the small sword as well as with his own particular weapon. For his faults, they were on his face— and I now knew them all. But the worst of them, his childish propensity to take offence and to pick quarrels, he greatly laid aside in my case, out of regard for the battle of the round-house. But whether it was because I had done well myself, or because I had been a witness of his own much greater prowess, is more than I can tell. For though he had a great taste for courage in other men, yet he admired it most in Alan Breck.

∾ 13

The Loss of the Brig

It was already late at night, and as dark as it ever would be at that season of the year, and that is to say, it was still pretty bright, when Hoseason clapped his head into the round-house door. He showed no fear of us, but seemed to have forgotten the whole business of the fight.

"Here," said he, "come out and see if ye can pilot."

"Is this one of your tricks?" asked Alan.

"Do I look like tricks?" cries the captain. "I have other things to think of—my brig's in danger!"

By the concerned look of his face, and above all by the sharp tones in which he spoke of his brig, it was plain to both of us he was in deadly earnest; and so Alan and I, without the smallest fear of treachery, stepped on deck.

The sky was clear; it blew hard and was bitter cold; a great deal of daylight lingered; and the moon, which was nearly full, shone brightly. The brig was close-hauled, so as to round the south-west corner of the Island of Mull; the hills of which, and Ben More above them all with a wisp of mist upon the top of it, lay full upon the larboard bow. Though it was no good point of sailing for the *Covenant*, she tore through the seas at a great rate, pitching and straining, and pursued by the westerly swell.

Altogether it was no such ill night to keep the seas in; and I had begun to wonder what it was that sat so heavily upon the captain, when the brig rising suddenly on the top of a high swell, he pointed and cried to us to look. Away on the lee bow, a thing like a fountain rose out of the moonlit sea, and immediately after we heard a low sound of roaring.

"What do ye call that?" asked the captain gloomily.

"The sea breaking on a reef," said Alan. "And now ye ken where it is; and what better would ye have?"

"Ay," said Hoseason, "if it was the only one."

And sure enough just as he spoke there came a second fountain further to the south.

"There!" said Hoseason. "Ye see for yourself. If I had kent of these reefs, if I had had a chart, or if Shuan had been spared, it's not sixty guineas, no, nor six hundred, would have made me risk my brig in sic a stoneyard! But you, sir, that was to pilot us, have ye never a word?"

"I'm thinking," said Alan, "these'll be what they call the Torran rocks."

"Are there many of them?" says the captain.

"Truly, sir, I am nae pilot," said Alan; "but it sticks in my mind, there are ten miles of them."

Mr Riach and the captain looked at each other.

"There's a way through them, I suppose?" said the captain.

"Doubtless," said Alan. "But where? But it somehow runs in my mind once more, that it is clearer under the land."

"So?" said Hoseason. "We'll have to haul our wind then, Mr Riach; we'll have to come as near in about the end of Mull as we can take her, sir; and even then, we'll have the land to kep the wind off us, and that stone-yard on our lee. Well, we're in for it now, and may as well crack on."

With that he gave an order to the steersman, and sent Riach to the foretop. There were only five men on deck, counting the officers; these were all that were fit (or at least, both fit and willing) for their work; and two of these were disabled. So, as I say, it fell to Mr Riach to go aloft, and he sat there looking out and hailing the deck with news of all he saw.

"The sea to the south is thick," he cried; and then after awhile, "It does seem clearer in by the land."

"Well, sir," said Hoseason to Alan, "we'll try your way of it. But I think I might as well trust to a blind fiddler. Pray God you're right."

"Pray God I am!" says Alan to me. "But where did I hear it? Well, well, it must be as it will be."

As we got nearer to the turn of the land, the reefs began to be sown here and there on our very path; and Mr Riach sometimes cried down to us to change the course. Sometimes, indeed, none too soon; for one reef was so close on the brig's weather board, that when a sea burst upon it, the lighter sprays fell upon her deck and wetted us like rain.

The brightness of the night showed us these perils as clearly as by day, which was perhaps the more alarming. It showed me, too, the face of the captain as he stood by the steersman, now on one foot, now on the other, and sometimes blowing in his hands, but still listening and looking and as steady as steel. Neither he nor Mr Riach had shown well in the fighting; but I saw they were brave in their own trade, and admired them all the more, because I found Alan very white.

"Ochone, David," said he, "this is no the kind of death I fancy."

"What, Alan!" I cried, "you're not afraid?"

"No," said he, wetting his lips, "but you'll allow yourself, it's a cold ending."

By this time, now and then shearing to one side or another to avoid a reef, but still hugging the wind and the land, we had got round Iona and begun to come alongside Mull. The tide at the tail of the land ran very strong, and threw the brig about. Two hands were put to the helm, and Hoseason himself would sometimes lend a help; and it was strange to see three strong men throw their weight upon the tiller, and it (like a living thing) struggle against and drive them back. This would have been the greater danger, had not the sea been for some while free of obstacles. Mr Riach, besides, announced from the top that he saw clear water ahead.

"Ye were right," said Hoseason to Alan. "Ye have saved the brig, sir; I'll mind that when we come to clear accounts." And I believe he not only meant what he said, but would have done it; so high a place did the *Covenant* hold in his affections.

But this is matter only for conjecture, things having gone otherwise than he forecast.

"Keep her away a point," sings out Mr Riach. "Reef to windward!"

And just at the same time the tide caught the brig, and threw the wind out of her sails. She came round into the wind like a top, and the next moment struck the reef with such a dunch as threw us all flat upon the deck, and came near to shake Mr Riach from his place upon the mast.

I was on my feet in a minute. The reef on which we had struck was close in under the southwest end of Mull, off a little isle they call Earraid, which lay low and black upon the larboard. Sometimes the swell broke clean over us; sometimes it only ground the poor brig upon the reef, so that we could hear her beat herself to pieces; and what with the great noise of the sails, and the singing of the wind, and the flying of the spray in the moonlight, and the sense of danger, I think my head was partly turned, for I could scarcely understand the things I saw.

Presently I observed Mr Riach and the seamen busy round the skiff, and still in the same blank, ran over to assist them; and as soon as I set my hand to work, my mind came clear again. It was no very easy task, for the skiff lay amidships and was full of hamper, and the breaking of the heavier seas continually forced us to give over and hold on; but we all wrought like horses while we could.

Meanwhile such of the wounded as could move, came clambering out of the fore-scuttle and began to help; while the rest that lay helpless in their bunks harrowed me with screaming and begging to be saved.

The captain took no part. It seemed he was struck stupid. He stood holding by the shrouds, talking to himself and groaning out aloud whenever the ship hammered on the rock. His brig was like wife and child to him; he had looked on, day by day, at the mishandling of poor Ransome; but when it came to the brig, he seemed to suffer along with her.

All the time of our working at the boat, I remember only one other thing: that I asked Alan, looking across at the shore, what country it was, and he answered, it was the worst possible for him, for it was a land of the Campbells.

We had one of the wounded men told off to keep a watch upon

the seas and cry us warning. Well, we had the boat about ready to be launched, when this man sang out pretty shrill: "For God's sake, hold on!" We knew by his tone that it was something more than ordinary; and sure enough, there followed a sea so huge that it lifted the brig right up and canted her over on one beam. Whether the cry came too late or my hold was too weak, I know not; but at the sudden tilting of the ship, I was cast clean over the bulwarks into the sea.

I went down, and drank my fill; and then came up, and got a blink of the moon; and then down again. They say a man sinks the third time for good. I cannot be made like other folk, then; for I would not like to write how often I went down or how often I came up again. All the while, I was being hurled along, and beaten upon and choked, and then swallowed whole; and the thing was so distracting to my wits, that I was neither sorry nor afraid.

Presently, I found I was holding to a spar; which helped me some. And then all of a sudden I was in quiet water, and began to come to myself.

It was the spare yard I had got hold of, and I was amazed to see how far I had travelled from the brig. I hailed her indeed; but it was plain she was already out of cry. She was still holding together; but whether or not they had yet launched the boat, I was too far off and too low down to see.

While I was hailing the brig, I spied a tract of water lying between us, where no great waves came, but which yet boiled white all over, and bristled in the moon with rings and bubbles. Sometimes the whole tract swung to one side, like the tail of a live serpent; sometimes, for a glimpse, it would all disappear, and then boil up again. What it was I had no guess, which for the time increased my fear of it; but I now know it must have been the roost, or tide race, which had carried me away so fast, and tumbled me about so cruelly, and at last, as if tired of that play, had flung out me and the spare yard upon its landward margin.

I now lay quite becalmed, and began to feel that a man can die of cold as well as of drowning. The shores of Earraid were close in; I could see in the moonlight the dots of heather and the sparkling of the mica in the rocks.

"Well," thought I to myself, "if I cannot get as far as that, it's strange!"

I had no skill of swimming, Essen water being small in our neighbourhood; but when I laid hold upon the yard with both arms, and kicked out with both feet, I soon began to find that I was moving. Hard work it was, and mortally slow; but in about an hour of kicking and splashing, I had got well in between the points of a sandy bay surrounded by low hills.

The sea was here quite quiet; there was no sound of any surf; the moon shone clear; and I thought in my heart I had never seen a place so desert and desolate. But it was dry land; and when at last it grew so shallow that I could leave the yard and wade ashore upon my feet, I cannot tell if I was more tired or more grateful. Both, at least, I was: tired as I never was before that night; and grateful to God as I trust I have been often, though never with more cause.

⌒ 14

The Islet

With my stepping ashore, I began the most unhappy part of my adventures.

It was half past twelve in the morning, and though the wind was broken by the land, it was a cold night. I dared not sit down (for I thought I should have frozen) but took off my boots and walked to and fro upon the sand, barefoot and beating my breast, with infinite weariness. There was no sound of man or cattle; not a cock crew, though it was about the hour of their first waking; only the surf broke outside in the distance, which put me in mind of my perils and those of my friend. To walk by the sea at that hour of the morning, and in a place so desert-like and lonesome, struck me with a kind of fear.

As soon as the day began to break, I put on my boots and climbed a hill—the ruggedest scramble I ever undertook—falling, the whole way, between big blocks of granite or leaping from one to another. When I got to the top, the dawn was come. There was no sign of the brig, which must have lifted from the reef and sunk. The boat, too, was nowhere to be seen. There was never a sail upon the ocean; and in what I could see of the land was neither house nor man.

I was afraid to think what had befallen my shipmates, and

afraid to look longer at so empty a scene. What with my wet clothes, and weariness, and my belly that now began to ache with hunger, I had enough to trouble me without that. So I set off eastward along the south coast, hoping to find a house where I might warm myself, and perhaps get news of those I had lost. And at the worst, I considered, the sun would soon rise and dry my clothes.

After a little, my way was stopped by a creek or inlet of the sea which seemed to run pretty deep into the land; and as I had no means to get across, I must needs change my direction to go about the end of it. It was still the roughest kind of walking; indeed the whole, not only of Earraid, but of the neighbouring part of Mull (which they call the Ross) is nothing but a jumble of granite rocks with heather in among. At first the creek kept narrowing as I had looked to see; but presently to my surprise it began to widen out again. At this I scratched my head, but had still no notion of the truth; until at last I came to a rising ground, and it burst upon me all in a moment that I was cast upon a little, barren isle, and cut off on every side by the salt seas.

Instead of the sun rising to dry me, it came on to rain with a thick mist; so that my case was lamentable.

I stood in the rain, and shivered, and wondered what to do, till it occurred to me that perhaps the creek was fordable. Back I went to the narrowest point and waded in. But not three yards from shore, I plumped in head over ears; and if ever I was heard of more, it was rather by God's grace than my own prudence. I was no wetter (for that could hardly be) but I was all the colder for this mishap; and having lost another hope, was the more unhappy.

And now, all at once, the yard came in my head. What had carried me through the roost, would surely serve me to cross this little quiet creek in safety. With that I set off, undaunted, across the top of the isle, to fetch and carry it back. It was a weary tramp in all ways, and if hope had not buoyed me up, I must have cast myself down and given up. Whether with the sea salt, or because I was growing fevered, I was distressed with thirst, and had to stop, as I went, and drink the peaty water out of the hags.

I came to the bay at last, more dead than alive; and at the first glance, I thought the yard was something further out than when I left it. In I went, for the third time, into the sea. The sand was smooth and firm and shelved gradually down; so that I could wade out till the water was almost to my neck and the little waves splashed into my face. But at that depth, my feet began to leave me, and I durst venture in no farther. As for the yard, I saw it bobbing very quietly some twenty feet in front of me.

I had borne up well until this last disappointment; but at that I came ashore, and flung myself down upon the sands, and wept.

The time I spent upon the island is still so horrible a thought to me, that I must pass it lightly over. In all the books I have read of people cast away, they had either their pockets full of tools, or a chest of things would be thrown upon the beach along with them, as if on purpose. My case was very different. I had nothing in my pockets but money and Alan's silver button; and being in-land bred, I was as much short of knowledge as of means.

I knew indeed that shellfish were counted good to eat; and among the rocks of the isle, I found a great plenty of limpets which at first I could scarcely strike from their places, not knowing quickness to be needful. There were, besides, some of the little shells that we call buckies: I think periwinkle is the English name. Of these two I made my whole diet, devouring them cold and raw as I found them; and so hungry was I, that at first they seemed to me delicious.

Perhaps they were out of season, or perhaps there was something wrong with the sea about my island. But at least I had no sooner eaten my first meal than I was seized with giddiness and retching, and lay for a long time no better than dead. A second trial of the same food (indeed I had no other) did better with me and revived my strength. But as long as I was on the island, I never knew what to expect when I had eaten; sometimes all was well and sometimes I was thrown into a miserable sickness; nor could I ever distinguish what particular fish it was that hurt me.

All day it streamed rain; the island ran like a sop; there was no dry spot to be found; and when I lay down that night, between two boulders that made a kind of roof, my feet were in a bog.

The second day, I crossed the island to all sides. There was no one part of it better than another; it was all desolate and rocky; nothing living on it but game birds, which I lacked the means to kill, and the gulls which haunted the outlying rocks in a prodigious number. But the creek, or straits, that cut off the isle from the main land of the Ross, opened out on the north into a bay, and the bay again opened into the sound of Iona; and it was the neighbourhood of this place that I chose to be my home; though if I had thought upon the very name of home in such a spot, I must have burst out crying.

I had good reasons for my choice. There was in this part of the isle a little hut of a house like a pig's hut, where fishers used to sleep when they came there upon their business; but the turf roof of it had fallen entirely in; so that the hut was of no use to me, and gave me less shelter than my rocks. What was more important, the shell-fish on which I lived grew there in great plenty; when the tide was out, I could gather a peck at a time, and this was doubtless a convenience. But the other reason went deeper.

I had become in no way used to the horrid solitude of the isle; but used to look round me on all sides (like a man that was hunted) between fear and hope that I might see some human creature coming. Now, from a little up the hillside over the bay, I could catch a sight of the great, ancient church and the roofs of the people's houses in Iona. And on the other hand, over the low country of the Ross, I saw smoke go up, morning and evening, as if from a homestead in a hollow of the land.

I used to watch this smoke, when I was wet and cold, and had my head half turned with loneliness; and think of the fireside and the company, till my heart burned. It was the same with the roofs of Iona. Altogether, this sight I had of men's homes and comfortable lives, although it put a point on my own sufferings, yet it kept hope alive, and helped me to eat my raw shellfish (which had soon grown to be a disgust) and saved me from the sense of horror I had, whenever I was quite alone with dead rocks, and fowls, and the rain, and the cold sea.

I say it kept hope alive; and indeed it seemed impossible that I should be left to die on the shores of my own country, and within view of a church tower and the smoke of men's houses. But the second day passed; and though as long as the light lasted, I kept a bright look-out for boats on the sound or men passing on the Ross, no help came near me. It still rained; and I turned in to sleep, as wet as ever and with a cruel sore throat, but a little comforted, perhaps, by having said good night to my next neighbours, the people of Iona.

Charles Second declared a man could stay out-doors more days in the year in the climate of England than in any other. This was very like a king with a palace at his back and changes of dry clothes. But he must have had better luck on his flight from Worcester than I had on that miserable isle. It was the height of the summer; yet it rained for more than twenty-four hours, and did not clear until the afternoon of the third day.

This was the day of incidents. In the morning I saw a red deer, a stag with a fine spread of antlers, standing in the rain on the top of the island; but he had scarce seen me rise from under my rock, before he trotted off upon the other side. I suppose he must have swum the straits; though what should bring any creature to Earraid, was more than I could fancy.

A little after, as I was jumping about after my limpets, I was startled by a guinea piece, which fell upon a rock in front of me and glanced off into the sea. When the sailors gave me my money again, they kept back not only about a third of the whole sum, but my father's leather purse; so that from that day out, I carried my gold loose in a pocket with a button. I now saw there must be a hole, and clapped my hand to the place in a great hurry. But this was to lock the stable door after the steed was stolen. I had left the shore at Queensferry with near on fifty pounds; now I found no more than two guinea pieces and a silver shilling.

It is true I picked up a third guinea a little after, where it lay shining on a piece of turf. That made a fortune of three pounds and four shillings, English money, for a lad, the rightful heir of an estate, and now starving on an isle at the extreme end of the wild Highlands.

This state of my affairs dashed me still further; and indeed my plight on that third morning was truly pitiful. My clothes were beginning to rot; my stockings in particular were quite worn through, so that my shanks went naked; my hands had grown quite soft with the continual soaking; my throat was very sore, my strength had much abated, and my heart so turned against the horrid stuff I was condemned to eat, that the very sight of it came near to sicken me.

And yet the worst was not yet come.

There is a pretty high rock on the north west of Earraid, which (because it had a flat top and overlooked the sound) I was much in the habit of frequenting. Not that ever I stayed in one place, save when asleep; my misery giving me no rest. Indeed I wore myself down with continual and aimless goings and comings in the rain.

As soon, however, as the sun came out, I lay down on the top of that rock to dry myself. The comfort of the sunshine is a thing I cannot tell. It set me thinking hopefully of my deliverance, of which I had begun to despair; and I scanned the sea and the Ross with a fresh interest. On the south of my rock, a part of the island jutted out and hid the open ocean; so that a boat could thus come quite near me upon that side, and I be none the wiser.

Well, all of a sudden, a coble with a brown sail and a pair of fishers aboard of it, came flying round that corner of the isle, bound for Iona. I shouted out, and then fell on my knees on the rock and reached up my hands and prayed to them. They were near enough to hear—I could even see the colour of their hair; and there was no doubt but they observed me; for they cried out in the Gaelic tongue and laughed. But the boat never turned aside, and flew on, right before my eyes, for Iona.

I could not believe such wickedness, and ran along the shore from rock to rock, crying on them piteously; even after they were out of reach of my voice, I still cried and waved to them; and when they were quite gone, I thought my heart would have burst. All the time of my troubles, I wept only twice. Once, when I could not reach the oar; and now, the second time, when these fishers turned a deaf ear to my cries. But this time I wept and roared like a wicked child, tearing up the turf with my nails and grinding my face in the earth. If a wish would kill men, then two fishers would never have seen morning; and I should likely have died upon my island.

When I was a little over my anger, I must eat again, but with such loathing of the mess as I could now scarce control. Sure enough, I should have done as well to fast, for my fishes poisoned me again. I had all my first pains; my throat was so sore I could scarce swallow; I had a fit of strong shuddering which clucked my teeth together; and there came on me that dreadful sense of illness, which we have no name for either in Scotch or English. I thought I should have died, and made my peace with God, forgiving all men, even my uncle and the fishers; and as soon as I had thus made up my mind to the worst, clearness came upon me: I observed the night was falling dry; my clothes were dried a good deal; truly, I was in a better case than ever before since I had landed on the isle; and so I got to sleep at last, with a thought of gratitude.

The next day (which was the fourth of this horrible life of mine) I found my bodily strength run very low. But the sun shone, the air was sweet, and what I managed to eat of the shell-fish, agreed well with me and revived my courage.

I was scarce back on my rock (where I went always the first thing after I had eaten) before I observed a boat coming down the sound and with her head, as I thought, in my direction.

I began at once to hope and fear exceedingly; for I thought these men might have thought better of their cruelty and be coming back to my assistance. But another disappointment, such as yesterday's, was more than I could bear. I turned my back, accordingly, upon the sea, and did not look again till I had counted many hundreds. The boat was still heading for the island. The next time I counted the full thousand, as slowly as I could, my heart beating so as to hurt me. And then it was out of all question. She was coming straight to Earraid!

I could no longer hold myself back, but ran to the sea side and out, from one rock to another, as far as I could go. It is a marvel I was not drowned; for when I was brought to a stand at last, my legs shook under me, and my mouth was so dry, I must wet it with the sea-water before I was able to shout.

All this time, the boat was coming on; and now I was able to perceive it was the same boat and the same two men as yesterday. This I knew by their hair, which the one had of a bright yellow and the other black. But now there was a third man along with them, who looked to be of a better class.

As soon as they were come within easy speech, they let down their sail and lay quiet. In spite of my supplications, they drew no nearer in, and what frightened me worst of all, the new man tee-hee'd with laughter as he talked and looked at me.

Then he stood up in the boat, and addressed me a long while, speaking fast and with many wavings of his hand. I told him I had no Gaelic; and at this he became very angry, and I began to suspect he thought he was talking English. Listening close, I caught the word "whateffer" several times; but all the rest was Gaelic, and might have been Greek and Hebrew for me.

"Whatever," said I, to show him I had caught a word.

"Yes, yes—yes, yes," says he, and then he looked at the other men, as much as to say "I told you I spoke English," and began again as hard as ever in the Gaelic.

This time I picked out another word, "tide." Then I had a flash of hope. I remembered he was always waving his hand toward the mainland of the Ross.

"Do you mean when the tide is out—" I cried, and could not finish.

"Yes, yes," said he. "Tide."

At that, I turned tail upon their boat (where my adviser had once more begun to tee-hee with laughter) leaped back the way I had come, from one stone to another, and set off running across the isle as I had never run before. In about half an hour, I came out upon the shores of the creek; and sure enough it was shrunk into a little trickle of water, through which I dashed, not above my knees, and landed with a shout on the main island.

A sea bred boy would not have stayed a day on Earraid; which is only what they call a tidal islet; and except in the bottom of the neaps, can be entered and left twice in every twenty-four hours, either dry-shod or, at the most, by wading. Even I, who had the tide going out and in before me in the bay, and even watched for the ebbs, the better to get my shell-fish—even I (I say) if I had but sat down to think, instead of raging at my fate, must have soon guessed the secret and got free.

It was no wonder the fishers had not understood me. The wonder was rather that they had ever guessed my pitiful illusion, and taken the trouble to come back. I had starved with cold and hunger on that island for close upon one hundred hours. But for the fishers, I might have left my bones there, in pure folly. And even as it was, I had paid for it pretty dear, not only in past sufferings but in my present case; being clothed like a beggarman, scarce able to walk, and in great pain of my sore throat.

I have seen wicked men and fools, a great many of both; and I believe they both get paid in the end; but the fools first.

15

The Lad with the Silver Button

THROUGH THE ISLE OF MULL

The Ross of Mull, which I had now got upon, was rugged and trackless like the isle I had just left; being all bog and brier and big stone. There may be roads for them that know that country well; but for my part I had no better guide than my own nose, and no other landmark than Ben More.

I aimed as well as I could for the smoke I had seen so often from the island; and with all my great weariness and the difficulty of the way, came upon the house in the bottom of a little hollow, about five or six at night. It was low and longish, roofed with turf and built of unmortared stones; and on a mound in front of it, an old gentleman sat smoking his pipe in the sun.

With what little English he had, he gave me to understand that my shipmates had got safe ashore, and had broken bread in that very house on the day after.

"Was there one," I asked, "dressed like a gentleman?"

He said they all wore rough greatcoats; but to be sure, the first of them, the one that came alone, wore breeches and stockings, while the rest had sailors' trousers.

"Ah," said I, "and he would have a feathered hat?"

He told me, no, that he was bare-headed like myself.

At first I thought Alan might have lost his hat; and then the rain came in my mind, and I judged it more likely he had it out of harm's way under his greatcoat. This set me smiling, partly because my friend was safe, partly to think of his vanity in dress.

And then the old gentleman clapped his hand to his brow, and cried out that I must be the lad with the silver button.

"Why, yes!" said I, in some wonder.

"Well, then," said the old gentleman, "I have a word for you: that you are to follow your friend to his country, by Torosay."

He then asked me how I had fared, and I told him my tale. A south-country man would certainly have laughed; but this old gentleman (I call him so because of his manners, for his clothes were dropping off his back) heard me all through with nothing but gravity and pity. When I had done, he took me by the hand, led me into his hut (it was no better) and presented me before his wife, as if she had been the Queen and I a Duke.

The good woman set oat-bread before me and a cold grouse, patting my shoulder and smiling to me all the time, for she had no English; and the old gentleman (not to be behind) brewed me strong punch out of their country spirit. All the while I was eating, and after that when I was drinking the punch, I could scarce come to believe in my good fortune; and the house, though it was thick with the peat-smoke and as full of holes as a colander, seemed like a palace.

The punch threw me in a strong sweat and a deep slumber; the good people let me lie; and it was near noon of the next day before I took the road, my throat already easier and my spirits quite restored by good fare and good news. The old gentleman, although I pressed him hard, would take no money, and gave me

"The good woman set oat-bread before me and a cold grouse,
patting my shoulder and smiling to me all the time."
Young Folks Paper, June 5, 1886.

an old bonnet for my head; though I am free to own I was no
sooner out of view of the house, than I very jealously washed this
gift of his in a wayside fountain.

Thought I to myself: "If these are the wild Highlanders, I
could wish my own folk wilder."

I not only started late, but I must have wandered nearly half
the time. True, I met plenty of people, grubbing in little miserable fields that would not keep a cat, or herding little kine about
the bigness of asses. The Highland dress being forbidden by law

since the rebellion, and the people condemned to the lowland habit which they much disliked, it was strange to see the variety of their array. Some went bare, only for a hanging cloak or great-coat and carried their trousers on their backs like a useless bur-then; some had made an imitation of the tartan with little parti-coloured strips patched together like an old wife's quilt; others, again, still wore the highland philabeg, but by putting a few stitches between the legs, transformed it into a pair of trousers like a Dutchman's. All those makeshifts were condemned and punished, for the law was harshly applied, in hopes to break up the clan spirit; but in that out-of-the-way, sea-bound isle, there were few to make remarks and fewer to tell tales.

They seemed in great poverty; which was no doubt natural, now that rapine was put down, and the chiefs kept no longer an open house; and the roads (even such a wandering, country by-track as the one I followed) were infested with beggars. And here again I marked a difference from my own part of the country. For our lowland beggars, even the gownsmen themselves who beg by patent, had a louting, flattering way with them, and if you gave them a plack and asked change, would very civilly return you a boddle. But these Highland beggars stood on their dignity, asked alms only to buy snuff (by their account) and would give no change.

To be sure, all this was no concern of mine, except in so far as it entertained me by the way. What was much more to the pur-pose, few had any English and these few (unless they were of the brotherhood of beggars) not very anxious to place it at my service. I knew Torosay to be my destination, and repeated the name to them and pointed; but instead of simply pointing in reply, they would give me a screed of the Gaelic that set me foolish; so it was small wonder if I went out of my road as often as I stayed in it.

At last, about eight at night and already very weary, I came to a lone house, where I asked admittance and was refused, until I bethought me of the power of money in so poor a country, and held up one of my guineas in my finger and thumb. Thereupon, the man of the house, who had hitherto pretended to have no English and driven me from his door by signals, suddenly began to speak as clearly as was needful, and agreed for five shillings to give me a night's lodging and guide me the next day to Torosay.

I slept uneasily that night, fearing I should be robbed; but I might have spared myself the pain; for my host was no robber, only miserably poor and a great cheat. He was not alone in his poverty; for the next morning, we must go five miles about to the house of what he called a rich man to have one of my guineas changed. This was perhaps a rich man for Mull; he would have scarce been thought so in the south; for it took all he had, the whole house was turned upside down, and neighbour brought under contribution, before he could scrape together twenty shillings in silver. The odd shilling, he kept for himself, protesting he could ill afford to have so great a sum of money lying "locked up." For all that he was very courteous and well spoken, made us both sit down with his family to dinner, and brewed punch in a fine china bowl; over which my rascal guide grew so merry that he refused to start.

I was for getting angry, and appealed to the rich man (Hector Maclean was his name) who had been a witness to our bargain and to my payment of the five shillings. But Maclean had taken his share of the punch, and vowed that no gentleman should leave his table after the bowl was brewed; so there was nothing for it but to sit and hear Jacobite toasts and Gaelic songs, till all were tipsy and staggered off to the bed or the barn for their night's rest.

Next day (the fourth of my travels) we were up before five upon the clock, but my rascal guide got to the bottle at once; and it was three hours before I had him clear of the house, and then (as you shall hear) only for a worse disappointment.

As long as we went down a heathery valley that lay before Mr McLean's house, all went well; only my guide looked constantly over his shoulder, and when I asked him the cause, only grinned at me. No sooner, however, had we crossed the back of a hill, and got out of sight of the house windows, than he told me Torosay lay right in front, and that a hilltop (which he pointed out) was my best landmark.

"I care very little for that," said I, "since you are going with me."

The impudent cheat answered me in the Gaelic that he had no English.

"My fine fellow," I said, "I know very well your English comes and goes. Tell me what will bring it back? Is it more money you wish?"

"Five shillings mair," said he, "and hersel' will bring ye there."

I reflected awhile and then offered him two, which he accepted greedily and insisted on having in his hands at once— "for luck," as he said, but I think it was rather for my misfortune.

The two shillings carried him not quite as many miles; at the end of which distance, he sat down upon the wayside and took off his brogues from his feet, like a man about to rest.

I was now red-hot. "Ha!" said I, "have you no more English?"

He said impudently, "no."

At that I boiled over and lifted my hand to strike him; and he, drawing a knife from his rags, squatted back and grinned at me like a wild cat. At that, forgetting everything but my anger, I ran in upon him, put aside his knife with my left and struck him in the mouth with the right. I was a strong lad and very angry, and he but a little man; and he went down before me heavily. By good luck, his knife flew out of his hand as he fell.

I picked up both that and his brogues, wished him a good morning and set off upon my way, leaving him bare-foot and disarmed. I chuckled to myself as I went, being sure I was done with that rogue for a variety of reasons. First, he knew he could have no more of my money; next, the brogues were worth in that country only a few pence; and lastly the knife, which was really a dagger, it was against the law for him to carry.

In about half an hour of walk, I overtook a great, ragged man, moving pretty fast but feeling before him with a staff. He was quite blind, and told me he was a catechist, which should have put me at my ease. But his face went against me; it seemed dark and dangerous and secret; and presently, as we began to go on alongside, I saw the steel butt of a pistol sticking from under the flap of his coatpocket. To carry such a thing meant a fine of fifteen pounds sterling upon a first offence, and transportation to the colonies upon a second. Nor could I quite see why a religious teacher should go armed, or what a blind man could be doing with a pistol.

I told him about my guide, for I was proud of what I had done, and my vanity for once got the heels of my prudence. At the mention of the five shillings he cried out so loud, that I made up my mind I should say nothing of the other two, and was glad he could not see my blushes.

"Was it too much?" I asked, a little faltering.

"Too much!" cries he. "Why I will guide you to Torosay myself for a dram of brandy. And give you the great pleasure of my company (me that is a man of some learning) in the bargain."

I said I did not see how a blind man could be a guide; but at that he laughed aloud, and said his stick was eyes enough for an eagle.

"In the isle of Mull at least," says he, "where I know every stone and heather-bush by mark of head. See now," he said, striking right and left as if to make sure, "down there a burn is running; and at the head of it, there stands a bit of a small hill with a stone cocked upon the top of that; and it's hard at the foot of the hill, that the way runs by to Torosay; and the way here, being for droves, is plainly trodden and will show grassy through the heather."

I had to own he was right in every feature, and told my wonder.

"Ha!" says he, "that's nothing. Would ye believe me now, that before the Act came out, and when there were weepons in this country, I could shoot? Ay, could I!" cries he, and then with a leer: "If ye had such a thing as a pistol here to try with, I would show ye how it's done."

I told him I had nothing of the sort, and gave him a wider berth. If he had known, his pistol stuck at that time quite plainly out of his pocket, and I could see the sun twinkle on the steel of the butt. But by the better luck for me, he knew nothing, thought all was covered, and lied on in the dark.

He then began to question me cunningly, where I came from,

whether I was rich, whether I could change a five shilling piece for him (which he declared he had that moment in his sporran) and all the time he kept edging up to me, and I avoiding him. We were now upon a sort of green cattle track which crossed the hills towards Torosay, and we kept changing sides upon that like dancers in a reel. I had so plainly the upper hand, that my spirits rose and indeed took a pleasure in this game of blind man's buff; but the catechist grew angrier and angrier, and at last began to swear in Gaelic and to strike for my legs with his staff.

Then I told him that, sure enough, I had a pistol in my pocket as well as he, and if he did not strike across the hill due south, I would even blow his brains out.

He became at once very polite; and after trying to soften me for some time, but quite in vain, he cursed me once more in the Gaelic and took himself off. I watched him striding along, through bog and briar, tapping with his stick, until he turned the end of a hill and disappeared in the next hollow. Then I struck on again for Torosay, much better pleased to be alone than to travel with that man of learning. This was an unlucky day; and these two, of whom I had just rid myself, one after the other, were the two worst men I met with in the Highlands.

At Torosay, on the sound of Mull and looking over to the mainland of Morven, there was an inn with an innkeeper who was a MacLean, it appeared, of a very high family; for to keep an inn is thought even more genteel in the highlands than it is with us, perhaps as partaking of hospitality or perhaps because the trade is idle and drunken. He spoke good English, and find-ing me to be something of a scholar, tried me first in French where he easily beat me, and then in the latin in which I don't know which of us did best. This pleasant rivalry put us at once upon friendly terms; and I sat up and drank punch with him (or to be more correct, sat up and watched him drink it) until he was so tipsy that he wept upon my shoulder.

I tried him, as if by accident, with a sight of Alan's button; but it was plain he had never seen or heard of it. Indeed, he bore some grudge against the family and friends of Ardshiel, and before he was drunk, he read me a lampoon, in very good latin but with a very ill meaning, which he had made in elegiac verses upon a person of that house.

When I told him of my catechist, he shook his head and said I was lucky to have got clear off. "That is a very dangerous man," he said; "Duncan McKiegh is his name; he can shoot by the ear at several yards, and has been often accused of highway robberies, and once of murder."

"The cream of it is," says I, "that he called himself a catechist."

"And why should he not," says he, "when that is what he is? It was MacLean of Duart gave it to him, because he was blind. But perhaps it was a peety," says my host; "for he is always on the road going from one place to another to hear the young folk say their religion; and doubtless that is a great temptation to the poor man."

At last, when my landlord could drink no more, he showed me to a bed and I lay down in very good spirits; having travelled the greater part of that big and crooked Island of Mull, from Earraid to Torosay, fifty miles as the crow flies and (with my wanderings) much nearer ninety, in four days and with little fatigue. Indeed I was by far in better heart and health of body at the end of that long tramp than I had been at the beginning.

16

The Lad with the Silver Button

ACROSS MORVEN

There is a regular ferry from Torosay to Kinlochaline on the mainland. Both shores of the sound are in the country of the strong clan of the McLeans, and the people that passed the ferry with me were almost all of that clan. The skipper of the boat, on the other hand, was called Neil Roy McRob; and since McRob was one of the names of Alan's clansmen, and Alan himself had sent me to that ferry, I was eager to come to private speech of Neil Roy.

In the crowded boat this was of course impossible, and the passage was a very slow affair. There was no wind, and as the boat was wretchedly equipped, we could pull but two oars on one side, and one on the other. The men gave way, however, with a good will, the passengers taking spells to help them, and the whole company giving the time in Gaelic boat-songs. And what with the songs, and the sea air, and the good nature and spirit of all concerned, and the bright weather, the passage was a pretty thing to have seen.

But there was one melancholy part. In the mouth of Loch Aline, we found a great sea-going ship at anchor; and this I supposed at first to be one of the King's cruisers which were kept along that coast, both summer and winter, to prevent communication with the French. As we got a little nearer, it became plain she was a ship of merchandise; and what still more puzzled me, not only her decks but the sea-beach also, were quite black with people, and skiffs were continually plying to and fro between them. Yet nearer, and there began to come to our ears a great sound of mourning, the people on board and those on the shore crying and lamenting one to another so as to pierce the heart.

Then I understood this was an emigrant ship bound for the American colonies.

We put the ferry boat alongside, and the exiles leaned over the bulwarks, weeping and reaching out their hands to my fellow passengers, among whom they counted some near friends. How long this might have gone on, I do not know, for they seemed to have no sense of time; but at last the captain of the ship who seemed near beside himself (and no great wonder) in the midst of this crying and confusion, came to the side and begged us to depart.

Thereupon, Neil sheared off; and the chief singer in our boat struck into a melancholy air, which was presently taken up both by the emigrants and their friends upon the beach, so that it sounded from all sides like a lament for the dying. I saw the tears run down the cheeks of the men and women in the boat, even as they bent at the oars; and the circumstances, and the music of the song (which is one called "Lochaber no more") were highly affecting even to myself.

At Kinlochaline I got Neil Roy upon one side on the beach, and said I made sure he was one of Appin's men.

"And what for no?" said he.

"I am seeking somebody," said I; "and it comes in my mind that you will have news of him. Alan Breck Stewart is his name."

And very foolishly, instead of showing him the button, I sought to pass a shilling in his hand.

At this he drew back. "I am very much affronted," he said; "and this is not the way that one shentleman should behave to another at all. The man you ask for is in France; but if he was in my sporran," says he, "and your belly full of shillings, I would not hurt a hair upon his body."

I saw I had gone the wrong way to work, and without wasting time upon apologies, showed him the button lying in the hollow of my palm.

"Aweel, aweel," said Neil; "and I think ye might have begun with that end of the stick, whatever! But if ye are the lad with the silver button, all is well, and I have the word to see that ye come safe. But if ye will pardon me to speak plainly," said he, "there is a name that you should never take into your mouth, and that is the name of Alan Breck; and there is a thing that ye would never do, and that is to offer your dirty money to a Hieland shentleman."

It was not very easy to apologise; for I could scarce tell him (what was the truth) that I had never dreamed he would set up to be a gentleman until he told me so. Neil on his part, had no wish to prolong his dealings with me, only to fulfil his orders and be done with it; and he made haste to give me my route. This was to lie the night in Kinlochaline in the public inn; to cross Morven the next day to Ardgour, and lie the night in the house of one John of the Claymore, who was warned that I might come; the third day, to be set across one loch at Corran and another at Balachulish, and then ask my way to the house of James of the Glens at Aucharn in Duror of Appin. There was a good deal of ferrying as you hear: the sea, in all this part, running deep into the mountains and winding about their roots. It makes the country strong to hold and difficult to travel, but full of prodigious wild and dreadful prospects.

I had some other advice from Neil: to speak with no one by the way, to avoid whigs, Campbells and the "red-soldiers;" to leave the road and lie in a bush, if I saw any of the latter coming "for it was never chancy to meet in with them;" and in brief, to conduct myself like a robber or a Jacobite agent, as perhaps Neil thought me.

The inn at Kinlochaline was the most beggarly, vile place that ever pigs were stied in, full of smoke, vermin and silent highlanders. I was not only dis-contented with my lodging, but with myself for my mismanagement of Neil, and thought I could hardly be worse off. But very wrongly, as I was soon to see; for I had not been half an hour at the inn (standing in the door most of the time, to ease my eyes from the peat smoke) when a thunderstorm came close by, the springs broke in a little hill on which the inn stood, and one end of the house became a running water. Places of public entertainment were bad enough all over Scotland in those days; yet it was a wonder to myself, when I had to go from the fireside to the bed in which I slept, wading over the shoes.

Early in my next day's journey, I overtook a little, stout, solemn man, walking very slowly with his toes turned out, sometimes reading in a book and sometimes marking the place with his finger, and dressed decently and plainly in something of a clerical style.

This I found to be another catechist, but of a different order from the blind man of Mull: being indeed one of those sent out by the Edinburgh Society for Propagating Christian Knowledge, to evangelise the more savage places of the Highlands. His name was Henderland; he spoke with the broad south-country tongue, which I was beginning to weary for the sound of; and besides common countryship, we soon found we had a more particular bond of interest. For my good friend, the minister of Essendean, had translated into the Gaelic in his by-time a number of hymns and pious books, which Henderland used in his work and held in great esteem. Indeed it was one of these he was carrying and reading when we met.

We fell in company at once, our ways lying together as far as to Kingairloch. As we went, he stopped and spoke with all the wayfarers and workers that we met or passed; and though of course I could not tell what they dis-coursed about, yet I judged Mr Henderland must be well liked in the countryside, for I observed many of them to bring out their mulls and share a pinch of snuff with him.

I told him as far in my affairs as I judged wise: as far, that is, as they were none of Alan's; and gave Balachulish as the place I was travelling to, to meet a friend; for I thought Aucharn or even Duror would be too particular and might put him on the scent.

On his part, he told me much of his work and the people he worked among, the hiding priests and Jacobites, the Disarming Act, the dress, and many other curiosities of the time and place. He seemed moderate: blaming parliament in several points, and especially because they had framed the Act more severely against those who wore the dress than against those who carried weapons.

This moderation put it in my mind to question him of the Red Fox and the Appin tenants: questions which, I thought, would seem natural enough in the mouth of one travelling to that country.

He said it was a bad business. "It's wonderful," said he, "where the tenants find the money, for their life is mere starvation. (Ye don't carry such a thing as snuff, do ye, Mr Balfour? No? Well, I'm better wanting it.) But these tenants (as I was saying) are doubtless partly driven to it. James Stewart in Duror (that's him they call James of the Glens) is half brother to Ardshiel, the captain of the clan; and he is a man much looked up to, and drives very hard. And then there's one they call Alan Breck—"

"Ah!" cried I, "what of him?"

"What of the wind that bloweth where it listeth?" said Henderland. "He's here and awa'; here today and gone tomorrow: a fair heather cat. He might be glowering at the two of us out of yon whin bush, and I wouldnae wonder!—Ye'll no carry such a thing as snuff, will ye?"

I told him no, and that he had asked the same thing more than once.

"It's highly possible," said he, sighing. "But it seems strange ye shouldnae carry it. However, as I was saying, this Alan Breck is a bold, desperate customer, and well kent to be James's right hand. His life is forfeit already; he would boggle at naething; and maybe, if a tenant-body was to hang back, he would get a dirk in his wame."

"You make a poor story of it all, Mr Henderland," said I. "If it is all fear upon both sides, I care to hear no more of it."

"Na," said Mr Henderland, "but there's love too, and self-denial that should put the like of you and me to shame. There's something fine about it; no perhaps Christian, but humanly fine. Even Alan Breck, by all that I hear, is a chield to be respected. There's many a lying sneckdraw sits close in kirk in our own part of the country, and stands well in the world's eye, and maybe is a far worse man, Mr Balfour, than yon misguided shedder of man's blood. Ay, ay, we might take a lesson by them.—Ye'll perhaps think I've been too long in the Hielands?" he added, smiling to me.

I told him, not at all; that I had seen much to admire among the Highlanders; and if he came to that, Mr Campbell himself was a highlander.

"Ay," said he, "that's true. It's a fine blood."

"And what is the King's agent about?" I asked.

"Colin Campbell?" says Henderland. "Putting his head in a bees' byke!"

"He is to turn the tenants out by force, I hear?" said I.

"Yes," says he, "but the business has gone back and forth, as folk say. First, James of the Glens rode to Edinburgh and got some lawyer (a Stewart, nae doubt—they all hing together like bats in a steeple) and had the proceedings stayed. And then Colin Campbell cam' in again, and had the upper hand before the Barons of Exchequer. And now they tell me the first of the tenants are to flit tomorrow. It's to begin at Duror under James's very windows, which doesnae seem wise by my humble way of it."

"Do you think they'll fight?" I asked.

"Well," says Henderland, "they're disarmed—or supposed to be, for there's still a good deal of cold iron lying by in quiet places. And then Colin Campbell has the sogers coming. But for all that, if I was his lady wife, I wouldnae be well pleased till I got him home again. They're queer customers, the Appin Stewarts."

I asked if they were worse than their neighbours.

"No they!" said he. "And that's the worst part of it. For if Colin Roy can get his business done in Appin, he has it all to begin again in the next country, which they call Mamore, and which is one of the countries of the Camerons. He's King's Factor upon both, and from both he has to drive out the tenants; and indeed, Mr Balfour, (to be open with ye) it's my belief that if he escapes the one lot, he'll get his death by the other."

So we continued talking and walking a great part of the day; until at last Mr Henderland, after expressing his delight in my company and satisfaction at meeting with a friend of Mr Campbell's ("whom" says he, "I will make bold to call that sweet singer of our Covenanted Zion") proposed that I should make a short stage, and lie the night in his house a little beyond Kingairloch. To say truth, I was overjoyed; for I had no great desire for John of the Claymore, and since my double misadventure, first with the guide, and next with the gentleman skipper, I stood in some fear of any Highland stranger. Accordingly we shook hands upon the bargain, and came in the afternoon to a small house, standing alone by the shore of the Linnhe Loch. The sun was already gone from the desert mountains of Ardgour upon the hither side, but shone on those of Appin on the farther; the loch lay as still as a lake, only the gulls were crying round the sides of it; and the whole place seemed solemn and uncouth.

We had no sooner come to the door of Mr Henderland's dwelling, than to my great surprise (for I was now used to the politeness of highlanders) he burst rudely past me, dashed into the room, caught up a jar and a small horn spoon, and began ladling snuff into his nose in most excessive quantities. Then he had a hearty fit of sneezing and looked round upon me with a rather silly smile.

"It's a vow I took," says he. "I took a vow upon me that I would-nae carry it. Doubtless it's a great privation; but when I think upon the martyrs, not only to the Scottish Covenant but to other points of Christianity, I think shame to mind it."

As soon as we had eaten (and porridge and whey was the best of the good man's diet) he took a grave face and said he had a duty to perform by Mr Campbell, and that was to inquire into my state of mind towards God. I was inclined to smile at him, since the business of the snuff; but he had not spoken long before he brought the tears into my eyes. There are two things that men should never weary of, goodness and humility; we get none too much of them in this rough world and among cold, proud people; but Mr Henderland had their very speech upon his tongue. And though I was a good deal puffed up with my adventures and with having come off, as the saying is, with flying colours; yet he soon had me on my knees beside a simple, poor old man, and both proud and glad to be there.

Before we went to bed, he offered me sixpence to help me on my way, out of a scanty store he kept in the turf wall of his house; at which excess of goodness, I knew not what to do. But at last he was so earnest with me, that I thought it the more mannerly part to let him have his way, and so left him poorer than myself.

17

The Death of the Red Fox

T he next day, Mr Henderland found for me a good man
who had a boat of his own and was to cross the Linnhe
loch that afternoon into Appin, fishing. Him, he prevailed on to
take me, for he was one of his flock; and in this way I saved a
long day's travel and the price of the two public ferries I must
otherwise have passed.

It was near noon before we set out: a dark day, with clouds and
the sun shining upon little patches. The sea was here very deep
and still, and had scarce a wave upon it; so that I must put the
water to my lips, before I could believe it to be truly salt. The
mountains on either side were high, rough and barren, very
black and gloomy in the shadow of the clouds, but all silver-laced
with little water-courses where the sun shone upon them. It
seemed a hard country, this of Appin, for people to care as much
about as Alan did.

There was but one incident. A little after we had started, the
sun shone upon a little moving clump of scarlet close in along
the waterside to the north. It was much of the same red as soldiers' coats; every now and then, too, there came little sparks and
lightnings, as though the sun had struck upon bright steel.

I asked my boatman what it should be; and he answered he supposed it was some of the red soldiers coming from Fort William into Appin, against the poor tenantry of the country. Well, it was a sad sight to me; and whether it was because of my thoughts of Alan, or from something prophetic in my bosom, although this was but the second time I had seen King George's troops, I had no good will to them.

At last, we came so near the point of land at the entering in of Loch Leven that I begged to be set on shore. My boatman (who was an honest fellow and mindful of his promise to the catechist) would fain have carried me on to Balachulish; but as this was to take me farther from my secret destination, I insisted and was set on shore at last under the wood of Lettermore (or Lettervore, for I have heard it both ways) in Alan's country of Appin.

This was a wood of birches, growing on a steep, craggy side of a mountain that overhung the loch. It had many openings and ferny dells; and a road or bridle track ran north and south through the midst of it, by the edge of which, where was a spring, I sat down to eat some oat-bread of Mr Henderland's and think upon my situation.

Here I was not only troubled by a cloud of stinging midges, but far more by the doubts of my mind. What I ought to do, why I was going to join myself with an outlaw and a would-be murderer like Alan, whether I should not be acting more like a man of sense to tramp back to the south country direct, by my own guidance and at my own charges, and what Mr Campbell or even Mr Henderland would think of me if they should ever learn of my folly and presumption: these were the doubts that now began to come in on me stronger than ever.

As I was so sitting and thinking, the noise of men and horses

came to me through the wood; and presently after, at a turning
of the road, I saw four men come into view. The way was in this
part so rough and narrow, that they came single and led their
horses by the reins. The first was a great, red-headed gentleman,
of an imperious and flushed face; who carried his hat in his hand
and fanned himself, for he was in a breathing heat. The second,
by his decent black garb and white wig, I correctly took to be a
lawyer. The third was a servant, and wore some part of his
clothes in tartan, which showed that his master was of a Highland family and either an outlaw or else in singular good odour
with the government, since the wearing of tartan was against the
Act. If I had been better versed in these things, I would have
known the tartan to be of the Argyle (or Campbell) colours. This
servant had a good sized portmanteau strapped on his horse,
and a net of lemons (to brew punch with) hanging at the saddle-
bow; as was often enough the custom with luxurious travellers in
that part of the country.

As for the fourth, who brought up the tail, I had seen his like
before, and knew him at once to be a Sheriff's officer.

I had no sooner seen these people coming than I made up my
mind (for no reason that I can tell) to go through with my adventure; and when the first came alongside of me, I rose up from the
bracken and asked him the way to Aucharn.

He stopped and looked at me, as I thought, a little oddly; and
then, turning to the lawyer, "Mungo," said he, "there's many a
man would think this more of a warning than two pyats. Here
am I on my road to Duror on the job ye ken; and here is a young
lad starts up out of the bracken, and spiers if I am on the way
to Aucharn."

"Glenure," said the other, "this is an ill subject for jesting."

These two had now drawn close up and were gazing at me, while the two followers had halted about a stone-cast in the rear.

"And what seek ye in Aucharn?" said Colin Roy Campbell of Glenure; him they called the Red Fox; for he it was that I had stopped.

"The man that lives there," said I.

"James of the Glens?" says Glenure musingly; and then to the lawyer: "Is he gathering his people, think ye?"

"Anyway," says the lawyer, "we shall do better to bide where we are and let the soldiers rally us."

"If you are concerned for me," said I, "I am neither of his people nor yours, but an honest subject of King George, owing no man and fearing no man."

"Why, very well said," replies the Factor. "But if I may make so bold as ask, what does this honest man so far from his country? and why does he come seeking the brother of Ardshiel? I have power here, I must tell you: I am King's Factor upon several of these estates, and have twelve files of soldiers at my back."

"I have heard a waif word in the country," said I, a little nettled, "that you were a hard man to drive."

He still kept looking at me, as if in doubt.

"Well," said he, at last, "your tongue is bold; but I am no unfriend to plainness. If ye had asked me the way to the door of James Stewart on any other day but this, I would have set ye right and bidden ye God-speed. But today—eh, Mungo?" And he turned again to look at the lawyer.

But just as he turned, there came the shot of a firelock from higher up the hill; and with the very sound of it, Glenure fell upon the road.

"O, I am dead!" he cried, several times over.

"The lawyer had caught him up and held him in his arms,
the servant standing over and clasping his hands."

Young Folks Paper, June 12, 1886.

The lawyer had caught him up and held him in his arms, the
servant standing over and clasping his hands. And now the
wounded man looked from one to another with scared eyes, and
there was a change in his voice that went to the heart.

"Take care of yourselves," says he. "I am dead."

He tried to open his clothes as if to look for the wound, but his
fingers slipped on the buttons. With that, he gave a great sigh, his
head rolled on his shoulder, and he passed away.

The lawyer said never a word, but his face was as sharp as a
pen and as white as the dead man's; the servant broke out into a

great noise of crying and weeping like a child; and I, on my side, stood staring at them in a kind of horror. The sheriff's officer had run back at the first sound of the shot, to hasten the coming of the soldiers.

At last the lawyer laid down the dead man in his blood upon the road, and got to his own feet with a kind of stagger.

I believe it was his movement that brought me to my senses; for he had no sooner done so than I began to scramble up the hill, crying out "The Murderer! the murderer!"

So little a time had elapsed, that when I got to the top of the first steepness, and could see some part of the open mountain, the murderer was still moving away at no great distance. He was a big man in a black coat with metal buttons, and carried a long fowling piece.

"Here!" I cried. "I see him!"

At that, the murderer gave a little, quick look over his shoulder and began to run. The next moment he was lost in a fringe of birches; then he came out again on the upper side, where I could see him climbing like a jackanapes, for that part was again very steep; and then he dipped behind a shoulder and I saw him no more.

All this time I had been running on my side, and had got a good way up, when a voice cried upon me to stand.

I was at the edge of the upper wood, and so now, when I halted and looked back, I saw all the open part of the hill below me. The lawyer and the sheriff's officer were standing just above the road, crying and waving on me to come back; and on their left, the red-coats, musket in hand, were beginning to struggle singly out of the lower wood.

"Why should I come back?" I cried. "Come you on!"

"Ten pounds if ye take that lad!" cried the lawyer. "He's an accomplice. He was posted here to hold us in talk."

At that word (which I could hear quite plainly, though it was to the soldiers and not to me that he was crying it) my heart came in my mouth with quite a new kind of terror. Indeed it is one thing to stand the danger of your life, and quite another to run the peril of both life and character. The thing besides had come so suddenly, like thunder out of a clear sky, that I was all amazed and helpless.

The soldiers began to spread, some of them to run, and others to put up their pieces and cover me; and still I stood.

"Jouk in here among the trees," said a voice close by.

Indeed, I scarce knew what I was doing, but I obeyed; and as I did so, I heard the firelocks bang and the balls whistle in the birches.

Just inside the shelter of the trees, I found Alan Breck standing, with a fishing rod. He gave me no salutation; indeed it was no time for civilities; only "Come!" says he, and set off running along the side of the mountain towards Balachulish; and I, like a sheep, to follow him.

Now we ran among the birches; now stooping behind low humps upon the mountainside; now crawling on all fours among the heather. The pace was deadly; my heart seemed bursting against my ribs; and I had neither time to think nor breath to speak with. Only I remember seeing with wonder, that Alan every now and then would straighten himself to his full height and look back; and every time he did so, there came a great faraway cheering and crying of the soldiers.

Quarter of an hour later, Alan stopped, clapped down flat in the heather, and turned to me.

"Now," said he, "it's earnest. Do as I do for your life."

And at the same speed, but now with infinitely more precaution, we traced back again across the mountainside by the same way that we had come, only perhaps higher; till at last Alan threw himself down in the upper wood of Lettermore where I had found him at the first, and lay, with his face in the bracken, panting like a dog.

My own sides so ached, my head so swam, my tongue so hung out of my mouth with heat and dryness, that I lay beside him like one dead.

18

I Talk with Alan in the Wood

of Lettermore

Alan was the first to come round. He rose, went to the border of the wood, peered out a little, and then returned
and sat down.

"Well," said he, "yon was a hot burst, David."

I said nothing, nor so much as lifted my face. I had seen murder done, and a great, ruddy, jovial gentleman struck out of life
in a moment; the pity of that sight was still sore within me, and
yet that was but a part of my concern. Here was murder done
upon the man Alan hated; here was Alan skulking in the trees
and running from the troops; and whether his was the hand that
fired or only the head that ordered, signified but little. By my way
of it, my only friend in that wild country was blood guilty in the
first degree; I held him in horror; I could not look upon his face;
I would have rather lain alone in the rain on my cold isle, than
in that warm wood beside a murderer.

"Are ye still wearied?" he asked again.

"No," said I, still with my face in the bracken, "no, I am not
wearied now, and I can speak. You and me must twine," I said.
"I liked you very well, Alan; but your ways are not mine, and
they're not God's; and the short and the long of it is just that we
must twine."

"I will hardly twine from ye, David, without some kind of reason for the same," said Alan, mighty gravely. "If ye ken anything against my reputation, it's the least thing that ye should do, for old acquaintance sake, to let me hear the name of it; and if ye have only taken a distaste to my society, it will be proper for me to judge if I'm insulted."

"Alan," said I, "what is the sense of this? Ye ken very well yon Campbell-man lies in his blood upon the road."

He was silent for a little; then says he, "Did ever ye hear tell of the story of the Man and the Good People?"

"No," said I, "nor do I want to hear it."

"With your permission, Mr Balfour, I will tell it you whatever," says Alan. "The man, ye should ken, was cast upon a rock in the sea, where it appears the Good People were in use to come and rest as they went through to Ireland. The name of this rock is called the Skerryvore, and it's not far from where we suffered shipwreck. Well, it seems the man cried so sore 'If he could just see his little bairn before he died!' that at last the King of the Good People took peety upon him, and sent one flying that brought back the bairn in a poke and laid it down beside the man where he lay sleeping. So when the man woke, there was a poke beside him and something into the inside of it that moved. Well, it seems he was one of these gentry that think aye the worst of things; and for greater security, he stuck his dirk throughout that poke before he opened it, and there was his bairn dead. I am thinking to myself, Mr Balfour, that you and the man are very much alike."

"Do you mean you had no hand in it?" cried I, sitting up.

"I will tell you first of all, Mr Balfour of Shaws, as one friend to another," said Alan, "that if I were going to kill a gentleman, it would not be in my own country, to bring trouble on my clan; and I would not go wanting sword and gun, and with a lang fishing rod upon my back."

"Well," said I, "that's true!"

"And now," continued Alan, taking out his dirk and laying his hand upon it in a certain manner, "I swear upon the Holy Iron I had neither art nor part, act nor thought in it."

"I thank God for that!" cried I, and offered him my hand.

He did not appear to see it. "And here is a great deal of work about a Campbell!" said he. "They are not so scarce, that I ken!"

"At least," said I, "you cannot justly blame me, for you know very well what you told me in the brig. But the temptation and the act are different, I thank God again for that. We may all be tempted; but to take a life in cold blood, Alan!" And I could say no more for the moment. "And do you know who did it?" I added. "Do you know that man in the black coat?"

"I have nae clear mind about his coat," said Alan cunningly; "but it sticks in my head that it was blue."

"Blue or black, did ye know him?" said I.

"I couldnae just conscientiously swear to him," says Alan. "He gaed very close by me, to be sure, but it's a strange thing that I should just have been tying my brogues."

"Can you swear that you don't know him, Alan?" I cried, half angered, half in a mind to laugh at his evasions.

"No yet," says he; "but I've a grand memory for forgetting, David."

"And yet there was one thing I saw clearly," said I; "and that was, that you exposed yourself and me to draw the soldiers."

"It's very likely," said Alan; "and so would any gentleman. You and me were innocent of that transaction."

"The better reason, since we were falsely suspected, that we should get clear," I cried. "The innocent should surely come before the guilty."

"Why, David," said he, "the innocent have aye a chance to get assoiled in court; but for the lad that shot the bullet, I think the best place for him will be the heather. Them that havenae dipped their hands in any little difficulty, should be very mindful of the case of them that have. And that is the good Christianity. For if it was the other way round about, and the lad whom I couldnae just clearly see had been in our shoes, and we in his (as might very well have been) I think we would be a good deal obliged to him oursel's if he would draw the soldiers."

When it came to this, I gave Alan up. But he looked so innocent all the time, and was in such clear good faith in what he said, and so ready to sacrifice himself for what he deemed his duty, that my mouth was closed. Mr Henderland's words came back to me: that we ourselves might take a lesson by these wild highlanders. Well, here I had taken mine. Alan's morals were all tail-first; but he was ready to give his life for them, such as they were.

"Alan," said I, "I'll not say it's the good Christianity as I understand it, but it's good enough; and here I offer ye my hand for the second time."

Whereupon, he gave me both of his, saying surely I had cast a spell upon him, for he could forgive me anything. Then he grew very grave, and said we had not much time to throw away, but must both flee that country: he, because he was a deserter and the whole of Appin would now be searched like a chamber, and every one obliged to give a good account of himself; and I, because I was certainly involved in the murder.

"O!" says I, willing to give him a little lesson, "I have no fear of the justice of my country."

"As if this was your country!" said he. "Or as if ye would be tried here, in a country of Stewarts!"

"It's all Scotland," said I.

"Man, I whiles wonder at ye," said Alan. "This is a Campbell that's been killed. Well, it'll be tried in Inverara, the Campbell's head place; with fifteen Campbells in the jury box and the biggest Campbell of all (and that's the Duke) sitting cocking on the bench. Justice, David? The same justice, by all the world, as Glenure found a while ago at the roadside."

This frighted me a little, I confess, and would have frighted me more if I had known how nearly exact were Alan's predictions; indeed it was but in one point that he exaggerated, there being but eleven Campbells on the jury; though as the other four were equally in the Duke's dependance, it mattered less than might appear. Still I cried out that he was unjust to the Duke of Argyle who (for all he was a whig) was yet a wise and honest nobleman.

"Hoot!" said Alan, "the man's a whig, nae doubt; but I would never deny he was a good chieftain to his clan. And what would the clan think, if there was a Campbell shot, and naebody hanged, and their own chief the Justice General? But I have often observed," says Alan, "that you low-country bodies have no clear idea of what's right and wrong."

At this I did at last laugh out aloud; when to my surprise, Alan joined in and laughed as merrily as myself.

"Na, na," said he, "we're in the Hielands, David; and when I tell ye to run, take my word and run. Nae doubt, it's a hard thing to skulk and starve in the heather, but it's harder yet to lie shackled in a red-coat prison."

I asked him whither we should flee; and as he told me "to the lowlands," I was a little better inclined to go with him; for indeed I was growing impatient to get back and have the upper hand of my uncle. Besides Alan made so sure there would be no question of justice in the matter, that I began to be afraid he might be right. Of all deaths, I would truly like least to die by the gallows; and the picture of that uncanny instrument came into my head with extraordinary clearness (as I had once seen it engraved at the top of a peddlar's ballad) and took away my appetite for courts of justice.

"I'll chance it, Alan," said I. "I'll go with you."

"But mind you," said Alan, "it's no small thing. Ye maun lie bare and hard, and brook many an empty belly. Your bed shall be the moorcock's, and your life shall be like the hunted deer's, and ye shall sleep with your hand upon your weepons. Ay, man, ye shall taigle many a weary foot, or we get clear! I tell ye this at the start, for it's a life that I ken well. But if ye ask what other chance ye have, I answer: Nane. Either take to the heather with me, or else hang."

"And that's a choice very easily made," said I; and we shook hands upon it.

"And now let's take another keek at the red-coats," says Alan, and he led me to the north-eastern fringe of the wood.

Looking out between the trees, we could see a great side of mountain, running down exceeding steep into the waters of the loch. It was a rough part, all hanging stone, and heather, and bit scrags of birchwood; and away at the far end towards Balachulish, little wee red soldiers were dipping up and down over hill and howe, and growing smaller every minute. There was no cheering now, for I think they had other uses for what breath was left them; but they still stuck to the trail, and doubtless thought that we were close in front of them.

Alan watched them, smiling to himself.

"Ay," said he, "they'll be gey weary before they've got to the end of that employ! And so you and me, David, can sit down and eat a bite and breathe a bit, and take a dram from my bottle. Then we'll strike for Aucharn, the house of my kinsman James of the Glens, where I must get my clothes, and arms, and money to carry us along; and then, David, we'll cry 'Forth, Fortune!' and take a cast among the heather."

So we sat again and ate and drank, in a place whence we could see the sun going down into a field of great, wild and houseless mountains, such as I was now condemned to wander in with my companion. Partly as we so sat, and partly afterwards, on the way to Aucharn, each of us narrated his adventures; and I shall here set down so much of Alan's as seems either curious or needful.

It appears he ran to the bulwarks as soon as the wave was passed; saw me, and lost me, and saw me again, as I tumbled in the roost; and at last had one glimpse of me clinging on the yard. It was this that put him in some hope I would maybe get to land after all, and made him leave these clues and messages which had brought me (for my sins) to that unlucky country of Appin.

In the meanwhile, those still on the brig had got the skiff launched, and one or two were on board of her already, when there came a second wave, greater than the first, and heaved the brig out of her place, and would certainly have sent her to the bottom, had she not struck and caught on some projection of the reef. When she had struck first, it had been bows-on, so that the stern had hitherto been lowest. But now her stern was thrown in the air, and the bows plunged under the sea; and with that, the water began to pour into the fore-scuttle like the pouring of a mill-dam.

It took the colour out of Alan's face, even to tell what followed. For there were still two men lying impotent in their bunks; and

these, seeing the water pour in and thinking the ship had foun-
dered, began to cry out aloud and that with such harrowing cries,
that all who were on deck tumbled one after another into the
skiff and fell to their oars. They were not two hundred yards
away, when there came a third great sea; and at that the brig
lifted clear over the reef; her canvas filled for a moment, and she
seemed to sail in chase of them, but settling all the while; and
presently she drew down and down, as if a hand was drawing
her; and the sea closed over the *Covenant* of Dysart.

Never a word they spoke as they pulled ashore, being stunned
with the horror of that screaming; but they had scarce set foot
upon the beach when Hoseason woke up, as if out of a muse, and
bade them lay hands upon Alan. They hung back indeed, having
little taste for the employment; but Hoseason was like a fiend;
crying that Alan was alone, that he had a great sum about him,
that he had been the means of losing the brig and drowning all
their comrades, and that here was both revenge and wealth upon
a single cast. It was seven against one; in that part of the shore
there was no rock that Alan could set his back to; and the sailors
began to spread out and come behind him.

"And then," said Alan, "the little man with the red head—I
havenae mind of the name that he is called."

"Riach," said I.

"Ay," said Alan, "Riach! Well, it was him that took up the clubs
for me, asked the men if they werenae feared of a judgement, and
says he 'Dod, I'll put my back to the Hielandman's mysel.' That's
none such an entirely bad little man, yon little man with the red
head," said Alan. "He has some spunks of decency."

"Well," said I, "he was kind to me in his way."

"And so he was to Alan," said he; "and by my troth, I found
his way a very good one! But ye see, David, the loss of the ship

and the cries of these poor lads sat very ill upon the man; and I'm thinking that would be the cause of it."

"Well, I would think so," says I; "for he was as keen as any of the rest at the beginning. But how did Hoseason take it?"

"It sticks in my mind that he would take it very ill," says Alan. "But the little man cried to me to run, and indeed I thought it was a good observe, and ran. The last that I saw they were all in a knot upon the beach, like folk that were not agreeing very well together."

"What do you mean by that?" said I.

"Well, the fists were going," said Alan; "and I saw one man go down like a pair of breeks. But I thought it would be better no to wait. Ye see there's a strip of Campbells in that end of Mull, which is no good company for a gentleman like me. If it hadnae been for that, I would have waited and looked for ye mysel—let alone giving a hand to the little man." (It was droll how Alan dwelt on Mr Riach's stature, for to say the truth, the one was no smaller than the other.) "So," says he, continuing, "I set my best foot forward, and whenever I met in with anyone, I cried out there was a wreck ashore. Man, they didnae stop to fash with me! Ye should have seen them linking for the beach! And when they got there, they found they had had the pleasure of a run, which is aye good for a Campbell. I'm thinking it was a judgement on the clan that the brig went down in the lump and didnae break. But it was a very unlucky thing for you, that same; for if any wreck had come ashore, they would have hunted high and low, and would soon have found ye."

❧ 19

The House of Fear

Night fell as we were walking, and the clouds which had broken up in the afternoon settled in and thickened, so that it fell, for the season of the year, extremely dark. The way we went was over rough mountainsides; and though Alan pushed on with an assured manner, I could by no means see how he directed himself.

At last about half past ten of the clock, we came to the top of a brae, and saw lights below us. It seemed a house door stood open and let out a beam of fire and candle light; and all round the house and steading, five or six persons were moving hurriedly about, each carrying a lighted brand.

"James must have tint his wits," said Alan. "If this was the soldiers instead of you and me, he would be in a bonny mess. But I daresay he'll have a sentry on the road, and he would ken well enough no soldiers would find the way that we came."

Hereupon he whistled three times, in a particular manner. It was strange to see how, at the first sound of it, all the moving torches came to a stand, as if the bearers were affrighted; and how at the third, the bustle began again as before.

Having thus set folks' minds at rest, we came down the brae, and were met at the yard gate (for this place was like a well-doing farm) by a tall, handsome man of more than fifty, who cried out to Alan in the Gaelic.

"James Stewart," said Alan, "I will ask ye to speak in Scotch, for here is a young gentleman with me that has nane of the other. This is him," he added, putting his arm through mine, "a young gentleman of the lowlands, and a laird in his country, too; but I am thinking it will be the better for his health, if we give his name the go-by."

James of the Glens turned to me for a moment, and greeted me courteously enough; the next he had turned to Alan.

"This has been a dreadful accident," he cried. "It will bring trouble on the country." And he wrung his hands.

"Hoots!" said Alan, "ye must take the sour with the sweet, man. Colin Roy is dead, and be thankful for that!"

"Ay," said James, "and by my troth, I wish he was alive again! It's all very fine to blow and boast beforehand; but now it's done, Alan; and who's to bear the wyte of it? The accident fell out in Appin—mind ye that Alan; it's Appin that must pay; and I am a man that has a family."

While this was going on, I looked about me at the servants. Some were on ladders digging in the thatch of the house or the farm buildings, from which they brought out guns, swords and different weapons of war; others carried them away; and by the sound of mattock blows from somewhere further down the brae, I suppose they buried them. Though they were all so busy, there prevailed no kind of order in their efforts; men struggled together for the same gun and ran into each other with their burning torches; and James was continually turning about from his talk with Alan, to cry out orders which were apparently never understood. The faces in the torchlight were like those of people overborne with hurry and panic; and though none spoke above his breath, their speech sounded both anxious and angry.

It was about this time that a lassie came out of the house carrying a pack or bundle; and it has often made me smile to think how Alan's instinct awoke at the mere sight of it.

"What's that, the lassie has?" he asked.

"We're just setting the house in order, Alan," said James, in his frightened and somewhat fawning way. "They'll search Appin with candles, and we must have all things straight. We're digging the bit guns and swords into the moss, ye see; and these, I am thinking, will be your ain French clothes."

"Bury my French clothes!" cried Alan. "Troth, no!" And he laid hold upon the packet and retired into the barn to shift himself, recommending me in the meanwhile to his kinsman.

James carried me accordingly into the kitchen, and sat down with me at table, smiling and talking at first in a very hospitable manner. But presently the gloom returned upon him; he sat frowning and biting his fingers; only remembered me from time to time; and then gave me but a word or two and a poor smile, and back into his private terrors. His wife sat by the fire and wept, with her face in her hands; his eldest son was crouched upon the floor, running over a great mass of papers and now and again setting one alight and burning it to the bitter end; all the while a servant lass with a red face was rummaging about the room, in a blind hurry of fear and whimpering as she went; and every now and again, one of the men would thrust in his face from the yard, and cry for orders.

At last James could keep his seat no longer, and begged my permission to be so unmannerly as walk about. "I am but poor company altogether, sir," says he, "but I can think of nothing but this dreadful accident, and the trouble it is like to bring upon quite innocent persons."

A little after, he observed his son burning a paper, which he thought should have been kept; and at that his excitement burst out so that it was painful to witness. He struck the lad repeatedly.

"Are ye gone gyte?" he cried. "Do ye wish to hang your father?" and forgetful of my presence, carried on at him a long time together in the Gaelic, the young man answering nothing; only the wife, at the name of hanging, throwing her apron over her face and sobbing out louder than before.

This was all wretched for a stranger like myself to hear and see; and I was right glad when Alan returned, looking like himself in his fine French clothes, though (to be sure) they were now grown almost too battered and withered to deserve that name. I was then taken out in my turn by another of the sons, and given that change of clothing of which I had stood so long in need, and a pair of Highland brogues, made of deer-leather, rather strange at first, but after a little practise very easy to the feet.

When I came back, Alan must have told his story; for it seemed understood that I was to fly with him, and they were all busy upon our equipment. They gave us each a sword and pistols, though I professed my inability to use the former; and with these, some ammunition, a bag of oatmeal, an iron pan, and a bottle of right French brandy, we were ready for the heather. Money, indeed, was lacking. I had about two guineas left; Alan's belt having been despatched by another hand, that trusty messenger had no more than seventeen pence to his whole fortune; and as for James, it appears he had brought himself so low with journeys to Edinburgh and legal expenses on behalf of the tenants, that he could only scrape together three and fivepence halfpenny; the most of it in coppers.

"This'll no do," said Alan.

"Ye must find a safe bit somewhere near by," said James, "and get word sent to me. Ye see, ye'll have to get this prettily off, Alan. This is no time to be stayed for a guinea or two. They're sure to get wind of ye, sure to seek ye, and by my way of it, sure to lay on ye the wyte of this day's accident. If it falls on you, it falls on me that am your near kinsman and harboured ye while ye were in the country. And if it comes on me . . ." he paused, and bit his fingers, with a white face. "It would be a painful thing for our friends if I was to hang," said he.

"It would be an ill day for Appin," says Alan.

"It's a day that sticks in my throat," said James. "O man, man, man—man, Alan! you and me have spoken like two fools!" he cried, striking his hand upon the wall so that the house rang again.

"Well, and that's true too," said Alan; "and my friend from the lowlands here" (nodding at me) "gave me a good word upon that head, if I would only have listened to him."

"But see here," said James, returning to his former manner, "if they lay me by the heels Alan, it's then that you'll be needing the money. For with all that I have said, and that you have said, it will look very black against the two of us: do ye mark that? Well, follow me out, and ye'll see that I'll have to get a paper out against ye mysel'; I'll have to offer a reward for ye; ay, will I! It's

a sore thing to do between such near friends; but if I get the dir-
dum of this dreadful accident, I'll have to fend for myself, man.
Do ye see that?"

He spoke with a pleading earnestness, taking Alan by the
breast of the coat.

"Ay," said Alan, "I see that."

"And ye'll have to be clear of the country, Alan—ay, and clear
of Scotland—you and your friend from the lowlands, too. For I'll
have to paper your friend from the lowlands. Ye see that, Alan—
say that ye see that!"

I thought Alan flushed a bit. "This is unco hard on me that
brought him here, James," said he, throwing his head back. "It's
like making me a traitor!"

"Now, Alan man!" cried James, "look things in the face! He'll
be papered anyway; Mungo Campbell'll be sure to paper him;
what matters if I paper him too? And then Alan, I am a man that
has a family." And then after a little pause on both sides: "And,
Alan, it'll be a jury of Campbells," said he.

"There's one thing," said Alan, musingly, "that naebody kens
his name."

"Nor yet they shallnae, Alan! There's my hand on that," cried
James, for all the world as if he had really known my name, and
was foregoing some advantage. "But just the habit he was in, and
what he looked like, and his age, and the like? I couldnae well
do less."

"I wonder at your father's son," cried Alan sternly. "Would
ye sell the lad with a gift? would ye change his clothes and then
betray him?"

"No, no, Alan," said James. "No, no: the habit he took off—

the habit Mungo saw him in." But I thought he seemed crest-fallen; indeed, he was clutching at every straw; and all the time I daresay, saw the faces of his hereditary foes on the bench and in the jury box, and the gallows in the background.

"Well, sir," says Alan, turning to me, "what say ye to that? Ye are here under the safeguard of my honour; and it's my part to see nothing done but what shall please ye."

"I have but one word to say," said I; "for to all this dispute I am a perfect stranger. But the plain common sense is to set the blame where it belongs, and that is on the man that fired the shot. Paper *him*, as ye call it; set the hunt on him; and let honest, inno-cent folk show their faces in safety."

But at this both Alan and James cried out in horror; bidding me hold my tongue, for that was not to be thought of; and asking me "What the Camerons would think?" (which again confirmed me, it must have been a Cameron from Mamore that did the act) and if I did not see that the lad might be caught?—"Ye havenae surely thought of that?" said they, with such innocent earnest-ness, that my hands dropped at my side and I despaired of ar-gument.

"Very well, then," said I, "paper me if you please, paper Alan, paper King George! We're all three innocent, and that seems to be what's wanted! But at least, sir," said I to James, recovering from my little fit of annoyance, "I am Alan's friend, and if I can be helpful to friends of his, I will not stumble at the risk."

I thought it best to put a fair face on my consent, for I saw Alan troubled; and besides (thinks I to myself) as soon as my back is turned, they will paper me, as they call it, whether I consent or not. But in this I saw I was wrong; for I had no sooner said the words, than Mrs Stewart leaped out of her chair, came running

" 'My heart is wae not to have your name, but I have your face.' "
Young Folks Paper, June 19, 1886.

over to us, and wept first upon my neck and then on Alan's, blessing God for our goodness to her family.

"As for you, Alan, it was no more than your bounden duty,"
she said. "But for this lad that has come here and seen us at our
worst, and seen the goodman fleeching like a suitor, him that by
rights should give his commands like any King—as for you, my
lad," she says, "my heart is wae not to have your name, but I have
your face; and as long as my heart beats under my bosom, I will
keep it, and think of it, and bless it." And with that she kissed me,
and burst out once more into such sobbing, that I stood abashed.

"Hoot, hoot," said Alan, looking mighty silly. "The day comes unco soon in this month of July; and tomorrow there'll be a fine to-do in Appin, a fine riding of dragoons, and crying of 'Crua-chan!' and running of red coats; and it behoves you and me to be the sooner gone."

Thereupon we said farewell, and set out again, bending some-what eastward, in a fine mild dark night, and over much the same broken country as before.

20

The Flight in the Heather

THE ROCKS

Sometimes we walked, sometimes ran; and as it drew on to morning, walked ever the less and ran the more. Though, upon its face, that country appeared to be a desert, yet there were huts and houses of the people, of which we must have passed more than twenty, hidden in quiet places of the hills. When we came to one of these, Alan would leave me in the way, and go himself and rap upon the side of the house and speak awhile at the window with some sleeper awakened. This was to pass the news; which, in that country, was so much of a duty that Alan must pause to attend to it even while fleeing for his life; and so well attended to by others, that in more than half of the houses where we called, they had heard already of the murder. In the others, as well as I could make out (standing back at a distance and hearing a strange tongue) the news was received with more of consternation than surprise.

For all our hurry, day began to come in while we were still far from any shelter. It found us in a prodigious valley, strewn with rocks and where ran a foaming river. Wild mountains stood around it; there grew there neither grass nor trees; and I have sometimes thought since then, that it may have been the valley called Glencoe, where the massacre was in the name of King

William. But for the details of our itinerary, I am all to seek; our way lying now by short cuts, now by great detours; our pace being so hurried; our time of journeying usually by night; and the names of such places as I asked and heard, being in the Gaelic tongue and the more easily forgotten.

The first peep of morning, then, showed us this horrible place, and I could see Alan knit his brow.

"This is no fit place for you and me," he said. "This is a place they're bound to watch."

And with that he ran harder than ever down to the waterside, in a part where the river was split in two among three rocks. It went through with a horrid thundering that made my belly quake; and there hung over the lynn a little mist of spray. Alan looked neither to the right nor to the left, but jumped clean upon the middle rock and fell there on his hands and knees to check himself, for that rock was small and he might have pitched over on the far side. I had scarce time to measure the distance or to understand the peril, before I had followed him, and he had caught and stopped me.

So there we stood, side by side upon a small rock slippery with spray, a far broader leap in front of us, and the river dinning upon all sides. When I saw where I was, there came on me a deadly sickness of fear, and I put my hand over my eyes. Alan took me and shook me; I saw he was speaking, but the roaring of the falls and the trouble of my mind prevented me from hearing; only I saw his face was red with anger, and that he stamped upon the rock. The same look showed me the water raging by, and the mist hanging in the air; and with that, I covered my eyes again and shuddered.

The next minute, Alan had set the brandy bottle to my lips and forced me to drink about a gill, which sent the blood into my head again. Then, putting his hands to his mouth and his mouth to my ear, he shouted "Hang or Drown!" and turning his back upon me, leaped over the farther branch of the stream and landed safe.

I was now alone upon the rock, which gave me the more room; the brandy was singing in my ears; I had this good example fresh before me, and just wit enough to see that if I did not leap at once, I should never leap at all. I bent low on my knees and flung myself forth, with that kind of anger of despair that has sometimes stood me in stead of courage. Sure enough, it was but my hands that reached the full length; these slipped, caught again, slipped again; and I was sliddering back into the lynn, when Alan seized me, first by the hair, then by the collar, and with a great strain dragged me into safety.

Never a word he said, but set off running again for his life, and I must stagger to my feet and run after him. I had been weary before, but now I was sick and bruised and partly drunken with the brandy; I kept stumbling as I ran, I had a stitch that came near to overmaster me; and when at last Alan paused under a great rock that stood there among a number of others, it was none too soon for David Balfour.

A great rock, I have said; but by rights it was two rocks leaning together at the top, both some twenty feet high, and at the first sight inaccessible. Even Alan (though you may say he had as good as four hands) failed twice in an attempt to climb them; and it was only at the third trial, and then by standing on my shoulders and leaping up with such force as I thought must have broke my collar bones, that he secured a lodgement. Once there, he let down his leathern girdle; and with the aid of that, and a pair of shallow footholds in the rock, I scrambled up beside him.

Then I saw why he had come there; for the two rocks, being both somewhat hollow on the top and sloping one to the other, made a kind of dish, or saucer, where as many as three or four men might have lain hidden.

All this while, Alan had not said a word, and had run and climbed with such a savage, silent frenzy of hurry, that I knew he was in mortal fear of some mis-carriage. Even now we were on the rock, he said nothing nor so much as relaxed the frowning look upon his face; but clapped flat down, and keeping only one eye above the edge of our place of shelter, scouted all round the compass. The dawn had come quite clear; we could see the stony sides of the valley, and its bottom which was bestrewed with rocks, and the river which went from one side to another and made white falls; but nowhere the smoke of a house, nor any living creature but some eagles screaming round a clift.

Then at last Alan smiled.

"Ay," said he, "now we have a chance;" and then looking at me with some amusement, "Ye're no very gleg at the jumping," said he.

At this I suppose I coloured with mortification, for he added at once: "Hoots! small blame to ye! To be feared of a thing and yet to do it, is what makes the prettiest kind of a man. And then there was water there, and water's a thing that daunts even me. No, no," said Alan, "it's no you that's to blame, it's me."

I asked him why.

"Why," said he, "I have proved myself a gomeral this night. For first of all I take a wrong road and that in my own country of

Appin; so that the day has caught us where we should never have been; and thanks to that, we lie here in some danger and mair dis-comfort. And next (which is the worst of the two, for a man that has been so much among the heather as myself) I have come wanting a water-bottle, and here we lie for a long summer's day with naething but neat spirit. Ye may think that a small thing; but before it comes night, David, ye'll give me news of it."

I was anxious to redeem my character, and offered, if he would pour out the brandy, to run down and fill the bottle at the river.

"I wouldnae waste the good spirit either," says he. "It's been a good friend to you this night; or in my poor opinion, ye would still be cocking on yon stone. And what's mair" says he, "ye may have observed (you that's a man of so much penetration) that Alan Breck Stewart was perhaps walking quicker than his or-dinar'."

"You!" I cried, "you were running fit to burst."

"Was I so?" said he. "Well then, ye may depend upon it, there was nae time to be lost. And now here is enough said: gang you to your sleep, lad, and I'll watch."

Accordingly, I lay down to sleep; a little peaty earth had drifted in between the top of the two rocks, and some bracken grew there, to be a bed to me: the last thing I heard was still the crying of the eagles.

I daresay it would be nine in the morning, when I was roughly awakened, and found Alan's hand pressed upon my mouth.

"Wheesht!" he whispered. "Ye were snoring."

"Well," said I, surprised at his anxious and dark face, "and why not?"

He peered over the edge of the rock, and signed to me to do the like.

It was now high day, cloudless and very hot. The valley was as clear as in a picture. About half a mile up the water was a camp of red coats; a big fire blazed in their midst, at which some were cooking; and near by, on the top of a rock about as high as ours, there stood a sentry with the sun sparking on his arms. All the way down along the riverside were posted other sentries; here near together, there widelier scattered; some planted like the first on places of command, some on the ground level and marching and countermarching so as to meet halfway. Higher up the glen, where the ground was more open, the chain of posts was continued by horse-soldiers, whom we could see in the distance riding to and fro. Lower down, the infantry continued; but as the stream was suddenly swelled by the confluence of a considerable burn, they were more widely set and only watched the fords and stepping stones.

I took but one look at them and ducked again into my place. It was strange indeed to see this valley, which had lain so solitary in the hour of dawn, bristling with arms and dotted with the red coats and breeches.

"Ye see," said Alan. "This was what I was afraid of, Davie: that they would watch the burnside. They began to come in about two hours ago, and man! but ye're a grand hand at the sleeping! We're in a narrow place. If they get up the sides of the hill, they could easy spy us with a glass; but if they'll only keep in the foot of the valley, we'll do yet. The posts are thinner down the water; and come night, we'll try our hand at getting by them."

"And what are we to do till night?" I asked.

"Lie here," says he, "and birstle."

That one good Scotch word, birstle, was indeed the most of the story of the day that we had now to pass. You are to remember that we lay on the bare top of a rock, like scones upon a girdle; the sun beat upon us cruelly; the rock grew so heated, a man could scarce endure the touch of it; and the little patch of earth and fern, which kept cooler, was only large enough for one at a time. We took turn about to lie on the naked rock, which was indeed like the position of that saint that was martyred on a gridiron; and it ran in my mind how strange it was that, in the same climate and at only a few days distance, I should have suffered so cruelly, first from cold upon my island, and now from heat upon this rock.

All the while, we had no water, only raw brandy for a drink, which was worse than nothing; but we kept the bottle as cool as we could, burying it in the earth, and got some relief by bathing our breasts and temples.

The soldiers kept stirring all day in the bottom of the valley, now changing guard, now in patrolling parties hunting among the rocks. These lay round in so great a number, that to look for men among them was like looking for a needle in a bottle of hay; and being so hopeless a task, it was gone about with the less care. Yet we could see the soldiers pike their bayonets among the heather, which sent a cold thrill into my vitals; and they would sometimes hang about our rock, so that we scarce dared to breathe.

It was in this way that I first heard the right English speech; one fellow as he went by actually clapping his hand upon the sunny face of the rock on which we lay, and plucking it off again with an oath.

"I tell you, it's 'ot!" says he; and I was amazed at the clipping tones and the odd sing-song in which he spoke, and no less at that strange trick of dropping out the letter h. To be sure, I had heard

Ransome, but he had taken his ways from all sorts of people, and spoke so imperfectly at the best, that I set down the most of it to childishness. My surprise was all the greater to hear that manner of speaking in the mouth of a grown man; and indeed I have never grown used with it; nor yet altogether with the English grammar, as perhaps a very critical eye might here and there spy out even in these memoirs.

The tediousness and pain of those hours upon the rock grew only the greater as the day went on; the rock getting still the hotter and the sun fiercer. There were giddiness and sickness and sharp pangs like rheumatism, to be supported. I minded then, and have often minded since, on the lines in our Scotch psalm:

> The moon by night thee shall not smite,
> Nor yet the sun by day;

and indeed it was only by God's blessing that we were neither of us sun-smitten.

At last, about two, it was beyond men's bearing, and there was now temptation to resist, as well as pain to thole. For the sun being now got a little into the west, there came a patch of shade on the east side of our rock, which was the side sheltered from the soldiers.

"As well one death as another," said Alan, and slipped over the edge and dropped on the ground on the shadowy side.

I followed him at once, and instantly fell all my length, so weak was I and so giddy with that long exposure. Here, then, we lay for an hour or two, aching from head to foot, as weak as water, and lying quite naked to the eye of any soldier who should have strolled that way. None came, however, all passing by on the other side; so that our rock continued to be our shield even in this new position.

Presently we began again to get a little strength; and as the soldiers were now lying closer along the riverside, Alan proposed that we should try a start. I was by this time afraid of but one thing in the world; and that was to be set back upon the rock; anything else was welcome to me; so we got ourselves at once in marching order, and began to slip from rock to rock one after the other, now crawling flat on our bellies in the shade, now making a run for it, heart in mouth.

The soldiers, having searched this side of the valley after a fashion and being perhaps somewhat sleepy with the sultriness of the afternoon, had now laid by much of their vigilance, and stood dozing at their posts or only kept a look out along the banks of the river; so that in this way, keeping down the valley and at the same time towards the mountains, we drew steadily away from their neighbourhood. But the business was the most wearing I had ever taken part in. A man had need of a hundred eyes in every part of him, to keep concealed in that uneven country and within cry of so many and scattered sentries. When we must pass an open place, quickness was not all, but a swift judgement not only of the lie of the whole country, but of the solidity of every stone on which we must set foot; for the afternoon was now fallen so breathless that the rolling of a pebble sounded abroad like a pistol shot, and would start the echo calling among the hills and cliffs.

By sundown, we had made some distance even by our slow rate of progress, though to be sure the sentry on the rock was still plainly in our view. But now we came on something that put all fears out of season; and that was a deep, rushing burn that tore down, in that part, to join the glen river. At the sight of this, we cast ourselves on the ground and plunged head and shoulders in the water; and I cannot tell which was the more pleasant, the great shock as the cool stream went over us, or the greed with which we drank of it.

We lay there (for the banks hid us) drank again and again, bathed our chests, let our wrists trail in the running water till they ached with the chill; and at last, being wonderfully renewed, we got out the meal-bag and made drammach in the iron pan. This, though it is but cold water mingled with oat-meal, yet makes a good enough dish for a hungry man; and where there are no means of making fire or (as in our case) good reason for not making one, it is the chief stand-by of those who have taken to the heather.

As soon as the shadow of the night had fallen, we set forth again, at first with the same caution, but presently with more boldness, standing our full height and stepping out at a good pace of walking. The way was very intricate, lying up the steep sides of mountains and along the brows of cliffs; clouds had come in with the sunset, and the night was dark and cool; so that I walked without much fatigue, but in continual fear of falling and rolling down the mountains, and with no guess at our direction.

The moon rose at last and found us still on the road; it was in its last quarter and was long beset with clouds; but after a while, shone out, and showed me many dark heads of mountains, and was reflected far underneath us on the narrow arm of a sea-loch.

At this sight we both paused: I struck with wonder to find myself so high and walking (as it seemed to me) upon clouds: Alan to make sure of his direction.

Seemingly he was well-pleased, and he must certainly have

judged us out of ear-shot of all our enemies; for throughout the rest of our night-march, he beguiled the way with whistling of many tunes, warlike, merry, plaintive; reel-tunes that made the foot go faster; tunes of my own south country that made me fain to be home from my adventures; and all these on the great, dark, desert mountains, making company upon the way.

21

The Flight in the Heather

THE HEUGH OF CORRYNAKIEGH

Early as day comes in the beginning of July, it was still dark when we reached our destination, a cleft in the head of a great mountain, with a water running through the midst, and upon the one hand a shallow cave in a rock. Birches grew there in a thin, pretty wood, which a little further on was changed into a wood of pines. The burn was full of trout; the wood of cushat-doves; on the open side of the mountain beyond, whaups would be always whistling and cuckoos were plentiful. From the mouth of the cleft we looked down upon a part of Mamore, and on the sea-loch that divides that country from Appin; and this from so great a height, as made it my continual wonder and pleasure to sit and behold them.

The name of the cleft was the Heugh of Corrynakiegh; and although from its height and being so near upon the sea, it was often beset with clouds, yet it was on the whole a very pleasant place, and the five days we lived in it went happily.

We slept in the cave, making our bed of heather bushes which we cut for that purpose, and covering ourselves with Alan's great coat. There was a low concealed place, in a turning of the glen, where we were so bold as to make fire; so that we could warm ourselves when the clouds set in, and cook hot porridge, and grill the little trouts that we caught with our hands under the stones and overhanging banks of the burn. This was indeed our chief pleasure and business; and not only to save our meal against worse times, but with a rivalry that much amused us, we spent a great part of our days at the waterside, stripped to the waist and groping or (as they say) guddling for these fish. The largest we got might have been three quarters of a pound; but they were of good flesh and flavour, and when broiled upon the coals, lacked only a little salt to be delicious.

In any by-time, Alan must teach me to use my sword; for my ignorance had much distressed him; and I think besides, as I had sometimes the upper hand of him in the fishing, he was not sorry to turn to an exercise where he had so much the upper hand of me. He made it somewhat more of a pain than need have been, for he stormed at me all through the lessons in a very violent manner of scolding, and would push me so close that I made sure he must run me through the body. I was often tempted to turn tail, but held my ground for all that, and got some profit of my lessons; if it was but to stand on guard with an assured countenance, which is often all that is required. So though I could never in the least please my master, I was not altogether displeased with myself.

In the meanwhile, you are not to suppose that we neglected our chief business, which was to get away.

"It will be many a long day," Alan said to me on our first morning, "before the red-coats think upon seeking Corrynakiegh; so now we must get word sent to James, and he must find the siller for us."

"And how shall we send that word?" says I. "We are here in a desert place, which yet we dare not leave; and unless ye get the fowls of the air to be your messengers, I see not what we shall be able to do."

"Ay," said Alan, "ye're a man of small contrivance, David."

Thereupon he fell in a muse, looking in the embers of the fire; and presently, getting a piece of wood, he fashioned it in a cross, the four ends of which he blackened on the coals. Then he looked at me, a little shyly.

"Could ye lend me my button?" says he. "It seems a strange thing to ask a gift again; but I own I am laith to cut another."

I gave him the button; whereupon he strung it on a strip of his great coat which he had used to bind the cross; and tying in a little sprig of birch and another of fir, he looked upon his work with satisfaction.

"Now," said he, "there is a little clachan" (what is called a hamlet in the English) "not very far from Corrynakiegh, and it has the name of Koalisnacoan. There, there are living many friends of mine whom I could trust with my life, and some that I am no just so sure of. Ye see, David, there will be money set upon our heads; James himsel' is to set money on them; and as for the Campbells, they would never spare siller where there was a Stewart to be hurt. If it was otherwise, I would go down to Koalisnacoan whatever, and trust my life into these people's hands as lightly as I would trust another with my glove."

"But being so?" said I.

"Being so," said he, "I would as lief they didnae see me. There's bad folk everywhere, and what's far worse, weak ones. So when it comes dark again, I will steal down into that clachan, and set this that I have been making in the window of a good friend of mine, John Breck Maccoll, a bouman of Appin's."

"With all my heart," says I; "and if he finds it, what is he to think?"

"Well," says Alan, "I wish he was a man of more penetration; for by my troth, I am afraid he will make little enough of it! But this is what I have in my mind. This cross is something in the nature of the crosstarrie, or fiery cross, which is the signal of gathering in our clans; yet he will know well enough the clan is not to rise, for there it is standing in his window, and no word with it. So he will say to himsel' *The clan is not to rise but there is something.* Then he will see my button, and that was Duncan Stewart's. And then he will say to himsel' *The son of Duncan is in the heather and has need of me.*"

"Well," said I, "it may be. But even supposing so, there is a good deal of heather between here and the Forth."

"And that is a very true word," says Alan. "But then John Breck will see the sprig of birch and the sprig of pine; and he will say to himsel' (if he is a man of any penetration at all, which I misdoubt) *Alan will be lying in a wood which is both of pines and birches.* Then he will think to himsel' *That is not so very rife hereabout;* and then he will come and give us a look up in Corrynakiegh. And if he does not, David, the devil may fly away with him for what I care; for he will no be worth the salt to his porridge."

"Eh man," said I, drolling with him a little, "you're very ingenious! But would it not be simpler for you, to write him a few words in black and white?"

"And that is an excellent observe, Mr Balfour of Shaws," says Alan, drolling with me; "and it would certainly be much simpler

for me to write to him, but it would be a sore job for John Breck
to read it. He would have to go to the school for two-three years;
and it's possible we might be wearied waiting on him."

So that night Alan carried down his fiery cross and set it in the
bouman's window. He was troubled when he came back; for the
dogs had barked, and the folk run out of their houses; and he
thought he had heard a clatter of arms and seen a red coat come
to one of the doors. On all accounts, we lay the next day in the
borders of the wood and kept a close lookout; so that if it was
John Breck that came, we might be ready to guide him, and if it
was the red-coats, we should have time to get away.

About noon a man was to be spied, straggling up the open
side of the mountain in the sun, and looking round him as he
came from under his hand. No sooner had Alan seen him than
he whistled; the man turned and came a little towards us; then
Alan would give another "peep!" and the man would come still
nearer; and so by the sound of whistling, he was guided to the
spot where we lay.

He was a ragged, wild, bearded man about forty, grossly dis-
figured with the smallpox, and looked both dull and savage. Although his English was very bad and broken, yet Alan (according
to his very handsome use, whenever I was by) would suffer him to
speak no Gaelic. Perhaps the strange language made him appear
more backward than he really was; but I thought he had little
good will to serve us, and what he had was the child of terror.

Alan would have him carry a message to James; but the bouman would hear of no message. "She was forget it," he said in his
screaming voice; and would either have a letter or wash his hands
of us.

I thought Alan would be gravelled at that, for we lacked the means of writing in that desert. But he was a man of more resources than I knew; searched the wood until he found a quill of a cushat-dove, which he shaped into a pen; made himself a kind of ink with gunpowder from his horn and water from that running stream; and tearing a corner from his French military commission (which he carried in his pocket, like a talisman to keep him from the gallows) he sat down and wrote as follows:

"Dear Kinsman,

"Please send the money by the bearer to the place he kens of.

"Your affectionate cousin
"A.S."

This he intrusted to the bouman who promised to make what manner of speed he best could, and carried it off with him down the hill.

He was three full days gone, but about five in the evening of the third, we heard a whistling in the wood which Alan answered; and presently the bouman came up the waterside, looking for us, right and left. He seemed less sulky than before, and indeed he was no doubt well pleased to have got to the end of such a dangerous commission.

He gave us the news of the country; that it was alive with redcoats; that arms were being found, and poor folk brought in trouble, daily; and that James and some of his servants were already clapped in prison at Fort William, under strong suspicion of complicity. It seemed it was noised on all sides that Alan Breck had fired the shot; and there was a bill issued for both him and me, with one hundred pounds reward.

This was all as bad as could be; and the little note the bouman had carried us from Mrs Stewart, was of a miserable sadness. In it she besought Alan not to let himself be captured, assuring him, if he fell in the hands of the troops, both he and James were no better than dead men. The money she had sent was all that she could beg or borrow, and she prayed heaven we could be doing with it. Lastly, she said she enclosed us one of the bills in which we were described.

This we looked upon with great curiosity and not a little fear, partly as a man may look in a mirror, partly as he might look into the barrel of an enemy's gun to judge if it be truly aimed. Alan was advertised as "a small, pock-marked, active man of thirty five or thereby dressed in a feathered hat, a French side-coat of blue with silver buttons and lace a great deal tarnished, a red waistcoat and breeches of black shag;" and I as "a tall strong lad of about eighteen, wearing an old blue coat, very ragged, an old Highland bonnet, a long homespun waistcoat, blue breeches; his legs bare; low-country shoes, wanting the toes; speaks like a low-lander, and has no beard."

Alan was well enough pleased to see his finery so fully remembered and set down; only when he came to the word tarnish, he looked upon his lace like one a little mortified. As for myself, I thought I cut a miserable figure in the bill, and yet was well enough pleased too; for since I had changed these rags, the description had ceased to be a danger and become a source of safety.

"Alan," said I, "you should change your clothes."

"Na, troth!" said Alan, "I have nae others. A fine sight I would be if I went back to France in a bonnet!"

This put a second reflection in my mind: that if I were to sepa-

"But the Bouman, after feeling about in a hairy purse that
hung in front of him . . . at last said 'Her nainsel will loss it,'
meaning he thought he had lost it."

Young Folks Paper, June 26, 1886.

rate from Alan and his tell-tale clothes, I should be safe against
arrest and might go openly about my business. Nor was this all;
for suppose I was arrested when I was alone, there was little
against me; but suppose I was taken in company with the reputed
murderer, my case would begin to be grave. For generosity's sake,
I dare not speak my mind upon this head; but I thought of it
none the less.

I thought of it all the more, too, when the bouman brought
out a green purse with four guineas in gold, and the best part of

another in small change. True, it was more than I had. But then Alan, with less than five guineas, had to get as far as France; I with my less than two, not beyond Queensferry; so, that taking things in their proportion, Alan's society was not only a peril to my life, but a burthen on my purse.

But there was no thought of the sort in the honest head of my companion. He believed he was serving, helping and protecting me. And what could I do but hold my peace, and chafe, and take my chance of it?

"It's little enough," said Alan, putting the purse in his pocket, "but it'll do my business. And now John Breck, if ye will hand me over my button, this gentleman and me will be for taking the road."·

But the Bouman, after feeling about in a hairy purse that hung in front of him in the Highland manner (though he wore otherwise the lowland habit, with sea trousers) began to roll his eyes strangely, and at last said "Her nainsel will loss it," meaning he thought he had lost it.

"What!" cried Alan, "you will lose my button, that was my father's before me? Now, I will tell you what is in my mind, John Breck: it is in my mind this is the worst day's work that ever ye did since ye were born."

And as Alan spoke, he set his hands on his knees and looked at the bouman with a smiling mouth, and that dancing light in his eyes that meant mis-chief to his enemies.

Perhaps the bouman was honest enough; perhaps he had meant to cheat and then, finding himself alone with two of us in a desert place, cast back to honesty as being safer; at least, and all at once, he seemed to find that button and handed it to Alan.

"Well, and it is a good thing for the honour of the Maccolls," said Alan; and then to me, "Here is my button back again, and I thank you for parting with it, which is of a piece with all your friendships to me." Then he took the warmest parting of the bouman. "For," says he, "ye have done very well by me, and set your neck at a venture, and I will always give ye the name of a good man."

Lastly, the Bouman took himself off by one way; and Alan and I (getting our chattels together) struck into another to resume our flight.

22

The Flight in the Heather

THE MUIR

More than eleven hours of incessant, hard travelling brought us early in the morning to the end of a range of mountains. In front of us there lay a piece of low, broken, desert land, which we must now cross. The sun was not long up and shone straight in our eyes; a little, thin mist went up from the face of the moorland like a smoke; so that (as Alan said) there might have been twenty squadron of dragoons there, and we none the wiser.

We sat down, therefore, in a howe of the hillside, till the mist should have risen, and made ourselves a dish of drammach, and held a council of war.

"David," says Alan, "this is the kittle bit. Shall we lie here till it comes night, or shall we risk it and stave on ahead?"

"Well," said I, "I am tired indeed, but I could walk as far again, if that was all."

"Ay, but it isnae," said Alan; "nor yet the half. This is how we stand: Appin's fair death to us. To the south, it's all Campbells, and no to be thought of. To the north; well, there's no muckle to be gained by going north; neither for you, that wants to get to Queensferry, nor yet for me, that wants to get to France. Well, then, we'll can strike east."

"East be it!" says I, quite cheerily; but I was thinking, into myself: "O man, if you would only take one point of the compass and let me take any other, it would be the best for both of us."

"Well, then, east, ye see, we have the muirs," said Alan. "Once there, David, it's mere pitch-and-toss. Out on yon bald, naked, flat place, where can a body turn to? Let the red coats come over a hill, they can spy you miles away; and the sorrow's in their horses' heels! they would soon ride you down. It's no good place, David; and I'm free to say, it's worse by daylight than by dark."

"Alan," said I, "hear my way of it. Appin's death for us; we have none too much money, nor yet meal; the longer they seek, the nearer they may guess where we are; it's all a risk; and I give my word to go ahead until we drop."

Alan was delighted. "There are whiles," said he, "when ye are altogether too canny and whiggish to be company for a gentleman like me; but there come other whiles when ye show yoursel' a mettle spark; and it's then, David, that I love ye like a brother."

The mist rose and died away, and showed us that country lying as waste as the sea; only the moorfowl and the peewees crying upon it, and far over to the east, a herd of deer moving like dots. Much of it was under heather; much of the rest broken up with hags and bogs and peaty pools; some had been burnt black in a heath fire; and in another place, there was quite a forest of dead firs, standing like skeletons. A wearier looking desert, man never saw; but at least it was clear of troops, which was our point.

We went accordingly into the waste, and began to make our toilsome and devious travel towards the eastern verge. There were the tops of mountains all round (you are to remember) from whence we might be spied at any moment; so it behoved us to keep in the hollow parts of the moor, and when these turned aside from our direction, to move upon its naked face with infinite care. Sometimes for half an hour together we must crawl from one heather bush to another, as hunters do when they are hard upon the deer. It was a clear day again, with a blazing sun; the water in the brandy bottle was some gone; and altogether if I had guessed what it would be to crawl half the time upon my belly and to walk much of the rest stooping nearly to the knees, I should certainly have held back from such a killing enterprise.

Toiling and resting and toiling again, we wore away the morning; and about noon lay down in a thick bush of heather to sleep. Alan took the first watch; and it seemed to me I had scarce closed my eyes, before I was shaken up to take the second. We had no clock to go by; and Alan stuck a sprig of heath in the ground to serve instead; so that as soon as the shadow of the bush should fall so far to the east, I might know to rouse him. But I was by this time so weary that I could have slept twelve hours at a stretch; I had the taste of sleep in my throat; my joints slept even when my mind was waking; the hot smell of the heather, and the drone of the wild bees, were like possets to me; and every now and again I would give a jump and find I had been dozing.

The last time I woke, I seemed to come back from farther away, and thought the sun had taken a great start in the heavens. I looked at the sprig of heath, and at that I could have cried aloud; for I saw I had betrayed my trust. My head was nearly turned with fear and shame; and at what I saw, when I looked out around me on the moor, my heart was like dying in my body. For sure enough, a body of horse soldiers had come down during my sleep, and were drawing near to us from the south east, spread out in the shape of a fan, and riding their horses to and fro in the deep parts of the heather.

When I waked Alan, he glanced first at the soldiers, then at the mark and the position of the sun, and knitted his brows with a sudden, quick look, both ugly and anxious, which was all the reproach I had of him.

"What are we to do now?" I gasped.

"We'll have to play at being hares," said he. "Do ye see yon mountain?" pointing to one on the north-eastern sky.

"Ay," said I.

"Well, then," says he, "let us strike for that. Its name is Ben Alder; it is a wild, desert mountain full of hills and hollows, and if we can win to it before the morn, we may do yet."

"But, Alan," cried I, "that will take us across the very coming of the soldiers!"

"I ken that fine," said he; "but if we are driven back on Appin, we are two dead men. So, now, David man, be brisk!"

With that he began to run forward on his hands and knees with an incredible quickness, as though it were his natural way of going. All the time, too, he kept winding in and out in the lower parts of the moorland, where we were the best concealed. Some of these had been burned or at least scathed with fire; and there rose in our faces (which were close to the ground) a blinding, choking dust as fine as smoke. The water was long out; and this posture of running on the hands and knees brings an over-mastering weakness and weariness, so that the joints ache and the wrists faint under your weight.

Now and then, indeed, where was a big bush of heather, we lay awhile and panted, and putting aside the leaves, looked back at the dragoons. They had not spied us, for they held straight on: a half-troop, I think, covering about two miles of ground and beating it mighty thoroughly as they went. I had awakened just

"We lay awhile and panted, and putting aside the leaves,
looked back at the dragoons."

Young Folks Paper, July 3, 1886.

in time; a little later, and we must have fled in front of them, instead of escaping on one side. Even as it was, the least misfortune might betray us; and now and again, when a grouse rose out of the heather with a clap of wings, we lay as still as the dead and were afraid to breathe.

The aching and faintness of my body, the labouring of my heart, the soreness of my hands, and the smarting of my throat and eyes in the continual smoke of dust and ashes had soon grown to be so unbearable that I would gladly have given up. Nothing but the fear of Alan lent me enough of a false kind of courage to continue. As for himself (and you are to bear in mind that he was cumbered with a greatcoat) he had first turned crimson, but as time went on, the redness began to be mingled with patches of white; his breath cried and whistled as it came; and his voice, when he whispered his observations in my ear during our halts, sounded like nothing human. Yet he seemed in no way dashed in spirits, nor did he at all abate in his activity; so that I was driven to marvel at the man's endurance.

At length, in the first gloaming of the night, we heard a trumpet sound, and looking back from among the heather, saw the troop beginning to collect. A little after, they had built a fire and camped for the night, about the middle of the waste.

At this I begged and besought that we might lie down and sleep.

"There shall be no sleep the night!" said Alan. "From now on, these weary dragoons of yours will keep the crown of the muirland, and none will get out of Appin but winged fowls. We got through in the nick of time, and shall we jeopard what we've gained? Na, na, when the day comes, it shall find you and me in a fast place on Ben Alder."

"Alan," I said, "it's not the want of will; it's the strength that I want. If I could, I would; but as sure as I'm alive, I cannot."

"Very well, then," said Alan. "I'll carry ye."

I looked to see if he were jesting; but no, the little man was in dead earnest, and the sight of so much resolution shamed me.

"Lead away!" said I. "I'll follow."

He gave me one look, as much as to say "Well done, David!" and off he set again at his top speed.

It grew cooler and even a little darker (but not much) with the coming of the night. The sky was cloudless; it was still early in July, and pretty far north; in the darkest part of that night, you would have needed pretty good eyes to read, but for all that, I have often seen it darker in a winter midday. Heavy dew fell, and drenched the moor like rain; and this refreshed me for awhile. When we stopped to breathe, and I had time to see all about me the clearness and sweetness of the night, the shapes of the hills like things asleep, and the fire dwindling away behind us, like a bright spot in the midst of the moor, anger would come upon me in a clap that I must still drag myself in agony and eat the dust like a worm. Every foot of ground was a pang to me; my tongue hung from my mouth; I hated Alan with black hate. By what I have read in books, I think few that have held a pen were ever really wearied, or they would write of it more strongly. I had no care of my life, neither past nor future, and I scarce remembered there was such a lad as David Balfour. I did not think of myself, but just of each fresh step which I was sure to be my last, with despair—and of Alan, who was the cause of it, with hatred. Alan was in the right trade as a soldier; this is the officer's part, to make men continue to do things, they know not wherefore, and when, if the choice was offered, they would lie down where they were and be killed. And I daresay I would have made a good enough private; for in these last hours, it never occurred to me that I had any choice, but just to obey as long as I was able, and die obeying.

Day began to come in, after years, I thought; and by that time, we were past the greatest danger and could walk upon our feet like men, instead of crawling like brutes. But, dear heart have mercy! what a pair we must have made, going double like old grandfathers, stumbling like babes, and as white as dead folk. Never a word passed between us; each set his mouth and kept his eyes in front of him, and lifted up his foot and set it down again, like people lifting weights at a county Play; all the while, with the moorfowl crying 'peep!' in the heather, and the light coming slowly clearer in the east.

I say Alan did as I did: Not that ever I looked at him, for I had enough to do not to fall upon the ground; but because it is plain he must have been as stupid with weariness as myself, and looked as little where we were going; or we should not have walked into an ambush like blind men.

It fell in this way. We were going down a heathery brae, Alan leading and I following a pace or two behind, like a fiddler and his wife; when upon a sudden the heather gave a rustle, three or four ragged men leaped out, and the next moment we were lying on our backs, each with a dirk at his throat.

I don't think I cared: the pain of this rough handling was quite swallowed up by the pains of which I was already full; and I was too glad to have stopped walking, to mind about a dirk. I lay looking up in the face of the man that held me; and I mind his face was black with the sun, and his eyes very light, but I was not afraid of him. I heard Alan and another whispering in the Gaelic; and what they said was all one to me.

Then the dirks were put up, our weapons were taken away, and we were set face to face, sitting in the heather.

"They are Cluny's men," said Alan. "We couldnae have fallen better. We're just to bide here with these, which are his out-sentries, till they can get word to the chief of my arrival."

Now Cluny Macpherson, the chief of the Clan Vourich, had been one of the leaders of the great rebellion six years before; there was a price on his life; and I had supposed him long ago in France, with the rest of the heads of that desperate party. Even tired as I was, the surprise of what I heard half wakened me.

"What?" I cried. "Is Cluny still here?"

"Ay is he so!" said Alan. "Still in his own country and kept by his own clan. King George can do no more."

I think I would have asked farther, but Alan gave me the put-off. "I am rather wearied," he said, "and I would like fine to get a sleep." And without more words, he rolled on his face in a deep heather bush, and seemed to sleep at once.

There was no such thing possible for me. You have heard grasshoppers whirring in the grass in the summertime? Well, I had no sooner closed my eyes, than my body, and above all my head, belly and wrists, seemed to be filled with whirring grass-hoppers; and I must open my eyes again at once, and tumble and toss, and sit up and lie down; and look at the sky which dazzled me, or at Cluny's wild and dirty sentries, peering out over the top of the brae and chattering to each other in the Gaelic.

That was all the rest I had, until the messenger returned; when, as it appeared that Cluny would be glad to receive us, we must get once more upon our feet and set forward. Alan was in excellent good spirits, much refreshed by his sleep, very hungry, and looking pleasantly forward to a dram and a dish of hot collops, of which, it seems, the messenger had brought him word. For my part, it made me sick to hear of eating. I had been dead-heavy before, and now I felt a kind of dreadful lightness, which would not suffer me to walk. I drifted like a gossamer; the ground seemed to me a cloud, the hills a featherweight, the air to have a current, like a running burn, which carried me to and fro. With all that, a sort of horror of despair sat on my mind, so that I could have wept at my own helplessness.

I saw Alan knitting his brows at me, and supposed it was in anger; and that gave me a pang of light-headed fear, like what a child may have. I remember too that I was smiling, and could not stop smiling, hard as I tried; for I thought it was out of place at such a time. But my good companion had nothing in his mind but kindness; and the next moment, two of the gillies had me by the arms, and I began to be carried forward with great swiftness (or so it appeared to me, although I daresay it was slowly enough in truth) through a labyrinth of dreary glens and hollows and into the heart of that dismal mountain of Ben Alder.

∾ 23

Cluny's Cage

W e came at last to the foot of an exceedingly steep wood, which scrambled up a craggy hillside and was crowned by a naked precipice.

"It's here," said one of the guides, and we struck up hill.

The trees clung upon the slope, like sailors on the shrouds of a ship; and their trunks were like the rounds of a ladder by which we mounted.

Quite at the top, and just before the rocky face of the cliff sprang above the foliage, we found that strange house which was known in the country as "Cluny's Cage."

The trunks of several trees had been wattled across, the intervals strengthened with stakes, and the ground behind this barricade, levelled up with earth to make the floor. A tree, which grew out from the hillside, was the living centre-beam of the roof. The walls were of wattle and covered with moss. The whole house had something of an egg shape; and it half hung, half stood in that steep, hillside thicket, like a wasp's nest in a green hawthorn.

Within, it was large enough to shelter five or six persons with some comfort. A projection of the cliff had been cunningly employed to be the fireplace; and the smoke rising against the face of the rock, and being not dissimilar in colour, readily escaped notice from below.

This was but one of Cluny's hiding places; he had caves, besides, and underground chambers in several parts of his country; and following the reports of his scouts, he moved from one to another, as the soldiers drew near or moved away. By this manner of living and thanks to the affection of his clan, he had not only stayed all this time in safety, while so many others had fled, or been taken and slain; but stayed four or five years longer, and only went to France at last, by the express command of his master. There he soon died; and it's strange to reflect that he may have regretted his cage upon Ben Alder.

When we came to the door, he was seated by his rock chimney, watching a gillie about some cookery. He was mighty plainly habited, with a knitted nightcap drawn over his ears, and smoked a foul cutty pipe. For all that, he had the manners of a king, and it was quite a sight to see him rise out of his place to welcome us.

"Well, Mr Stewart, come awa' sir!" said he, "and bring in your friend that as yet I dinna ken the name of."

"And how is yourself, Cluny?" said Alan. "I hope ye do brawly, sir. And I am proud to see ye, and to present to ye my friend the laird of Shaws, Mr David Balfour."

Alan never referred to my estate without a touch of a sneer, when we were alone; but with strangers, he rang the words out like a herald.

"Step in by, the both of ye, gentlemen," says Cluny. "I make ye welcome to my house, which is a queer, rude place for certain, but one where I have entertained a royal personnage, Mr Stewart—ye doubtless ken the personnage I have in my eye. We'll take a dram for luck, and as soon as this handless man of mine has the collops ready, we'll dine and take a hand at the cartes as gentlemen should. My life is a bit driegh," says he, pouring out the brandy; "I see little company, and sit and twirl my thumbs, and mind upon a great day that is gone by, and weary for another great day that we all hope will be upon the way. And so here's a toast to ye: The Restoration!"

Thereupon we all touched glasses and drank. I am sure I wished no ill to King George; and if he had been there himself in proper person, it's like he would have done as I did. No sooner had I taken out the dram than I felt hugely better, and could look on and listen, still a little mistily perhaps, but no longer with the same groundless horror and distress of mind.

It was certainly a strange place, and we had a strange host. In his long hiding, Cluny had grown to have all manner of precise habits, like those of an old maid. He had a particular place, where no one else must sit; the Cage was arranged in a particular way, which none must disturb; cookery was one of his chief fancies, and even while he was greeting us in, he kept an eye to the collops.

It appears, he sometimes visited or received visits from his wife and one or two of his nearest friends, under the cover of night, but for the more part lived quite alone and communicated only with his sentinels and the gillies that waited on him in the Cage. The first thing in the morning, one of these, who was a barber, came and shaved him, and gave him the news of the country, of which he was immoderately greedy. There was no end to his questions; he put them as eagerly as a child; and at some of the answers, laughed out of all bounds of reason, and would break out again laughing at the mere memory, hours after the barber was gone.

To be sure, there might have been a purpose in his questions; for though he was thus sequestered, and like the other landed gentlemen of Scotland, stripped by the late Act of Parliament of legal powers, he still exercised a patriarchal justice in his clan. Disputes were brought to him in his hiding-hole to be decided; and the men of his country, who would have snapped their fingers at the Court of Session, laid aside revenge and paid down money at the bare word of this forfeited and hunted outlaw. When he was angered, which was often enough, he gave his commands and breathed threats of punishment like any king; and his gillies trembled and crouched away from him like children before a hasty father. With each of these, as he entered, he ceremoniously shook hands, both parties touching their bonnets at the same time in a military manner. Altogether, I had a fair chance to see some of the inner workings of a Highland Clan; and this with a proscribed, fugitive chief; his country conquered; the troops riding upon all sides in quest of him, sometimes within a mile of where he lay; and when the least of the ragged fellows whom he rated and threatened, could have made a fortune by betraying him.

On that first day, as soon as the collops were ready, Cluny gave them with his own hand a squeeze of a lemon (for he was well supplied with luxuries) and bade us draw in to our meal.

"They," said he, meaning the collops, "are such as I gave his Royal Highness in this very house: bating the lemon juice, for at that time we were glad to get the meat and never fashed for kitchen. Indeed there were mair dragoons than lemons in my country in the year forty-six."

I do not know if the collops were truly very good, but my heart rose against the very sight of them, and I could eat but little. All the while Cluny entertained us with stories of Prince Charlie's stay in the Cage, giving us the very words of the speakers and rising from his place to show us where they stood. By these, I gathered the Prince was a gracious, spirited boy, like the son of a race of polite kings, but not so wise as Solomon. I gathered, too, that while he was in the cage, he was often drunk; so the fault that has since, by all accounts, made such a wreck of him, had even then begun to show itself.

We were no sooner done eating, than Cluny brought out an old, thumbed, greasy pack of cards, such as you may find in a mean inn; and his eyes brightened in his face as he proposed that we should fall to playing.

Now, this was one of the things I had been brought up to eschew like disgrace; it being held by my father neither the part of a christian nor yet of a gentleman, to set his own livelihood and fish for that of others, on the cast of painted pasteboard. To be sure, I might have pleaded my fatigue, which was excuse enough; but I thought it behoved that I should bear a testimony. I must have got very red in the face, but I spoke steadily, and told them I had no call to be a judge of others, but for my own part, it was a matter in which I had no clearness.

Cluny stopped mingling the cards. "What in deil's name is this?" says he. "What kind of whiggish, canting talk is this, for the house of Cluny Macpherson?"

"I will put my hand in the fire for Mr Balfour," says Alan. "He is an honest and a mettle gentleman, and I would have ye bear in mind wha says it. I bear a King's name," says he, cocking his hat; "and I and any that I call friend are company for the best. But the gentleman is tired, and should sleep; if he has no mind to the cartes, it will never hinder you and me. And I'm fit and willing, sir, to play ye any game that ye can name."

"Sir," says Cluny, "in this poor house of mine, I would have you to ken that any gentleman may follow his pleasure. If your friend would like to stand on his head, he is welcome. And if either he, or you, or any other man, is not preceesely satisfied, I will be proud to step outside with him."

I had no will that these two friends should cut their throats for my sake.

"Sir," said I, "I am very wearied as Alan says; and what's more, as you are a man that likely has sons of your own, I may tell you it was a promise to my father."

"Say nae mair, say nae mair," said Cluny, and pointed me to a bed of heather in a corner of the Cage. For all that he was displeased enough, looked at me askance, and grumbled when he looked. And indeed it must be owned that both my scruples and the words in which I declared them, smacked somewhat of the Covenanter, and were little in their place among wild, Highland Jacobites.

What with the brandy and the venison, a strange heaviness had come over me; and I had scarce lain down upon the bed, before I fell into a kind of trance in which I continued almost the whole time of our stay in the cage. Sometimes I was broad awake and understood what passed; sometimes I only heard voices or men snoring, like the noise of a silly river; and the plaids upon the wall dwindled down and swelled out again, like firelight shadows on the roof. I must sometimes have spoken or cried out, for I remember I was now and then amazed at being answered; yet I was conscious of no particular nightmare, only of a general, black, abiding horror—a horror of the place I was in, and the bed I lay in, and the plaids on the wall, and the voices, and the fire, and myself.

The barber-gillie, who was a doctor too, was called in to prescribe to me; but as he spoke in the Gaelic, I understood not a word of his opinion, and was too sick even to ask for a translation. I knew well enough I was ill, and that was all I cared about.

I paid little heed while I lay in this poor pass. But Alan and Cluny were most of the time at the cards, and I am clear that Alan must have begun by winning; for I remember sitting up, and seeing them hard at it, and a great glittering pile of as much as sixty or a hundred guineas on the table. It looked strange enough, to see all this wealth in a nest upon a cliffside, wattled about growing trees. And even then, I thought it seemed deep water for Alan to be riding, who had no better battle-horse than a green purse and the matter of five pounds.

The luck, it seems, changed upon the second day. About noon, I was wakened as usual for dinner, and as usual refused to eat, and was given a dram with some bitter infusion, which the barber had prescribed. The sun was shining in at the open door of the cage, and this dazzled and offended me. Cluny sat at the table, biting the pack of cards. Alan had stooped over the bed, and had his face close to my eyes; to which, troubled as they were with the fever, it seemed of the most shocking bigness.

He asked me for a loan of my money.

"What for?" said I.

"O, just for a loan," said he.

"But why?" I repeated. "I don't see."

"Hut, David!" said Alan, "ye wouldnae grudge me a loan?"

I would though, if I had had my senses! But all I thought of then was to get his face away, and I handed him my money.

On the morning of the third day, when we had been forty eight hours in the Cage, I awoke with a great relief of spirits, very weak and weary indeed, but seeing things of the right size and with their honest, everyday appearance. I had a mind to eat, moreover; rose from bed of my own movement; and as soon as we had breakfasted stepped to the entry of the cage and sat down outside in the top of the wood. It was a gray day with a cool mild air; and I sat in a dream all morning, only disturbed by the passing by of Cluny's scouts and servants coming with provisions and reports; for as the coast was at that time clear, you might almost say he held court openly.

When I returned, he and Alan had laid the cards aside and were questioning a gillie; and the chief turned about and spoke to me in the Gaelic.

"I have no Gaelic, sir," said I.

Now, since the card question, everything I said or did had the power of annoying Cluny. "Your name has more sense than yourself then," said he, angrily; "for it's good Gaelic. But the point is this. My scout reports all clear in the south, and the question is have ye the strength to go?"

I saw cards on the table, but no gold; only a heap of little written papers, and these all on Cluny's side. Alan besides had an odd look, like a man not very well content; and I began to have a strong mis-giving.

"I do not know if I am as well as I should be," said I, looking at Alan; "but the little money we have, has a long way to carry us."

Alan took his under lip into his mouth, and looked upon the ground.

"David," says he at last, "I've lost it: there's the naked truth."

"My money, too?" said I.

"Your money too," says Alan, with a groan. "Ye shouldnae have given it me. I'm daft when I get to the cartes."

"Hoot-toot, hoot-toot," said Cluny. "It was all daffing; it's all nonsense. Of course, ye'll have your money back again, and the double of it, if ye'll make so free with me! It would be a singular thing for me to keep it. It's not to be supposed that I would be any hindrance to gentlemen in your situation: that would be a singular thing!" cries he, and began to pull gold out of his pocket, with a mighty red face.

Alan said nothing, only looked on the ground.

"Will you step to the door with me, sir?" said I.

Cluny said he would be very glad, and followed me readily enough, but he looked flustered and put out.

"And now, sir," says I, "I must first acknowledge your generosity."

"Nonsensical nonsense!" cries Cluny. "Where's the generosity? This is just a most unfortunate affair; but what would ye have me do—boxed up in this beeskep of a cage of mine—but just set my friends to the cartes, when I can get them? And if they lose, of course, it's not to be supposed——" And here he came to a pause.

"Yes," said I, "if they lose, you give them back their money; and if they win, they carry away yours in their pouches! I have said before that I grant your generosity; but to me, sir, it's a very painful thing to be placed in this position."

There was a little silence, in which Cluny seemed always as if he was about to speak, but said nothing. All the time, he grew redder and redder in the face.

"I am a young man," said I, "and I ask your advice. Advise me as you would advise your son. My friend fairly lost this money, after having fairly gained a far greater sum of yours: can I accept it back again? would that be the right part of me to play? Whatever I do, you see for yourself, it must be hard upon a man of any pride."

"It's rather hard on me, too, Mr Balfour," said Cluny, "and ye give me very much the look of a man that has entrapped poor people to their hurt. I wouldnae have my friends come to any house of mine to accept affronts; no," he cried, with a sudden heat of anger, "nor yet to give them!"

"And so you see, sir," said I, "there is something to be said upon my side; and this gambling is a very poor employ for gentlefolks. But I am still waiting your opinion."

I am sure if ever Cluny hated any man, it was David Balfour. He looked me all over with a warlike eye, and I saw the challenge at his lips. But either my youth disarmed him, or perhaps his own sense of justice. Certainly it was a mortifying matter for all concerned, and not least for Cluny; the more credit that he took it as he did.

"Mr Balfour," said he, "I think you are too nice and covenanting, but for all that you have the spirit of a very pretty gentleman. Upon my honest word, ye may take this money;—it's what I would tell my son;—and here's my hand along with it!"

∾ 24

The Flight in the Heather

THE QUARREL

Alan and I were put across Loch Errocht under cloud of night, and went down its eastern shore to another hiding place near the head of Loch Rannoch whither we were led by one of the gillies from the cage. This fellow carried all our luggage and Alan's great coat in the bargain, trotting along under the burthen, far less than the half of which used to weigh me to the ground, like a stout hill poney with a feather; yet he was a man that, in plain contest, I could have broken on my knee.

Doubtless it was a great relief to walk disencumbered; and perhaps without that relief, and the consequent sense of liberty and lightness, I could not have walked at all. I was but new risen from a bed of sickness; and there was nothing in the state of our affairs to hearten me for much exertion; travelling as we did, over the most dismal deserts in Scotland, under a cloudy heaven, and with divided hearts among the travellers.

For long, we said nothing; marching alongside or one behind the other, each with a set countenance: I, angry and proud, and drawing what strength I had from these two violent and sinful feelings: Alan angry and ashamed, ashamed that he had lost my money, angry that I should take it so ill.

The thought of a separation ran always the stronger in my

mind; and the more I approved of it, the more ashamed I grew of my approval. It would be a fine, handsome, generous thing, indeed, for Alan to turn round and say to me: "Go. I am in the most danger, and my company only increases yours." But for me to turn to the friend who certainly loved me, and say to him: "You are in great danger, I am in but little; your friendship is a burthen; go, take your risks and bear your hardships alone——" no, that was impossible; and even to think of it privily to myself, made my cheeks to burn.

And yet Alan had behaved like a child and (what is worse) a treacherous child. Wheedling my money from me while I lay half-conscious, was scarce better than theft; and yet here he was trudging by my side, without a penny to his name, and by what I could see, quite blythe to sponge upon the money he had driven me to beg. True, I was ready to share it with him; but it made me rage to see him count upon my readiness.

These were the two things uppermost in my mind; and I could open my mouth upon neither without black ungenerosity. So I did the next worst, and said nothing, nor so much as looked once at my companion save with the tail of my eye.

At last, upon the other side of Loch Errocht, going over a smooth, rushy place, where the walking was easy, he could bear it no longer and came close to me.

"David," says he, "this is no way for two friends to take a small accident. I have to say that I'm sorry; and so that's said. And now if you have anything, ye'd better say it."

"O," says I, "I have nothing."

He seemed dis-concerted; at which I was meanly pleased.

"No," said he, with rather a trembling voice, "but when I say I was to blame?"

"Why, of course, ye were to blame," said I, coolly: "and you will bear me out that I have never reproached you."

"Never," says he; "but ye ken very well that ye've done worse. Are we to part? Ye said so once before. Are ye to say it again? There's hills and heather enough between here and the two seas, David; and I will own I'm no very keen to stay where I'm no wanted."

This pierced me like a sword, and seemed to lay bare my private disloyalty.

"Alan Breck!" I cried; and then: "Do you think I am one to turn my back on you in your chief need? You durstn't say it to my face. My whole conduct's there to give the lie to it. It's true, I fell asleep upon the muir; but that was from weariness, and you do wrong to cast it up to me———"

"Which is what I never did," said Alan.

"But aside from that," I continued, "what have I done that you should even me to dogs by such a supposition? I never yet failed a friend, and it's not likely I'll begin with you. There are things between us that I can never forget, even if you can."

"I will only say this to ye, David," said Alan, very quietly, "that I have long been owing ye my life, and now I owe ye money. Ye should try to make that burthen light for me," said he.

This ought to have touched me, and in a manner it did, but the wrong manner. I felt I was behaving badly; and was now not only angry with Alan, but angry with myself in the bargain; and it made me the more cruel.

"You asked me to speak," said I. "Well, then, I will. You own yourself that you have done me a disservice; I have had to swallow an affront; I have never reproached you, I never named the thing till you did. And now you blame me," cried I, "because I cannae laugh and sing as if I was glad to be affronted! The next thing will be that I'm to go down upon my knees and thank you for it! Ye should think more of others, Alan Breck. If ye thought more of others, ye would perhaps speak less about yourself; and when a friend that likes you very well, has passed over an offence without a word, you would be blythe to let it lie, instead of making it a stick to break his back with. By your own way of it, it was you that was to blame: then it shouldnae be you to seek the quarrel."

"Aweel," said Alan, "say nae mair."

And we fell back into our former silence; and came to our journey's end and supped, and lay down to sleep, without another word.

The gillie put us across Loch Rannoch in the dusk of the next day, and gave us his opinion as to our best route. This was to get us up at once into the tops of the mountains; to go round by a circuit, turning the heads of Glen Lyon, Glen Lochay and Glen Dochart; and come down upon the lowlands by Kippen and the upper waters of the Forth. Alan was little pleased with a route which led us through the country of his blood-foes, the Glenorchy Campbells. He objected that by turning to the east, we should come almost at once among the Athole Stewarts, a race of his own name and lineage, although following a different chief, and come besides, by a far easier and swifter way to the place whither we were bound. But the gillie, who was indeed the chief man of Cluny's scouts, had good reasons to give him on all hands, naming the force of troops in every district, and alledging finally (as well as I could understand) that we should nowhere be so little troubled as in a country of the Campbells.

Alan gave way at last but with only half a heart. "It's one of the dowiest countries in Scotland," said he. "There's naething there that I ken, but heath, and crows, and Campbells. But I see that ye're a man of some penetration; and be it as ye please!"

We set forth accordingly by this itinerary; and for the best part of three nights travelled on eerie mountains and among the well-heads of wild rivers; often buried in mist, almost continually blown and rained upon, and not once cheered by any glimpse of sunshine. By day, we lay and slept in the drenching heather; by night, we incessantly clambered upon breakneck hills and among rude crags. We often wandered; we were often so involved in fog, that we must lie quiet till it lightened. A fire was never to be thought of. Our only food was drammach and a portion of cold meat that we had carried from the cage; and as for drink, Heaven knows we had no want of water.

This was a dreadful time, rendered the more dreadful by the gloom of the weather and the country. I was never warm; my teeth chattered in my head; I was troubled with a very sore throat, such as I had on the isle; I had a painful stitch in my side, which never left me; and when I slept in my wet bed, with the rain beating above and the mud oozing below me, it was to live over again in fancy the worst part of my adventures—to see the tower of Shaws lit by lightning, Ransome carried below on the men's backs, Shuan dying on the round-house floor, or Colin Campbell grasping at the bosom of his coat. From such broken slumbers, I would be aroused in the gloaming, to sit up in the same puddle where I had slept and sup cold drammach; the rain driving sharp in my face or running down my back in icy trickles; the mist enfolding us like as in a gloomy chamber—or perhaps, if the wind blew, falling suddenly apart, and showing us the gulf of some dark valley, where the streams were crying aloud.

The sound of an infinite number of rivers came up from all round. In this steady rain, the springs of the mountain were broken up; every glen gushed water like a cistern; every stream was in high spate, and had filled and overflowed its channel. During our night tramps, it was solemn to hear the voice of them below us in the valleys, now booming like thunder, now with an angry cry. I could well understand the story of the Water Kelpie, that demon of the streams, who is fabled to keep wailing and roaring at the ford until the coming of the doomed traveller. Alan I saw believed it, or half believed it; and when the cry of the river rose more than unusually sharp, I was little surprised (though, of course, I would still be shocked) to see him cross himself in the manner of the catholics.

During all these horrid wanderings, we had no familiarity, scarcely even that of speech. The truth is that I was sickening for my grave, which is my best excuse. But besides that I was of an unforgiving disposition from my birth, slow to take offence, slower to forget it, and now incensed both against my companion and myself. For the best part of two days, he was unweariedly kind; silent indeed, but always ready to help, and always hoping (as I could very well see) that my displeasure would blow by. For the same length of time, I stayed in myself, nursing my anger, roughly refusing his services, and passing him over with my eyes as if he had been a bush or a stone.

The second night, or rather the peep of the third day, found us upon a very open hill, so that we could not follow our usual plan and lie down immediately to eat and sleep. Before we had reached a place of shelter, the gray had come pretty clear, for though it still rained, the clouds ran higher; and Alan, looking in my face, showed some marks of concern.

"Ye had better let me take your pack," said he, for perhaps the ninth time since we had parted from the scout beside Loch Rannoch.

"I do very well, I thank you," said I, as cold as ice.

Alan flushed darkly. "I'll not offer it again," he said. "I am not a patient man, David."

"I never said you were," said I, which was exactly the rude, silly speech of a boy of ten.

Alan made no answer at the time, but his conduct answered for him. Thenceforth, it is to be thought, he quite forgave himself for the affair at Cluny's; cocked his hat again, walked jauntily, whistled airs, and looked at me upon one side with a provoking smile.

The third night, we were to pass through the western end of the country of Balquidder. It came clear and cold, with a touch in the air like frost, and a northerly wind that blew the clouds away and made the stars bright. The streams were full, of course, and still made a great noise among the hills; but I observed that Alan thought no more upon the Kelpie and was in high good spirits. As for me, the change of weather came too late; I had lain in the mire so long that (as the Bible has it) my very clothes "abhorred me;" I was dead weary, deadly sick and full of pains and shiverings; the chill of the wind went through me, and the sound of it confused my ears. In this poor state, I had to bear from my companion something in the nature of a persecution. He spoke a good deal, and never without a taunt. "Whig" was the best name he had to give me. "Here," he would say, "here's a dub for ye to jump, my Whiggie! I ken you're a fine jumper." And so on; all the time with a gibing voice and face.

I knew it was my own doing, and no one else's; but I was too miserable to repent. I felt I could drag myself but little farther; pretty soon, I must lie down and die on these wet mountains, like a sheep or a fox, and my bones must whiten there like the bones of a beast. My head was light, perhaps; but I began to love the prospect, I began to glory in the thought of such a death, alone in the desert, with the wild eagles besieging my last moments. Alan would repent then, I thought; he would remember, when I was dead, how much he owed me, and the remembrance would be torture. So I went like a sick, silly and bad-hearted schoolboy, feeding my anger against a fellow-man, when I would have been better on my knees, crying on God for mercy. And at each of Alan's taunts, I hugged myself. "Ah!" thinks I to myself, "I have a better taunt in readiness; when I lie down and die, you will feel it like a buffet in your face; ah, what a revenge! ah, how you will regret your ingratitude and cruelty!"

All the while, I was growing worse and worse. Once I had fallen, my legs simply doubling under me, and this had struck Alan for the moment; but I was afoot so briskly, and set off again with such a natural manner, that he soon forgot the incident. Flushes of heat went over me, and then spasms of shuddering. The stitch in my side was hardly bearable. At last I began to feel that I could trail myself no farther: and with that, there came on me all at once, the wish to have it out with Alan, let my anger blaze, and be done with my life in a more sudden manner. He had just called me "Whig." I stopped.

"Mr Stewart," said I, in a voice that quivered like a fiddle-string, "you are older than I am, and should know your manners. Do you think it either very wise or very witty to cast my politics in my teeth? I thought, where folk differed, it was the part of gentlemen to differ civilly; and if I did not, I may tell you I could find a better taunt than some of yours."

Alan had stopped opposite to me, his hat cocked, his hands in his breeches pockets, his head a little on one side. He listened smiling evilly, as I could see by the starlight; and when I had done he began to whistle a Jacobite air. It was the air made in mockery of General Cope's defeat at Preston Pans:

> "Hey, Johnnie Cope, are ye waukin' yet?
> And are your drums a-beatin' yet?"

And it came in my mind that Alan, on the day of that battle, had been engaged upon the royal side.

"Why do ye take that air, Mr Stewart?" said I. "Is that to remind me you have been beaten on both sides?"

The air stopped on Alan's lips. "David!" said he.

"But it's time these manners ceased," I continued; "and I mean you shall henceforth speak civilly of my King and my good friends the Campbells."

"I am a Stewart . . ." began Alan.

"O!" says I, "I ken ye bear a King's name. But you are to remember, since I have been in the Highlands, I have seen a good many of those that bear it; and the best I can say of them is this, that they would be none the worse of washing."

"Do you know that you insult me?" said Alan, very low.

"I am sorry for that," said I, "for I am not done; and if you distaste the sermon, I doubt the pirliecue will please you as little. You have been chased in the field by the grown men of my party; it seems a poor kind of pleasure to outface a boy. Both the Campbells and the Whigs have beaten you; you have run before them like a hare. It behoves you to speak of them as of your betters."

Alan stood quite still, the tails of his great coat clapping behind him in the wind.

"This is a pity," he said at last. "There are things said that cannot be passed over."

"I never asked you to," said I. "I am as ready as yourself."

"Ready?" said he.

"Ready," I repeated. "I am no blower and boaster like some that I could name. Come on!" And drawing my sword, I fell on guard as Alan himself had taught me.

"David!" he cried. "Are ye daft? I cannae draw upon ye, David. It's fair murder."

"That was your lookout when you insulted me," said I.

"It's the truth!" cried Alan, and he stood for a moment, wringing his mouth in his hand like a man in sore perplexity. "It's the bare truth," he said, and drew his sword. But before I could touch his blade with mine, he had thrown it from him and fallen to the ground. "Na, na," he kept saying, "na, na—I cannae, I cannae."

At this the last of my anger oozed all out of me; and I found myself only sick, and sorry, and blank, and wondering at myself. I would have given the world to take back what I had said; but a word once spoken, who can recapture it? I minded me of all Alan's kindness and courage in the past, how he had helped and cheered and borne with me in our evil days; and then recalled my own insults, and saw that I had lost forever that doughty friend. At the same time, the sickness that hung upon me seemed to redouble, and the pang in my side was like a sword for sharpness. I thought I must have swooned where I stood.

This it was that gave me a thought. No apology could blot out what I had said; it was needless to think of one, none could cover the offence; but where an apology was vain, a mere cry for help might bring Alan back to my side. I put my pride away from me. "Alan!" I said, "if you cannae help me, I must just die here."

He started up sitting, and looked at me.

"It's true," said I. "I'm by with it. O, let me get into the bield of a house—I'll can die there easier." I had no need to pretend; whether I chose or not, I spoke in a weeping voice that would have melted a heart of stone.

"Can ye walk?" asked Alan.

"No," said I, "not without help. This last hour, my legs have been fainting under me; I've a stitch in my side like a red-hot iron; I cannae breathe right. If I die, ye'll can forgive me, Alan? In my heart, I liked ye fine—even when I was the angriest."

"Wheest, wheesht!" cried Alan. "Dinnae say that! David man, ye ken . . ." He shut his mouth upon a sob. "Let me get my arm about ye," he continued: "that's the way! Now lean upon me hard. Gude kens where there's a house! We're in Balwhidder too; there should be nae want of houses, no, nor friends' houses here. Do ye gang easier so, Davie?"

"Ay," said I, "I can be doing this way;" and I pressed his arm with my hand.

Again he came near sobbing. "Davie," said he, "I'm no right man at all; I have neither sense nor kindness; I couldnae remember ye were just a bairn, I couldnae see ye were dying on your feet: Davie, ye'll have to try and forgive me."

"O man, let's say no more about it!" said I. "We're neither one of us to mend the other—that's the truth! We must just bear and forbear, man Alan! O, but my stitch is sore! Is there nae house?"

"I'll find a house to ye, David," he said stoutly. "We'll follow down the burn, where there's bound to be houses. My poor man, will ye be no better on my back?"

"O, Alan," says I, "and me a good twelve inches taller!"

"Ye're no such a thing!" cried Alan, with a start. "There may be a trifling maitter of an inch or two; I'm no saying I'm just exactly what ye would call a tall man, whatever; and I daresay," he added, his voice tailing off in a laughable manner, "now when I come to think of it, I daresay ye'll be just about right. Ay, it'll be a foot, or near hand; or maybe even mair!"

It was sweet and laughable to hear Alan eat his words up in the fear of some fresh quarrel. I could have laughed, had not my stitch caught me so hard; but if I had laughed, I think I must have wept too.

"Alan," cried I, "what makes ye so good to me? what makes ye care for such a thankless fellow?"

"Deed, and I don't know!" said Alan. "For just precisely what I thought I liked about ye, was that ye never quarrelled;—and now I like ye better!"

ᔥ 25

In Balquidder

At the door of the first house we came to, Alan knocked, which was no very safe enterprise in such a part of the Highlands as the Braes of Balquidder. No great clan held rule there; it was filled and disputed by small septs, and broken remnants, and what they call "chiefless folk," driven into the wild country about the springs of Forth and Teith by the advance of the Campbells. Here were Stewarts and Maclarens, which came to the same thing, for the Maclarens followed Alan's chief in war, and made but one clan with Appin. Here, too, were many of that old, proscribed, nameless, red-handed clan of the Macgregors. They had always been ill considered, and now worse than ever, having credit with no side or party in the whole country of Scotland. Their chief, Macgregor of Macgregor, was in exile; the more immediate leader of that part of them about Balquidder, James More, Rob Roy's eldest son, lay waiting his trial in Edinburgh Castle; they were in ill-blood with Highlander and lowlander, with the Grahames, the Maclarens and the Stewarts; and Alan, who took up the quarrel of any friend however distant, was extremely wishful to avoid them.

Chance served us very well; for it was a household of Maclarens that we found, where Alan was not only welcome for his name's sake but known by reputation. Here then I was got to bed without delay, and a doctor fetched, who found me in a sorry plight. But whether because he was a very good doctor, or I a very young, strong man, I lay bed-ridden for no more than a week, and before a month, I was able to take the road again with a good heart.

All this time, Alan would not leave me, though I often pressed him; and indeed his foolhardiness in staying was a common subject of outcry with the two or three friends that were let into the secret. He hid by day in a hole of the braes under a little wood; and at night when the coast was clear, would come into the house to visit me. I need not say if I was pleased to see him; Mrs Maclaren, our hostess, thought nothing good enough for such a guest; and as Duncan Dhu (which was the name of our host) had a pair of pipes in his house and was much of a lover of music, the time of my recovery was quite a festival, and we commonly turned night into day.

The soldiers let us be; although once a party of two companies and some dragoons went by in the bottom of the valley, where I could see them through the window as I lay in bed. What was much more astonishing, no magistrate came near me, there was no question put of whence I came or whither I was going; and in that time of excitement, I was as free of all inquiry as though I had lain in a desert. Yet my presence was known before I left to all the people in Balquidder and the adjacent parts; many coming about the house on visits and these (after the custom of the country) spreading the news among their neighbours. The bills, too, had now been printed. There was one pinned near the foot of my bed, where I could read my own not very flattering portrait, and in large characters, the amount of the blood money that had

been set upon my life. Duncan Dhu and the rest that knew I had
come there in Alan's company, could have entertained no doubt
of who I was; and many others must have had their guess. For
though I had changed my clothes, I could not change my age or
person; and lowland boys of eighteen were not so rife in these
parts of the world, and above all about that time, that they could
fail to put one thing with another and connect me with the bill.
So it was, at least. Other folk keep a secret among two or three
near friends, and somehow it leaks out; but among these clansmen, it is told to a whole countryside, and they will keep it for
a century.

There was but one thing happened worth narrating; and that
is the visit I had of Robin Oig, one of the sons of the notorious
Rob Roy. He was sought upon all sides on a charge of carrying a
young woman from Balfron and marrying her (as was alleged)
by force; yet he stept about Balquidder like a gentleman in his
own walled policy. It was he who had shot James Maclaren at
the ploughstilts, a quarrel never satisfied; yet he walked into the
house of his blood enemies as a rider might into a public inn.

Duncan had time to pass me word of who it was; and we
looked at one another in concern. You should understand, it was
then close upon the time of Alan's coming; the two were little
likely to agree; and yet if we sent word or sought to make a signal,
it was sure to arouse suspicion in a man under so dark a cloud as
the Macgregor.

He came in with a great show of civility, but like a man among
inferiors; took off his bonnet to Mrs Maclaren, but clapped it on
his head again to speak to Duncan; and having thus set himself
(as he would have thought) in a proper light, came to my bedside
and bowed.

"I am given to know, sir," says he, "that your name is Balfour."

"They call me David Balfour," said I, "at your service."

"I would give ye my name in return, sir," he replied, "but it's one somewhat blown upon of late days; and it'll perhaps suffice if I tell ye that I am own brother to James More Drummond, or Macgregor, of whom ye will scarce have failed to hear."

"No, sir," said I, a little alarmed; "nor yet of your father, Macgregor-Campbell." And I sat up and bowed in bed; for I thought best to compliment him, in case he was proud of having had an outlaw to his father.

He bowed in return. "But what I am come to say, sir," he went on, "is this. In the year '45, my brother raised a part of the Gregara', and marched six companies to strike a stroke for the good side; and the surgeon that marched with our clan and cured my brother's leg when it was broken in the brush at Prestonpans, was a gentleman of the same name precisely as yourself. He was brother to Balfour of Baith; and if you are in any reasonable degree of nearness one of that gentleman's kin, I have come to put myself and my people at your command."

You are to remember that I knew no more of my descent than any cadger's dog; my uncle, to be sure, had prated of some of our high connections, but nothing to the present purpose; and there was nothing left me but that bitter disgrace of owning that I could not tell.

Robin told me shortly he was sorry he had put himself about, turned his back on me without a sign of salutation, and as he went towards the door, I could hear him telling Duncan that I was "only some kinless loon that didn't know his own father." Angry as I was at these words and ashamed of my own ignorance, I could scarce keep from smiling that a man who was under the lash of the law (and was indeed hanged some three years later) should be so nice as to the descent of his acquaintances.

Just in the door, he met Alan coming in; and the two drew back and looked at each other like strange dogs. They were neither of them big men, but they seemed fairly to swell out with pride. Each wore a sword, and by a movement of his haunch, thrust clear the hilt of it, so that it might be the more readily grasped and the blade drawn.

"Mr Stewart, I am thinking?" says Robin.

"Troth, Mr Macgregor, it's not a name to be ashamed of," answered Alan.

"I did not know ye were in my country, sir," says Robin.

"It sticks in my mind that I am in the country of my friends the Maclarens," says Alan.

"That's a kittle point," returned the other. "There may be two words to say to that. But I think I will have heard that you are a man of your sword?"

"Unless ye were born deaf, Mr Macgregor, ye will have heard a good deal more than that," says Alan. "I am not the only man that can draw steel in Appin; and when my kinsman and captain, Ardshiel, had a talk with a gentleman of your name, not so many years back, I could never hear that the Macgregor had the best of it."

"Do ye mean my father, sir?" says Robin.

"Well, I wouldnae wonder," said Alan. "The gentleman I had in my mind had the ill-taste to clap Campbell to his name."

"My father was an old man," returned Robin. "The match was unequal. You and me would make a better pair, sir."

"I was thinking that," said Alan.

I was half out of bed, and Duncan had been hanging at the elbows of these fighting cocks, ready to intervene upon the least occasion. But when that word was uttered, it was a case of now or never; and Duncan, with something of a white face, to be sure, thrust himself between.

"Gentlemen," said he, "I will have been thinking of a very different matter, whateffer. Here are my pipes, and here are you two gentlemen who are baith acclaimed pipers. It's an auld dispute which one of ye's the best. Here will be a braw chance to settle it."

"Why, sir," said Alan, still addressing Robin, from whom indeed he had not so much as shifted his eyes, nor yet Robin from him—"why, sir," says Alan, "I think I will have heard some sough of the sort. Have ye music, as folk say? Are ye a bit of a piper?"

"I can pipe like a Macrimmon!" cries Robin.

"And that is a very bold word," quoth Alan.

"I have made bolder words good before now," returned Robin, "and that against better adversaries."

"It is easy to try that," says Alan.

Duncan Dhu made haste to bring out the pair of pipes that was his principal possession, and to set before his guests a muttonham and a bottle of that drink which they call Athole Brose and which is made of old whiskey, strained honey and sweet cream, slowly beaten together in the right order and proportion. The two enemies were still on the very breach of a quarrel; but down they sat, one upon each side of the peat fire, with a mighty show of politeness. Maclaren pressed them to taste his muttonham and "the wife's brose," reminding them the wife was out of Athole and had a name far and wide for her skill in that confection. But Robin put aside these hospitalities as bad for the breath.

"I would have ye to remark, sir," said Alan, "that I havenae broken bread for near upon ten hours, which will be worse for the breath than any brose in Scotland."

"I will take no advantages, Mr Stewart," replied Robin. "Eat and drink: I'll follow you."

Each ate a small portion of the ham and drank a glass of the brose to Mrs Maclaren; and then after a great number of civilities, Robin took the pipes and played a little spring in a very ranting manner.

"Ay, ye can blow," said Alan; and taking the instrument from his rival, he first played the same spring in a manner identical with Robin's: and then wandered into variations which, as he went on, he decorated with a perfect flight of grace-notes, such as pipers love and call the "warblers."

I had been pleased with Robin's playing, Alan's ravished me.

"That's no very bad, Mr Stewart," said the rival, "but ye show a poor device in your Warblers."

"Me!" cried Alan, the blood starting to his face. "I give ye the lie."

"Do ye own yourself beaten at the pipes, then," said Robin, "that ye seek to change them for the sword?"

"And that's very well said, Mr Macgregor," returned Alan; "and in the meantime," (laying a strong accent on the words) "I take back the lie. I appeal to Duncan."

"Indeed, ye need appeal to naebody," said Robin. "Ye're a far better judge than any Maclaren in Balwhidder; for it's a God's truth that you're a very creditable piper for a Stewart. Hand me the pipes."

Alan did as he asked; and Robin proceeded to imitate and correct some part of Alan's variations, which it seemed that he remembered perfectly.

"Ay, ye have music," said Alan gloomily.

"And taking up the variations from the beginning, [Robin] worked them throughout to so new a purpose, with such ingenuity and sentiment . . . and so quick a knack in the grace notes, that I was amazed to hear him."
Young Folks Paper, July 10, 1886.

"And now be the judge yourself, Mr Stewart," said Robin; and taking up the variations from the beginning, he worked them throughout to so new a purpose, with such ingenuity and sentiment and with so odd a fancy and so quick a knack in the grace notes, that I was amazed to hear him.

As for Alan, his face grew dark and hot, and he sat and gnawed his fingers, like a man under some deep affront. "Enough!" he cried. "Ye can blow the pipes—make the most of that." And he made as if to rise.

But Robin only held out his hand as if to ask for silence, and struck into the slow measure of a pibroch. It was a fine piece of music in itself, and nobly played; but it seems besides it was a piece peculiar to the Appin Stewarts and a chief favourite with Alan. The first notes were scarce out, before there came a change in his face; when the time quickened, he seemed to grow restless in his seat; and long before that piece was at an end, the last signs of his anger died from him, and he had no thought but for the music.

"Robin Oig," he said, when it was done, "ye are a great piper. I am not fit to blow in the same kingdom with ye. Body of me! ye have mair music in your sporran than I have in my head! And though it still sticks in my mind that I could maybe show ye another of it with the cold steel, I warn ye before hand—it'll no be fair! It would go against my heart to haggle a man that can blow the pipes as you can!"

Thereupon that quarrel was made up; all night long the brose was going and the pipes changing hands; and the day had come pretty bright, and the three men were none the better for what they had been taking, before Robin as much as thought upon the road.

It was the last I saw of him, for I was in the low countries at the University of Leyden, when he stood his trial and was hanged in the Grassmarket. And I have told this at so great length, partly because it was the last incident of any note that befell me on the wrong side of the Highland Line, and partly because (as the man came to be hanged) it's in a manner history.

◆26

We Pass the Forth

The month, as I have said was not yet out, but it was already far through August and beautiful warm weather with every sign of an early and great harvest, when I was pronounced able for my journey. Our money was now run to so low an ebb that we must think first of all on speed; for if we came not soon to Mr Rankeillor's, or if when we came there he should fail to help me, we must surely starve. In Alan's view, besides, the hunt must have now greatly slackened; and the line of the Forth, and even Stirling Bridge, which is the main pass over that river, would be watched with little interest.

"It's a chief principle in military affairs," said he, "to go where ye are least expected. Forth is our trouble; ye ken the saying 'Forth bridles the wild Hielandman'? Well, if we seek to creep round about the head of that river and come down by Kippen or Balfron, it's just precisely there that they'll be looking to lay hands on us. But if we stave on straight to the auld Brig' of Stirling, I'll lay my sword they let us pass unchallenged."

The first night accordingly, we pushed to the house of a Maclaren in Strathire, a friend of Duncan's, where we slept the twenty first of the month, and whence we set forth again about the fall of night to make another easy stage. The twenty second we lay in a heather bush on a hillside in Uam Var, within view of a herd of deer; the happiest ten hours of sleep, in a fine, breathing sunshine and on bone-dry ground, that I have ever tasted. That night we struck Allan Water, and followed it down; and coming to the edge of the hills, saw the whole Carse of Stirling under-foot, as flat as a pancake, with the town and castle on a hill in the midst of it, and the moon shining on the Links of Forth.

"Now," said Alan, "I kennae if ye care, but ye're in your own land again. We passed the Highland Line in the first hour; and now if we could but pass yon crooked water, we might cast our bonnets in the air."

In Allan Water, near by where it falls into the Forth, we found a little sandy islet, overgrown with burdock, butterburr and the like low plants, that would just cover us if we lay flat. Here it was we made our camp, within plain view of Stirling Castle, whence we could hear the drums beat as some part of the garrison pa-raded. Shearers worked all day in a field on one side of the river, and we could hear the stones going on the hooks and the voices and even the words of the men talking. It behoved to lie close and keep silent. But the sand of the little isle was sun-warm, the green plants gave us shelter for our heads, we had food and drink in plenty; and to crown all, we were within sight of safety.

As soon as the shearers quit their work and the dusk began to fall, we waded ashore and struck for the Bridge of Stirling, keep-ing to the fields and under the field hedges.

The bridge is close under the castle hill, an old, high, narrow bridge with pinnacles along the parapet; and you may conceive with how much interest I looked upon it, not only as a place fa-mous in history, but as the very doors of salvation to Alan and myself. The moon was not yet up when we came there; a few lights showed along the front of the fortress, and lower down a few lighted windows in the town; but it was all mighty still, and there seemed to be no guard upon the passage.

I was for pushing straight across; but Alan was more wary.

"It *looks* unco' quiet," said he; "but for all that we'll lie down here cannily behind a dyke, and make sure."

So we lay for about quarter of an hour, whiles whispering, whiles lying still and hearing nothing earthly but the washing of the water on the piers. At last there came by an old, hobbling woman with a crutchstick; who first stopped a little, close to where we lay, and bemoaned herself and the long way she had travelled; and then set forth again up the steep spring of the bridge. The woman was so little, and the night still so dark, that we soon lost sight of her; only heard the sound of her steps, and her stick, and a cough that she had by fits, draw slowly farther away.

"She's bound to be across now," I whispered.

"Na," said Alan, "her foot still sounds boss upon the bridge."

And just then—"Who goes?" cried a voice, and we heard the butt of a musket rattle on the stones. I must suppose the sentry had been sleeping, so that had we tried, we might have passed unseen; but he was awake now, and the chance forfeited.

"This'll never do," said Alan. "This'll never, never do for us, David."

And without another word, he began to crawl away through the fields; and a little after, being well out of eye-shot, got to his feet again, and struck along a road that led to the eastward. I could not conceive what he was doing; and indeed I was so sharply cut by the dis-appointment, that I was little likely to be pleased with anything. A moment back, and I had seen myself knocking at Mr Rankeillor's door to claim my inheritance, like a hero in a ballad; and here was I back again, a wandering, hunted blackguard, on the wrong side of Forth.

"Well?" said I.

"Well," said Alan, "what would ye have? They're none such fools as I took them for. We have still the Forth to pass, Davie— weary fall the rains that fed and the hillsides that guided it!"

"And why go east?" said I.

"Ou, just upon the chance!" said he. "If we cannae pass the river, we'll have to see what we can do for the firth."

"There are fords upon the river, and none upon the firth," said I.

"To be sure there are fords, and a bridge forbye," quoth Alan; "and of what service, when they're watched?"

"Well," said I, "but a river can be swum."

"By them that have the skill of it," returned he; "but I have yet to hear that either you or me is much of a hand at that exercise; and for my own part, I swim like a stane."

"I'm not up to you in talking back, Alan," I said; "but I can see we're making bad worse. If it's hard to pass a river, it stands to reason it must be worse to pass a sea."

"But there's such a thing as a boat," says Alan—"or I'm the more deceived."

"Ay, and such a thing as money," says I. "But for us that have neither one nor other, they might just as well not have been invented."

"Ye think so?" said Alan.

"I do that," said I.

"David," said he, "ye're a man of small invention and less

faith. But let me set my wits upon the hone, and if I cannae beg, borrow nor yet steal a boat, I'll make one!"

"I think I see ye!" said I. "And what's more than all that: if ye pass a bridge, it can tell no tales; but if we pass the firth, there's the boat on the wrong side—somebody must have brought it—the countryside will all be in a bizz—"

"Man!" cried Alan, "if I make a boat, I'll make a body to take it back again! So deave me with no more of your nonsense, but walk—(for that's what you've got to do) and let Alan think for ye."

All night, then, we walked through the north side of the Carse under the high line of the Ochil mountains; and by Alloa and Clackmannan and Culross, all of which we avoided; and about ten in the morning, mighty hungry and tired, came to the little clachan of Limekilns. This is a place that sits near in by the waterside, and looks across the Hope to the town of the Queensferry. Smoke went up from both of these, and from other villages and farms upon all hands. The fields were being reaped; two ships lay anchored and boats were coming and going on the Hope. It was altogether a right pleasant sight to me; and I could not take my fill of gazing at these comfortable, green, cultivated hills and the busy people both of the field and sea.

For all that, there was Mr Rankeillor's house on the south shore, where I had no doubt wealth awaited me; and here was I upon the north, clad in poor enough attire of an outlandish fashion, with three silver shillings left to me of all my fortune, a price set upon my head, and an outlawed man for my sole company.

"O Alan!" said I, "to think of it! Over there, there's all that heart could want waiting me; and the birds go over, and the boats go over—all that please can go, but just me only! O man, but it's a heartbreak!"

In Limekilns we entered a small change-house, which we only knew to be a public by the wand over the door, and bought some bread and cheese from a good-looking lass that was the servant. This we carried with us in a bundle, meaning to sit and eat it in a bush of wood on the seashore, that we saw some third part of a mile in front. As we went, I kept looking across the water and sighing to myself; and though I took no heed of it, Alan had fallen into a muse. At last he stopped in the way.

"Did ye take heed of the lass we bought this of?" says he, tapping on the bread and cheese.

"To be sure," said I, "and a bonny lass she was."

"Ye thought that?" cries he. "Man David, that's good news!"

"In the name of all that's wonderful, why so?" says I. "What good can that do?"

"Well," said Alan, with one of his droll looks, "I was rather in hopes it would maybe get us that boat."

"If it were the other way about, it would be liker it," said I.

"That's all that you ken, ye see," said Alan. "I don't want the lass to fall in love with ye, I want her to be sorry for ye, David; to which end, there is no manner of need that she should take you for a beauty. Let me see" (looking at me curiously over) "I wish ye were a wee thing paler; but apart from that ye'll do fine for my purpose—ye have a fine, hang-dog, rag-and-tatter, clapper-maclaw kind of a look to ye, as if ye had stolen the coat from a potato-bogle. Come; right about, and back to the change-house for that boat of ours."

I followed him laughing.

"She drew quite near, and stood leaning with
her back on the next table."

Young Folks Paper, July 17, 1886.

"David Balfour," said he, "ye're a very funny gentleman by
your way of it, and this is a very funny employ for ye, no doubt.
For all that, if ye have any affection for my neck (to say nothing
of your own) ye will perhaps be kind enough to take this matter
gravely. I am going to do a bit of play-acting, the bottom ground
of which is just exactly as serious as the gallows for the pair of us.
So bear it, if ye please, in mind, and conduct yourself according."

"Well, well," said I, "have it as you will."

As we got near the clachan, he made me take his arm and hang upon it like one almost helpless with weariness; and by the time he pushed open the change-house door, he seemed to be half carrying me. The maid appeared surprised (as well she might be) at our speedy return; but Alan had no words to spare for her in explanation, helped me to a chair, called for a tass of brandy with which he fed me in little sips, and then breaking up the bread and cheese helped me to eat it like a nursery-lass: the whole with that grave, concerned, affectionate countenance, that might have imposed upon a judge. It was small wonder if the maid were taken with the picture we presented, of a poor, sick, overwrought lad and his most tender comrade. She drew quite near, and stood leaning with her back on the next table.

"What's like wrong with him?" said she at last.

Alan turned upon her, to my great wonder, with a kind of fury. "Wrong?" cries he. "He's walked more hundreds of miles than he has hairs upon his chin, and slept oftener in wet heather than dry sheets. Wrong, quo' she! Wrong enough, I would think! Wrong indeed!" And he kept grumbling to himself as he fed me, like a man ill-pleased.

"He's young for the like of that," said the maid.

"Ower young," said Alan, with his back to her.

"He would be better riding," says she.

"And where would I get a horse for him?" cried Alan, turning on her with the same appearance of fury. "Would ye have me steal?"

I thought this roughness would have sent her off in dudgeon, as indeed it closed her mouth for the time. But my companion knew very well what he was doing; and for as simple as he was in some things of life, he had a great fund of roguishness in such affairs as these.

"Ye neednae tell me," she said at last—"ye're gentry."

"Well," said Alan, softened for a little (I believe against his will) by the artless compliment, "and suppose we were? did ever you hear that gentrice put money in folks' pockets?"

She sighed at this, as if she were herself some disinherited great lady. "No," says she, "that's true indeed!"

I was all this while chafing at the part I played, and sitting tongue-tied between shame and merriment; but somehow at this I could hold in no longer, and bade Alan let me be, for I was better already. My voice stuck in my throat, for I ever hated to take part in lies; but my very embarrassment helped on the plot, for the lass no doubt set down my husky voice to sickness and fatigue.

"Has he nae friends?" said she, in a tearful voice.

"That has he so!" cried Alan—"if we could but win to them! —friends and rich friends, beds to lie in, food to eat, doctors to see to him—and here he must tramp in the dubs and sleep in the heather like a beggarman."

"And why that?" says the lass.

"My dear," says Alan, "I cannae very safely say; but I'll tell ye what I'll do instead," says he, "I'll whistle ye a bit tune." And with that he leaned pretty far over the table, and in a mere breath of a whistle but with a wonderful pretty sentiment, gave her a few bars of "Charlie is my darling."

"Wheesht," says she, and looked over her shoulder to the door.

"That's it," said Alan.

"And him so young!" cries the lass.

"He's old enough to——" and Alan struck his forefinger on the back part of his neck, meaning that I was old enough to lose my head.

"It would be a black shame," she cried, flushing high.

"It's what will be though," said Alan, "unless we manage the better."

At this the lass turned and ran out of that part of the house, leaving us alone together, Alan in high good humour at the furthering of his schemes and I in bitter dudgeon at being called a Jacobite and treated like a child.

"Alan," I cried, "I can stand no more of this."

"Ye'll have to sit it then, Davie," said he. "For if ye upset the pot now, ye may scrape your own life out of the fire, but Alan Breck is a dead man."

This was so true that I could only groan; and even my groan served Alan's purpose, for it was overheard by the lass as she came flying in again with a dish of white puddings and a bottle of strong ale.

"Poor lamb!" says she, and had no sooner set the meat before us, than she touched me on the shoulder with a little friendly touch, as much as to bid me cheer up. Then she told us to fall to, and there would be no more to pay; for the inn was her own, or at least her father's, and he was gone for the day to Pittencrieff. We waited for no second bidding, for bread and cheese is but cold comfort, and the puddings smelt excellently well; and while we sat and ate, she took up that same place by the next table, looking on, and thinking, and frowning to herself, and drawing the string of her apron through her hand.

"I'm thinking ye rather have a long tongue," she said at last to Alan.

"Ay," said Alan; "but ye see I ken the folk I speak to."

"I would never betray ye," said she, "if ye mean that."

"No," said he, "ye're not that kind. But I'll tell ye what ye would do: ye would help."

"I couldnae," said she, shaking her head. "Na, I couldnae."

"No," said he, "but if ye could?"

She answered him nothing.

"Look here, my lass," said Alan, "there are boats in the Kingdom of Fife, for I saw two (no less) upon the beach, as I came in by your town's end. Now if we could have the use of a boat to pass under cloud of night into Lothian, and some secret, decent kind of man to bring that boat back again and keep his counsel, there would be two souls saved—mine, to all likelihood—his, to a dead surety. If we lack that boat, we have but three shillings left in this wide world; and where to go, and how to do, and what other place there is for us except the chains of a gibbet—I give you my naked word, I kenna! Shall we go wanting, lassie? Are ye to lie in your warm bed and think upon us, when the wind gowls in the chimney and the rain tirls on the roof? Are ye to eat your meat by the cheeks of a red fire, and think upon this poor sick lad of mine, biting his finger ends on a blae muir for cauld and hunger? Sick or sound, he must aye be moving; with the death grapple at his throat he must aye be trailing in the rain on the lang roads; and when he gants his last on a rickle of cauld stanes, there will be nae friends near him but only me and God."

At this appeal, I could see the lass was in great trouble of mind, being tempted to help us, and yet in some fear she might be helping malefactors; and so now I determined to step in myself and to allay her scruples with a portion of the truth.

"Did you ever hear," said I, "of Mr Rankeillor of the Queensferry?"

"Rankeillor the writer!" said she. "I daursay that!"

"Well," said I, "it's to his door that I am bound, so you may judge by that if I am an ill-doer; and I will tell you more, that though I am indeed, by a dreadful error, in some peril of my life, King George has no truer friend in all Scotland than myself."

Her face cleared up mightily at this, although Alan's darkened.

"That's more than I would ask," said she. "Mr Rankeillor is a kennt man. Finish your bit meat, get you clear of the Clachan as soon as maybe, lie close in the bit wood there is on the sea beach, and this very night I'll find some means to put you over."

At this we waited for no more, but shook hands with her upon the bargain, made short work of the puddings, and set forth again from Limekilns as far as to the wood. It was a small piece of perhaps a score of elders and hawthorns, and a few young ashes not thick enough to veil us from passers-by upon the road or beach. Here we must lie, however, making the best of the brave warm weather and the good hopes we now had of a deliverance, and planning more particularly what remained for us to do.

We had but one trouble all day; when a strolling piper came and sat in the same wood with us: a red-nosed, blear-eyed, drunken dog, with a great bottle of whiskey in his pocket, and a long story of wrongs that had been done him by all sorts of persons from the Lord President of the Court of Session who had denied him justice, down to the Baillies of Inverkeithing who had given him more of it than he desired. It was impossible but he should conceive some suspicion of two men lying all day concealed in a thicket and having no business to alledge. As long as he stayed there, he kept us in hot water with prying questions; and after he was gone, as he was a man not very likely to hold his tongue, we were in the greater impatience to be gone ourselves.

The day came to an end with the same brightness; the night fell quiet and clear; lights came out in houses and hamlets, and then, one after another, began to be put out; but it was past eleven, and we were long since strangely tortured with anxieties, before we heard the grinding of oars upon the rowing pins. At that, we looked out and saw the lass herself coming rowing to us in a boat. She had trusted no one with our affairs, not even her sweetheart, if she had one; but as soon as her father was asleep, had left the house by a window, stolen a neighbor's boat, and come to our assistance single-handed.

I was abashed how to find expression for my thanks; but she was no less abashed at the thought of hearing them; begged us to lose no time and to hold our peace, saying (very properly) that the heart of our matter was in haste and silence; and so, what with one thing and another, she had set us on the Lothian shore not far from Carriden, had shaken hands with us, and was out again at sea and rowing for Limekilns, before there was one word said either of her service or our gratitude.

Even after she was gone, we had nothing to say, as indeed nothing was enough for such a kindness. Only Alan stood a great while upon the shore shaking his head.

"It is a very fine lass," he said at last. "David, it is a very fine lass." And a matter of an hour later, as we were lying in a den on the seashore and I had been already dozing, he broke out again in commendations of her character. For my part, I could say nothing; she was so simple a creature, that my heart smote me both with remorse and fear; remorse, because we had traded upon her innocence and fear lest we should have anyway involved her in the dangers of our situation.

27

I Come to Mr Rankeillor

The next day was to be the touchstone of my fortunes. I was come apparently to an end of dangerous adventures, but perhaps only to the beginning of dis-appointments more difficult to bear. And as it drew nearer to the hour of trial, I found the less courage in my heart.

It was agreed that Alan should fend for himself until sunset; but as soon as it began to grow dark, he should lie in the fields by the roadside near to Newhalls, and stir for naught until he heard me whistling. At first I proposed I should give him for a signal the *Bonnie House of Airlie* which was a favourite of mine; but he objected that as the piece was very commonly known, any ploughman might whistle it by accident; and taught me instead a little fragment of a Highland air, which has run in my head from that day to this, and will likely run in my head when I lie dying. Every time it comes to me, it takes me off to that last day of my uncertainty, with Alan sitting up in the bottom of the den, whistling and beating the measure with a finger, and the gray of the dawn coming on his face.

I was in the long street of Queensferry before the sun was up. It was a fairly built burgh, the houses of good stone, many slated; the town hall not so fine, I thought, as that of Peebles nor yet the

street so noble; but take it altogether, it put me to shame for my
foul tatters.

As the morning went on, and the fires began to be kindled,
and the windows to open, and the people to appear out of the
houses, my concern and despondency grew ever the blacker. I
saw now that I had no grounds to stand upon; and no clear proof
of my rights, nor so much as of my own identity. If it was all a
bubble, I was indeed sorely cheated and left in a sore pass. Even
if things were as I conceived, it would in all likelihood take time
to establish my contentions; and what time had I to spare with
three shillings in my pocket, and a condemned, hunted man
upon my hands to ship out of the country? Truly, if my hope
broke with me, it might come to the gallows yet for both of us.
And as I continued to walk up and down, and saw people looking
askance at me upon the street or out of windows, and nudging
or speaking one to another with smiles, I began to take a fresh
apprehension: that it might be no easy matter even to come to
speech of the lawyer, far less to convince him of my story.

For the life of me, I could not muster up the courage to address
any of these reputable burghers; I thought shame even to speak
with them in such a pickle of rags and dirt; and if I had asked for
the house of such a man as Mr Rankeillor, I supposed they would
have burst out laughing in my face. So I went up and down, and
through the street, and down to the harbourside, like a dog that
has lost its master, with a strange gnawing in my inwards and
every now and then a movement of despair. It grew to be high
day at last, perhaps nine in the forenoon; and I was worn with
these wanderings, and chanced to have stopped in front of a very
good house on the landward side, a house with beautiful, clear,
glass windows, flowering knots upon the sills, the walls new-

harled, and a chase-dog sitting yawning on the step like one that was at home. Well, I was even envying this dumb brute, when the door fell open and there issued forth a little, shrewd, ruddy, kindly, consequential man in a fair wig and spectacles. I was in such a plight that no one set eyes on me once, but he looked at me again; and this gentleman, as it proved, was so much struck with my poor appearance, that he came straight up to me and asked me what I did.

I told him I was come to the Queensferry on business and taking heart of grace, asked him to direct me to the house of Mr Rankeillor.

"Why," said he, "that is his house that I have just come out of; and for a rather singular chance, I am that very man."

"Then, sir," said I, "I have to beg the favour of an interview."

"I do not know your name," said he, "nor yet your face."

"My name is David Balfour," said I.

"David Balfour?" he repeated, in rather a high tone, like one surprised. "And where have you come from, Mr David Balfour?" he asked, looking me pretty drily in the face.

"I have come from a great many strange places, sir," said I; "but I think it would be as well to tell you where and how in a more private manner."

He seemed to muse awhile, holding his lip in his hand, and looking now at me and now upon the causeway of the street.

"Yes," says he, "that will be the best, no doubt." And he led me back with him into his house, cried out to some one whom I could not see that he would be engaged all morning, and brought me into a little dusty chamber full of books and documents. Here he sate down, and bade me be seated; though I thought he looked a little ruefully from his clean chair to my muddy rags. "And now," says he, "if you have any business, pray be brief and come swiftly to the point. *Nec germino bellum Trojanum orditur ab ovo*— do you understand that?" says he, with a keen look.

"I will even do as Horace says, sir," I answered, smiling, "and carry you *in medias res*." He nodded as if he was well pleased, and indeed his scrap of latin had been set to test me. For all that, and though I was somewhat encouraged, the blood came in my face when I added: "I have reason to believe myself some rights on the estate of Shaws."

He got a paper book out of a drawer and set it before him open. "Well?" said he.

But I had fired my bolt and sat speechless.

"Come, come, Mr Balfour," said he, "you must continue. Where were you born?"

"In Essendean, sir," said I, "the year 1734, the 12th of March."

He seemed to follow this statement in his paper book; but what that meant, I knew not. "Your father and mother?" said he.

"My father was Alexander Balfour, schoolmaster of that place," said I, "and my mother Grace Pitarrow; I think her people were from Angus."

"Have you any papers proving your identity?" asked Mr Rankeillor.

"No, sir," said I, "but they are in the hands of Mr Campbell the minister and could be readily produced. Mr Campbell, too, would give me his word; and for that matter, I do not think my uncle would deny me."

"Meaning Mr Ebenezer Balfour?" says he.

"The same," said I.

"Whom you have seen?" he asked.

"By whom I was received into his own house," I answered.

"Did you ever meet a man of the name of Hoseason?" asked Mr Rankeillor.

"I did so, sir, for my sins," said I; "for it was by his means and the procurement of my uncle, that I was kidnapped within sight of this town, carried to sea, suffered shipwreck and a hundred other hardships, and stand before you today in this poor accoutrement."

"You say you were shipwrecked," said Rankeillor: "where was that?"

"Off the south end of the isle of Mull," said I. "The name of the isle on which I was cast up is the Island Earraid."

"Ah!" says he smiling, "you are deeper than me in the geography. But so far, I may tell you, this agrees pretty exactly with other informations that I hold. But you say you were kidnapped: in what sense?"

"In the plain meaning of the word, sir," said I. "I was upon my way to your house, when I was trepanned on board the brig, cruelly struck down, thrown below, and knew no more of anything till we were far at sea. I was destined for the plantations; a fate that, in God's providence, I have escaped."

"The brig was lost on June the 27th," says he, looking in his book, "and we are now at August the 24th. Here is a considerable hiatus, Mr Balfour, of near upon two months. It has already caused a vast amount of trouble to your friends; and I own I shall not be very well contented until it is set right."

"Indeed, sir," said I, "these months are very easily filled up; but yet before I told my story, I would be glad to know that I was talking to a friend."

"This is to argue in a circle," said the lawyer. "I cannot be convinced till I have heard you. I cannot be your friend till I am properly informed. If you were more trustful, it would better befit your time of life. And you know, Mr Balfour, we have a proverb in the country that Evil doers are aye evil dreaders."

"You are not to forget, sir," said I, "that I have already suffered by my trustfulness; and was shipped off to be a slave by the very man that (if I rightly understand) is your employer."

All this while, I had been gaining ground with Mr Rankeillor, and in proportion as I gained ground, gaining confidence. But at this sally, which I made with something of a smile myself, he fairly laughed aloud.

"No, no," said he, "it is not so bad as that. *Fui, non sum.* I *was* indeed your uncle's man of business; but while you (*inberbus juvenis custode remoto*) were gallivanting in the west, a good deal of water has run under the bridges; and if your ears did not sing, it was not for lack of being talked about. On the very day of your sea disaster, Mr Campbell stalked into my office, demanding you from all the winds. I had never heard of your existence; but I had known your father; and from matters in my competence (to be touched upon here after) I was disposed to fear the worst. Mr Ebenezer admitted having seen you; declared (what seemed improbable) that he had given you considerable sums; and that you had started for the continent of Europe, intending to fulfil your education, which was probable and praiseworthy. Interrogated how you had come to send no word to Mr Campbell, he deponed that you had expressed a great desire to break with your past life. Further interrogated where you now were, protested ignorance but believed you were in Leyden. That is a close sum of his replies. I am not exactly sure that any one believed him," continued Mr Rankeillor with a smile; "and in particular he so much disrelished some expressions of mine that (in a word) he showed me to the door. We were then at a full stand; for whatever shrewd suspicions we might entertain, we had no shadow of probation. In the very article, comes Captain Hoseason with the story of your drowning; whereupon all fell through; with no consequences but concern to Mr Campbell, injury to my pocket, and another blot upon your uncle's character, which could very ill afford it. And now, Mr Balfour," said he, "you understand the whole process of these matters, and can judge for yourself to what extent I may be trusted."

Indeed he was more pedantic than I can represent him, and placed more scraps of latin in his speech; but it was all uttered with a fine geniality of eye and manner which went far to conquer my distrust. Moreover I could see he now treated me as I was myself beyond a doubt; so that first point of my identity seemed fully granted.

"Sir," said I, "if I tell you my story, I must commit a friend's life to your dis-cretion. Pass me your word it shall be sacred; and for what touches myself, I will ask no better guarantee than just your face."

He passed me his word very seriously. "But," said he, "these are rather alarming prolocutions; and if there are in your story any little jostles to the law, I would beg you to bear in mind that I am a lawyer, and pass lightly."

Thereupon I told him my story from the first, he listening with his spectacles thrust up and his eyes closed, so that I sometimes feared he was asleep. But no such matter! he heard every word (as I found afterward) with such quickness of hearing and precision of memory as often surprised me. Even strange, outlandish Gaelic names, heard for that time only, he remembered and would remind me of, years after. Yet when I called Alan Breck in full, we had an odd scene. The name of Alan had of course rung through Scotland, with the news of the Appin murder and the offer of the reward; and it had no sooner escaped me than the lawyer moved in his seat and opened his eyes.

"I would name no unnecessary names, Mr Balfour," said he:

"above all of Highlanders, many of whom are obnoxious to the law."

"Well, it might have been better not," said I; "but since I have let it slip, I may as well continue."

"Not at all," said Mr Rankeillor. "I am somewhat dull of hearing, as you may have remarked; and I am far from sure I caught the name exactly. We will call your friend, if you please, Mr Thomson—that there may be no reflections. And in future, I would take some such way with any Highlander that you may have to mention—dead or alive."

By this, I saw he must have heard the name all too clearly, and had already guessed I might be coming to the murder. If he chose to play this part of ignorance, it was no matter of mine; so I smiled, said it was no very Highland sounding name, and consented. Through all the rest of my story Alan was Mr Thomson; which amused me the more, as it was a piece of policy after his own heart. James Stewart, in like manner, was mentioned under the style of Mr Thomson's kinsman; Colin Campbell passed as a Mr Glen; and to Cluny, when I came to that part of my tale, I gave the name of "Mr Jameson, a Highland chief." It was truly the most open farce, and I wondered that the lawyer should care to keep it up; but after all it was quite in the taste of that age, when there were two parties in the state, and quiet persons, with no very high opinions of their own, sought out every cranny to avoid offence to either.

"Well, well," said the lawyer, when I had quite done, "this is a great epic, a great Odyssey of yours. You must tell it, sir, in a sound latinity when your scholarship is riper; or in English if you please, though for my part I prefer the stronger tongue. You have rolled much; *quae regio in terris*—what parish in Scotland (to make a homely translation) has not been filled with your wan-

derings? You have shown besides a singular aptitude for getting into false positions; and, yes, upon the whole, for behaving
well in them. This Mr Thomson seems to me a gentleman of
some choice qualities, though perhaps a trifle bloody-minded. It
would please me none the worse, if (with all his merits) he were
soused in the North Sea; for the man, Mr Balfour, is a sore embarrassment. But you are doubtless quite right to adhere to him;
indubitably, he adhered to you. *It comes*—we may say—he was
your true companion; nor less, *paribus curis vestigia figit*, for I daresay you would both take an orra thought upon the gallows. Well,
well, these days are fortunately by; and I think (speaking humanly) that you are near the end of your troubles."

As he thus moralised on my adventures, he looked upon me
with so much humor and benignity that I could scarce contain
my satisfaction. I had been so long wandering with lawless
people, and making my bed upon the hills and under the bare
sky, that to sit once more in a clean, covered house and to talk
amicably with a gentleman in broadcloth, seemed a mighty ele-
vation. Even as I thought so, my eye fell on my unseemly tatters,
and I was once more plunged in confusion. But the lawyer saw
and understood me. He rose, called over the stair to lay another
plate for Mr Balfour would stay to dinner, and led me into a bedroom in the upper part of the house. Here he set before me water
and soap and a comb; and laid out some clothes that belonged
to his son; and here, with another apposite tag, he left me to my
toilet.

28

I Go in Quest of My Inheritance

I made what change I could in my appearance; and blythe was I to look in the glass and find the beggarman a thing of the past, and David Balfour come to life again. And yet I was ashamed of the change too, and above all, of the borrowed clothes. When I had done, Mr Rankeillor caught me on the stair, made me his compliments, and had me again into the cabinet.

"Sit ye down, Mr David," said he; "and now that you are looking a little more like yourself, let me see if I can find you any news. You will be wondering, no doubt, about your father and your uncle? To be sure, it is a singular tale; and the explanation is one that I blush to have to offer you. For," says he, really with embarrassment, "the matter hinges on a love affair."

"Truly," said I, "I cannot very well join that notion with my uncle."

"But your uncle, Mr David, was not always old," replied the lawyer, "and what may perhaps surprise you more, not always ugly. He had a fine, gallant air; people stood in their doors to look after him, as he went by upon a mettle horse. I have seen it with these eyes, and I ingenuously confess, not altogether without envy; for I was a plain lad myself and a plain man's son; and in those days, it was a case of *Odi te, qui bellus es, Sabelle.*"

"It sounds like a dream," said I.

"Ay, ay," said the lawyer, "that is how it is with youth and age. Nor was that all, but he had a spirit of his own that seemed to promise great things in the future. In 1715, what must he do but run away to join the rebels? It was your father that pursued him, found him in a ditch, and brought him back *multum gementem*; to the mirth of the whole country. However, *majora canamus*—the two lads fell in love, and that with the same lady. Mr Ebenezer, who was the admired and the beloved, and the spoiled one, made, no doubt, mighty certain of the victory; and when he found he had deceived himself, screamed like a peacock. The whole country heard of it; now he lay sick at home, with his silly family standing round the bed in tears; now he rode from public house to public house and shouted his sorrows into the lug of Tom, Dick and Harry. Your father, Mr David, was a kind gentleman; but he was weak, dolefully weak; took all this folly with a long countenance; and one day—by your leave!—resigned the lady. She was no such fool, however; it's from her you must inherit your excellent good sense; and she refused to be bandied from one to another. Both got upon their knees to her; and the upshot of the matter for that while was that she showed both of them the door. That was in August; dear me! the same year I came from college. The scene must have been highly farcical."

I thought myself it was a silly business, but I could not forget my father had a hand in it. "Surely, sir, it had some note of tragedy," said I.

"Why, no, sir, not at all," returned the lawyer. "For tragedy implies some ponderable matter in dispute, some *dignus vindice nodus*; and this piece of work was all about the petulance of a young ass that had been spoiled, and wanted nothing so much

as to be tied up and soundly belted. However, that was not your
father's view; and the end of it was, that from concession to concession on your father's part, and from one height to another of
squalling, sentimental selfishness upon your uncle's, they came
at last to drive a sort of bargain, from whose ill-results you have
recently been smarting. The one man took the lady, the other
the estate. Now, Mr David, they talk a great deal of charity and
generosity; but in this disputable state of life, I often think the
happiest consequences seem to flow when a gentleman consults
his lawyer and takes all the law allows him. Anyhow, this piece
of Quixotry upon your father's part, as it was unjust in itself, has
brought forth a monstrous family of injustices. Your father and
mother lived and died poor folk; you were poorly reared; and in
the meanwhile, what a time it has been for the tenants on the
estate of Shaws! And I might add (if it was a matter I cared much
about) what a time for Mr Ebenezer!"

"And yet that is certainly the strangest part of all," said I, "that
a man's nature should thus change."

"True," said Mr Rankeillor. "And yet I imagine it was natural
enough. He could not think that he had played a handsome part.
Those who knew the story gave him the cold shoulder; those who
knew it not, seeing one brother disappear, and the other succeed
in the estate, raised a cry of murder; so that upon all sides, he
found himself evited. Money was all he got by his bargain; well,
he came to think the more of money. He was selfish when he was
young; he is selfish now that he is old; and the latter end of all
these pretty manners and fine feelings you have seen for yourself."

"Well, sir," said I, "and in all this, what is my position?"

"The estate is yours, beyond a doubt," replied the lawyer. "It matters nothing what your father signed; you are the heir of entail. But your uncle is a man to fight the indefensible; and it would be likely your identity that he would call in question. A lawsuit is always expensive, and a family lawsuit always scandalous; besides which, if any of your doings with your friend Mr Thomson were to come out, we might find that we had burned our fingers. The kidnapping, to be sure, would be a court card upon our side, if we could only prove it. But it may be difficult to prove; and my advice (upon the whole) is to make a very easy bargain with your uncle, perhaps even leaving him at Shaws, where he has taken root for a quarter of a century, and contenting yourself in the meanwhile with a fair provision."

I told him I was very willing to be easy, and that to carry family concerns before the public was a step from which I was naturally much averse. In the meantime (thinking to myself) I began to see the outlines of that scheme on which we afterwards acted.

"The great affair," I asked, "is to bring home to him the kidnapping?"

"Surely," said Mr Rankeillor, "and if possible, out of court. For mark you here, Mr David: we could no doubt find some men of the *Covenant* who would swear to your reclusion; but once they were in the box, we could no longer check their testimony, and some word of your friend Mr Thomson must certainly crop out: which (from what you have let fall) I cannot think to be desirable."

"Well, sir," said I, "here is my way of it." And I opened my plot to him.

"But this would seem to involve my meeting the man Thomson?" says he, when I had done.

"I think so, indeed, sir," said I.

"Dear doctor!" cries he, rubbing his brow. "Dear doctor! No, Mr David, I am afraid your scheme is inadmissible. I say nothing against your friend Mr Thomson; I know nothing against him; and if I did——mark this, Mr David!——it would be my duty to lay hands on him. Now I put it to you: is it wise to meet? He may have matters to his charge. He may not have told you all. His name may not be even Thomson!" cries the lawyer, twinkling; "for some of these fellows will pick up names by the roadside as another would gather haws."

"You must be the judge, sir," said I.

But it was clear my plan had taken hold upon his fancy, for he kept musing to himself till we were called to dinner and the company of Mrs Rankeillor; and that lady had scarce left us again to ourselves and a bottle of wine, ere he was back harping on my proposal. When and where was I to meet my friend Mr Thomson; was I sure of Mr T's discretion; supposing we could catch the old fox trimming, would I consent to such and such a term of an agreement——these and the like questions he kept asking at long intervals, while he thoughtfully rolled his wine upon his tongue. When I had answered all of them, seemingly to his contentment, he fell into a still deeper muse, even the claret being now forgotten. Then he got a sheet of paper and a pencil, and set to work writing and weighing every word; and at last touched a bell and had his clerk into the chamber.

"Torrance," said he, "I must have this written out fair against tonight; and when it is done, you will be so kind as put on your hat and be ready to come along with this gentleman and me, for you will probably be wanted as a witness."

"What! sir," cried I, as soon as the clerk was gone, "are you to venture it?"

"Why, so it would appear," says he, filling his glass. "But let us speak no more of business. The very sight of Torrance brings in my head a little, droll matter of some years ago, when I had made a tryst with the poor oaf at the Cross of Edinburgh. Each had gone his proper errand; and when it came four o'clock, Torrance had been taking a glass and did not know his master, and I, who had forgot my spectacles, was so blind without them, that I give you my word I did not know my own clerk." And thereupon he laughed heartily.

I said it was an odd chance, and smiled out of politeness; but what held me all the afternoon in wonder, he kept returning and dwelling on this story, and telling it again with fresh details and laughter; so that I began at last to be quite put out of countenance and feel ashamed for my friend's folly.

Towards the time I had appointed with Alan, we set out from the house, Mr Rankeillor and I arm in arm, and Torrance following behind, with the deed in his pocket and a covered basket in his hand. All through the town, the lawyer was bowing right and left, and continually being buttonholed by gentlemen on matters of burgh or private business; and I could see he was one greatly looked up to in the country. At last we were clear of the houses, and began to go along the side of the haven and towards the Hawes Inn and the Ferry pier, the scene of my misfortune. I could not look upon the place without emotion, recalling how many that had been there with me that day were now no more: Ransome taken, I could hope, from the evil to come; Shuan passed where I dared not follow him; and the poor souls that had gone down with the brig in her last plunge. All these, and the brig herself, I had outlived, and come through these hardships and fearful perils without scathe. My only thought should have been of gratitude; and yet I could not behold the place without sorrow for others and a chill of recollected fear.

I was so thinking when, upon a sudden, Mr Rankeillor cried out, clapped his hand to his pockets, and began to laugh.

"Why," he cries, "if this be not a farcical adventure! After all that I said, I have forgot my glasses!"

At that, of course, I understood the purpose of his anecdote, and knew that if he had left his spectacles at home, it had been done on purpose, so that he might have the benefit of Alan's help without the awkwardness of recognizing him. And indeed it was well thought upon; for now (suppose things to go the very worst) how could Rankeillor swear to my friend's identity, or how be made to bear damaging evidence against myself? For all that, he had been a long while of finding out his want, and had spoken to and recognized a good few persons as we came through the town; and I had little doubt myself that he saw reasonably well.

As soon as we were past the Hawes (where I recognized the landlord smoking his pipe in the door, and was amazed to see him look no older), Mr Rankeillor changed the order of march, walking behind with Torrance, and sending me forward in the manner of a scout. I went up the hill, whistling from time to time my Gaelic air; and at length I had the pleasure to hear it answered and to see Alan rise from behind a bush. He was somewhat dashed in spirits, having passed a long day alone skulking in the country, and made but a poor meal in an alehouse near Dundas. But at the mere sight of my clothes, he began to brighten up; and as soon as I had told him in what a forward state our matters were, and the part I looked to him to play in what remained, he sprang into a new man.

"And that is a very good notion of yours," says he; "and I dare to say that you could lay your hands upon no better man to put it through than Alan Breck. It is not a thing (mark ye) that any one could do, but takes a gentleman of penetration. But it sticks in my head your lawyer-man will be somewhat wearying to see me," says Alan.

Accordingly I cried and waved on Mr Rankeillor, who came up alone and was presented to my friend, Mr Thomson.

"Mr Thomson, I am pleased to meet you," said he. "But I have forgotten my glasses; and our friend Mr David, here" (clapping me on the shoulder), "will tell you that I am little better than blind, and that you must not be surprised if I pass you by to-morrow."

This he said, thinking that Alan would be pleased; but the Highlandman's vanity was ready to startle at a less matter than that.

"Why, sir," says he, stiffly, "I would say it mattered the less as we are met here for a particular end, to see justice done to Mr Balfour: and by what I can see, not very likely to have much else in common. But I accept your apology, which was a very proper one to make."

"And that is more than I could look for, Mr Thomson," said Rankeillor, heartily. "And now as you and I are the chief actors in this enterprise, I think we should come into a nice agreement; to which end, I propose that you should lend me your arm, for (what with the dusk and the want of my glasses) I am not very clear as to the path; and as for you, Mr David, you will find Torrance a pleasant kind of body to speak with. Only let me remind you, it's quite needless he should hear more of your adventures or those of—ahem—Mr Thomson."

Accordingly these two went on ahead in very close talk, and Torrance and I brought up the rear.

Night was quite come when we came in view of the house of Shaws. Ten had been gone some time; it was dark and mild, with a pleasant, rustling wind in the southwest that covered the sound of our approach; and as we drew near we saw no glimmer of light in any portion of the building. It seemed my uncle was already in bed, which was indeed the best thing for our arrangements. We made our last whispered consultations some fifty yards away; and then the lawyer and Torrance and I crept quietly up and crouched down beside the corner of the house; and as soon as we were in our places, Alan strode to the door without concealment and began to knock.

29

I Come into My Kingdom

For some time Alan volleyed upon the door, and his knock-ing only roused the echoes of the house and neighbour-hood. At last, however, I could hear the noise of a window gently thrust up, and knew that my uncle had come to his observatory. By what light there was, he would see Alan standing, like a dark shadow, on the steps; the three witnesses were hidden quite out of his view; so that there was nothing to alarm an honest man in his own house. For all that, he studied his visitor awhile in si-lence, and when he spoke, his voice had a quaver of misgiving.

"What's this?" says he. "This is nae kind of time of night for decent folk; and I hae nae trokings wi' night-hawks. What brings ye here? I have a blunderbush."

"Is that yoursel', Mr Balfour?" returned Alan, stepping back and looking up into the darkness. "Have a care of that blunder-buss; they're nasty things to burst."

"What brings ye here? and whae are ye?" says my uncle, angrily.

"I have no manner of inclination to rowt out my name to the countryside," said Alan; "but what brings me here is another story, being more of your affairs than mine; and if ye're sure it's what ye would like, I'll set it to a tune and sing it to you."

"And what is't?" asked my uncle.

"David," says Alan.

"What was that?" cried my uncle, in a mighty changed voice.

"Shall I give ye the rest of the name, then?" said Alan.

There was a pause; and then, "I'm thinking I'll better let ye in," says my uncle, doubtfully.

"I daresay that," said Alan; "but the point is, Would I go? Now I will tell you what I am thinking. I am thinking that it is here upon this doorstep that we must confer upon this business; and it shall be here or nowhere at all whatever; for I would have you to understand that I am as stiffnecked as yoursel', and a gentleman of better family."

This change of note disconcerted Ebenezer; he was a little while digesting it; and then says he, "Weel, weel, what must be must," and shut the window. But it took him a long time to get down stairs, and a still longer to undo the fastenings, repenting (I daresay) and taken with fresh claps of fear at every second step and every bolt and bar. At last, however, we heard the creak of the hinges, and it seems my uncle slipped gingerly out and (seeing that Alan had stepped back a pace or two) sate him down on the top doorstep, with the blunderbuss ready in his hands.

"And now," says he, "mind I have my blunderbush, and if ye take a step nearer ye're as good as deid."

"And a very civil speech," says Alan, "to be sure."

"Na," says my uncle, "but this is no a very chancy kind of a proceeding, and I'm bound to be prepared. And now that we understand each other, ye'll can name your business."

"Why," says Alan, "you that are a man of so much understanding, will doubtless have perceived that I am a Hieland gentleman. My name has nae business in my story; but the country of my friends is no very far from the Isle of Mull, of which ye will have heard. It seems there was a ship lost in those parts; and the next day a gentleman of my family was seeking wreck-wood for his fire along the sands, when he came upon a lad that was half drowned. Well, he brought him to; and he and some other gentlemen took and clapped him in an auld, ruined castle, where from that day to this he has been a great expense to my friends. My friends are a wee wild-like, and not so particular about the law as some that I could name; and finding that the lad owned some decent folk, and was your born nephew, Mr Balfour, they asked me to give ye a bit call and to confer upon the matter. And I may tell ye at the off-go, unless we can agree upon some terms, ye are little likely to set eyes upon him. For my friends," added Alan, simply, "are no very well off."

My uncle cleared his throat. "I'm no very caring," said he. "He wasnae a good lad at the best of it, and I've nae call to interfere."

"Ay, ay," said Alan, "I see what ye would be at: pretending ye don't care, to make the ransome smaller."

"Na," said my uncle, "it's the mere truth. I take nae manner of interest in the lad, and I'll pay nae ransome, and ye can make a kirk and a mill of him for what I care."

"Hoot, sir!" says Alan. "Blood's thicker than water, in the deil's name! Ye cannae desert your brother's son for the fair shame of it; and if ye did, and it came to be kennt, ye wouldnae be very popular in your countryside, or I'm the more deceived."

"I'm no just very popular the way it is," returned Ebenezer; "and I dinnae see how it would come to be kennt. No by me, onyway; nor yet by you or your friends. So that's idle talk, my buckie," says he.

"Then it'll have to be David that tells it," said Alan.

"How that?" says my uncle, sharply.

"Ou, just this way," says Alan. "My friends would doubtless keep your nephew as long as there was any likelihood of siller to be made of it; but if there was nane, I am clearly of opinion they would let him gang where he pleased, and be damned to him!"

"Ay, but I'm no very caring about that either," said my uncle. "I wouldnae be muckle made up with that."

"I was thinking that," said Alan.

"And what for why?" asked Ebenezer.

"Why, Mr Balfour," replied Alan, "by all that I could hear, there were two ways of it: either ye liked David and would pay to get him back; or else ye had very good reasons for not wanting him, and would pay for us to keep him. It seems it's not the first; well, then, it's the second; and blythe am I to ken it, for it should be a pretty penny in my pocket and the pockets of my friends."

"I dinnae follow ye there," said my uncle.

"No?" said Alan. "Well, see here: you dinnae want the lad back; well, what do ye want done with him, and how much will ye pay?"

My uncle made no answer, but shifted uneasily on his seat.

"Come, sir," cried Alan. "I would have ye to ken that I am a gentleman; I bear a king's name; I am nae rider to kick my shanks at your hall door. Either give me an answer in civility, and that out of hand; or by the top of Glencoe, I will ram three feet of iron through your vitals."

"Eh, man," cried my uncle, scrambling to his feet, "give me a meenit! What's like wrong with ye? I'm just a plain man, and nae dancing master; and I'm trying to be as ceevil as it's morally possible. As for that wild talk, it's fair disrepitable. Vitals, says you! And where would I be with my blunderbush?" he snarled.

"Powder and your auld hands are but as the snail to the swallow against the bright steel in the hands of Alan," said the other. "Before your jottering finger could find the trigger, the hilt would dirl on your breastbane."

"Eh, man, whae's denying it?" said my uncle. "Pit it as ye please; hae't your ain way; I'll do naething to cross ye. Just tell me what like ye'll be wanting, and ye'll see that we'll can agree fine."

"Troth, sir," said Alan, "I ask for nothing but plain dealing. In two words: do ye want the lad killed or kept?"

"O, sirs!" cried Ebenezer. "O, sirs, me! that's no kind of language!"

"Killed or kept?" repeated Alan.

"O, keepit, keepit!" wailed my uncle. "We'll have nae bloodshed, if you please."

"Well," says Alan, "as ye please; that'll be the dearer."

"The dearer?" cries Ebenezer. "Would ye fyle your hands wi' crime?"

"Hoot!" said Alan, "they're baith crime, whatever! And the killing's easier, and quicker, and surer. Keeping the lad'll be a fashious job, a fashious, kittle business."

"I'll have him keepit, though," returned my uncle. "I never had naething to do with onything morally wrong; and I'm no gaun to begin to pleasure a wild Hielandman."

"Ye're unco scrupulous," sneered Alan.

"I'm a man o' principle," said Ebenezer, simply; "and if I have to pay for it, I'll have to pay for it. And besides," says he, "ye forget the lad's my brother's son."

"Well, well," said Alan, "and now about the price. It's no very easy for me to set a name upon it; I would first have to ken some small matters. I would have to ken, for instance, what ye gave Hoseason at the first off-go?"

"Hoseason?" cries my uncle, struck aback. "What for?"

"For kidnapping David," says Alan.

"It's a lee! it's a black lee!" cried my uncle. "He was never kidnapped. He leed in his throat that tauld ye that. Kidnapped! He never was!"

"That's no fault of mine, nor yet of yours," said Alan; "nor yet of Hoseason's, if he's a man that can be trusted."

"What do you mean?" cried Ebenezer. "Did Hoseason tell ye?"

"Why, ye donnered auld runt, how else would I ken?" cried Alan. "Hoseason and I are partners; we gang shares; so ye can see for yoursel' what good ye can do leeing. And I must plainly say ye drove a fool's bargain when ye let a man like the sailorman so far forward in your private matters. But that's past praying for; and ye must lie on your bed the way ye made it. And the point in hand is just this: what did ye pay him?"

"Has he tauld ye himsel'?" asked my uncle.

"That's my concern," said Alan.

"Weel," said my uncle, "I dinnae care what he said, he leed, and the solemn God's truth is this, that I gave him twenty pound. But I'll be perfec'ly honest with ye: forby that, he was to have the selling of the lad in Caroliny, whilk would be muckle mair, but no from my pocket, ye see."

"Thank you, Mr Thomson. That will do excellently well," said the lawyer, stepping forward; and then mighty civilly, "Good evening, Mr Balfour," said he.

And "Good evening, uncle Ebenezer," said I.

And "It's a braw nicht, Mr Balfour," added Torrance.

Never a word said my uncle, neither black nor white; but just sat where he was on the top doorstep and stared upon us like a man turned to stone. Alan flinched away his blunderbuss; and the lawyer, taking him by the arm, plucked him up from the doorstep, led him into the kitchen, whither we all followed, and set him down in a chair beside the hearth, where the fire was out and only a rushlight burning.

There we all looked upon him for awhile, exulting greatly in our success, but yet with a sort of pity for the man's shame.

"Come, come, Mr Ebenezer," said the lawyer, "you must not be down-hearted, for I promise you we shall make easy terms. In the meanwhile give us the cellar key, and Torrance shall draw us a bottle of your father's wine in honour of the event." Then, turning to me and taking me by the hand, "Mr David," says he, "I wish you all joy in your good fortune, which I believe to be deserved." And then to Alan, with a spice of drollery, "Mr Thomson, I pay you my compliment; it was most artfully conducted; but in one point you somewhat outran my comprehension. Do I understand your name to be James? or Charles? or is it George, perhaps?"

"And why should it be any of the three, sir?" quoth Alan, drawing himself up, like one who smelt an offence.

"Only, sir, that you mentioned a king's name," replied Rankeillor; "and as there has never yet been a King Thomson, or his fame at least has never come my way, I judged you must refer to that you had in baptism."

This was just the stab that Alan would feel keenest, and I am free to confess he took it very ill. Not a word would he answer, but stepped off to the far end of the kitchen, and sat down and sulked; and it was not till I stepped after him, and gave him my hand, and thanked him by title as the chief spring of my success, that he began to smile a bit, and was at last prevailed upon to join our party.

By that time we had the fire lighted, and a bottle of wine uncorked; a good supper came out of the basket, to which Torrance

"They had come to a good understanding, and my uncle and I
set our hands to the agreement in a formal manner."

Young Folks Paper, July 24, 1886.

and I and Alan set ourselves down; while the lawyer and my uncle passed into the next chamber to consult. They stayed there
closeted about an hour; at the end of which period they had come
to a good understanding, and my uncle and I set our hands to
the agreement in a formal manner. By the terms of this, my uncle
bound himself to satisfy Rankeillor as to his intromissions, and
to pay me two clear thirds of the yearly income of Shaws.

So the beggar in the ballad had come home; and when I lay
down that night on the kitchen chests, I was a man of means and
had a name in the country. Alan and Torrance and Rankeillor
slept and snored on their hard beds; but for me, who had lain out
under heaven and upon dirt and stones, so many days and nights,
and often with an empty belly, and in fear of death, this good
change in my case unmanned me more than any of the former
evil ones; and I lay till dawn, looking at the fire on the roof and
planning the future.

ᗑ 30

Good-bye

So far as I was concerned myself, I had come to port; but I had still Alan, to whom I was so much beholden, on my hands; and I felt besides a heavy charge in the matter of the murder and James of the Glens. On both these heads I unbosomed to Rankeillor the next morning, walking to and fro about six of the clock before the house of Shaws, and with nothing in view but the fields and woods that had been my ancestors' and were now mine. Even as I spoke on these grave subjects, my eye would take a glad bit of a run over the prospect, and my heart jump with pride.

About my clear duty to my friend, the lawyer had no doubt; I must help him out of the country at whatever risk; but in the case of James, he was of a different mind.

"Mr Thomson," says he, "is one thing, Mr Thomson's kinsman quite another. I know little of the facts; but I gather that a great noble (whom we will call, if you like, the D. of A.) has some concern and is even supposed to feel some animosity in the matter. The D. of A. is doubtless an excellent nobleman; but, Mr David, *timeo qui nocuere deos*. If you interfere to baulk his vengeance, you should remember there is one way to shut your testimony out; and that is to put you in the dock. There, you would be in the same pickle as Mr Thomson's kinsman. You will object that you are innocent; well, but so is he. And to be tried for your life before a Highland jury, on a Highland quarrel, and with a Highland judge upon the bench, would be a brief transition to the gallows."

Now I had made all these reasonings before and found no very good reply to them; so I put on all the simplicity I could. "In that case, sir," said I, "I would just have to be hanged—would I not?"

"My dear boy," cries he, "go in God's name, and do what you think is right. It is a poor thought that at my time of life I should be advising you to choose the safe and shameful; and I take it back with an apology. Go and do your duty; and be hanged, if you must, like a gentleman. There are worse things in the world than to be hanged."

"Not many, sir," said I, smiling.

"Why, yes, sir," he cried, "very many. And it would be ten times better for your uncle (to go no farther afield) if he were dangling decently upon a gibbet."

Thereupon he turned into the house (still in a great fervour of mind, so that I saw I had pleased him heartily), and there he wrote me two letters, making his comments on them as he wrote.

"This," says he, "is to my bankers, the British Linen Company, placing a credit to your name. Consult Mr Thomson; he will know of ways; and you, with this credit, can supply the means. I trust you will be a good husband of your money; but in the affair of a friend like Mr Thomson, I would be even prodigal. Then, for his kinsman, there is no better way than that you should seek the Advocate, tell him your tale, and offer testimony; whether he may take it or not is quite another matter, and will turn on the D. of A. Now that you may reach the Lord Advocate well recommended, I give you here a letter to a namesake of your own, the learned Mr Balfour of Pilrig, a man whom I esteem. It will look better that you should be presented by one of your own name; and the laird of Pilrig is much looked up to in the Faculty and stands well with Lord Advocate Grant. I would not trouble him, if I were you, with any particulars; and (do you know?) I think it would be needless to refer to Mr Thomson. Form yourself upon the laird—he is a good model; when you deal with the Advocate, be discreet; and in all these matters, may the Lord guide you, Mr David!"

Thereupon he took his farewell, and set out with Torrance for the Ferry, while Alan and I turned our faces for the city of Edinburgh. As we went by the footpath and beside the gateposts and the unfinished lodge, we kept looking back at the house of my fathers. It stood there, bare and great and smokeless, like a place not lived in; only in one of the top windows, there was the peak of a nightcap bobbing up and down and back and forward, like the head of a rabbit from a burrow. I had little welcome when I came, and less kindness while I stayed; but at least I was watched as I went away.

Alan and I went slowly forward upon our way, having little heart either to walk or speak. The same thought was uppermost in both, that we were near the time of our parting; and remembrance of all the bygone days sate upon us sorely. We talked indeed of what should be done; and it was resolved that Alan should keep to the country, biding now here, now there, but coming once in the day to a particular place where I might be able to communicate with him, either in my own person or by messenger. In the meanwhile, I was to seek out a lawyer, who was an Appin Stewart, and a man therefore to be wholly trusted; and it should be his part to find a ship and to arrange for Alan's safe embarkation. No sooner was this business done, than the words seemed to leave us; and though I would seek to jest with Alan under the name of Mr Thomson, and he with me on my new clothes and my estate, you could feel very well that we were nearer tears than laughter.

We came the by-way over the hill of Corstorphine; and when we got near to the place called Rest-and-be-Thankful, and looked down on Corstorphine bogs and over to the city and the castle on the hill, we both stopped, for we both knew, without a word said, that we had come to where our ways parted. Here he repeated to me once again what had been agreed upon between us: the address of the lawyer, the daily hour at which Alan might be found, and the signals that were to be made by any that came seeking him. Then I gave what money I had (a guinea or two of Rankeillor's) so that he should not starve in the meanwhile; and then we stood a space and looked over at Edinburgh in silence.

"Well, good-bye," said Alan, and held out his left hand.

"Good-bye," said I, and gave the hand a little grasp, and went off down hill.

Neither one of us looked the other in the face, nor so long as he was in my view did I take one back glance at the friend I was leaving. But as I went on my way to the city, I felt so lost and lonesome that I could have found it in my heart to sit down by the dyke, and cry and weep like any baby.

It was coming near noon when I passed in by the West Kirk and the Grassmarket into the streets of the capital. The huge height of the buildings, running up to ten and fifteen storeys, the narrow arched entries that continually vomited passengers, the wares of the merchants in their windows, the hubbub and endless stir, the foul smells and the fine clothes, and a hundred other particulars too small to mention, struck me into a kind of stupor of surprise, so that I let the crowd carry me to and fro; and yet all the time what I was thinking of was Alan at Rest-and-be-Thankful; and all the time (although you would think I would not choose but be delighted with these braws and novelties) there was a cold gnawing in my inside like a remorse for something wrong.

The hand of Providence brought me in my drifting to the very doors of the British Linen Company's bank.

*

Just there, with his hand upon his fortune, the present editor inclines for the time to say farewell to David. How Alan escaped, and what was done about the murder, with a variety of other delectable particulars, may be some day set forth. That is a thing, however, that hinges on the public fancy. The editor has a great kindness for both Alan and David, and would gladly spend much of his life in their society; but in this he may find himself to stand alone. In the fear of which, and lest any one should complain of scurvy usage, he hastens to protest that all went well with both, in the limited and human sense of the word "well;" that whatever befell them, it was not dishonour, and whatever failed them, they were not found wanting to themselves.

"Etched From the Life on Board a Scotch Ship. The Cook, Captain, & Mait."
Etching by Paul Sandby.

NOTES

The serial illustrations of the text from *Young Folks Paper* are reproduced here for the first time from the original drawings by William Boucher, by permission of The City of Edinburgh Museums and Galleries. *Young Folks Paper* used text from the novel to create the captions. They were often extensive and have been revised and shortened for this edition. Two etchings by Paul Sandby (RB 323330), and the title page and map from the first English edition (RB 8135), are from the Huntington Library. The title page of the copyright edition published by James Henderson and two pages from Henry James's inscribed copy of the first English edition are reproduced by permission of the Houghton Library, Harvard University. The binding design of the first American edition (Scribner's) is reproduced with permission of the Hamilton Library, University of Hawaii.

On 19 February 1887 James Murray, editor of *A New English Dictionary* (later renamed the *Oxford English Dictionary*), wrote to Stevenson for an explanation of the word *brean* in "the horror of the charnel brean" from his long story "The Merry Men," which had been published in the June 1882 issue of *The Cornhill Magazine*. Stevenson replied that he had not read proof, and "brean" was a misprint for "ocean" (*Letters*, 5:365). If the novelist was a major source for Scottish lexicographers in the twentieth century (see the Glossary), his work was combed even earlier by the readers for Murray's massive enterprise (*Kidnapped* alone is quoted one hundred seventy-five times, with more than a third of the quotations consisting of non-Scots terms). In effect, Stevenson was recognized as an important source for language even before he was "Stevenson," that is, well before he made his worldwide reputation with *Jekyll and Hyde*. G. L. Apperson, for example, one of the "principal readers" and "sub-editors" for the *OED* before 1884, later published an important collection of English proverbs that drew extensively from Stevenson's work. And Joseph Wright, editor of *The English Dialect Dictionary*, lists all the Scots novels as sources for his great lexicon. In *Kidnapped*, the fluency of the narrative screens the intricacy of its construction. It is in fact built up of homely and archaic words, of legal terms and nautical jargon, of proverbial and dialectal and slang phrases. What follows are notes on words and phrases whose meaning may not be immediately apparent, whose usage may be uncommon, or whose proverbiality might pass unnoticed. The texts listed below are the major sources for the definitions, or are otherwise cited in these notes. Citations from *Kidnapped* are indicated by an asterisk, while a dagger (†) signifies that the novel is the sole source for a citation.

Ansted	A. Ansted, *A Dictionary of Sea Terms* (Glasgow, 1919).
Apperson	G. L. Apperson, *English Proverbs and Proverbial Phrases* (London, 1929).

Burt   E. Burt, *Letters from a Gentleman in the North of Scotland*, 2 vols. (London, 1754).

EDD   Joseph Wright, *The English Dialect Dictionary* (6 vols., Oxford, 1898–1905).

HBP   Burton Stevenson, *Home Book of Proverbs, Maxims and Familiar Phrases* (New York, 1948).

Kelly   James Kelly, *A Complete Collection of Scotish Proverbs* (London, 1721).

Kinsley   James Kinsley, ed., *The Poems and Songs of Robert Burns*, 3 vols. (Oxford, 1968).

Letters   *The Letters of Robert Louis Stevenson*, ed. B. Booth and E. Mehew, 8 vols. (New Haven, 1994–1995).

ODP   F. P. Wilson, *Oxford Dictionary of English Proverbs* (3d ed., Oxford, 1970).

OED   *Oxford English Dictionary* (2d ed., Oxford, 1989).

Smyth   W. A. Smyth, *The Sailor's Word-Book* (London, 1867).

SND   William Grant, *Scottish National Dictionary* (Edinburgh, [1931]–1976).

Stewart   David Stewart, "References to the Map of the Clans," in *Sketches of the Character, Manners, and Present State of the Highlanders of Scotland*, 3d ed., 2 vols. (Edinburgh, 1825).

Tilley   Morris Palmer Tilley, *A Dictionary of the Proverbs in England in the Sixteenth and Seventeenth Centuries* (Ann Arbor, Mich., 1950).

5 **the Appin murder . . . printed trial:** *Kidnapped* has its genesis in a resonant historical incident of 14 May 1752: the murder of a King's agent, Colin Campbell, in a remote wood in the "country" of Appin, and the subsequent indictment of two men identified with the recent Jacobite rebellion, James Stewart and Alan Breck Stewart. James was tried, convicted, and executed; Alan, accused of being the actual assassin, was never caught. Although Stevenson implies that the question of Alan's guilt or innocence is a critical one, in reality the murder and the trial had a larger political and cultural significance in the aftermath of the short-lived rebellion (1745–1746). Enmity persisted between the supporters of King George and those who remained loyal to the exiled Stewarts. Clan hatred between the Campbells and Stewarts was as deep as ever. And the destitution of agrarian life seemed an insuperable barrier to change. Under these conditions, an audacious crime was seized on by the government and vigorously prosecuted in order to set an example: to choke any impulse for resisting the laws from London, and to destroy the remnants of Highland customs. In the extensive speeches of the prosecutors and defense lawyers, in the vivid and often riveting testimony of the witnesses, and in the final "dying speech" of the principal defendant, the *Trial of James Stewart* (1753) concentrated in its pages the contentious political and cultural life of the period. Stevenson's copy of the *Trial*, purchased by him in the city of Inverness, is now part of the Parrish Collection in the Firestone Library at Princeton University.

6 **Speculative:** Independent club of long standing that was housed at Edinburgh University and counted among its past members Walter Scott, Francis Jeffrey, and Lord Brougham. Stevenson warmly recalled his early "Speculative" evenings ("I look back upon these good times with much regret") in a farewell address (1873) that was published posthumously by Charles Baxter. See "A College Magazine" in *Memories and Portraits* for Stevenson's description of the "Spec."

6 **Robert Emmet:** Radical Irish nationalist (1778–1803), excelled as a student of history and an orator at Trinity College, marched on Dublin Castle in a futile bid for Irish independence, fled to his fiancée's arms before heading for the continent, was caught and then hanged one day after his trial. His dramatic speeches at his sentencing and on the scaffold, together with his twin passions for love and politics, made his name synonymous with romantic adventure.

6 **Macbean:** William Macbean, secretary of the Speculative Society, died in 1842 at age nineteen and was commemorated by a plaque on the lobby wall. In 1892 Stevenson (through Charles Baxter) forwarded a photograph of himself to the Speculative and insisted upon knowing where it was hung: "Am I within eyeshot of Macbean?" (*Letters*, 8:19).

6 **L.J.R.:** Informal club (including Stevenson, his cousin Bob, Charles Baxter, and Walter Ferrier) that met at a pub in the Advocates' Close, the initials standing for Liberty, Justice, Reverence. A clearer picture of the club's objectives can be gleaned from verses that Stevenson inscribed "To the Members of the L.J.R." in a letter to Charles Baxter on 7 April 1872: "One rood of Holy-ground in this bleak earth / Sequestered still (an homage surely due!) / To the twin Gods of mirthful wine and mirth" (*Letters*, 1:225).

12 **peradventure:** *Arch.* By chance or accident.

12 **testamentary:** Of or relating to a testament or will.

12 **superscrived:** Written upon the outside or cover of the letter.

13 **If the worst . . . worst:** *Prov.* *Apperson.

14 **honour to whom honour:** Romans 13:7.

15 **jogging:** Jerking. **OED.*

15 **think shame:** Be ashamed. **OED.*

15 **To Make Lilly ... Water:** Stevenson drew this recipe from E. Smith's *The Compleat Housewife: or, Accomplish'd Gentlewoman's Companion* (London, 1737), a cookbook and collection of medicinal home remedies. He added the note about the recipe serving equally well for men and women, along with the final line "in the minister's own hand." The Stevenson copy of *The Compleat Housewife* is in the Firestone Library, Princeton University.

17 **Grenadiers ... Pope's-hats:** Grenadiers were originally soldiers armed with grenades: the name was retained for an élite company of powerful men, whose distinctive headgear was a peaked or mitre-shaped cap, 15–17 inches tall. **OED.*

18 **heard tell of:** *Dial. and colloq.* Heard or learned by report. **OED.*

19 **put the matter ... touch:** "To put to the touch" = a test or trial. **OED.*

20 **pith:** Vigor, strength. **OED.*

21 **hurdles:** A portable frame of wattled twigs used for fencing land or livestock.

22 **in full carreer:** I.e., going at it full blast.

24 **horn spoon:** An animal's hollow horn used as a drinking spoon.

25 **sharp-set:** Very hungry, craving food.

28 **under lee of:** In the shelter or under the protection of.

28 **fair:** Handsome, beautiful.

30 **Hieland:** Pertaining to or characteristic of people of the Highlands, descendants of Celts and distinguished from their kinsmen to the south by language, custom, and history. **SND.* See HIELANDS (p. 292).

30 **keep your tongue between your teeth:** *Provb*. Be silent. Apperson.

30 **Blood's thicker than water:** *Provb*. Apperson.

31 **session clerk:** The secretary of a church court that operates at the parish level.

31 **bear and forbear:** *Provb*. Epictetus' golden rule, cited by Erasmus as embracing almost all that philosophy or human reason can teach. *HBP.*

33 **chapbook . . . of Patrick Walker's:** Any of three tracts issued between 1725 and 1732 by an indefatigable and passionate chronicler of the "martyrs" of the SCOTTISH COVENANT (p. 299). Quite apart from the content, Walker's lives were remarkable for their racy language and vernacular style. Stevenson was an admirer of this self-taught writer, and his marked copy of *Biographia Presbyteriana* (1827), a collected edition of Walker's work, is in the Beinecke Library at Yale University.

36 **my word is my bond:** *Provb*. "An honest man's word is as good as his bond" (*ODP*).

40 **Aqua Vitae:** "Water of Life." Strong liquor, such as brandy, rum, or whiskey.

40 **huddled:** *Dial*. Jumbled, in a heap. **OED.*

41 **besides:** *Obs*. Besides (of) = beside myself.

43 **Johnnie-Raw:** *Colloq*. Innocent; simpleton or fool. **OED.*

43 **mother-wit:** Native wit, common sense.

43 **porridge stick:** *Dial*. A piece of hard wood used to stir porridge.

43 **sea-hornpipe:** A lively dance associated with sailors, usually performed by one person to the accompaniment of a wind instrument.

44 **For it's my . . . year:** From an eighteenth-century folk song, by turns classified as a children's ditty or a song about the rural poor: "When I was bound apprentice, in famous Zummersetshire, / I sarv'd my master truly, for nearly seven long year: / Till I took up to poaching, As you shall quickily hear, / For it's my delight of a shiny night, In the season of the year!" ("The Poacher," in *The Cavendish Music Books. No. 81. Old English Ballads* [London, n.d.], pp. 10–11).

44 **mortal:** *Colloq.* Intensive. Very, extremely.

44 **hawser:** *Naut.* A small cable or thick rope used in mooring.

45 **naked word:** *Rare.* Free from concealment; plain, straightforward.

46 **crack on:** *Naut.* Carry as much sail as wind and sea will allow.

47 **moon-calf:** Idiot; born fool. **OED.*

48 **rope's end:** Short rope used for whipping.

48 **kidnapped or trepanned:** In the eighteenth century these words referred to the enticement and abduction of children and young adults for enforced labor in the British colonies in North America. Stevenson was aware of the notorious case of Peter Williamson, who in 1743 had been kidnapped from Aberdeen as a boy and sent to the colonies. Williamson later escaped from "slavery," made his way back to Scotland, and sued the magistrates of the city for their complicity in his abduction. The trial (1762) exposed the existence of a flourishing "kidnapping-trade" in Aberdeen between 1740 and 1746, replete with a "kidnapping-book" and a record of charges for the "listing" (enlistment) of children. There was no criminal statute in Scotland against kidnapping, and the first trial for this offense in 1752 carried an indictment for theft, or " 'the stealing or away-taking of a living child' " (Archibald Alison, *Principles of the Criminal Law of Scotland* [Edinburgh, 1832], 281). The terror of the word derives from this social and cultural context, from the realization that kidnapping meant the forced removal from home and country, with no prospects beyond servitude, exile, or death.

48 **Hope:** ST. MARGARET'S HOPE (see Gazetteer).

48 **an islet with some ruins:** INCHGARVIE (see Gazetteer).

48 **thwarts:** *Naut.* The seat across (athwart) the boat; the rower's bench.

50 **old coal bucket burning:** In the seventeenth century a tower was built on this small island, on the top of which a coal fire was constantly kept burning as a beacon light for the guidance of sailors. See ISLE OF MAY in the Gazetteer.

50 **carbonadoed:** Cut, hacked, or slashed. A "carbonado" is a piece of meat, fish, or fowl, scored across and grilled or broiled.

51 **full:** *Scots.* Conceited, i.e., full of myself.

51 **weeds:** Plants that grow wild in fresh or salt water. **OED.*

51 **case knives:** Knives carried in sheaths or cases.

52 **mopped and mowed:** *Dial.* Grimaced and made faces.

52 **Scotch way:** A "Scotch cousin" is a distant relative.

52 **ill-seen:** Unpopular. **SND.*

58 **deep sea:** *Provb.* "Between the devil and the deep sea," i.e., between two equally dangerous difficulties. *ODP.*

59 **pannikin:** A small drinking cup.

59 **Scotch tongue:** *Provb.* I.e., a knowledge of Scots. See Kelly ("You have a Scotish tongue in your Head") and *Kidnapped* ("Ye've ... a Scotch tongue in your head," p. 74).

60 **keep your breath . . . porridge:** *Provb.* Hold your tongue; usually delivered as a rebuke. *ODP.*

60 **Flit:** *Dial.* Move, shift; also applied to a tethered animal.

61 **scuttle:** *Naut.* A small hole, or hatchway, in a ship's deck for lighting and ventilation.

62 **at a word and a blow:** *Provb.* Quick to anger and ready to fight. Tilley.

62–63 **slavery:** A parallel or synonymous term for *indenture* in eighteenth-century judicial proceedings. Thus the legal scholar Hugo Arnot, after describing the bungled procedure in a minor criminal case of 1774, acidly noted the sentence given the defendant: "It was only, indeed, a matter of adjudging [i.e., sentencing] to slavery for seven years, and transportation for life" (*History of Edinburgh* [Edinburgh, 1816], p. 377). Under *indentured*, the *OED* cites an example from a magazine in 1808 that joins the two terms: "Indentured bond-slaves are shipped from Liverpool and Glasgow, for Canada, and independent North-America, in considerable numbers."

63 **the whole jing-bang:** *Dial.* The whole crowd; contemptuously = a worthless lot. **OED.*

63 **"The north countrie":** A ballad sung to the tune "There Was a Lass in the North-Country" can be found in both *The Roxburghe Ballads* (Hertford: The Ballad Society, 1895, vol. 7, part 1, p. 173) and William Chappell's *Old English Popular Music* (London, 1893, 2:220–21), albeit under alternate titles ("The Fickle Northern Lass" and "The Northern Lass"). Yet another ballad begins, "A North-Countrey Lass up to *London* did pass," and continues in the second stanza: "Fain would I be in the North Country, / Where the lads and the lasses are making of hay" ("The Northern Lasse's Lamentation," *Roxburghe Ballads*, p. 168).

65 **life is all a variorum:** In Scots usage, "variorum" = uncertain, changing, mutable. "Life is all a VARIORUM, / We regard not how it goes; / Let them cant about DECORUM, / Who have character to lose" (Robert Burns, "Love and Liberty—A Cantata," in Kinsley, 1:208).

65 **man-Jack:** *Dial. and slang.* Everyman, usually in the phrase "every man jack"; used occasionally with contemptuous emphasis.

66 **round-house:** *Naut.* A square cabin (which could be walked around) on the afterpart (or stern side) of the deck.

67 **starboard tack:** *Naut.* Sailing with the wind blowing from the right-hand side of the ship.

67 **foresail:** *Naut.* The principal sail on the forward lower mast.

67 **north-about:** *Naut.* In a northerly direction; specifically, round the north of Scotland.

69 **sea-boots:** High rubber boots worn by sailors.

69 **hob-a-nobbed:** *Slang.* Drank together easily and familiarly.

69 **aftermost:** *Naut.* The rear part, nearest the stern.

70 **salt junk:** *Naut.* Salt beef, hard from long keeping. "Junks" are old shipboard ropes hardened from usage and salt water.

70 **duff:** Stiff flour pudding.

70 **lee-way:** *Naut.* The difference (or distance) between the course steered by a ship and that actually run, as a consequence of winds and currents. Figuratively, Riach and the Captain are closing the distance (in their minds) between their intentions toward Ransome and their actual treatment of him.

71 **at the stick's end:** *Provb.* At a distance, usually at "staff's" end. **HBP.*

71 **unbuckle:** Unbend, become less stiff. †*OED.*

72 **beat:** *Naut.* Tacking against the wind in a zigzag line, or turning to windward in a storm.

72 **a fair wind of a foul:** *Naut.* The latter prevents a ship from making headway, the former keeps it on course.

72 **bulwarks:** *Naut.* A raised wood parapet running around a ship's deck.

72 **breakers:** *Naut.* Waves that produce a distinctively loud roaring as they "break" violently over reefs or rocks lying at or under the surface of the sea.

73 **frieze:** A heavy fabric woven of coarse wool.

73 **bowsprit:** *Naut.* A large SPAR (see note on p. 295) projecting out from the front of the ship (where the bows join) to support the foremast ropes and extend the headsails.

74 **is that how the wind sets:** *Provb.* "To know which way the wind blows." *Apperson.

74 **Jacobite:** Partisan or supporter of the Stewart claim to the throne of England after 1688 when James II was supplanted by William and Mary. The term derives from the Latin "Jacobus" for James, but in the mouths of Whigs it alluded to the biblical story of Jacob and Esau and carried an insinuation that the Stewart claim was fraudulent.

75 **true-blue:** Unswerving loyalty to party and principles. From the Covenanters' use of the color blue as a mark of constancy and fidelity. Cf. "True blue will never stain" (Kelly).

75 **go-by:** *Colloq.* Slip, i.e., missed us. *OED.

75 **guinea:** An English gold coin, unminted after 1813.

75 **doit:** A minor Dutch coin; a very small sum.

77 **fool's bargain:** Cf. "It is an ill Bargain, where no Man wins" (Kelly) or "It is a silly bargain, where no body gets" (Apperson). Cf. also, "When two Fools meet, the Bargain goes off" (*HBP*).

77 **forfeited:** *Law.* Confiscation by the British government of the estates and property of the Highland lairds who supported the Stewart rebellions in 1715 and 1745. "Forfeiture" was the penalty for treason. See JACOBITE (p. 290).

77 **what must be must:** *Prov.* "What must be must be" (*HBP*).

78 **by your long . . . whig:** In a letter to Sidney Colvin requesting Stevenson's autograph, Thomas Hutchinson copied out four inscriptions that the novelist had previously penned in Hutchinson's books, including this one from *Kidnapped:* "By sea and shore, through tears and smiles, / Behold my hero roam. / 'Mong long Scots faces, over long Scots miles / Across the hills of home" (30 May 1894; National Library of Scotland, MS.9894.ff.66–69).

78 **Betwixt and Between:** *Dial.* Neither one thing nor the other.

78 **waist:** *Naut.* The middle part of the main deck; without an upper deck, it looks like a low deck or well.

79 **horn:** Flask for gunpowder.

80 **back and forth:** *Dial.* Backwards and forwards; this way and that. **SND.*

84 **My badge is the oak:** Identifying emblem of the Stewart clan, signifying hardness and endurance.

84 **let your hand . . . head:** *Prov.* "Hand over head" = recklessly, rashly (*EDD, SND*). Stevenson inverts the meaning (= be prudent, be cautious). Cf. "Hand over head, as men took the *Covenant* . . . preserves the manner in which the Scotch covenant . . . was violently taken by above sixty thousand persons about Edinburgh, in 1638" (*ODP*).

84 **grip:** Battle. "Grip" = handle of a sword (Smyth).

87 **paid the piper:** Paid for the dance, i.e., died.

90 **King's English:** Pure or correct English speech or usage. **HBP.*

94 **Charlemagne:** Charles the Great (742–814), crowned Holy Roman Emperor, consolidated the Christian empire in the West from the Ebro in Spain to the Elbe in central Germany.

94 **parley:** *Scots and dial.* Truce.

95 **to be shut of him:** *Dial. and colloq.* To be rid of him.

95 **parole:** Pledged word, i.e., a verbal commitment to honor the terms of the truce.

95 **instancy:** Urgency, insistence.

95 **gill:** Liquid measure = one-quarter of a British pint; dialectally = half a pint, generally of ale or wine.

95 **a breakable:** I.e., a pledge or a promise.

95 **apple-wife:** A woman who sells apples.

96 **draught:** *Naut.* The depth of water a ship displaces in order to float.

97 **weathercock:** One who is fickle or changeable. From a weather vane in the form of a cock.

97 **run jeopardy:** Risk danger or death.

97 **rope's-end:** A hangman's noose.

99 **by-west:** To the west of.

100 **black-cocks:** A game bird (the male black grouse) "which resembles in Size and Shape, a Pheasant, but is black and shining like a Raven" (Burt, 2:169).

100 **underhand:** A position of dependence or subordination. †*OED.*

101 **Hielands:** Separated from the Lowlands by a geological fault extending from Stonehaven in the east (just below Aberdeen on the North Sea) to Dumbarton and the Firth of Clyde in the west, the Highlands constitute the mountainous district north and west of this rift, a massive lofty ground deeply cut with valleys and sea lochs and including all the western islands. *SND*. See HIELAND (p. 284).

101 **Black Watch:** Sobriquet given to the independent companies originally recruited by the British (1725/1729) to police or "watch" the Highlands after the first Jacobite rebellion (1715), and presumably so named for the somber appearance of their dark green, black, and navy tartan dress. See RED-SOLDIERS (p. 298).

101 **Butcher Cumberland:** William Augustus, Duke of Cumberland (1721–1765), son of George II, commander of the English army at Culloden, received the epithet "Butcher" for his troops' brutal suppression of the Highlanders following their victory in April 1746: "Numbers were hanged without ceremony, by orders from the general officers, as spies, deserters, or rebels. The homes of the Highland chiefs were plundered and burned: nay, through a large tract of country every village and hovel shared the same fate, and in some of them the miserable families perished in the flames. The cattle were everywhere taken away, and brought to the Duke's army, sometimes by the amount of 2000 in a drove. Every species of provision was carried off; so that many who were not consumed by fire nor sword, perished by famine" (Hugo Arnot, *The History of Edinburgh* [Edinburgh, 1816], 168).

102 **Preston Pans:** Site of a major Jacobite victory over the English on 21 September 1745. See PRESTON PANS in the Gazetteer.

102 **short shrift:** A brief respite for confession before execution.

103 **at his whistle:** *Provb*. At his signal, summons. *HBP.*

104 **men of the clans were broken:** On 16 April 1746 the Highland clans, who had been fighting together as an army under Prince Charles, were beaten by Cumberland's superior force. This final battle of the Jacobite rebellion ended the Stewart cause. See CULLODEN in the Gazetteer.

104 **sings small:** Talks humbly or obsequiously.

104 **hail-fellow-well-met:** *Provb*. One who is overly familiar and intimate. *ODP.*

105 **commons:** Common people, as opposed to the nobility or gentry.

105 **sides of Clyde . . . Edinburgh:** I.e., from one end of Scotland to the other. The river Clyde extends into a broad firth southward and westward between Kintyre and the Ayrshire coast. See CANTYRE in the Gazetteer.

106 **not enough heather in all Scotland:** "For it is more difficult to find a Highlander among the Heather, except newly tracked, than a Hare in her Form" (Burt, 1:321).

106 **blow off:** *Dial. and fig.* Let fly, i.e., burst out with.

106 **observe:** Observation, remark. **OED.*

106 **spread his butter thinner:** *Provb*. An inversion of the more common expression, "They that have good store of butter may lay it thick on their bread" (*HBP*).

107 **byword:** *Dial.* Trite or commonplace saying.

108 **muse:** State of profound meditation or abstraction.

108 **small sword:** Light sword tapering from the hilt to the point and designed for thrusting.

109 **close-hauled:** *Naut.* Trimmed to sail close to (i.e., against) the wind.

109 **larboard bow:** *Naut.* Left side of the forward part of the ship.

109 **point:** *Naut.* Navigational line charted or followed by the ship.

109 **swell:** *Naut.* Rising and heaving of the sea, a succession of long rolling waves, before, during, or after a storm.

110 **lee bow:** *Naut.* Forward side opposite to that upon which the wind blows.

110 **haul our wind:** *Naut.* Bring the ship closer to the wind, usually said when a ship has been sailing free.

111 **foretop:** *Naut.* Platform resting on the head of the lower mast and projecting out like a scaffold.

111 **weather board:** *Naut.* Windward side.

113 **amidships:** *Naut.* In the middle of the ship.

113 **hamper:** *Naut.* Articles of a ship that are ordinarily indispensable but may get in the way during a storm.

113 **fore-scuttle:** *Naut.* Small hatchway in the forward deck.

113 **shrouds:** *Naut.* Strong ropes supporting a mast.

113 **mishandling:** Rough handling, maltreatment. **OED.*

114 **canted:** Tilted or pitched to one side, so as not to stand square.

114 **spar:** *Naut.* Any round piece of timber used for a mast, boom, or YARD (see below).

114 **yard:** *Naut.* A spar suspended from a mast for the purpose of extending a sail.

114 **tract:** Expanse or stretch. **OED.*

114 **bristled:** I.e., sizzled.

115 **roost, or tide race:** *Naut.* Powerful conflicting currents that produce a tumultuous rippling or "race" in the sea, where the water is propelled with immense force (see Stevenson's "The Merry Men").

115 **margin:** Area extending along the edge of the water.

117 **fordable:** Crossable. **OED.*

118 **limpets:** Mollusks with conical shells that adhere tightly to rocks.

119 **peck:** Large quantity or number.

120 **between fear and hope:** *Provb.* "Between hope and fear" (*HBP*).

120 **Charles Second declared ... other:** In *English Traits* (1856) Ralph Waldo Emerson commented on the climate of England ("neither hot nor cold, there is no hour in the whole year when one cannot work") and then attributed the following note on the weather to Charles the Second: " 'It invited men abroad more days in the year and more hours in the day than another country' " (*Collected Works of Ralph Waldo Emerson*, ed. D. Nicoloff et al. [Cambridge, Mass., 1994], 5:20). The quotation is untraced.

120 **flight from Worcester:** Worcester was the site of the last great battle of the Civil War on 3 September 1651. Charles had a very narrow escape from the field and spent the next six weeks eluding Cromwell's troops before crossing to safety in France.

121 **lock the stable ... stolen:** *Provb. HBP.*

124 **tee-hee'd:** Laughed in a high voice, derisively. **OED.*

124 **Greek and Hebrew for me:** *Provb. ODP.* Cf. *Julius Caesar* 1.2.284 ("but, for mine own part, it was Greek to me").

125 **neaps:** *Naut.* Smallest tides.

127 **out of harm's way:** *Provb. HBP.*

128 **jealously:** *Obs.* Eagerly, fervently.

128 **grubbing:** Digging, in the sense of mean and gruelling labor. **OED.*

128 **Highland dress being ... law:** See DISARMING ACT (p. 298).

129 **strips:** Stripes.

129 **wandering:** Winding, meandering. **OED.*

129 **by-track:** Out of the way, little used road.

129 **gownsmen:** Licensed beggars. †*OED*, †*SND*.

130 **set me foolish:** Confused or bewildered me.

132 **catechist:** One who went from house to house instructing children in religious faith.

132 **got the heels of:** *Dial.* Tripped up, i.e., got the better of.

133 **the Act:** See DISARMING ACT (p. 298).

133 **weepons:** The only instance cited by the *SND* of this Scots form. Stevenson repeats the usage in chapter 18, but the first book edition (London, 1886) printed it there as *weapons.*

135 **lampoon:** Polemical or malicious satire.

135 **cream:** *Fig.* The best or choicest part.

135 **MacLean of Duart:** "Maclean of Dowart has generally been considered as the chief of all the Macleans" (Donald Gregory, *The History of the Western Highlands* [London, 1881], p. 69). See TOROSAY in the Gazetteer.

136 **Both shores . . . McLeans:** "Morven on the Mainland, and part of the Isle of Mull . . . was formerly the inheritance of this clan" (Stewart, 1:[xxii]).

137 **sea-beach:** Beach.

137 **Lochaber no more:** "Farewell to *Lochaber*, and farewell, my *Jean*, / Where heartsome with thee I've mony Day been; / For *Lochaber* no more, *Lochaber* no more. / We'll may be return to *Lochaber* no more. / These tears that I shed, they are a' for my Dear, / And no for the Dangers attending on Weir, / Tho' bore on rough Seas to a far bloody Shore, / May be to return to *Lochaber* no more" (*The Works of Allan Ramsay*, vol. 2, ed. Burns Martin and John Oliver [Edinburgh, 1953], 281). "Weir" = war.

138 **that end of the stick:** *Dial.* The right end or the right way.

139 **red-soldiers:** Nickname for the regular English troops (Gaelic = "*Seideran Dearag*") who were distinguished by their scarlet coats and breeches from their Highland counterparts, the "*Freicudan Dhu,*" or BLACK WATCH (p. 293, also Stewart, 1:248).

139 **Edinburgh Society for ... Knowledge:** First established in 1709, its purpose was to send missionaries and schoolmasters to the remote areas of Scotland "promoting Christian Knowledge, and the Encrease of Piety and Vertue," especially in the Highlands and Islands, "where Error, Idolatry, Superstition, and Ignorance do mostly abound, by Reason of the Largeness of Parishes and Scarcity of Schools" (*State of the Society in Scotland* [Edinburgh, 1721], p. 8).

140 **the Disarming Act ... weapons:** One of the first Acts to follow the collapse of the Jacobite rebellion, it required the Highlanders to turn in their arms, authorized government officers to conduct unannounced house searches, and, in its most vindictive strike at clan culture, prohibited any wearing of traditional clothes: "No Man or Boy within that Part of *Great Britain* called *Scotland* . . . shall, on any Pretence whatsoever, wear or put on the Clothes commonly called *Highland Clothes*" ("An Act for the more effectual disarming the Highlands in *Scotland*; and for more effectually securing the Peace of the said Highlands; and for restraining the Use of the Highland Dress; etc" [*19 & 20 Geo.II.c.39*]). Aggravating the offensiveness of the Act were the respective penalties: for a first offense for failing to disarm, a heavy fine (£15 to £100) and imprisonment until the fine was paid; for a second, transportation to the colonies for seven years. For wearing the Highland clothes, on the other hand, six months' imprisonment for a first offense, and after that transportation for seven years.

141 **boggle:** *Dial.* Hesitate, shrink from.

142 **Barons of Exchequer:** The judges of the Court of Exchequer with jurisdiction over all matters concerning the King's revenue.

143 **Covenanted Zion:** Subscribers or adherents to the SCOTTISH COVENANT (see below). Zion = one of the hills of Jerusalem, captured by David, and later a metonym for "Jerusalem." Symbolically "Zion" = house of God, and of all believers.

143 **upon the hither side:** I.e., on this side. David is on the western shore of the loch, facing Appin across the water to the east.

144 **Scottish Covenant:** Agreement signed at Edinburgh in 1638 ("National Covenant") in which subscribers bound themselves to maintain Presbyterian doctrine as the sole religion of Scotland. The "Covenanters," as these adherents were known, were the dominant party in Scotland until 1651, and they were fiercely opposed to the episcopal practices favored by Charles I, and to any form of Roman Catholic worship. In 1643 the English parliament, in the midst of the Civil War and in need of Scots aid, ratified the "Solemn League and Covenant," a document that extended the Edinburgh agreement and proposed the complete reformation of England's church doctrine and worship.

144 **men should never . . . humility:** *Provb.* "Never be weary of well doing" (Apperson).

144 **with flying colours:** *Provb.* With great success. *HBP.*

146 **charges:** *Arch.* Expenses (with the sense of financial burden).

148 **stone-cast:** *Dial.* Stone's throw, i.e., a short distance.

148 **waif word:** Rumor. "Waif" = stray, floating. The **OED*, listing the word as *Scots* and *rare*, cites two examples, *Kidnapped* and the *Trial of James Stewart* (1753): "Depones, That he heard a waif report in the country." The **SND* correctly notes that Stevenson's usage derived from the 1753 source.

150 **jackanapes:** Ape, monkey. *OED*.

155 **Holy Iron:** Sword.

155 **in cold blood:** *Provb. HBP.*

156 **tail-first:** Backward. *OED*.

157 **dependance:** Control, subjection. *OED*.

157 **low-country:** *Dial.* Low-lying districts as opposed to hill country. *OED*.

158 **or we get clear:** I.e., before we get clear. *OED*.

159 **cast:** *Dial.* Chance. Literally, a throw of the dice.

159 **bows-on:** *Naut.* "On the bow" = within 45 degrees of the point right ahead.

163 **the sour with the sweet:** *Provb.* "Take the sweet with the sour" (*ODP*).

163 **mattock:** Farm tool for digging and chopping.

166 **lowlands:** Less mountainous region of Scotland, the plain, low-lying land south and east of the Highlands.

166 **lay me by the heels:** *Dial.* Kill me. "To turn up the heels" = to die. *EDD.*

167 **musingly:** In a meditative, contemplative manner. *OED*.

170 **Cruachan:** See Glossary. Ben Cruachan (Gaelic = "cone-shaped mountain"), one of the most spectacular pinnacles in Scotland, rises above Loch Awe in Argyllshire, the country of the Campbells.

171–172 **massacre . . . King William:** In 1692 members of the clan Macdonald, after subscribing their allegiance to King William, were betrayed and murdered in their homes by troops under the command of Campbell of Glenlyon. See GLENCOE in the Gazetteer.

172 **dinning:** *Dial.* Continuous, resounding noise.

173 **Hang or Drown:** *Provb.* "He that is born to be hanged, shall never be drowned" (*ODP*).

173 **stood me in stead of:** I.e., taken the place of.

175 **neat spirit:** Pure, undiluted alcoholic drink (in this case, brandy).

177 **saint that was . . . gridiron:** Saint Lawrence, third-century Roman Christian who (according to church tradition) rejoiced in his slow death over the coals and directed the executioner to turn his body over after one side had been broiled enough.

177 **a needle in . . . hay:** *Provb.* Bottle = bundle (Tilley). **HBP.*

177 **dropping out the letter h:** "A still worse habit . . . prevails, chiefly among the people of London, that of sinking the *h* at the beginning of words where it ought to be sounded" (John Walker, *A Critical Pronouncing Dictionary of the English Language* [London, 1791], xiii).

178 **minded then . . . minded:** *Dial.* Recalled to mind; remembered.

178 **our Scotch psalm:** "The Sun shal not smite thee by day, nor the Moon by night" (Ps. 121, *The Psalms of David* [Edinburgh, 1635]).

178 **by God's blessing . . . sun-smitten:** "The faithfull ought to looke for all their succour of God alone" (ibid., commentary on Ps. 121).

179 **sultriness:** Oppressive heat and humidity. **OED.*

179 **out of season:** I.e., aside.

182 **the sea-loch:** LOCH LEVEN (see Gazetteer).

187 **gravelled:** *Dial. and Scots.* Baffled, perplexed.

187 **noised:** *Dial.* Spread around, rumored.

190 **sea trousers:** Presumably breeches worn by fishermen; cf. "sea-breeks" (*EDD*).

191 **chattels:** Movable goods and possessions.

193 **pitch-and-toss:** A game of skill and chance, where a player who *pitches* a coin nearest the mark has first chance at *tossing* all the coins played into the air and winning those that turn up heads.

194 **possets:** *Dial.* Warm milk curdled with ale or brandy, often used as a remedy for colds.

199 **as white as dead folk:** *Provb.* Cf. "As pale as death" (*ODP*).

199 **all one to me:** *Provb.* Made no difference to me. *HBP.*

200 **out-sentries:** Guards placed at a distance to defend the outer approach. **OED.*

202 **The trunks of . . . hawthorn:** "Wattled across" = bound together with interlaced twigs and branches (**OED*). "Wattle" = rods or poles interwoven with slender branches and twigs (**OED*). "There were first some rows of trees laid down, in order to level a floor for the habitation; . . . and these trees, in the way of joists or planks, were levelled with earth and gravel. There were betwixt the trees, growing naturally on their own roots, some stakes fixed in the earth, which, with the trees, were interwoven with ropes, made of heath and birch twigs, all to the top of the Cage, it being of a round or rather oval shape; and the whole thatched and covered over with fog [i.e., moss]. This whole fabric hung, as it were, by a large tree, which reclined from the one end, all along the roof to the other, and which gave it the name of the Cage" (John Home, *The History of the Rebellion in the Year 1745* [London, 1802], 381–82).

203 **personnage:** French = English *personage.*

204 **handless:** Awkward, clumsy.

205 **the late Act . . . powers:** The 1747 act that "abrogated . . . and extinguished" the Scottish lords' right to administer the law in their own jurisdictions, i.e., on their estates, and to pass that right down to their heirs, was the most far-reaching of the post-Culloden acts designed to break up the clan system and bring the Highlands under the control of Westminster ("An Act for taking away and abolishing the Heretable Jurisdictions in . . . *Scotland* etc" [*20 & 21 Geo.II.c.43*]).

205 **Court of Session:** The supreme civil judicature in Scotland.

205 **rated:** Scolded, reproved vehemently or angrily.

205 **bating:** Excepting.

206 **thumbed:** Soiled, worn. **OED.*

206 **pasteboard:** Playing cards.

206 **canting talk:** Whining, hypocritical piety.

213 **privily:** Privately, secretly.

213 **ungenerosity:** Meanness, spite. **OED.*

213 **with the tail of my eye:** *Slang.* I.e., out of the corner of my eye.

214 **even:** *Dial. and Scots.* Lower, i.e., bring down a level.

216 **well-heads:** Source of a running river. **OED.*

216 **breakneck:** Steep.

216 **rude:** Rugged.

217 **in high spate:** Swollen with flood water.

217 **Water Kelpie:** In the Highlands the water demon known as the kelpie is "almost always associated with solitary rivers [and] deep, dark, eddying cauldron-pools" (J. M. Mackinlay, "Traces of River-Worship in Scottish Folk-Lore," *Proceedings of the Society of Antiquaries of Scotland* [Edinburgh, 1896], 30:40). "The ride was **stey, and the bottom deep, / Frae bank to brae the water pouring, / And the bonny grey mare did sweat for fear, / For she heard the water-kelpy roaring" [**steep] ("Annan Water," in *The English and Scottish Popular Ballads*, ed. F. J. Childs [Boston, 1892], 4:184).

218 **my very clothes "abhorred me":** Job 9:31.

218 **"Whig" was the . . . me:** The Highlanders' contemptuous epithet for Lowlanders. *Whig* "was by no means among them a term solely appropriated to political differences. . . . It was used to designate a character made up of negatives: One who had neither ear for music, nor taste for poetry;—no pride of ancestry;—no heart for attachment;—no soul for honour: One who merely studied comfort and conveniency, and was more anxious for the absence of positive evil, than the presence of relative good: A Whig, in short, was what all highlanders cordially hated,—a cold, selfish, formal character" ([Anne Grant], *Essay on the Superstitions of the Highlanders* [London, 1811], 1:138–39).

220 **Hey, Johnnie Cope . . . yet:** The background for this taunting refrain from the popular song "Johnnie Cope" was the English general's scornful dismissal of the Highland army prior to their battle. "Cope sent a letter frae Dunbar:— / Charlie, meet me and ye daur, / And I'll learn you the art o' war, / If you'll meet me in the morning" (*The Scottish Songs*, ed. Robert Chambers [Edinburgh, 1829], 1:50).

222 **Gude:** *Dial.* God. *EDD.*

223 **near hand:** *Dial. and Scots.* Nearly, almost.

224 **septs:** Clans.

224 **broken remnants:** Outlaws; the remains of clans with no chiefs to control and protect them.

224 **that old, proscribed . . . Macgregors:** After the Scottish parliament first outlawed any use of the name Macgregor in 1603—a consequence of the clan's bloody reputation—members adopted the surnames of the chiefs who afforded them protection on their estates. Thus Rob Roy Macgregor, the famous cattle-thief, took the name Campbell after his patron the Duke of Argyle, and was known by that name outside his own immediate vicinity, although within his district he always went by the name Macgregor.

224 **red-handed:** Murderous, bloodthirsty. Originally "red hand" = "a hand red (with blood)," and later, of a criminal = "with the evidences of murder or . . . of any crime still about him" (*SND*).

224 **James More:** With so many members of a clan bearing the same surname, the adoption of "by-names" (sobriquets or nicknames) was an absolute necessity in order to distinguish individuals. Thus Alan Breck (= smallpox) Stewart; Rob Roy (= red [hair]) Macgregor; James More (= big) Macgregor; Robin Oig (= young) Macgregor; Duncan Dhu (= black) Maclaren.

227 **blown upon:** Defamed, disparaged; also, formally denounced as a rebel.

227 **an outlaw to his father:** In Scots idiomatic usage, "to" = "for," hence "an outlaw *for* a father" (**SND*).

227 **the Gregara':** The clan Gregor.

227 **Balfour of Baith:** A young surgeon to the Macgregors during the Jacobite rebellion, identified as "Brother to Balfour of Baith, near Dunfermline" (*Jacobite Memoirs*, ed. Robert Forbes [Edinburgh, 1834], p. 349n).

229 **I can pipe like a Macrimmon:** The Macrimmons, celebrated in the Highlands for their playing and composing, ran a school for pipers on the western island of Skye. "Donald, ye may gang and entertain her with a pibroch of Macreeman's composition; and if she has any taste for moosic, ye'll soon gar her forget her disaster" (Tobias Smollett, *The Reprisal* [1757], ed. Byron Gassman [Athens, Georgia, 1993], p. 182).

229 **Athole Brose:** Powerful Highland drink identified with the mountainous district in north Perthshire. Athole was also famous for its bagpipers. **SND.*

230 **grace-notes:** Notes added as an embellishment or improvement to a musical composition. *OED.

230 **a poor device:** A lack of imagination or invention.

230 **I give ye the lie:** *Provb.* To accuse someone to his face of lying. HBP. Cf. *Hamlet* 2.2.574 ("gives me the lie i' th' throat").

232 **pibroch:** Traditional musical theme with variations, often improvised. *SND.

232 **stood his trial . . . Grassmarket:** Robin Oig, also known as Robert Macgregor, was tried in January 1754 on charges relating to the kidnapping of Jean Key, a well-to-do young widow. After conviction, he was executed in early February.

232 **the Highland Line:** The division between the Highlands and Lowlands was marked largely by shire boundaries and rivers. Although it ran parallel to the geological fault that separated the plains from the hills (see HIELANDS, p. 292), practically speaking it divided those who supported the Stewarts from those who remained loyal to the King. Thus the 1746 disarmament act specified the Highland areas where arms and dress were proscribed: "the Shire of Dunbartain, on the North Side of the Water of Leven, Stirling, on the North Side of the River of Forth, Perth, Kincardin, Aberdeen, Inverness, Nairn, Cromarty, Argyle, Forfar, Bamff, Sutherland, Caithness, Elgine, and Ross." In the event this broad swath might overlook some hidden fastness—Highland geography at this time was more faith than knowledge—the act also applied to anyone within the "bounds" or borderlands of these territories.

233 **Forth bridles the wild Hielandman:** *Provb.* The river Forth served as a restraint upon the Highland raider. *ODP.

233 **auld Brig' of Stirling:** A structure of four arches dating from the end of the fourteenth century and commonly referred to as "the key to the Highlands." A new bridge was erected nearby in 1829 from designs by Robert Stevenson, the novelist's grandfather.

234 **Carse of Stirling:** *Carse* = stretch of low alluvial land along the banks of a river (frequently in place-names).

234 **underfoot:** Down below. **OED.*

234 **Links of Forth:** Popular name for the windings of the river between Stirling and Alloa.

234 **Shearers:** Reapers.

234 **place famous in history:** In 1297 William Wallace and his Scottish army, poised on the north side of the Forth, routed a massive force of English troops as they crossed Stirling Bridge. Afterward Wallace wrote that the victory freed Scotland "from the power of the English."

236 **weary fall:** *Scots.* Dismal and trying.

237 **hone:** Stone for sharpening cutting tools, especially razors.

237 **bizz:** *Scots form of English* "buzz." Commotion, frenzy.

237 **Hope:** st. margaret's hope (see Gazetteer).

238 **wand:** *Dial. and Scots.* Slender, pliant stick. A branch or bush was a traditional sign for a tavern. **EDD.*

238 **clappermaclaw:** *Dial.* = clapperclawed. Scolded.

238 **right about:** A military command = about face or turn around.

240 **imposed upon:** I.e., deceived.

240 **the like of that:** *Dial.* The equal of, the match to.

240 **in dudgeon:** Angered, resentful.

241 **tongue-tied:** Speechless, mute. **OED.*

241 **Charlie is my darling:** Adapted by Robert Burns from "a long romantic street ballad" (Kinsley, 3:1503), this high-spirited song recounts a casual sexual encounter between the Prince and a "bonie" Highland lass ("Charlie he's my darling," in Kinsley, 2:846).

242 **fall to:** Begin eating.

242 **cold comfort:** *Provb.* Chilling, discouraging. *ODP.*

242 **a long tongue:** *Provb.* "Little can a long Tongue Conceal" (Kelly). I.e., to talk more than is good for you.

243 **Kingdom of Fife:** Ancient name for the union of Picts and Scots under Kenneth MacAlpine in the ninth century. See FIFE in the Gazetteer.

243 **dead surety:** *Provb.* As sure as death. *HBP.*

243 **writer:** *Scots.* Lawyer.

244 **maybe:** *Dial.* I.e., the possibility allows.

244 **Baillies:** A *baillie* (or *bailie*) is a magistrate next in rank to a provost with jurisdiction in financial matters and civil disputes between individuals.

246 ***Bonnie House of Airlie:*** A ballad that recounts the destruction of the house of Airlie in 1640 by the Duke of Argyle for the Earl of Airlie's refusal to subscribe to the Covenant. But most versions situate the house's burning in the period of the Stewart rebellion and highlight Lady Airlie's defiance: "Gin my good lord had been at hame, / As he's awa' wi' Charlie, / There durstna a Campbell o' a' Argyle / Set a fit on the bonnie green o' Airlie. / Eleven bairns hae I born, / And the twelfth ne'er saw his daddy; / But though I had gotten as mony again / They sud a' gang to fecht for Charlie" (*The Oxford Book of Ballads*, ed. James Kinsley (Oxford, 1969], p. 616).

247 **pickle:** *Dial. and slang.* Miserable or comical condition (said of someone covered in dirt).

247 **inwards:** Innards, guts.

248 **taking heart of grace:** *Provb.* To pluck up courage. Apperson.

249 ***Nec germino bellum . . . ovo:*** "Trojan war does not begin with the twinned egg" (Horace, *The Art of Poetry*, 147). Horace refers to the fact that the *Iliad* begins not with the historical start of the conflict, which is the birth of Helen and her twin brothers, but in the middle of the war itself.

249 ***in medias res:*** "In the midst of things" (Horace, ibid., 148).

249 **I had fired my bolt:** *Provb.* "A fool's bolt is soon shot" (Apperson). Also, I have done all I can, I am finished.

250 **procurement:** Management, contrivance. **OED.*

250 **Evil doers are . . . dreaders:** *Provb.* I.e., those who are guilty are always suspicious. **ODP.*

251 ***Fui, non sum:*** "I was, but I am not now." Cf. *non sum qualis eram* ("I am not as I was," Horace, *Odes*, IV.1).

251 ***inberbus . . . remoto:*** "A beardless youth with [your] tutor away" (Horace, *The Art of Poetry*, 161).

251 **your ears did not sing:** *Provb.* "If your ears glow, someone is talking of you" (*ODP*).

251 **disrelished:** Disliked, found distasteful. **OED.*

251 **full stand:** Standoff.

251 **probation:** *Scots law.* Evidence, proof, or demonstration of it.

252 **no better guarantee . . . face:** *Provb.* "The face is index of the heart" (Apperson).

252 **prolocutions:** *Rare.* Preliminary remarks. **OED.*

253 **obnoxious to the law:** I.e., liable or subject to punishment by the law.

253 **a piece of policy:** "Policy" = shrewdness or inventiveness.

253 **rolled:** Roamed, wandered. **OED.*

253 *quae regio in terris*: From Aeneas' rhetorical question to Achates: *quae regio in terris nostri non plena laboris* ("what part of the world is not full of our sorrow?" [*Aeneid*, 1.460]).

254 **adhere**: *Scots law*. Be loyal. *Of a husband or wife*, remain with and be faithful to the other.

254 *It comes . . . paribus curis . . . figit*: "[As] a faithful friend goes does he make tracks with equal care" (*Aenied*, 6.158).

255 *Odi te . . . Sabelle*: "I hate you Sabellus, because you are handsome" (Martial, *Epigrams*, 12.39).

256 *multum gementem*: "Groaning greatly." Cf. *multa gemens* ("sighing often" [*Aeneid*, 1.465]).

256 *majora canamus*: "Let us now sing of greater subjects" (Virgil, *Eclogues*, 4.1).

256 *dignus vindice nodus*: "Knot [or problem] worthy of [a god's] intercession" (Horace, *The Art of Poetry*, 191).

257 **Quixotry**: Blind or impulsive chivalry.

258 **court card**: Face card.

258 **reclusion**: Solitary imprisonment.

258 **crop out**: *Dial*. Come into the open.

259 **haws**: Fruit of the hawthorn.

259 **trimming**: Modifying his position.

259 **fair**: Clean, unblemished; as in *fair-copy*.

260 **scathe**: Harm, injury.

264 **volleyed**: Banged rapidly and continuously. **OED*.

264 **observatory**: Place of observation. **OED*.

266 **make a kirk and a mill**: *Scots*. *Prov*. Do whatever you like. Kelly.

269 **past praying for:** Cf. *provb.* "Past cure, past care" (*ODP*).

272 **intromissions:** *Scots law.* The possession and management of property belonging to another.

273 **D. of A.:** Duke of Argyle.

273 *timeo qui nocuere deos*: "I fear the gods who have harmed [me]" (Ovid, *Tristia*, 1.74).

275 **Balfour of Pilrig:** James Balfour (1705–1795), philosopher and advocate, studied law at Leyden (where young Scots journeyed for their legal education) and taught philosophy and law at Edinburgh University.

275 **Faculty:** Faculty of Advocates.

275 **Lord Advocate Grant:** William Grant of Prestongrange ([1701]–1764), named Lord Advocate in 1746, was instrumental in framing the post-Culloden legislation, particularly the bills governing the heritable jurisdictions and the forfeited estates. In 1752 he prosecuted the government's case against James Stewart in Inverary in Argyleshire, the first time a lord advocate argued a criminal case in a circuit court away from Edinburgh. Grant took the title Lord Prestongrange upon his appointment to the bench two years later.

276 **by-way:** Secluded, unfrequented road.

"John Balfours Coffee house at EDINBURGH 1752."
Etching by Paul Sandby.

GLOSSARY

"No one but a Scotchman born," wrote one reader during the serial publication of *Kidnapped*, "could write dialect in the manner Mr. Stevenson does" (*Young Folks*, 12 June 1886). This reader recognized almost intuitively what the lexicographers were systematically to demonstrate: that Stevenson's use of Scots was historical, comprehensive, and even singular. He was occasionally the first source for a dictionary's illustration of a word, and often the only recent source. No glossary can convey the inflection, let alone the nuance, of Stevenson's language; but it can provide a necessary aid to meaning. The primary sources here are: the *Scottish National Dictionary*, along with its later abbreviated version, the *Concise Scots Dictionary*; *the English Dialect Dictionary*; and more selectively the *Oxford English Dictionary*. The *Glossary* appended to the New Edition of the Waverley Novels (1829–1833) also proved helpful. Stevenson himself glossed a number of words on the autograph pages; these are marked with a cross (+) and Stevenson's definition is followed by his initials. Words that have been cited from *Kidnapped* in the *OED* (*) and the *SND* (†) have also been marked.

allenarly singly, solitarily; *Scots law*: exclusively, solely (a technical term in the conveyance of property)

argle-bargled† argued, disputed, bandied words

assoiled+ acquitted (*RLS* and *Scots law*)

aumry cupboard, pantry

aweel well then; well

awhilie diminutive form of *while*: a length of time

bairn(s) child; children

bauchled+† bungled (*RLS*)

beeskep† beehive

begowk+† befool (*RLS*); dupe

behoved be under an obligation or necessity

bield shelter, protection

bill(s) written or printed list, inventory; *Scots law*: document used to initiate proceedings before the Court of Session

birling drinking; pouring out, serving

birstle+ scorch (*RLS*)

bit a small piece (used as a diminutive); small spot, place

bittie a short time

blae bleak, cold, exposed

blow, blower boast, brag; braggart

blunderbush† Sc. form of Eng. *blunderbuss*: a short heavy gun with a wide bore

blythe Sc. form of Eng. *blithe*: glad

boddle a small copper coin; something of little value

boss+† hollow (*RLS*)

bouman+* a *bouman* is a tenant who takes stock from the landlord and shares with him the increase (*RLS*); the man who rented land for a part of the crop

brae the (steep or sloping) bank of a river or shore of the sea; a hillside

bracken fern

braw, brawly fine, splendid; finely, very well

braws good things

breeks breeches, trousers

brogues shoes

buckie perverse, obstinate person

buckies whelks, edible or otherwise; sometimes applied to other mollusks

burn brook, stream

busking† preparing, making ready

by past, gone

byke bees' nest

byre(s) cowshed(s)

by-time† spare moments, spare time

by with+ finished (ch. 3); done for (*RLS*) (ch. 24)

ca' cannie be moderate

cadger travelling peddler; itinerant beggar

callant young lad

canny cautious, prudent, astute; skilful; lucky

cannily skilfully; cautiously

cartes playing cards

chancy+ safe (*RLS*)

chappie *familiar*: little boy

chapping knocking

clachan hamlet, small village

clour+ blow (*RLS*); bump or swelling on the head from a blow

cobles+ coble: a small boat used in fishing (*RLS*)

cocking+ perched (*RLS*); showing off, domineering

cold-rife chilly, susceptible to cold; cold in manner

collops slices of meat

county Play+* village holiday (*RLS*); fair or festival

crofters tenants or occupants of small, enclosed pasture fields

crosstarrie† fiery cross

Cruachan+ the rallying word of the Campbells (*RLS*)

cushat-doves ringdoves, wood pigeons

cutty pipe pipe cut or broken short

daffing* fooling, sporting; thoughtless fun

dauntons intimidates

deave deafen (with noise); bother, weary with talk or questions

den glen, small hollow

deponed testified, gave evidence on oath

dirdum+* blame (*RLS*)

dirk short dagger worn in the kilt by Highlanders

dirl vibrate, ring

Dod a perversion of *God*, used as an exclamation

doer+ agent (*RLS*)

dominie schoolmaster

donnered* stupid, dazed

dowiest dreariest, most dismal

drammach* thick raw mixture of oatmeal and cold water

driegh+* dull (*RLS*); slow; dreary, tiresome

drolling joking, jesting

dub,* dubs† small pool of muddy or stagnant rain water

dunch*† blow, sharp bump

dunt+*† stroke (*RLS*); wound caused by such a blow

durstn't† dare not

eldritch† weird, ghostly, hideous

evited shunned, avoided

factor one entrusted with another's business affairs

fain eager (with the sense of *glad* or *cheerful*)

fash*† trouble, bother

fashed for kitchen+* bothered for sauce (*RLS*)

fashious+ troublesome (*RLS*)

firth† estuary of a river; opening of a river into the sea

fleeching+* beseeching (*RLS*); flattering, coaxing

flit move, transport (from one place to another)

forby* besides, in addition, as well

fyle† soil, defile

gaed (gae) went

gang go

gants*† gasps (for breath)

gars makes, compels

gentrice+† good family (*RLS*)

gey considerably, rather

gifties gifts

gillie male servant-attendant on a Highland chief; a Highlander

girdle* iron plate used for baking

girning* grimacing, snarling

gleg+*† brisk (*RLS*); nimble, quick

gliff* look (*RLS*); resemblance

gloaming twilight, dusk

goer passerby

gomeral+* blockhead (*RLS*)

Good People+ The Faries [*sic*] (*RLS*)

gowls*† howls

guddling*† groping (for fish) with the hands in water

gyte+* mad (*RLS*)

haggle† hack or mangle

hags* marshy hollow ground in a moor

handless awkward, clumsy

harled (new-)+ rough-cast (*RLS*); to plaster a wall with lime

heather cat*† wild cat; *fig.*: wild, roaming person

herried harried

heugh crag or cliff, precipice; deep cleft in the rocks (frequently in place-names)

hind end rear end; buttocks

hoot† exclamation expressing annoyance, disgust, incredulity, or remonstrance; dismissal of another's opinion

hoot aye indeed, certainly

Hoots, Hoot-toot nonsense

howe* hollow or low-lying piece of ground

Hut† see *hoot* (alternate spelling)

jottering† fumbling; also, jerky; dawdling

jouk+* Duck (*RLS*)

kale cabbage

keek* peep

ken(s) know, knows

kenna know not, i.e., don't know

kenned (well-)* well known, familiar

kennt* known

kep+ catch (*RLS*)

kite belly

kittle+ ticklish (*RLS*)

laith unwilling, reluctant

lief (I would as) I would rather

like† used parenthetically with a depreciatory or apologetic force

liker† more likely

limmer loose woman; contemptuous term for a woman

linking+† running (*RLS*); moving fast, walking briskly

louting* stooping, deferential

lug ear

lynn† pool below a waterfall

mair more

maitter matter

mannie*† affectionate address to a small boy, disparaging to an adult

maun dow+ put up (*RLS*); *literally*: must do

mettle*† spirited, lively, game

midden dunghill

moss+ bog (*RLS*)

muckle† large, big; much, a great deal

mulls+ horns to carry snuff (*RLS*)

nainsel ownself (a Highlander's supposed way of speaking of himself)

notour well known, notorious

ochone (uchone) *interj.* (emphatic) of sorrow, regret, or weariness

off-go*† start, outset

ordinar' custom, habit

orra*† odd; occasional

Ou *interj.*: Oh!

ought* own, possess

out by* outside, a little way out

ower too

paper*† a printed proclamation or notice; to describe in writing, to insert a notice in a newspaper

peat-hag a hole or pit left where peat has been dug

peaty of or like peat

peewees* lapwing or pewit, named for its thin, wailing cry

penny stone* a flat round stone used as a quoit

philabeg† little kilt

pickle small quantity of something

piper† one who plays the bagpipes

pirliecue+*† concluding sermon (*RLS*)

pit-mirk+* dark as the pit (*RLS*)

plack a copper coin, equal to a third part of an English penny

plaid-neuk*† a fold in a plaid used as a pocket

plenishing furniture

ploughstilts the shafts or handle of a plough

poke+ bag (*RLS*); a small sack

policy† the enclosed grounds of a large country house

potato-bogle+*† scarecrow (*RLS*)

pretty,* prettily general epithet of admiration: *fine, commendable*; having the appearance or qualities of a man, conventionally applied to soldiers: *brave, gallant*

put-off* a dismissal, evasion

pyats+† magpies (*RLS*)

pyke, pike*† pick, eat in a nibbling way; probe with a pointed instrument

ranting lively, in quick measure

raxing+† reaching (*RLS*); extending, handing over

redd up settled; *Scots law*: vacated, made ready for the next occupant

rickle a loose heap or pile

rife+ common (*RLS*)

rispf† grate, scratch

rowans† mountain ashes

rowpit sold up (by auction), i.e., turned out of house

rowt*† shout, make a great noise

scones* round, semi-sweet cakes made of wheat flour

screed† confused or meaningless talk; or, a long harangue

session clerk the clerk or secretary of a kirk session, the lowest court exercising the functions of church government within a parish

siller silver coin

sliddering sliding, slipping

slockens+ moistens (*RLS*)

sneckdraw† crafty, sly, covetous person

snuff† a rage, huff

soger† soldier

soople* supple; astute, subtle; *fig.*: yielding to persuasion, compliant

sough+† report (*RLS*); rumor

spark *fig.*: sharp, quick-witted

spiers (speer) asks, questions

sporran† a purse or pouch worn in front of a man's kilt

spunks+*† sparks (*RLS*)

stave* move forward quickly, dash ahead

steading the buildings on a farm separate from the farmhouse

swier+ unwilling (*RLS*)

syne since, before now

taigle+*† drag (*RLS*)

tarry (tarry breeks) sobriquet for a sailor

tass cup, especially for liquor

tenty+*† careful (*RLS*); cautious, prudent

thole suffer patiently

tint+* lost (*RLS*)

tirls*† rattles, beats

tit exclamation of disapproval; nonsense

tod+*† fox (*RLS*)

tow+*† rope (*RLS*); gallows rope

tow-row*† din, uproar

trokings+† dealings (*RLS*); implying friendly and possibly illicit intercourse

twine+* part, separate

uncanny† threatening; inauspicious; ominous

unchancy unlucky, ill-fated; dangerous

unco† very, exceedingly; strangely

uncouth unfriendly; eerie, full of dread

wae sorrowful

wame belly

wanting* without, deprived of

warlock*† wizard, magician

waukin' waking

wee bit tiny, very small amount

weel well

whae who

whaups curlews

wheen (a)* a parcel, a small number

wheesht *interj.*: silence, be quiet

whig,+ whigamore*† *note:* whig or whigamore was the cant name for those who were loyal to **King George** (*RLS*)

while a space of time

whiles* times; at times, sometimes

whilk which

whin bush gorse or furze bush

win (into)† get in, obtain entry

win (to) reach

wyte+*† blame (*RLS*)

GAZETTEER

Four years after Stevenson's death a young Scot named John Buchan paid homage to the "uncommon topographical accuracy" of his elder countryman ("The Country of *Kidnapped*," *The Academy*, 7 May 1898). Stevenson was precise in his use of place, and quick to notice both error and lacuna, first asking Charles Scribner to restore "Long Islands" to its correct form, "Long Island," and then, after the American illustrated edition was printed a year later, carping about the disappearance of the map: "I have but one complaint. Where is the map of *Kidnapped*? I must have my map, when you next issue it: a book of mine without a map, ye Gods!" (*Letters*, 6:40). In fact, Stevenson was lucky with this book, for the fold-out tracing David Balfour's "wanderings" (reproduced here as endsheets) appeared intact in the initial English and American editions. The map in *Kidnapped* was a blueprint of the narrative, and the exactitude of bay and river, islet and mountain, village and town—an exactitude Stevenson knew by foot and from text—constituted the building of that narrative, whose architectural space was nothing less than the whole of Scotland. For the place-names below, the principal sources are Samuel Lewis's two-volume *Topographical Dictionary of Scotland* (London, 1846) and Francis Groome's six-volume *Ordnance Gazetteer of Scotland* (Edinburgh, 1882–1885). A small number of citations are from the *Trial of James Stewart* (Edinburgh, 1753). An asterisk indicates that the place-name appeared on the original map.

Allan Water* Small river running south from Dunblane (in Perthshire) into the Forth just north of Stirling.

Alloa* Seaport and chief town of Clackmannanshire, on the north side of the Forth and east of Stirling.

Angus Formerly Forfarshire, maritime county on the east side of Scotland.

Appin* Extensive district in Argyllshire, noted for its spectacular scenery and as home to the Stewart clan; bounded by Loch Linnhe on the west, Perthshire and Loch Leven on the north, Loch Creran and the sound of Mull on the south.

Ardgour District and hamlet in north Argyllshire, the latter lying near the Corran Ferry at the connection between Loch Linnhe and Loch Eil, and southwest of Fort William.

Ardnamurchan* Peninsular headland in Argyllshire, the westernmost point of the Scottish mainland and site of "multitudes" of shipwrecks on its rocky coastline.

Arisaig [Arasaig] District and hamlet on west coast of Inverness-shire.

Athole Mountainous district in north Perthshire.

Aucharn "The house of . . . James Stewart at Aucharn" (*Trial*).

Baith [Beath] Parish in Fifeshire, bounded on the southwest with Dunfermline.

Balachulish [Ballachulish] Large, straggling village in the parish of Lismore and Appin, Argyllshire, along the south shore of Loch Leven, with a ferry at the loch's entrance.

Balfron* District and village in west Stirlingshire; Kippen forms one of its northern boundaries.

Balquidder* [= **Balquhidder** on map] District in west Perthshire, cut by valleys and hills, level lands and deep glens, rocky prominences and numerous lakes. The "Braes of Balquidder" are in the northern part of the district, above Loch Voil.

Ben Alder* The highest peak of the chain of the central Grampians, Inverness-shire, just west of Loch Ericht.

Ben More* Highest peak on Mull, commanding an extensive view of the Hebrides and a great part of the mainland of Argyllshire.

Breadalbane Mountainous district in west Perthshire, scored by deep glens with numerous lochs. Also, the home of a major branch of the Campbells.

Canna Small island southwest of Skye, Inverness-shire.

Cantyre [Kintyre] Peninsula, southernmost district of Argyllshire, at its tip in the Atlantic the nearest point of Scotland to Ireland.

Cape Wrath* High promontory in Sutherland, the extreme northwest point of the Scottish mainland.

Carriden* Small coastal district in Linlithgowshire, west of Queensferry.

Clackmannan* County town and parish of Clackmannanshire, the town two miles east of Alloa, elevated and overlooking the Forth.

Colinton Village and parish southwest of Edinburgh.

Corran Narrow strait between Ardgour on the west and the district of Lochaber in Inverness-shire on the east, with a ferry crossing.

Corrynakiegh "D.B continues his dreary carreer; and is now encamped in the Heugh of Korrynakiegh with Alan Breck" (RLS to his parents, 3 February 1886 [Beinecke Library]).

Corstorphine Small village just west of Edinburgh, at the base of the "Corstorphine Hill," which rises more than 500 feet above the sea. See REST-AND-BE-THANKFUL.

Cramond Village in the northwest corner of Edinburghshire, on the south side of the Firth of Forth, and a parish bordering and overlapping Linlithgowshire. The road from Edinburgh to Queensferry passes through this parish.

Culloden (**Muir**) Inverness-shire, battlefield, on the northeastern border of Nairnshire, a few miles east of Inverness.

Culross Small town on the north shore of the Firth of Forth, five miles southeast of Clackmannan.

Duart See TOROSAY.

Dundas In Linlithgowshire, ancient castle and hill less than two miles southwest of Queensferry.

Duror* Hamlet and district in north Appin, five miles southwest of Ballachulish; occupies the angle between Loch Linnhe and Loch Leven, traversed by a small stream called the Duror.

Dysart Historic seaport in Fifeshire, on the northern shore of the Firth of Forth, northeast of Edinburgh.

Earraid* [= **Erraid** on map] In the district of Mull, served as shore station during the construction of the SKERRYVORE and Dhu Heartach (1867–1872) lighthouses.

Ettrick, Forest of Popular and historic name for most of Selkirkshire, in south Scotland, and parts of Peebles and Edinburgh shires. A favorite hunting ground for Scottish kings.

Fife Fifeshire, maritime county on the east side of Scotland, bounded on its southern coastline by the Firth of Forth and on its eastern coastline by the North Sea.

Firth of Forth Estuary of the river Forth, starting just below Alloa, slowly widening and extending some fifty miles until it reaches the North Sea.

Forth* One of Scotland's great rivers, it forms the boundary between Perthshire and Clackmannanshire on the north and Stirlingshire on the south.

Fort William Inverness-shire, small garrison town on the upper end of Loch Linnhe, north of Appin.

Glencoe* Rugged and desolate valley in north Argyllshire, near Ballachulish, overhung by some of the craggiest and wildest mountains in Scotland, mountains that "seem as if composed of huge disjointed rocks heaped one upon another, and appear to be in danger of falling every moment" (Lewis).

Glen Dochart Perthshire, south of Glen Lochay and north of Balquidder.

Glen Lochay [Lochy] Breadalbane, running along the river Lochy, south of Glen Lyon and north of Glen Dochart.

Glen Lyon Breadalbane, long, narrow glen running along the river Lyon, the mountains on either side among the tallest in the county.

Glenorchy* Parish in northeastern Argyllshire, near Glen Lochy. Once the home of the Macgregors and later of the Campbells.

Grassmarket Large open space at the base of the Castle rock leading to the western exit from the city of Edinburgh. For over a century after 1660 it was the place of public execution.

Hebrides Western Islands, extending more than 200 miles along the west coast of Scotland, from Cape Wrath on the north to Kintyre [CANTYRE] on the south.

Inchgarvie A mile off the shore from Queensferry, the "ruins" are of a fort built in the late fifteenth or early sixteenth century, and used for a time as a state prison.

Inverkeithing Fifeshire, coastal town just east of Limekilns that includes the greater part of St. Margaret's Hope.

Iona Small island off the southwestern corner of Mull, in the Atlantic Ocean, and separated from the ROSS OF MULL by a deep but dangerous channel. Site of influential monastery established in the sixth century by St. Columba.

Isle Eriska [Eriskay] Outer Hebrides, small isle narrowly separated from South Uist, and the site of Prince Charles's landing in 1745.

Isle of May Fifeshire, small island at the northern end of the mouth of the Firth of Forth.

Kingairloch Hamlet in Lismore and Appin parish, southwest of Ardgour, at the head of an offshoot of Loch Linnhe.

Kinlochaline* Hamlet in Morven (*Kinloch* = Gaelic form for naming towns and villages at the head of a loch).

Kippen* District and village in north Stirlingshire, west of Stirling and south of the river Forth.

Koalisnacoan* [= **Coalisnacoan** on map] In Appin, "a remote or solitary place called Koalisnacoan" (*Trial*).

Leith Edinburghshire, seaport on the south side of the Forth estuary, less than two miles from Edinburgh.

Lettermore "The wood of Lettermore, standing upon the lands of

Ardshiel . . . about a mile distant from the house and ferry of Ballachelish" (*Trial*).

Limekilns* Coastal village in Fifeshire, on the north shore of the Firth of Forth.

Linnhe Loch* Sea loch separating Appin on one side from Morven and Ardgour on the other.

Lismore Small island in the Linnhe Loch just off the Argyllshire mainland. Part of the united parish of Lismore and Appin, and home to the Stewarts.

Loch Aline* Small arm of the sea striking north into Morven from the Sound of Mull.

Loch Errocht [Ericht; = Erricht on map] On the border of Inverness-shire and Perthshire. Prince Charles hid from the English near the banks of this loch.

Loch Leven* "A narrow arm of the sea called Lochlevin, that separates the country of Appin on the south, from that of Mamore, part of Lochiel's estate, on the north side of it" (*Trial*).

Loch Rannoch* Northwest Perthshire, south and east of Loch Ericht, with densely wooded shores.

Long Island Outer Hebrides, chain of islands of varying sizes extending from Lewis on the north to Barra on the south. Separated only by narrow sounds and channels, the islands appear as one continuous ridge of land.

Lothian District on the south side of the Firth of Forth, including Haddington, Edinburgh, and Linlithgow shires (now East, Mid, and West Lothian).

Mamore* "In the shire of Inverness, to the southward of Fort-

William, and betwixt that fort and the ferry of Ballachelish"
(*Trial*). See LOCH LEVEN.

Minch, Little Channel between Skye island on the east and the
middle portion of the Outer Hebrides on the west (North Uist,
Benbecula, and part of Harris).

Morar District in Inverness-shire, adjoining Arisaig to the south
and bisected from east to west by Loch Morar, dividing the
territory into North and South Morar.

Morven [Morvern] Parish in the district of Mull, in northern
Argyllshire, forming a triangular peninsula bounded by Lochs
Sunart and Linnhe on the north and east, and the Sound of
Mull on the south, which divides it from the island of Mull.

Mull* In Argyllshire, third largest island in the Hebrides, bounded
on the north and east by the Sound of Mull, and on the south and
west by the Atlantic Ocean. "Mull has a boisterous coast, a wet
and stormy climate, and a rough, unpromising, trackless surface"
(Groome).

Newhalls Village on the Firth of Forth just east of Queensferry.

Ochil Range of high hills extending northeast from Stirling
through Clackmannanshire and Perthshire, overlooking Alloa,
Clackmannan, and Culross.

Orkney* Group of islands off the northeastern coast of Scotland,
separated from the mainland (Caithness) by the Pentland Firth,
bounded on the east by the North Sea, on the west by the Atlantic,
and on the north by the waters dividing it from the Shetland
islands.

Outer Hebrides See LONG ISLAND.

Peebles County town of Peeblesshire, south of Edinburgh. It boasts a "spacious" High Street and a town hall dating from 1753.

Pentland Firth Strait separating the Orkney islands from the north coast of Scotland and connecting the North Sea and Atlantic Ocean. It is the most dangerous passage in the Scottish seas.

Pittencrieff Fifeshire, glen near the town of Dunfermline, and site of a "tower" or castle ruins.

Preston Pans [Prestonpans] Haddingtonshire, parish and coast town east of Edinburgh, on the south bank of the Firth of Forth.

Queensferry* Small, historic seaport on the south shore of the Firth of Forth, west of Edinburgh.

Rest-and-be-Thankful Steep point on the eastern side of Corstorphine Hill with a commanding view of Edinburgh and its castle.

Ross (of Mull) Peninsular arm stretching into the sea, facing Earraid and Iona at its western end.

Rum* Inner Hebrides, Argyllshire, separated from Skye on the north and the island of Canna on the northwest.

St. Margaret's Hope Small bay or natural dock west of North Queensferry, in the Firth of Forth.

Shetland* Archipelago lying northeast of the Orkney islands, surrounded by the North Sea and Atlantic Ocean; the northernmost part of all Scotland.

Skerryvore A dangerous rock in the midst of reefs, eleven miles southwest of the island of Tiree, and site of the "Skerryvore" lighthouse (1844) built by Robert Stevenson, the writer's grandfather.

Skye* Off the west coast of Inverness-shire, one of the larger and most varied of the Hebrides islands, indented with sea lochs and dominated by the wild and spectacular Cuchullin (Cuillin) Hills.

Sound of Mull "Boomerang-shaped belt of sea separating the island of Mull from the Scottish mainland" (Groome). Tides and fierce winds make navigation very difficult.

Stirling* County town of Stirlingshire, on the south bank of the river Forth, lying on the slope of a rocky hill, and crowned by a castle, one of the chief residences of the Stewart kings. Stirling historically was considered the key to the Highlands.

Teith River in southwest Perthshire; joins the Forth two miles northwest of Stirling.

Tiree* [Tyree] Inner Hebrides, the westernmost of the cluster of islands (including **Canna** and **Coll**) identified as the "Mull" group.

Torosay* Parish on Mull; includes Duart, a small bay, and the remains of Duart Castle, situated on a prominent headland facing directly across the Sound toward Oban.

Torran rocks* Off the southwest coast of Mull.

Uam Var* [= Uamvar on map] Or Uamh Mhor, mountain in hilly district in south Perthshire, northwest of Stirling, cut on one side with a large cavern said to have been a robbers' den until about 1750.

THE MODERN LIBRARY EDITORIAL BOARD

Maya Angelou

•

Daniel J. Boorstin

•

A. S. Byatt

•

Caleb Carr

•

Christopher Cerf

•

Ron Chernow

•

Shelby Foote

•

Stephen Jay Gould

•

Vartan Gregorian

•

Charles Johnson

•

Jon Krakauer

•

Edmund Morris

•

Joyce Carol Oates

•

Elaine Pagels

•

John Richardson

•

Salman Rushdie

•

Arthur Schlesinger, Jr.

•

Carolyn See

•

William Styron

•

Gore Vidal

A Note on the Type

This book was set in Baskerville, a typeface which was designed by John Baskerville, an amateur printer and typefounder, and cut for him by John Handy in 1750. The type became popular again when the Lanston Monotype Corporation of London revived the classic Roman face in 1923. The Mergenthaler Linotype Company in England and the United States cut a version of Baskerville in 1931, making it one of the most widely used typefaces today.